Camels and Corpses

G.K. Parks

A Modus Operandi imprint

ISBN: 0989195864
ISBN-13: 978-0-9891958-6-7

For my two favorite aunts.

BOOKS IN THE ALEXIS PARKER SERIES:

Likely Suspects
The Warhol Incident
Mimicry of Banshees
Suspicion of Murder
Racing Through Darkness
Camels and Corpses
Lack of Jurisdiction
Dying for a Fix
Intended Target
Muffled Echoes
Crisis of Conscience
Misplaced Trust
Whitewashed Lies
On Tilt
Purview of Flashbulbs
The Long Game
Burning Embers
Thick Fog
Warning Signs
Past Crimes
Sinister Secret
Zero Sum

BOOKS IN THE JULIAN MERCER SERIES:

Condemned
Betrayal
Subversion
Reparation
Retaliation
Hunting Grounds

BOOKS IN THE CROSS SECURITY INVESTIGATIONS SERIES:

Fallen Angel
Calculated Risk

BOOKS IN THE LIV DEMARCO SERIES:

Dangerous Stakes
Operation Stakeout
Unforeseen Danger
Deadly Dealings
High Risk
Fatal Mistake
Imminent Threat
Mistaken Identity

ONE

"Oh, come on. Do I look like a cop to you?"

Tommy Claxton narrowed his eyes and turned his head to the side like a cockatoo, considering the question. "I've never seen a cop built like you, babe." He licked his lips and reached into his pocket, causing the hanging chain to rattle from his belt loop. I took an uneasy breath, wondering if he was about to pull a gun. Instead, he produced a pack of cigarettes and a lighter. "Want a smoke?"

"No." I brushed my long brown hair out of my face. "Are we doing this or not?"

"My god, you're impatient." He grinned. "One of the things I look for in a broad."

"I aim to please." I ran my leather clad hand up his chest and grabbed the cigarette from between his lips. "Work first, then play." He caught my wrist in a vise-like grip and kissed me hard. The impending heist made him handsy. "Work first," I repeated when we broke for air.

He snatched the cigarette from my hand and

relaxed his grip on my ass. “I’ve only known you a few days, Alex, but damn. If you’re half as good as you claim,” his eyes lit up, “mmm.”

“Tommy, keep it in your pants. We’re working on a timetable, and your screwing around is going to get us all fucked,” Robert Gregson snapped, walking into the repair garage. He cast his gaze at me. “Just because you like my boy doesn’t mean we’re square. Consider tonight your audition.”

“You’ll be impressed. I never make promises I can’t keep.” My tone held much more conviction than I felt. Stealing cars was not my forte. Sure, I’d been practicing for the last two weeks, but with so many different makes, models, and security systems, there was a good chance I wouldn’t be able to pull it off, especially when Gregson was keeping the relevant information so close to the vest.

“Somehow, I doubt it.” He turned to Tommy. “You brought her in, so she’s your problem.”

“Hear that, babe? You’re all mine.” Tommy slung his arm around my waist and guided me to the back of the SUV.

“Just the way I like it.” I nipped at his earlobe before getting into the truck. Gregson climbed into the driver’s seat, and Tommy got in the passenger’s side.

It was after three a.m. I tied my hair up and tucked my ponytail into the back of my leather jacket. When I was trying to catch Tommy’s eye, I had to blend in at the bars he frequented. That required a lot of leather, chains, piercings, and dark eye makeup. Although he wasn’t a biker, his style reflected a cross between rocker and Hell’s Angel. I opted for a slightly more rocker-esque appearance and donned dark jeans, stylish boots, and a tank top covered by a leather jacket and matching driving gloves.

As we drove through the city in search of whatever

the perfect audition score would be, I pulled out my electronic frequency scanner and my code sequencer. If it was a high-end vehicle with such features as keyless entry, remote ignition start, or pretty much anything that used a radio frequency to operate the vehicle, I'd be set. Unfortunately, Gregson wanted to see some old school techniques since he pulled to a stop two blocks from a classic American muscle car.

"Didn't I mention I'm more of a modern-day thief?" I asked.

He handed me a slip of paper with an address. "Delivery is twenty minutes or less. You leave a tracker or any anti-theft measures in place and you're done. If you don't deliver, don't come back."

"I'll see you in fifteen."

Stepping out of the car, I pulled my collar up. Tommy got out and joined me on the sidewalk. I spotted a gun tucked into a holster at his hip. Maybe I wouldn't have to worry about making a bad impression since failure was no longer an option. Tommy kissed my cheek as we made our way to the vehicle.

"What does Robert want you to do?" I knelt next to the driver's side door and checked to see if it was unlocked. It was not.

"Keep an eye on you. He has trust issues."

"Yeah? How come?" I pulled the thin piece of wire from inside my jacket and inserted it between the molding and the window, manipulating it into the interior of the car in order to unlock the door.

"Don't know." Tommy lit a cigarette and stood with his back to me, watching for signs of trouble. "I think it has something to do with a rat on his last crew."

"That'll do it." The lock popped, and I opened the door, sliding across the seat and unlocking the passenger's side for Tommy. By the time he got in the car, I was scanning for radio signals.

He looked at my gear quizzically. "Who'da thought I'd be into some fancy, high-tech chick?"

A transmitter of some sort, probably an installed lowjack, was hidden in the trunk or under the hood. Getting out, I started at the front of the vehicle and located the security system. At least I was familiar enough with the proper method of disengaging these.

"You got ten minutes," he muttered as I got back inside.

"Plenty of time." Reaching under the steering console, I felt around for the seam and pulled the panel off, exposing the wires and burning the tips of my fingers with the initial spark. The engine roared to life, and I pulled out of the parking space. "Grab the address out of my pocket, will ya?"

DOT cameras were everywhere. If the cops had some idea what to look for, they'd spot us easily enough. Classic cars were few and far between.

Tommy reached into my pocket, copping a feel before extracting the paper. I drove one-handed since my cell phone was in the other. Hopefully, the GPS app could provide directions to our destination.

"Give me that," he insisted, but I refused to hand him my phone. There was too much incriminating evidence on it.

"I got it. Just tell me the address."

He rattled it off, and I input the information. After executing the proper turns, I drove to the roof level of a parking garage and pulled into a space. I wiped the interior and climbed out of the car.

"Now what?"

"We wait."

"Shit. First, you accuse me of being a cop, and now, you want me to sit around with a hot number like this. Are you insane? How do I know you're not a cop?"

"He's not a cop," a voice said from behind. Tommy waved at the approaching man. "I'm unaware of any who'd be willing to commit such costly felonies." The stranger circled the vehicle, scanning it with his own RF reader. "Excellent."

"I told you she was rocking my world," Tommy said, "in more ways than one."

"Did I miss the introduction?" I asked.

"There wasn't one. Not yet. You have to earn it. Tonight was a cakewalk. If you step up your game, maybe I'll consider formally introducing myself. In the meantime," he tossed a bag to Tommy, "tell Robert to split it any way he sees fit."

"Thanks, man." Tommy grabbed my wrist and dragged me toward the stairwell. Normally, I didn't let anyone push me around, but it was necessary for the part I was playing.

Back on the street, Gregson brought the SUV to a stop in front of us. "You're still breathing. Things went well."

"I said they would."

When we arrived at the garage, Gregson took the bag from Tommy which contained an unknown amount of cash. He removed two stacks, thumbed through them, and handed them to Tommy. "Tomorrow, I'll call with additional details. We'll be moving fast, so stay by your phone."

"Right-o." Tommy handed one of the stacks to me, and I slipped it inside my jacket pocket without counting it. He led the way out of the garage and to his car. "You were so fucking amazing tonight." He snaked his hand under my top while we made out against the passenger's side door. His fingers moved to my belt, and I reached down and grabbed his hand.

"Tommy, no, I have to get to work. We don't have time. My shift starts at five."

“We just finished work.” He continued to pull at my belt, and I considered slamming his skull into the car roof.

“I have a real job. You know that. I can’t be late.”

“Come on, watching you work tonight’s made me so hard.” He pressed his pelvis into my thigh to demonstrate.

Gritting my teeth and ignoring my natural inclination to resort to a violent protest, I chose a verbal assault instead. “You called me a cop before. You might as well have called me a freaking pig, and now you think you’re going to get some. No way.” I shoved him back. “You don’t even trust me enough to tell me who we’re working for besides Robert, and yet, you think I should trust you enough to let you in my pants. Get real.”

“Babe,” he stepped back as if I’d slapped him, “I’m sorry. I can’t tell you. But if tomorrow night goes well, I’m sure you’ll be in, and then you’ll know everything.”

“Fine, when I get in, so do you.”

He smiled. “Tomorrow night?” He offered a chaste kiss, which I couldn’t refuse.

“Tomorrow night.” I went to my car and drove toward the hospital. Medical transcriptionist by day, car thief by night, and yet, neither of those things was actually true.

* * *

After switching vehicles in the hospital’s garage to avoid possible tails, I took a circuitous route back to my apartment. Paranoia was my constant friend, but I could never be too careful. Before stepping out of my car, and not the rental I claimed was mine for Tommy’s benefit, I took off my jacket, clipped my hair into a bun, and put on a sweater. Maybe going so far as to change my appearance in addition to my car would be considered overkill, but it couldn't hurt.

Once safely inside my apartment with the doors locked, I dialed the police station and left a tip on a stolen vehicle. I did my best to memorize the VIN, but there were too many digits and too little time. Instead, I provided the location, description of the perpetrators, and the make, model, and year. At least the owner could file a police report and hopefully be reimbursed for the loss. Hanging up, I went into the bathroom to shower and change.

After gargling half a bottle of mouthwash to remove the memory of Tommy's tongue shoved down my throat, I stared at my reflection in the mirror. At this moment, I hated myself. Not only did I just commit grand theft auto, but I was becoming increasingly physically involved with the mark. It was revolting, and while there were some lines that would never be crossed, I had to act like the possibility was only moments away. My stomach knotted at the thought.

Knowing I wouldn't be able to sleep, I opened the dossier I had compiled and began reading. Two hours passed before the adrenaline and self-loathing dropped away. I just went to bed when my cell phone rang. Cursing, I grabbed it and tried to sound like I was fully awake and in the midst of performing a boring desk job. "What is it, Tommy?"

"I just wanted to make sure you weren't mad about earlier. You know I didn't mean nothing by it."

"It's okay. Hang on a second." I got out of bed and shut my bedroom door, so the sound of a door closing would be heard on the other end. "Sorry, I didn't want to talk in front of the other girls. You know my boss hates it when I take personal calls at work."

"Then I'll make this short. Rob wants you to locate

a high-end vehicle, we're talking a street value of at least 100K, and deliver it by four a.m."

"He's not choosing?"

"Nah. He wants to see if you got taste to match your skills. Maybe we can meet up earlier and scout some places, see what we can find, and once Rob gives the go-ahead, you'll know exactly where to go."

I already knew how to find an appropriate car. "Sure, I'd like that." I opened and closed the door again for effect. "I gotta get back to work, but I'll call you tonight."

"Hang on. One last thing. Ribbed or regular?"

Resisting the urge to vomit, I said, "You decide."

So much for sleeping. I threw on some clothes and found my keys. It was a little after six a.m. On my way to Auto Protection Services, I dialed my current boss, Jeremy Islind. By the time I arrived, he was waiting.

"Ms. Parker," he began after I explained my need for an expensive vehicle in the next twenty-four hours, "when we hired you to investigate these claims and get an insider's view of the current vehicular thievery trends, we budgeted in such possibilities, but we don't have vehicles available for your disposal."

"What am I supposed to do?" Only hours earlier, I had stolen a car which I had no legal right to do. "As it is, I might be arrested for GTA. If I have to conduct another heist tonight, it's just a matter of time before I end up behind bars. No matter how much you offer to pay me, that's not a risk I want to take."

"Don't you have friends in high places?" Islind asked. "According to your résumé, you've been a police consultant numerous times. You were a federal agent at the Office of International Operations for four years prior to that. Can't you just make the charges go away?"

"You're shitting me, right?" I pushed away from the

conference table and paced the room. "The police were tipped on the '67 Mustang that went missing tonight, but by the time they bother to check into it, there won't be anything left. What are you doing on your end to mitigate my involvement?"

"Your investigation has proven most advantageous to APS. Our clients want assurances that we offer the safest and most effective security systems money can buy. The fact that you've exploited the RF weaknesses has impressed our design team and our financial backers."

"I wasn't hired for this corporate bull." I bit off the last word.

"No, you were not. Too many cars with our security systems have been taken lately by the ring you've infiltrated. The authorities had other things to do besides taking this seriously, so that's why we hired you. Now that we have actual proof of the ring's existence, maybe the police will take our concerns under advisement." He glanced at the clock. "I'll phone our legal team at eight and see if we can reach some kind of deal or partnership with the district attorney's office. After all, you phoned in the tip, so clearly, we're making their case for them."

"Right, because they just love when other people do their jobs. And while all of this is absolutely fascinating, how does it alleviate our current problem?"

"Like I told you when you agreed to work for us, Auto Protection Services will pay restitution for any damage or theft incurred during your employment with us. You're completely indemnified from civil liability."

"Fine." It was time to move on to plan B. "See what kind of deal you can make to indemnify me from criminal charges too."

TWO

It was 7:30 a.m. when James Martin came down the steps. He was dressed in a designer suit, minutes away from leaving for work. His smile brightened when he found me drinking a cup of coffee. Normally, I didn't risk visiting him when I was working a job for fear he would get caught in someone's crosshairs, but once again, I needed a favor.

"Look what the cat dragged in. Should I reset my security codes?" he teased.

"It'd be easier to take your key back, instead of going through all that trouble."

"Never." He leaned down for a kiss, but I turned away. He pecked my cheek, confused. "I haven't seen you in weeks, and I can't even get a good morning kiss?"

"I'm catching a cold," I lied. Even though it was imperative to lock lips with Tommy to maintain my cover, it still felt like cheating, semantics aside.

Martin was confused by my unannounced visit this early in the morning, especially when he had to leave for work soon. Despite being CEO of Martin Technologies, a multimillion dollar corporation, he knew I'd never ask him to take the morning off. We were both workaholics, and I often insisted our careers came before our relationship. It was my way of excluding him from the dangers associated with my line of work.

Before the request formed on my lips, I reconsidered asking for one of his cars. He would bend over backward for me, but 100K was something I could never repay. My work as a private investigator and the occasional stint as a police consultant barely provided enough to afford the rent for my office and my bills. Even though Islind promised to reimburse all affected parties, Martin shouldn't be subjected to acting as my sugar daddy, even if it was just a temporary loan.

"So you just stopped by for a cup of coffee?" He popped a bagel into the toaster and poured a glass of orange juice.

"Apparently."

"Liar." He put the juice down in front of me. "What's wrong? Are you still working a case?"

"Yes." I slowly exhaled. "The reason I stopped by was to ask a favor, but it's too much."

"Why don't you let me be the judge of that? I'm game for most things, but oddly enough, I'm drawing the line at a threesome. While sexy in theory, someone's bound to be left out at some point, and I have zero desire to share you with anyone. Not to mention, we'd probably need a world-class athlete to keep up with the two of us," his timbre lowered, "especially when it's been a few weeks since we've spent any time together."

"I need a car."

"Did someone shoot through your engine block

again?"

"No, it's for the job, and it has to be worth at least a hundred thousand."

He whistled and went to the toaster to retrieve his bagel.

"Like I said, I changed my mind about asking. It's too much," I said.

"Red or blue?"

"Whichever you like the least. There's a good chance you'll never see it again."

"Blue then." He went into the other room and came back with a set of keys. "I'm not entirely certain if you're required to pay gift taxes on this, so we won't report it to the IRS."

I shook my head, refusing to take the offered keys.

"It's just a car, sweetheart. I don't have any particular attachment to this one. It came out this year and can easily be replaced."

I hated doing this. "I'm almost certain you'll be reimbursed for any loss or damage the vehicle sustains."

"Aren't you afraid I'll be committing insurance fraud if I report it stolen?" He was only teasing, but I put my finger to his lips to stop the banter.

"No. I don't want it. I'll figure something else out. I must have been out of my mind to come here and ask you this." Hugging him, I hoped he would forget the whole thing. Instead, he dropped the keys into my jacket pocket. "I can't."

"You will." He looked into my eyes. "Although, I do drive a hard bargain. I'd like that kiss now." As I looked away, he brushed his thumb across my cheek to get my attention. "I'm not worried about catching a cold." How could I tell him I spent the past week making out with some slimeball car thief? He saw the guilt in my eyes and backed away. "Alexis, you're scaring me a little."

"This job's starting to take its toll. I've been forced to do some questionable things, and it makes me sick." Shifting my gaze to the ceiling, I couldn't look at him.

"Like ask for a car?" Sometimes letting him believe he knew everything was the best plan. When it was over, we'd talk about it. "Really, it's not a big deal, but I won't force you to take it if it'll create friction between us." He grinned. "And not the good kind of friction." His gaze momentarily snapped to the clock on the wall.

"Get to work. I need to go home and sleep. I've been up all night." Taking his car was the only real option, unless I stole another car, but there was no guarantee I'd be able to pull that off. This would solidify my status with Gregson and put me that much closer to closing the case. "You're sure?" I held up the keys. My indecisiveness was giving me whiplash.

"Absolutely."

"I'll do my best to get it back to you in one piece." Temporarily silencing my guilty conscience, I kissed him.

"Alex, just make sure you come back in one piece." His tone held the slightest edge of worry and sadness. My career had the unfortunate habit of making relationships harder than they had to be.

"I love you, and it's not because of your material possessions. I don't want you to think I'm only with you because of this."

"I know exactly why you're with me." He winked. "It's my sculpture worthy physique, brilliant mind, and god-like stamina."

"You forgot to mention your modesty and grace."

"That goes without saying."

He left for work in his chauffeured town car, and I

elected to leave my car in his garage and drive the newly acquired sports car home. I just had to figure out where to leave it for pick-up tonight, but right now, I needed to get some sleep.

* * *

Before leaving the sports car in a five-star hotel garage, I disengaged the security system. Martin was smart enough to utilize the best technology and most reliable security measures, much better than the crap my current employer was selling. Thankfully, I knew his codes from my days serving as his personal security consultant.

After disconnecting the device, I removed the vehicle registration information and made sure no personal effects had been left inside. Considering Martin had a fleet of vehicles at his disposal, I wondered if he even drove this one for any real length of time. The interior was spotless, and the outside was polished to a reflective gleam. It was a pity it would be chopped.

Stopping inside the hotel, I gave the desk clerk Martin's name since he kept credit cards on file at the most prestigious places in town and asked if it'd be okay to leave his car here for the evening. I flashed my old Martin Technologies ID card at the woman. She smiled and called for a valet. That was easy enough.

Hailing a cab, I went home and locked Martin's vehicle registration in my gun safe, changed into jeans and leather, and clipped on some earrings. I already had the scars from where a few extra holes had been punched through my body, courtesy of being shot and stabbed, so I didn't have any real piercings. Hopefully, these expensive facsimiles would continue to go unnoticed by Tommy.

After applying some blood red lipstick and shimmery black eyeshadow with thick eyeliner, I hailed another cab and went to the hospital to pick up my rental. On the ride over, I left Martin a voicemail asking if Marcal and Bruiser, his driver and bodyguard, could drop my car off at my place when they got a chance. In the interim, there was always public transportation and taxis.

My phone rang, and I glanced at the caller ID. "Yo, Tommy." I laughed internally at my attempt to sound like a mobster's lackey. "What's going on?"

"Hi ya, babe." He flicked his lighter. "I wasn't sure if you'd be awake yet. I hope you had some sweet dreams." There was something sleazy about his tone that grated on my nerves.

"Always. Just dreaming of some fast cars and you. Do we have time to grab dinner before our scavenger hunt?" I asked.

"Music to my ears. Want to go to Franco's and we'll scope out the city after splitting a pizza?"

"Sure."

"See you in thirty?"

"Can't wait."

Franco's was a pizza and beer place a block from the bar where we first met. Tommy tended to stay in the same neighborhood. Apparently, he never learned not to shit where he eats. Everything from Gregson's repair shop, which doubled as a chop shop, to the bars and restaurants Tommy frequented were all within a ten block radius of his apartment.

Maneuvering into a spot that was half a foot too small for my car, I knew the two cars I parked between would curse and likely ding the front and back fenders, but it didn't matter. It was only a rental. If Islind felt particularly generous, he'd reimburse the rental agency for the damage.

When I stepped inside, Tommy was waiting in a back booth. He smiled appreciatively, waving me over. His anxiety was made obvious by the tapping of his fingertips on the tabletop. I wondered if that had more to do with the impending heist or the promise of what would follow. Between now and then I had to find a way out of that potentially sticky situation, but like I insisted the previous night, work came first.

We made small talk while we ate, and he pretended to be fascinated by my job transcribing medical records and filling out insurance forms. He asked dozens of questions about my family, friends, and hobbies. The former federal agent in me was wary of the questions, but I reminded myself this was the equivalent of the coveted third date. Tommy wanted to appear attentive and interested, just like any suitor would. Still, I deflected the questions, knowing anything I said would be a lie I'd have to remember.

After we finished eating, we checked out some gated communities, the exclusive clubs and restaurants, a couple hotels, and the financial district. Quite a few options were available, but I already had something better in mind. I needed to steer him in the right direction without giving away the plant.

"Hey, what about these hotels?" I asked as we went by some valet parking stands. "The problem with restaurants and businesses is no one's around in the middle of the night. That means they won't just leave their cars behind."

"How many times have you done this?"

"Boosting cars?" I shrugged. "Not that often. I'm an upstanding citizen with a day job. The problem is the day job no longer pays the bills ever since they cut my hours."

"How did you get started?"

"The guy I used to date was a car aficionado. He

drove a fancy car and always had cash. I thought he was rich, and we'd get married. Turns out he was a thief. We had some fun, and he taught me a lot. But the whole thing became so complicated. We'd boost a car, but unless a buyer was already lined up, we'd be stuck sitting on a hot ride for weeks. It was too dangerous."

"What happened to him?"

"He got pinched on our seventh GTA. At least the bastard never gave me up."

"I don't imagine anyone would willingly give you up, babe." He circled around another parking garage.

"What about that cute little silver number?" I drew his attention to a BMW.

"Good eye." As he looped around, he pointed out a black Audi and a classic yellow Corvette. "But you got to pay attention to the security cams. There's way too many in here. We gotta look elsewhere." We left that garage and checked three more before he drove into the right parking structure. "Hey, check out that royal blue number." Martin's sports car caught Tommy's eye, like I thought it would. Men were so predictable, sometimes.

"Ooh, that'd be the perfect score." Before he could point out the security camera posted on the wall, I pointed to the support pillar that provided ample cover. Honestly, I wasn't sure if it did, but I was insistent. "What's the spot number?" I made a pretense of scribbling down the location. Now the only thing left to do was pick up Martin's car and take it to whatever location Gregson provided. With any luck, everything would go off without a hitch.

THREE

Night had fallen. Tommy and I waited for Gregson to arrive. To pass the time, Tommy attempted to be suave, but that quickly fizzled after he hit the backrest release on my seat and dropped us into a horizontal position. Luckily, before things progressed too far, Gregson knocked on the window.

"Zip it up, we have work to do," Gregson ordered.

"Dammit," Tommy cursed.

"Like I told you, sweetie, work first." I opened my car door and went inside.

As soon as Tommy joined us, Gregson gave us a different location for delivery and a timetable with further stipulations. I had two hours to find a car and deliver it. If everything went perfectly, I would be introduced to the man in charge.

The goal was to get on the crew and get the buyer's identity. Once I knew that, I could turn the case over to the authorities. The police would get the car thieves off the street, and Auto Protection Services could reassure their customers they were instrumental in shutting down a chop shop, all while bringing them the best innovations in vehicle protection.

Originally, I was hired to identify the thieves and retrieve the stolen property, but after doing some digging, it became apparent Robert Gregson and Tommy Claxton were just a small part of a larger ring. Unfortunately, they were at the bottom of the totem pole. Gregson was just a middleman. Someone else was orchestrating the thefts, deciding which vehicles to steal, where to move them, if they'd be broken down into parts, or sold on the black market. Neither Gregson nor Tommy had any say in the matter, so my job became much more complicated.

Even after stealing the '67 Mustang, I had yet to uncover the identity of the buyer, or maybe he was our benefactor. At this point, I was uncertain of the mystery man's role in the operation. Either way, he gave Gregson orders and cash. He was the key to stopping the car theft ring. Once I got him, my job would be done. I couldn't wait to be free from Tommy. After all, Martin didn't like to share, and neither did I.

"Alex, you're doing this by yourself," Gregson said. "I have something more important for Tommy to do, but we'll meet at this location." He handed me another slip of paper. "If there's trouble, you're on your own."

"See you guys later."

Something felt off. I couldn't put my finger on it, but this didn't seem like the best way to vet a new teammate. Was Gregson suspicious of my sudden appearance and skills? Or was Tommy questioning his good fortune of finding the girl of his dreams who could hold her own stealing cars? Maybe it was because I refused to sleep with him or perform any type of sexual act on him. Had they figured out who I really was?

I went to the hotel and parked across the street. My

spare nine millimeter was in the glove box, and although I didn't want to carry during the commission of a crime, the uneasy feeling demanded it. I slipped into my shoulder holster, checked the magazine, and clipped my gun in place. After readjusting my jacket to conceal my weapon without hindering my ability to reach it quickly, I darted across the street and into the elevator. Scanning the area, I didn't spot a tail. Maybe Gregson was on the level, and I was simply paranoid.

Using the key to Martin's car, I got inside without any muss or fuss. With plenty of time to spare, I monitored the area for signs of movement. With the exception of a few late night guests arriving, the place was quiet. There was no sign of my car thief cohorts. Once a reasonable amount of time passed, I started the car and pulled out of the space.

Ten minutes before deadline, I arrived at thc predetermined destination and found Gregson standing next to his SUV. There was no sign of Tommy. Shutting off the engine, I opened the car door.

"Look what someone left." I offered a broad smile, holding up the keys. "Snatched 'em right from the valet stand. Ta da." I played up the scenario as a great victory, but Gregson barely cracked a smile.

"Nicely done." He nodded to a parked car across the street, and the high beams came on. I threw up a hand to shield myself from the sudden brightness in the otherwise dimly lit alleyway, just as something hard and cold pressed against the back of my neck.

"What the hell is this?" I exhaled slowly, not wanting to risk whoever was holding the gun becoming trigger happy.

"You're good," Gregson said, "maybe too good. Within the course of two weeks, it's rare to find someone willing to boost cars. What's even stranger is your willingness to work alone to find something worth this much," he gestured to the blue Ferrari, "and then, to top it off, you show up with the keys."

"Paranoid much, Robert?" I glared daggers at him. "Tommy gave me the heads-up on tonight's assignment. We cased the car earlier. It's a lot easier to borrow a car than it is to steal one, which I can claim by lifting the keys. Maybe I just have sticky fingers, or I got into the wrong car by mistake. If I were stopped, joyriding doesn't carry the years of prison time GTA does. Frankly, proving myself to you isn't worth my freedom."

Gregson nodded to the person holding me at gunpoint. The headlights switched off, and Tommy stepped into view with the gun at his side.

"We had to make sure you weren't a cop." Tommy looked remorseful. "If you were, your backup would have intervened by now."

Remaining in character, I slapped him. "Don't you ever touch me again. We're done." I spun toward Gregson. "I don't need this shit." I threw the keys at him. "Keep the car and the cut. I want nothing to do with sadists like you."

"Babe," Tommy grabbed my elbow, which I jerked out of his grasp, "c'mon, don'tcha wanna meet the boss?"

"I don't care." Petulant was something I did well. "What were you going to do? Shoot me?" He reached for me again, and I batted his hand away. "Don't touch me." It was a fine line to walk, reacting as if this no longer mattered and wanting nothing to do with any of the drama while at the same time needing to get deeper and uncover more. An oversell was just as detrimental as an undersell.

From across the street, a man cleared his throat. Gregson shot Tommy a look. "If she wants to go, let her. We'll find someone else."

Tommy's eyes pleaded that I reconsider, and audibly sighing and crossing my arms over my chest, I gave in. "Fine."

"This is Reggie." Gregson indicated the man from last night. "He's our benefactor."

Reggie crossed the street and circled Martin's car, scanning it for RF signals. "Very impressive. It's a brand new model. We'll make more selling the entire unit than breaking it down for parts." His eyes met mine. "Young lady, you have a great eye." At least Martin did. "Let's get off the street and talk about this somewhere more secure." Tommy headed for Gregson's SUV, but I hedged, not certain how to play this off. "Why don't you come with me?" Reggie offered.

"What about the car?" Why weren't they concerned about moving it out of sight?

"Hoyt," Reggie bellowed, and a man stepped out of the shadows, "take her to the garage."

"Right away, sir," Hoyt said with the faintest of Irish accents.

There was something familiar about him, but I couldn't place him. I only caught a glimpse of his silhouette in the dark alley. Maybe he'd been arrested or was a suspect on another case I worked. His name didn't ring any bells. Hopefully, I was mistaken. At this point, I couldn't afford for my cover to be blown.

As Hoyt recovered the keys from the ground and unlocked Martin's car, Reggie went back to the vehicle that had blinded me only minutes earlier. "You coming?" he asked.

"Looks like it." I opened the passenger's side door, and before it even shut, Reggie hit the gas pedal.

Ten minutes later, we were at Gregson's repair garage. Martin's car was brought inside, and Hoyt and

Gregson shut the garage doors. In this neighborhood, a bright blue sports car would stick out like a sore thumb.

"What's your name?" Reggie asked.

"Alexandra Riley."

I hoped to get a first and last name for Reggie, but instead, he performed a quick search on his phone, finding my falsified background. He read the info, but my cover had no arrest record and nothing indicating who I was or what I could do. Riley was a blank slate. Thankfully, it was an old alias the OIO established years ago when I was still getting a government paycheck.

"It doesn't look like you've ever been on anyone's radar."

"I'm a good girl. I keep my nose clean." Reggie barely paid attention to my comment, tapping away at the screen. "Will I end up on *America's Most Wanted* because of who you are, Reggie?" I asked.

He looked up and smiled like the cat that swallowed the canary but didn't respond. At least in this light I had a decent chance of figuring out if he had a record. He was approximately 5'10, average build, late thirties, brown eyes, brown hair, and a tattoo of a pair of dice on his left wrist. How many criminals could that possibly describe?

"Alex," Tommy called.

"Don't."

Gregson returned from locking the garage door, but Hoyt lingered in the shadows. Reggie shifted his gaze to the three of us, not looking particularly pleased with his options. Shutting his phone, he leaned against the hood of the car.

"Looks like you're capable of finishing the job," Reggie said. "Another three cars and I'm moving on. Like I told Robert, when this is over, you'll get a cut of the profit. It's nearly half a million for the entire job. Although you've already fulfilled most of the orders on my wish list, I need a coordinated team to nab the last few vehicles." His eyes bore into me. "Ms. Riley, can you work with Mr. Claxton without further incident?"

Sighing audibly, I kicked the toe of my shoe into the ground. "I guess."

"Don't guess," he chastised. "Yes or no?"

"Yes."

"Excellent." His face erupted in a bright smile. "Three vehicles are being delivered to a dealership at the end of the week. Claxton, Hoyt, and Riley will retrieve them. Gregson and I will ensure they are untraceable and cleaned for transport. Your cuts will be left in private overseas accounts. The account information will be provided at the conclusion of our business transaction. After this, there will be no further contact."

Reggie had it down to a T. He had done this before. My guess was it was one city, then another, and another. He was a thief who couldn't stop. It was an addiction for men like him. One score that became just one more score. There were only two ways they ever stopped, incarceration or incapacitation.

"How about some details?" Gregson asked.

"You'll get them the day of and not before," Reggie said. "This isn't my first rodeo, and while you all seem so trustworthy, that's one risk I won't take."

Reggie left, and Hoyt followed him out. Was Hoyt his personal bodyguard, or would he be dismissed at the conclusion of business too? The way they traveled together indicated they had a strong familiarity with one another. How long was this auto theft ring in operation?

I watched as they exited the side door. Even Hoyt's walk looked familiar. It was making me crazy. As it was, my guard was already up. I didn't know if I could handle any more surprises.

"You heard the man, nothing 'til Friday," Gregson said. "Stay out of trouble until then and keep your phones on in case of anything." He focused on me. "In the event some idiot from the valet stand remembers you, don't come crying to me. You made your bed."

"Whatever." I marched to the door, hoping to get a better look at Hoyt, but he was long gone. Before I made it across the street, Tommy caught up.

"Alex, wait. Quit being such a bitch."

"Screw you, Tommy." If the cops wanted to roll in on account of disorderly conduct, I wasn't opposed. "You were two minutes away from blowing my brains out, and you expect me to talk to you. I'm pretty sure you don't want to hear what I have to say."

"I wouldn't have."

"Bullshit. If Robert told you to, you would. It's that simple. I don't want someone in my life I don't trust, so stay away from me." Keeping up this pointless argument was the only thing keeping Tommy off of me. If I accepted his apology, there would be other expectations I had no desire to fulfill. "I'll work with you Friday, and that's it. If you're looking to get laid, go find some whore at Franco's."

Muttering expletives and derogatory comments, he stalked down the street to his car, slammed the door, and sped away. Thank goodness that was over. Unfortunately, my rental was parked twenty blocks away, across the street from the hotel. I was almost positive I'd never find a cab in this neighborhood. On the bright side, my nine millimeter was great company.

I passed some streetwalkers and the occasional drug dealer who offered to improve my mood. Despite the fact that I could have used a pick-me-up, I had no interest in what they were hocking. My mood would improve once this case was over and I figured out who Hoyt was and why he seemed so familiar.

After being catcalled and spooked more times than I'd ever admit, I made it to my car. Instead of going home, I went to the precinct. With it being this early in the morning, there was a decent chance I could get access to police records without too much hassle. Maybe I'd flip through the mug books and see if I could identify Reggie. I had worked many cases with three major crimes detectives, O'Connell, Thompson, and Heathcliff. If one of them was assigned the graveyard shift, I'd call in a favor, especially after promising to turn over evidence on an active auto theft ring.

"Holy crap," Detective Nick O'Connell glanced behind me, "where's the arresting officer? I'd love to shake the hand of the person who finally got you off the street. Let me guess, solicitation?" He shook his head and made a tsk sound. "I know money's tight for private investigators, but if Martin wouldn't give you a loan, y'know Jen and I would have scraped something together to keep you from selling your body."

"I'll keep that in mind." I took a seat at his partner's desk. "I was hoping to proposition you, Detective."

"Now what do you want?"

"Should I take my clothes off first? Or is that what happens after we come to an arrangement?" All's fair in love and war or when dealing with my police brethren. Since Nick opened that can of worms by suggesting I looked like a hooker, I'd enjoy watching him squirm.

"There isn't a right answer to that question." He leaned back in his chair. "So I'm going to remind you I'm married, and you're in a committed relationship and completely insane."

"True." I smiled. "I was wondering if you could run a search on a guy who goes by the name Reggie. He has a tattoo of some dice on his left wrist." I described him while Nick typed some things into the computer. He hit enter and leaned back. "Anything?" I asked.

"Nada." He spun the monitor so I could see the blank search results. "Do you want to go through the mug books?"

"Yes."

After disappearing into the records room, he returned with half a dozen thick binders and dropped them on his partner's desk. I flipped pages while he worked, or maybe he was playing solitaire. Whatever he was doing involved an astronomical amount of mouse clicking.

"Do you want to tell me what you're working on or who this guy is?" he asked. "Y'know, I'm a detective, so I will figure it out eventually."

"I plead the fifth. Did burglary get a tip the other night about a stolen '67 Mustang?" I asked. He cocked an eyebrow up and stopped clicking the mouse. "Just wondered." I went back to scanning the photographs.

He typed something into the computer and leaned back, picking up his pen and tapping it against the desk. "Is there a reason one of the perps fits your description?"

"No, she doesn't. And I didn't think you called them perps. Isn't that just artistic licensing by TV writers?" He knew I was trying to derail his questioning and glared. "Do I look like a perp to you?"

"At the moment, a little bit." He waited for an explanation. "Well?"

"There've been some complaints about stolen vehicles within the last month. The police aren't handling the situation to everyone's satisfaction. A dozen or so cars have gone missing that I know about, and all of the owners are customers of Auto Protection Services which installs security systems with the latest technology, meaning radio frequency transmitters that anyone can hack with the right program. Needless to say, APS wants the culprits caught before they get a bad reputation. So they hired someone who actually knows what she's doing and isn't limited by the city's finite resources. Ultimately, they want the thieves identified, but if any of the vehicles can be recovered, that's even better."

"So you're dressed like a cross between a cat burglar and hooker in order to lurk in the shadows, waiting for the thieves to show up?"

"Not exactly."

"Will the exactly require handcuffs and reminding you of your rights?"

"I'd hate to make you go through all that trouble." He wouldn't arrest me for conjecture. We'd had our tiffs in the past, but we were good now. Nick wasn't one to harbor ill will. "Friday, I'll present you with a case on a silver platter."

"Joy." He didn't sound particularly pleased by this prospect, but he had been up all night. Perhaps he was just tired.

FOUR

A few minutes later, Nick was called to assist on a double homicide, which I took as my cue to leave. It was six a.m. I detoured to my office, checked my messages, ran Reggie through the criminal databases, and stopped at the rental car agency to return my vehicle. I didn't need it anymore since my interaction with Tommy was over, and Alexandra Riley didn't want anyone to trace her rental car back to Alexis Parker.

I shook my head. Sometimes, I was certain too many undercover assignments would lead to multiple personality disorder. Finally, I called a cab and went home.

As I tried to fall asleep, I ran through every case I'd worked at the Office of International Operations while serving as a federal agent and everything I had done as part of the private sector since, but I hadn't come across any Hoyts. Assuming Hoyt might be a nickname or false identity, I focused on the man's build and voice, but he only spoke a few words. And in the shadows, he fit almost anyone's description. Who was he? Why did he seem so familiar? The puzzle did nothing to squelch my occasional insomnia, and by the time I fell asleep, it was mid-afternoon. My dreams were a scattered haze of past cases and experiences I tried very hard to forget.

When I woke up, it was nighttime. I made dinner and settled in front of the computer. I ran Reggie through Interpol's criminal database, glad to have access thanks to my former connections. While the search ran in the background, I minimized the window and did some digging on Hoyt, but I lacked enough information to conduct a decent internet people search. Out of ideas, I left the Interpol search running and phoned Jeremy Islind's private number.

"Ms. Parker, how is your investigation going?" he asked.

"I'm getting closer. From the intel I've gathered, three cars are being delivered to a dealership on Friday night, but they won't arrive. Once I get the details, I'll call the authorities. With any luck, they'll catch the thieves in the act."

"Very good. I've spoken to our legal counsel who has instilled upon the district attorney's office our desire to find justice for our clients. As long as we cooperate, no criminal charges will be filed against you."

"Do the cops know this?"

"They will when the time comes. Right now, your case isn't solid."

If I couldn't point the finger at the actual guilty parties, the DA could pin all of this on me. "It will be." I filled him in on the use of James Martin's personal vehicle as part of the venture, and Islind guaranteed as soon as the paperwork was filed he'd get the ball rolling on issuing a reimbursement check. "Thanks.

Let me know if anyone else loses a car between now and Friday. Until then, I'm maintaining a low profile."

"Good luck, Ms. Parker."

"Thanks, but I hope I won't need it."

After hanging up, I dialed Martin. He was in the middle of an international conference call, according to the assistant who answered his cell phone. Without leaving my name, I told her to remind him to check his home phone for details concerning his car and hung up. How many other people could he have possibly lent a car to in the last few days? After leaving all the relevant information regarding filing the paperwork for reimbursement on his answering machine, I left a few wildly inappropriate suggestions about what we should do the next time we were together and hung up.

As predicted, Martin called a few hours later, proving Pavlov's theory, even though I didn't conduct my experiment using doorbells and meaty treats. Voicemail messages promising sexual favors worked just as well for the male half of the species. After making sure he had all the proper documentation necessary and telling him I would leave his car registration information on my countertop for Marcal to retrieve whenever he delivered my car, our conversation devolved into phone sex after which we made plans for a repeat performance on Saturday without the phone.

I checked the progress on the search and called it a night. Hopefully, I could flip-flop my days and nights to something resembling normal or at least more normal. After all, Alexandra Riley had to be up early to transcribe patient records.

When I woke up the next morning, I felt hungover. I wasn't, but it sure felt like it. Too much sleep or too little sleep or some combination of the two over the last couple of weeks had taken their toll. After showering and making a pot of coffee, I returned to the computer. There were a dozen hits in the international databases. Skimming through the details, I eliminated half the possibilities based on race and age. The remaining few had arrest records, but one, in particular, caught my attention.

Reginald Barlow had a record for petty theft, assault with a deadly weapon, and grand theft auto. The mug shot appeared on my screen, and while it was outdated by close to a decade, it was the same guy. The tattoo was photographed separately, and it matched perfectly. Barlow was born in England but held Canadian citizenship. Although, he had no discernible accent. I incorrectly assumed he was American, but from his passport records, he should be considered international. In the last six months, he visited Germany, Switzerland, France, and Belgium. This factoid complicated matters.

The stolen vehicles were all rare finds. With the proper acid wash, re-etching of VINs, and falsified documentation, they could easily be exported and resold internationally. I sighed. “Why can’t a chop shop just be a chop shop?”

International sales made this a federal matter too. Sure, the local police department could take the collar, but some three letter agency would have to become involved to search cargo ships, access shipping manifests, and track down the international buyers. It must be me. Nothing I was involved in could ever be simple. I was a jinx and proved it again. No luck would be preferable to my luck.

As I assessed the situation, listing the stolen vehicles in chronological order to conduct my own search before contacting my friends at the OIO, FBI, and Interpol, a key scraped in my lock. Always paranoid, I grabbed my nine millimeter from my desk drawer and waited. Marcal, Martin's driver and valet, opened my door. He smiled and held up my car keys.

"Thanks." I put the gun down. "The paperwork's on my counter."

"Anything else I can do for you?" he asked, retrieving the documentation.

"That was it. Can I get you a cup of coffee or tea? Maybe some toast or," I tried to recall what my fridge contained, "some leftover Indian takeout?"

He shook his head. "Jones is waiting downstairs." Jones, a.k.a Bruiser, was Martin's bodyguard. "Have a good day, Ms. Parker."

"You too." He let himself out, and I relocked my door.

Something pinged in my brain, but it disappeared before I latched onto the thought wisp. Europe, Hoyt, exported cars, Reggie, what was it? Frustrated, I returned to mapping out the stolen vehicles, but my focus was shattered.

* * *

Over the course of the next two days, I compiled additional information on Reginald Barlow, Robert Gregson, Tommy Claxton, and the stolen vehicles. Although I couldn't be sure they were being sent overseas or shipped internationally, given Barlow's recent travel history, it wouldn't have been surprising. I called SSA Mark Jablonsky, my former mentor at the OIO, and gave him the non-incriminating version of my current gig. He agreed to work with the Interpol liaison, Patrick Farrell, to track any suspicious auto sales in the EU and Canada that matched the makes and models of the stolen cars. At this point, going to the precinct would be premature, so I kept O'Connell in the dark. My boss could make that call when the time came.

Tommy tried to talk to me a handful of times, each time leaving more aggressive messages. By Thursday evening, I was tired of the harassment and answered. We were supposed to work together the following night, and I was edgy enough without dealing with a spurned would-be lover.

"Tommy, stop calling. What part of leave me alone don't you understand?"

"We were doing good, and then you overreacted. What the hell?"

"Are you going to keep it together tomorrow night?" I asked.

"Can't we talk about this? Rob tells me to do one thing, and then you flip out because of it. Shit. What was I supposed to do? I can't go against Rob."

"You picked him over me. That's the problem."

"I didn't pick nobody."

"So what happens tomorrow if Reggie decides I didn't do a good job and wants you to end it? Or if Rob doesn't want to split the cut three ways? What are you going to do then?"

"I never killed nobody. It's all an act. You should know I'm not a tough guy. I'm just a big teddy bear. A Tommy bear. Alexandra, I'd never hurt you. I'm falling head over heels for you." The romantic commentary was supposed to melt the ice around my heart, but it didn't.

"I'll think about it." I sighed into the phone. "Just do me a favor tomorrow night and act professional. After the job, you and I will have a nice long chat. Maybe you can take me out to breakfast at that little diner a block from the garage."

"It's a date."

After agreeing, I hung up. Was I leading the poor

schlub on? Absolutely. Did I care? Not at all.

Before going to sleep, I compiled my files on the nine previously stolen cars in preparation for turning them over to the authorities. Since I was responsible for two of the cars, that left seven counts of GTA the authorities could pass around to Rob, Tommy, Reggie, and Hoyt. With any luck, my weekend wouldn't be spent in lockup on two pending counts of GTA. Well, really only one since Martin willingly surrendered his vehicle for my use. But regardless of the possible charges, cops didn't do well in jail, and neither did former federal agents or current private investigators, so avoiding getting arrested in the raid seemed like a no-brainer.

After making sure all the relevant information was in triplicate, I repeated the process with the knowledge I possessed on Robert Gregson, Tommy Claxton, and the peripheral players, Reginald 'Reggie' Barlow and Hoyt. I placed my personal set of documents in my small fireproof lockbox and put the other two sets in envelopes. Tomorrow, I'd drop copies off with Mr. Islind and leave the extra set at my office in case of anything. Reassured that all the bases were covered, I logged almost two hours on the treadmill to burn off the nervous energy before calling it quits.

The next day, I ran a few remaining errands and camped out at a nearby coffee shop to wait for Gregson's message. The sun had just set when my phone rang. Delivery was at eleven p.m. Tommy and I were to wait for further instructions. A few minutes later, Tommy called. He wanted to work on a plan to ensure everything went smoothly, and since the more information I had, the better, I reluctantly agreed.

An hour later, I was in the passenger's seat of his car, parked across the street from the high-end dealership. Hoyt declined the invitation to join us which was a relief since I still wasn't sure who he was, and I couldn't risk him blowing this operation when I was so close to ending the case. Tommy yapped about how Hoyt planned to pretend to be an employee assigned to unload the truck. He'd get keys and access, and if the three of us acted swiftly enough, we'd be long gone by the time the real employees realized others were doing their jobs for them.

"What happens if they're outside, waiting for the shipment?"

"Reggie says his boy's gonna provide a distraction, so we can take off with the cars."

"Okay, but who's covering for Hoyt so he can nab the last car?"

"You worry too much. Why do you have to overthink everything, babe? You did the same thing to us."

"Whatever." It didn't matter since I was sabotaging the entire operation anyway. Hopefully, they'd catch Hoyt in the act and find the remaining cars with Barlow, Gregson, and Tommy at the garage. The trick was to avoid getting arrested too. "We just have to drop them off at Rob's, right?"

"Yep, then they'll deactivate the security beacons, we get our cut, and you and I will be celebrating by dawn." He smiled lecherously. "I went with ribbed for your pleasure."

"Tommy, I said we'd talk. I never said anything else was going to happen."

"We're stealing some fucking cars tonight, babe. We're going to make bank on this. You'll want to celebrate. You'll see."

"Yeah, we'll see," I replied, unconvinced. "Right now, I'm going to change into something less visible. I'll be back an hour before go-time. I don't suggest you hang around here until then because Reggie will be pissed if someone gets suspicious and it tanks the job."

"Good call," he watched as I stepped out of the car, "to go with that fantastic ass."

"Charmer," I retorted, heading for the bus stop.

Utilizing public transportation, I made it to my office without Tommy or anyone else being the wiser. Inside, I changed into all black, knotted my hair in a tight braid, and checked the time. With a couple of hours to kill, I prioritized my calls. First was Jeremy Islind. He promised to phone the legal department and have the DA's office brought up to speed while I called the police department. Being familiar with protocol and procedure, I cut through the red-tape and asked for Det. O'Connell. Unfortunately, he wasn't in. I tried his partner, Thompson, who was out on a call. Third try's a charm. Det. Derek Heathcliff was at his desk, incorrectly believing he was twenty minutes away from going home.

"Parker," he said, "O'Connell warned us you might call. Can it wait until tomorrow when he's at work?"

"No, but if you're lucky, maybe this will bump you up on my list of favorite detectives."

"I'm already your favorite. What've you got?" I updated him on the impending heist, leaving my own culpability out of the equation. After I provided addresses, a reasonable timeframe, and the reason Auto Protection Services hired me, Heathcliff whistled. "Why can't everyone make our cases for us?"

"Civilians have no manners." Checking the time, I had to cut our conversation short. "Look, I need some leeway when you roll up on the heist in progress. My boss wants to make sure we get the head of the chop shop, and since his legal counsel's been negotiating with the DA's office, do you think you can grab all the moving parts in one fell swoop?"

"As long as the team splits up like you say, we should be fine. I'll get some guys to sit on the garage and the dealership, and a couple of mobile units will tail the drivers." He lowered his voice. "Do you want your cover to remain intact if you get grabbed in the sting?"

"Just in case, but I'm hoping to get away without being sidled with those lovely silver bracelets you carry with you at all times."

"Any other women on the team?"

"Not that I know of."

"All right. I'll see what I can do. But if you get cornered, don't resist arrest. Your boyfriend would have our asses if you were taken down by friendly fire."

FIVE

It was almost eleven. I was sitting in an all-night diner a block from the dealership, watching out the window. I paid my bill twenty minutes ago, but I remained, sipping coffee, ready to dash across the street as soon as I got the signal. Tommy was parked on the opposite side of the road, waiting for the delivery truck. I didn't have eyes on Hoyt and wondered if he was even going to show up. A dark gray van idled three blocks away. It belonged to the police department.

My plan was simple. Follow directions, get the car, drop it off at Rob's, and get the hell out of there. If the raid commenced before I arrived, I would ditch the vehicle nearby, find a cab, and go home. There I could change, speak to Islind, and determine if I needed to spend my night at the police station. A lot depended on how much evidence the police acquired during the raid. I wasn't sure if they had warrants; although, they might by now. But even if they didn't, they would be intervening during the commission of a crime. Most things were fair game under those conditions.

My phone buzzed. It was time to move. The truck, loaded with eight brand new cars, just arrived. Zipping my jacket, I pulled the baseball cap lower and met Tommy at his car.

"Hang on," he put his hand on my arm, "Hoyt's speaking to the driver." A man stood outside the cab of the truck, gesturing animatedly as he spoke. Then he waved us over. "Okay, I'll go first. We're taking the bottom three 911s. That's all Reggie wants. After I clear the ramps, I'll pull around to the side like I'm going around back. You get in the next car and follow."

"Okay."

I waited patiently as Tommy received a set of keys and lowered the ramps on the back of the sixteen-wheeler. As soon as he was inside the car, I made my way to the truck. Hoyt was still facing away from me, talking to the driver, but he held out a second set of keys. The fact that he never even turned toward me set my internal radar buzzing. Either he recognized me, or he was afraid of anyone else on the team being able to identify him. Neither of those possibilities bode well. If Hoyt made me, I didn't know what would be waiting at the garage, and if he didn't and simply wanted to keep his identity concealed, then he might be planning to put two in the back of each of our heads.

Ignoring the mounting panic, I went to the back of the truck, climbed inside the second Porsche, and carefully backed out. Shifting gears, I spotted three men shouting and rushing toward the truck. Our plan wasn't working out so well. As I turned the corner, the van from earlier hurtled down the street. It was definitely time to get out of here.

Putting the car into fourth, I headed for Rob's garage. Half a dozen police cruisers were in hot pursuit of Tommy. Thankfully, they were all ahead of me.

Cursing, I calculated the risk associated with each of my options. Delivering the car would cast aside any distrust, and in the event Gregson and Barlow thwarted the cops, I might need to make sure Alexandra Riley remained intact. Praying not to get stopped, I sped to the drop-off location.

I pulled into the open door of the garage and found Barlow and Gregson looking particularly antsy. "Where's Tommy?" Gregson asked as I stepped out of the car. Barlow grabbed the keys, and Gregson scanned the vehicle. In under a minute, they opened the hood and trunk and disconnected the security beacons.

"He was ahead of me." I inched nonchalantly toward the door. "I'm sure he'll be here any second."

"What about Hoyt?" Barlow asked. Before I could answer, the sound of sirens grew louder. "Shit."

Tossing them both a quick glance as they scurried around the room, I knew it was time to go. I ducked out the side door and sprinted across the street, taking a seat at the bus stop two blocks away while I took off my jacket, tossed the cap into the garbage receptacle, and tugged my hair free. It wasn't much, but it ought to be enough. As I did this, I made sure neither man exited the garage. Barlow shut the large vehicle entryway, but before either could escape, police cruisers surrounded the place.

Letting out a sigh of relief, I dialed a cab company and waited. As the raid commenced and the men were led outside in handcuffs, the cab pulled up. *Mission accomplished*, I thought happily as the city whizzed past and I found myself forty minutes away from the chaos. Paying the cabbie and overtipping him on account of my good fortune not to be sitting in the back of a cruiser, I went inside my apartment.

After spending the next few hours on the phone with Islind, the attorney he hired, and the police department, I was assured my involvement was being assessed in conjunction with the evidence obtained tonight. Four men were in custody, along with two stolen Porsches. The entire garage was being scoured for signs of the previously stolen vehicles or any left behind parts. As far as everyone was concerned, the private investigator who'd been instrumental in solidifying the case wasn't being brought up on any charges. Happily calling it a night, I went to bed, feeling accomplished and free.

The ringing phone woke me. It was seven a.m. on a Saturday. Phones should not work this early in the morning.

"Hello?"

"Parker," O'Connell sounded annoyed, "I need you to come to the station."

"Am I in trouble?"

"We have a suspect in holding who refuses to talk to anyone. The only person he said he'd speak to is you."

"Me or Alex Riley?" If it was Tommy making a fuss, I'd pay someone to look the other way while I stabbed him.

"*Agent* Alexis Parker," O'Connell specified.

My throat went dry. Who did they arrest? "I'll be right there."

Dressing quickly, I grabbed my credentials and a set of the documents for last night's raid, just in case someone misplaced something, and drove at breakneck speed to the precinct. Automatic transmission didn't pull the tight turns the manual did, but I still made it in record time. As I headed to the major crimes floor, I couldn't figure out who would be asking for me. More specifically, the former version of me.

"He's in the interview room," O'Connell said as soon as I walked in. "I'm coming with you." I dropped the file on top of his desk and took a deep breath. "He has no identification. We ran his prints through the system, but it looks like someone deleted them."

"How can that be?"

"I don't know. We grabbed him at the dealership last night. He wouldn't say a word. He didn't even acknowledge that he understood his rights. The officers thought he might be a mute or deaf. Then after spending the last four hours sitting alone in interview, I walk in, introduce myself, and he says *get me Agent Parker*." O'Connell snorted. "I didn't realize I was your personal assistant."

"That's because you forgot my coffee this morning. I might have to fire you." I opened the door to the room. The officer inside stepped out, and I entered.

"Alexis," the Irish accent was unmistakable, "I need to get out of here."

"Ryan?" My breath hitched, and I barely choked out his name. "My god, Ryan." Memories of working with the Paris police flooded my thoughts, followed by being tortured by a crime lord who had fled France only to come to the United States in the hopes of finishing what he started in that Parisian warehouse. "What are you doing here?"

"I didn't think anyone would believe me. I didn't want you to get involved, but I didn't see any other way, and since you were working undercover, you must already be involved."

I turned to O'Connell who was standing behind me, perplexed. "Take the cuffs off." He looked at me like I lost my mind. "Nick, this is Inspector Ryan Donough of the Police Nationale. Take the cuffs off."

"Donough," the name rang a bell for O'Connell, but he hedged, "we've spoken on the phone before."

"Indeed," Ryan replied. "You put down the sadistic animal that tortured Alex."

O'Connell nodded. After giving me a final uncertain look, he unlocked Ryan's handcuffs.

No longer able to contain the emotional barrage, I launched myself into Ryan's arms. He saved my life once, and with the exception of the occasional e-mail, we hadn't seen each other in almost a year. Whatever was going on, he needed help.

"I thought I was crazy thinking Hoyt seemed so familiar," I mumbled. He gave me a tight squeeze and released me.

"Why didn't you say something sooner, buddy?" O'Connell asked, not liking any bit of the current situation. "Y'know, you're not walking out of here until we verify who you are and what you're doing with a group of car thieves."

"If you phone my captain, he can verify my involvement. I was assigned to assist the International Criminal Court in an investigation they were conducting." The fact that Ryan had yet to divulge anything concrete piqued my interest, and O'Connell left us alone to consult with his supervisor over this new wrinkle.

"Does Interpol know what you're doing?" I asked. "Maybe I can phone some friends and get you out of here sooner instead of later."

"I'm not asking you for any other favors. I wasn't even sure about asking to speak to you. After all, the last time we worked together, things didn't turn out so well."

"You showed up in time. That's all that mattered. But honestly, asking for Agent Parker," I laughed, "you're years too late."

His brow furrowed. "When we spoke on the phone, you said you were going back to the OIO."

"It was temporary. Consulting only. I've done a couple of jobs for them. A few for the police department too. Ever since I quit my corporate gig, I've been trying to remain firmly planted in private investigations."

"Then what were you doing with Barlow?" he asked.

"My client wanted to shut down the chop shop. No big deal." He squinted, trying to determine if I was lying, and I shot him a questioning look. "Why would the ICC have any interest in a few internationally sold stolen vehicles?"

"Who knows?" He stared at the table. I sat across from him, determined to get a straight answer. Instead, his focus shifted to my wrists, looking for the faint scars from my botched Parisian assignment. "You heal well." He rubbed his fingers against my skin, tracing the faint pink lines. "Thanks for getting me out of the cuffs, but you've done enough. I can take it from here."

"Actually, you can't," O'Connell said, rejoining us. My bet was he had been observing from the other side of the glass while phone calls were made. "You are who you claim to be, but we're having trouble getting a straight answer out of your superior. It turns out you have zero jurisdiction here. Whatever you think you're doing, it's not police work."

"There must be some mistake," Ryan insisted. "Try calling Interpol, please." For someone who just said he didn't want any favors, he was desperate to get out of lockup.

"Parker, I need a minute." O'Connell led me into the hallway. After the door closed, he turned to me. "I remember your Paris case just as well as you do. I had your back the entire week we spent tracking that psychopath. And yes, I remember the phone calls back and forth to the Paris police. But are you sure Donough can be trusted? It's been a while since you worked with him."

"What did they say when you called?"

"His supervisor said he's been undercover for the last six months, but three weeks ago, they lost track of him. He went to Belgium, Spain, and Germany, but communication ceased after his passport was stamped leaving Germany. He went dark, and Captain Reneaux of the Police Nationale hasn't heard from him since."

"Ryan says he's working with the ICC. Did you contact them?"

"They say he's assisting on building an international case, but you know they have no jurisdiction in our country without express permission. We scanned the printouts for pending federal and international operations, but the state department has no idea they're here. I left a message with Agent Jablonsky for verification, but..." his words dropped off.

"They probably don't know what's going on either."

"What do you want me to do? The lieutenant says we can theoretically confiscate his passport and cut him loose since he won't be going anywhere, or we can leave him in custody for the next thirty-six hours."

"You're not bringing him up on charges?"

"No." He kicked the toe of his shoe into the molding. "The officer who arrested him said he wasn't doing anything wrong at the time." I stared incredulously. "Yeah, I know he handed the keys to you and that moron who won't shut up for two seconds, but you were dressed like employees. He could claim it was an honest mistake. None of the other guys are willing to roll on him. They aren't even willing to roll on you or each other. There really is honor among thieves. Go figure."

"So he's free to go?"

"For now, unless something changes. We planned to hold him the full forty-eight, until he asked for you," O'Connell said. "So it's your call."

"Set him free. Ryan's a good cop. He ends up in these long-term undercover assignments with little to no support, but he's one of the good guys."

"Okay." He nodded to himself and studied me. "Are you okay? The entire Paris situation is something you avoid talking about like the plague. It almost destroyed you, and with this guy here, right in front of your face, I just don't want to see you forced to endure anything else."

"I'm fine. It happened a year ago, and a lot has happened since." I smiled reassuringly. "You were my knight in shining armor on that one, rushing in and shooting that sick, twisted bastard. Maybe I should be asking if you're okay."

He scoffed at the question. "Not at all." His eyes shifted toward the interview room. "I don't like this. I don't know him, and I don't trust him."

"But you trust me?"

"Yes, even if you are a car thief." He rubbed a hand over his face. "But I'm sending a unit to keep him under surveillance until we get some straight answers. For all I know, he's the ringleader of this car theft ring, and I'm not letting a collar like that walk out of this precinct just because he used to be your friend."

"Fair enough."

"Hey," O'Connell grabbed my elbow before I could go back inside the interrogation room, "stay away from him until we verify his story."

Nodding, I turned to leave. Since I was up early, I might as well get everything straightened out with

Islind, make some calls on Ryan's behalf, perhaps meet with the attorneys, and hopefully make it to Martin's by late this afternoon.

SIX

I was thankful someone had the wherewithal to order coffee and donuts. Islind, APS's legal counsel, and I sat in the conference room, going over the information from last night's bust. Reginald Barlow, Robert Gregson, and Tommy Claxton had charges pending against them. Barlow and Gregson's fingerprints were found on the car I delivered, the discarded lowjack, and transmitter wiring. It was nice to know criminals weren't always smart enough to wear gloves.

The rest of the evidence from the chop shop had not been divulged. If evidence from any of the missing vehicles that APS serviced turned up, the police would pass it along or notify the victims directly.

Tommy had been nabbed in possession of a stolen vehicle after a long police chase. The chase pissed off the cops, who trumped up as many charges as they could. Tommy was an idiot and an asshole. It couldn't have happened to a nicer person.

Ryan "Hoyt" Donough was released. Perhaps it was

his police training, but there was no actual evidence against him. He didn't say a word to anyone, and unless Barlow or Gregson pointed the finger at him, he might appear even more innocent than I was. Not even the employees at the dealership were certain he wasn't a temporary worker from the trucking company. Obviously, his years of undercover work paid off, and he picked up a few tricks of the trade.

"No charges are pending against you, Ms. Parker." The lawyer flipped to the next page. "The district attorney's office has issued a statement thanking you for your service to the city."

"Hooray. Does that mean I get a parade?"

"No. It means you hold zero culpability for the thefts that occurred last night, and as far as I'm aware, they won't be pressing charges on the '67 Mustang or for James Martin's vehicle."

"We've worked out restitution with the Mustang's owner," Islind said. "We'll replace his car as soon as we locate one in similar condition."

"Do we know what they did with the vehicles?" I asked.

"The police department is working on that. It isn't what we do," Islind said. "The PR department is writing a press release to reassure all our clients who suffered a theft that we've taken appropriate measures on their behalf and have upgraded our security standards so nothing like this will happen in the future."

"Nothing's ever completely safe, but that's neither here nor there, I suppose." My mind was on the missing vehicles and Ryan.

"We appreciate your hard work." Islind slid an envelope across the table. "Should you encounter any issues, don't hesitate to contact us."

"Thanks." I picked up the envelope and headed for

the door.

After dropping by the ATM to deposit my check, I went to my office and made a slew of phone calls to corroborate Ryan's story and to figure out what was going on. But it was Saturday, so Agent Jablonsky, Farrell, and even Director Kendall were out of the office. I considered calling the Police Nationale to get an update from Capt. Reneaux but decided better of it. This was something O'Connell said he would handle, and until the truth was authenticated, I wanted to distance myself. Perhaps it was self-preservation or my desire to forget the past. Nick was right, seeing Ryan was my kryptonite. It opened Pandora's Box to some of my repressed traumas, and there was a hell of a lot more in that box than a deranged Frenchman.

Stopping at home, I changed into something casual and sexy, packed a bag for the weekend, and went to Martin's. We had plans, and I didn't want to be alone. Although, I wasn't sure which topic of conversation would be worse, locking lips with a mark or mentioning Ryan Donough was in town.

* * *

"For the last two weeks, you've been letting some guy slobber all over you?" Martin exhaled, fighting to remain emotionless.

We were in the living room, drinking a bottle of champagne since I finished a job which was usually reason to celebrate. However, under the circumstances, Martin would have preferred a fifth of scotch. I searched his eyes, but I couldn't figure out if he was mad or hurt.

"I'm sorry." I sighed. "I feel like I've been cheating on you, but it wasn't me. It was, but it wasn't." This was where undercover work got tricky.

"Did you enjoy it? How much slobbering was there?"

"No, I didn't enjoy it. Would you enjoy making out with a Saint Bernard?" Getting aggravated and defensive wasn't the way to go. "Alexandra Riley had to be affectionate to Tommy, but it was nothing serious. Just kissing. Slobbering mostly. I draw the line at first base."

He considered what I said, mulling over my words and their implication. "Like when you went undercover as Lola?" At one point, I impersonated a model, and Martin had been part of that cover identity. It was what led to our getting together and staying together.

"Yes, but without the fringe benefits of me turning back into me." Wow, this conversation was becoming too convoluted to follow. Maybe it was because of the empty bottle of champagne. "Are you mad?"

"No." But he didn't sound completely certain as he considered what I said and weighed his options. His brows scrunched together. "It wasn't you. It's like actors kissing on screen, right? Just a part you were playing." He frowned, trying to wrap his mind around everything and struggling to decide what to make of these odd circumstances. Admittedly, he was taking this better than I imagined. "Honestly," he put the glass down, "at least I understand why you didn't want to kiss me the other morning. You felt guilty." He smirked, pleased that I thought so highly of him.

"You can be so arrogant sometimes."

"But I'm right." He grinned. "Admit it." He pinned me against the sofa cushion. "I'm the best thing that's ever happened to you."

"Aren't you charming?" I teased.

"I can charm the pants right off you." He kissed me gently. All was forgiven. "And now we're going upstairs, so I can remind you how lovely a slobber-free make-out session can be."

"Aren't we going to do more than just make-out?" I quipped, giving him my best seductive look. There was no reason to broach the subject of Ryan now and ruin his good mood.

"See, I knew I could charm the pants off you, and I was barely even trying."

* * *

The nightmares were back. It had been months since my dreams were so terrifying to startle me awake, drenched in sweat, and screaming. Shaking as a result of the sudden adrenaline surge, I cautioned a glance at Martin who was sound asleep. At least the screaming was only in my dream and not for the rest of the world to hear. Getting out of bed, I stepped into the hallway and sat at the top of stairs, resting my head against the railing. Pull it together, Parker.

The dreams were a result of Ryan and the Pandora's Box he was unfortunately connected with. Reminding myself it was over and the psychopath was dead and could never hurt me again, I took a few deep breaths. My heart rate slowed, and my breathing steadied. Only my hands held the slight tremors as the remainder of the nervous energy worked its way from my body.

"Alex," Martin said from behind, "are you okay?"

"I'm fine."

"Why didn't you wake me?" He sat on the step and put his arm around my shoulders. "For a minute, I thought you left to spend the rest of the night with the Saint Bernard."

"I thought about it, but he's in jail." I snuggled against him. "You were sleeping so peacefully. I didn't want to bother you with this stupid shit my subconscious decided to create."

"Wake me next time." He led me back into the bedroom. "Is it the house? We can stay at your place instead."

"Not the house. Just some old memories. Nothing important." I laid my head against his chest, and no more nightmares disturbed my sleep for the rest of the night.

* * *

The next morning at breakfast, Martin's phone rang. Despite the fact it was Sunday, the day of rest, he had to meet with his acquisitions manager concerning the impending product line. Although he promised it would only be for a few hours, I declined the offer to enjoy all the amenities his house provided while I awaited his return. Sure, he had a full-size swimming pool, boxing ring, a home gym, and all the premium channels on cable, but if he was spending Sunday working, I should too.

"Maybe I'll stay the week," I mused. "Why don't you call tomorrow after work? Depending on how busy your schedule is, maybe I'll elect to stay here while I'm between jobs. Especially since your mattress is really starting to grow on me."

"Fine," he wasn't happy by my leaving, "but I can tell you right now, regardless of how busy this coming week is, I'd still like to wake up to you in the morning."

Rolling my eyes at his gushy, romantic side, I left my weekend bag at his house as a show of good faith and went home.

Being alone in the car made me rethink everything about the auto thefts. No matter how I twisted the facts around, there was no reason for Ryan to be working undercover here. This job wasn't big enough to warrant sending an inspector overseas. If it was simply about selling stolen property, Interpol could have kept an eye out, and the local law enforcement agencies should have gotten a memo. This left two possibilities. Either this situation was much grander than a simple GTA ring, or Ryan had been out in the cold too long and crossed the line.

Arriving at home, I turned on my computer and scanned my e-mail inbox for our correspondence. I was a packrat. Even online, I saved all my messages in properly labeled folders. After the Paris case, Ryan and I exchanged dozens of e-mails. The last time we corresponded was six months ago. He said he volunteered for a new undercover assignment to which I teased him about not expecting me to bail him out again. There hadn't been a single reply. I assumed he was working. I had been busy and didn't give it a second thought. Maybe that was partially my fault.

I stared at my computer screen, hoping answers would appear, but they didn't. When I couldn't take the questions my brain continued to pose, I dialed O'Connell. In the last twenty-four hours, he verified Donough's story that he was working undercover to get close to Barlow, but the details regarding the goal were not relinquished. Since the DA's office was claiming jurisdiction due to the number of crimes that occurred in our city and our police force being instrumental in putting an end to it, Ryan wasn't leaving anytime soon.

"We're keeping his passport and papers," O'Connell said. "Even though he's not a criminal, something's fishy. His documentation isn't even under his real name. His passport says Ryan Hoyt."

"Is a unit keeping tabs on him?"

"Absolutely. The guy hasn't left his hotel since we dropped him off." O'Connell paused briefly. "You probably don't want to talk about this, but did he really pull you out of that warehouse in Paris?" Obviously, Nick reread the old case file.

"By the time the police rolled in, I pulled myself out, but Ryan made sure I was okay and didn't get arrested."

"I take it the irony isn't lost on you."

"Not in the least. I've been skimming our occasional correspondence. I have an e-mail from six months ago that corroborates the story he told you, at least in part." Nick made a hmm sound but didn't speak. "There are a handful of people I trust with my life," I said, "and Ryan Donough is one of them. I need to hear him out and find out what is going on."

"Okay. No one's ever doubted your instincts, Parker, but just be careful." O'Connell provided the room number and hotel.

As soon as we hung up, I got back in my car. Before going up to Ryan's room, I spoke to the officers on duty and informed them Mr. Donough would be going for a ride and gave them my address. At least they wouldn't get in trouble if they lost us in cross-city traffic. Then I took a deep breath and went to Ryan's room.

"Room service," I called from the hallway.

"Funny, I didn't order room service." He cracked a smile, seeming much more rested and in better spirits than he had at the precinct.

"You realize you're supposed to inform me when you're planning a visit instead of just showing up out of the blue. It's proper etiquette. Do I have to sign you up for daily e-mail reminders on how to behave in civilized society?" I quipped.

"Bloody hell, Alex." He tried to hide his grin, but it

wasn't working. He rubbed the stubble on his cheek with the back of his hand and gestured to the chair next to the tiny table next to the bed in the tiny room. "I was convinced you had me pegged from that first night when you showed up with that sports car."

"No." I sat down and studied him. He took a seat on the unmade bed. "Didn't I make myself clear about having to save your ass when it comes to these long-term assignments?"

"I'm fine," his demeanor shifted, "but you shouldn't be here. You're a civilian. None of this concerns you."

"Correct me if I'm wrong, but the last time you needed my help, I was a civilian then too."

His eyes darted around the room, and he took a deep breath, struggling to make up his mind about something.

"What's this really about, Ryan? The ICC wouldn't send a cop across the Atlantic for a few car thieves."

He picked at the threadbare spread on the bed. "I'm not here for a car thief."

"I figured that much out on my own. Are you even working for the International Criminal Court?"

"Yes." He pressed his lips together. "Well, maybe since I'm in North America, it's Interpol now. It's hard to keep track when dealing with joint task forces. You remember how bloody fantastic those can be."

I nodded. "Go on."

"We're attempting to track someone else."

"Who?"

He shook his head.

"Well, they clearly aren't in this room. Do they have ties to Barlow?" I asked.

"That's what the intel says."

"Did I blow your cover or your case?" His eyes darted to mine, and I saw the remorse. "Just tell me what you need, so I can fix it."

"No. I won't ask anything else of you. Not on this."

I glared at him. "Ryan, c'mon."

"Do you still have a wicked right cross?"

"I'm not sure. I broke my knuckles recently and haven't hit anyone since. Are you volunteering to find out?"

He chuckled.

"Grab your stuff and let's get out of here. This room is making me claustrophobic." Before he could protest, I stood up. "We're friends, and you're in my neck of the woods. The least you can do is come over for dinner."

"What about my police escort?"

"They can buy their own dinner. Plus, I already told them you'd be at my place if they're looking for you." I tossed his jacket to him. "Vite. Vite."

He rambled a response in French that I didn't understand since it wasn't something I practiced on a daily basis.

"Have I mentioned I'm thankful English is your first language?"

SEVEN

After unlocking my door, I let Ryan inside my apartment. He walked around, taking in the view from my fire escape and otherwise doing what trained investigators do—snoop. I watched him, wondering what he was thinking, as I took off my shoulder holster and laid it on the table, leaving my gun in the slot. He glanced at it, acknowledging that it was that simple gesture that spoke volumes about my level of trust for him.

"Nice place," he said. "Did you just move in? Or is this a safe house you keep for uninvited guests?"

"It's my apartment, jackass. I've lived here for almost seven years." Guys always gave me grief about my apartment and office. Apparently, I lacked the ability to make a place seem lived in or homey. I went into the kitchen and opened the fridge. As usual, it was empty. "Want something to drink? I can offer you water, beer, or whatever's stocked in my liquor cabinet. Unless you want some tea or coffee."

He shook his head, and I shut the fridge, pulling out the stack of menus for the local delivery joints.

"Alexis," he caught my eye as I spread the menus across the counter for his perusal, "why didn't you tell me you stopped working for the OIO?"

"It didn't seem important. You and I rarely discuss the cases we're working. I guess I just assumed you knew."

"The last I heard, you were working a bloody kidnapping. Isn't that in your FBI's jurisdiction?"

I shrugged. "Occasionally."

"Before that, you mentioned a corruption case."

I put my hand up. "Okay, fine. Maybe you had reason to think I was still an agent." I narrowed my eyes at him. "If I was, would you tell me what's going on?"

"Bollocks," he muttered. "I'm already indebted to you. I'm not asking for anything else."

"You're not. I'm offering." He hesitated, so I turned up my powers of persuasion. "Look, at the moment, I'm unemployed. Do you want to see what I'm like when I go stir crazy? The only way I stay out of trouble is by having something to do. So let me focus on helping out a friend. I'm a consultant. How 'bout I consult for you?" I gave him my dazzling smile.

"Is this how you got the keys to that blue Ferrari?"

"Actually, it kinda is."

"Only you." He shook his head and sighed. "But there's a hard line here. I'll tell you what's going on, and you will point me in the right direction. If you have colleagues who might be of some assistance, I would appreciate that, but you are not becoming directly involved."

"How could I?" My innocent act could be very convincing at times. "I have zero authority when it comes to criminal matters. Now, if you're chasing a cheating spouse or looking for photographic evidence of fraud being committed, that would be my area of expertise."

"Bullshit." He rolled his eyes. Maybe I needed to polish my halo before trying the innocent act again. I stared up at him expectantly. "Fine, but we're ordering dinner first. I'm famished. I haven't had a decent meal since Friday afternoon."

"See, I'm already saving your ass."

After deciding on hibachi and sushi, I phoned in our order. Since it was peak dinner hours for a Sunday, they were backed up, but our food should be arriving within the hour. While we waited, I found a notepad and pen and cleared everything off the dining room table.

"Where should I begin?" He pulled out the chair across from me and sat down. It was rhetorical, so I didn't answer. After he organized his thoughts, he finally spoke. "Have you ever heard of the Camel?"

"As in *careful, they spit*?" Maybe I should have taken Ryan for a head CT instead.

"No. He's a contract killer. He earned the nickname because of his disposal method." He bit the inside of his lip, wondering where to go from here. "The International Criminal Court has a unit that monitors similar criminal activity across the EU. Needless to say, there were two murders in Paris almost seven months ago. We didn't have any leads, but the ICC passed along the information and Interpol showed up."

"Don't you hate it when uninvited guests thwart your investigation?"

"I know. It's so annoying." He played along. "But it turns out this man means serious business. Interpol hasn't determined his true identity. The ICC still wants to call dibs, and the Police Nationale are wondering when everyone will leave us the hell alone. Excluding present company, we are capable of handling our own crime scenes."

"What did your captain say about this?"

"He asked if I wanted to assist Interpol. I'm sure you remember Agent Delacroix."

I rolled my eyes and grunted. "How could I forget?"

"Needless to say, I was assigned to liaise between HQ and Interpol, except Delacroix passed me off to the ICC."

"That's because you're such a useful asset."

"Or because he doesn't know how the bloody hell to conduct an operation."

"Which goes without saying." Agent Delacroix was a huge pain in the ass. On my bitchier days, I hoped he would get run over by every single biker in the Tour de France. Alas, no such luck. "Does the ICC know the Camel's actual identity?"

"No." Ryan went to the fridge and pulled out a beer. "The dates of the Camel's murders correspond to Reginald Barlow's travel itinerary. All the cities he visited turned up a corpse with the Camel's M.O. It can't be a coincidence."

"Barlow's the Camel?" It couldn't be that simple.

"That's what I thought. It's why I was keeping tabs on him, why I infiltrated his inner circle, tracked his movements, and learned more than I ever wanted to know about disassembling cars." I sensed the but coming. "And after all these months, he's never done anything to prove he's a contract killer."

I looked down at the notes I absently scribbled while Ryan spoke. "What about the other members of his team? I only know about the people he hired on this end, but if you were part of his inner circle, you must know everyone involved."

"The timeframe doesn't fit for any of them. At least

not that I'm aware." He blew out a breath and returned to the table. "Some have gotten caught or arrested. Others have taken their cut and left for whatever the reason. The victims, the people the Camel targeted, I don't know why Barlow would have had contact with any of them."

"Since you're pursuing a contract killer, how does he collect his payment? How do his client's get in touch with him?"

"We don't know." His eyes pleaded with me. "I can't stay here. I doubt Barlow is the Camel, and the longer your detective friend keeps me here, the less chance we have of finding the actual killer."

"Then why didn't you tell O'Connell this?"

"Because I can't risk him questioning Barlow or the others about it. What if I'm wrong and Barlow is the Camel or he's in contact with him? It could tip him off. He might go into hiding, and we'd never find him."

"Now who doesn't think a police force can conduct a proper investigation?" Putting myself in Ryan's shoes, I understood his misplaced desire for secrecy. Getting a killer off the street was important, but this wasn't the way to do anything. "How come the ICC and Interpol haven't said anything to the local authorities? If there's a killer loose in our city, don't you think someone needs to know about this?"

"Politics," he suggested. "Or fear of botching the investigation," he added more pointedly as reinforcement to his previous dumbass move.

"And you weren't planning to share any of this with me either?"

"I was afraid of what you'd do."

"Right now, I'm going to call Nick and make sure they keep a close watch on the men in custody and every visitor who comes and goes. Then you and I will dig into everyone's background and see what we can find. We'll look for repeat numbers, possible dead drops or pick-ups, and anything out of the ordinary."

"Alex," he protested, "you're only consulting."

"No, I'm advising. Then I'm going to spend too many hours sitting behind the computer, helping you track leads. And," I grabbed the phone and headed to my bedroom, "if you behave yourself, tomorrow, I'll take you to the OIO offices, and you can speak with some people who can actually provide help."

"Thank you."

"De rien." I smiled, recalling bits and pieces of my French.

As Ryan attempted to make himself useful by locating flatware and plates, I paced the walkway in my bedroom, rattling off everything he just divulged. Nick wasn't happy about having a potential contract killer in lockup. He was even less pleased Ryan told me what was going on.

"Parker," O'Connell warned, "don't do it."

"Do what?"

"You're like a dog with a bone. Just because Mr. French is spouting out crazy tales of camels and corpses doesn't mean you need to involve yourself. Why don't you let those of us with badges do the heavy lifting?"

"I am," I insisted. "Tomorrow morning, I'll introduce Ryan to Mark and Agent Farrell, and they can sort this out. Haven't you heard? I'm a private investigator. We don't track killers. Union rules."

"You don't have a union."

"Are you sure? Someone came by to collect dues from my paycheck last week?"

"You don't get a regular paycheck either."

The doorbell rang.

"See, there's my union representative right now,

delivering dinner." Ryan called that he'd get it while Nick continued to instill upon me his infinite wisdom on leaving well enough alone. Well enough should never be alone. If it was well enough, shouldn't I share it with everyone? I heard muffled voices coming from my living room. "I'll talk to you later." Hanging up the phone, I opened my bedroom door to find Martin standing at my front door.

"I said she was in the bedroom," Ryan retorted angrily. "Now who the hell are you?"

"Is this the Saint Bernard?" Martin seethed, ignoring Ryan, who wouldn't let him step foot inside my apartment.

"No." I slid into the space between the two men. I had never seen Martin in an actual fight. Sure, I'd seen him spar with Bruiser on occasion, but this was different. His posture was rigid and his muscles taut. Honestly, I wouldn't be surprised if he started swinging. "This is my friend, Ryan. He's a cop." I forced Martin to look at me, and he relaxed slightly. Ryan stepped back, still watching Martin uncertainly. "Come inside. The neighbors hate me enough as it is. We don't need to cause a commotion."

"Ryan?" Martin's eyes narrowed, recalling the name.

"From Paris," I added quietly, pressing my lips together and fearing what he'd do next. His green eyes flashed rage, sorrow, and something I couldn't place. Looking away from him, I found Ryan confused and on edge. "Ryan Donough meet James Martin."

"The CEO," Ryan practically spat. Being stuck in a room with two overprotective, alpha males was not the way I intended to spend my Sunday. Maybe I should shoot both of them and track down the Camel to ask for tips on body disposal. "It figures you'd keep the job protecting the man who almost got you killed."

"Ryan," I snapped, "don't pretend to know what's going on here." Martin stepped forward, and I put my palms against his chest to stop him.

"That's rich, coming from the coward who sent my girlfriend into a trap. You left her there to die, you son of a bitch." Martin's chest heaved as he sucked in ragged breaths. If I weren't standing between them, Martin would rip Ryan to pieces.

To his benefit, Ryan looked appropriately nauseous and guilty. "Alex," he began, but I shook my head. Someone in the room needed to be the adult, and since it was my house, that meant it should be me.

"Take it easy," I said to Martin. "Regardless of what you think, Ryan isn't my enemy. He did what he could." I turned to Ryan. "And you misinterpreted what I told you about my bodyguard work. Show some respect. Martin's not my boss anymore. He's my boyfriend." That word always sounded so juvenile, but it was appropriate, especially with the way these grown men were acting.

"Fine," Martin muttered.

"Okay." Ryan stepped into my kitchen and rummaged through the fridge, seeking some distance.

"What are you doing here?" I asked Martin.

"After last night, I was worried. I didn't want you to stay by yourself." He shot a look of disgust at Ryan. "Little did I know you weren't by yourself, and he definitely won't be part of our threesome." He was hoping the joke would lighten the mood, but there was too much built up hostility for it to be effective. He ran his thumb across my cheek. "He's the reason for your nightmares last night, isn't he?"

I looked away, knowing it was true but not wanting to admit it. "Thanks for checking on me, but maybe now's not a good time."

Martin emitted a strange sound, prepared to

protest, but before he said a word, Ryan shut the fridge door and faced us.

"Alex has offered to consult on my current case," Ryan said. "Since you're together, you should join us for dinner."

Martin looked at me. It would have taken a crowbar to get him out of my apartment.

"We've ordered plenty," Ryan continued. At least he was trying.

Thankfully, Martin turned off his kill instinct and went with his business professional persona instead. Trying to find common ground, he and Ryan chitchatted about international trade, capitalism, the world economy, and hockey. I stared at the two of them, wondering how men did it. One minute, they were ready to fight, and the next, they were pals, at least superficially.

Dinner arrived twenty minutes late. The hibachi was cold, and the sushi was warm. No one complained. We ate in companionable silence. Or at least I hoped it was companionable silence and not Ryan plotting Martin's death and vice versa. I glanced at my gun on the end table, regretting not putting it in a less accessible location. When we were finished, Martin went to the liquor cabinet and retrieved the bottle of scotch.

"Tell me about your case," Martin insisted, finding two glasses and placing one in front of Ryan.

"I don't think—" I interjected, but Ryan cut me off by giving a brief synopsis as the two sat drinking and assessing one another. Fifteen minutes later, I couldn't take the competitiveness that hung in the air any longer. "Do I need to find a measuring tape, or can the two of you put those things away before someone gets hurt?"

Martin looked sheepish, knowing exactly what he

did. Ryan, on the other hand, appeared clueless. Maybe it was part of the language barrier.

Summoning Ryan to my computer, I wanted to get started on the work we needed to accomplish, even though Martin was still in my apartment. Normally, I tried to keep my work from him as much as possible. I hated to admit it, but O'Connell was right. Under these conditions, I probably should remove myself from the equation and let someone else help Ryan.

After providing a couple of names and finding some basic information within the ICC and Interpol databases on the Camel, Ryan stood up. "I should get going. I'm still on Paris time. Will the officers downstairs give me a ride to my hotel?"

"I'm sure they will, if you ask nicely."

"Alex," he put his jacket on and went to the door, "you don't have to do anything else. I'm capable of handling this situation on my own."

"Tomorrow, I'm introducing you to Mark Jablonsky. He'll put you in contact with the right people." Something occurred to me, and I narrowed my eyes. "Why don't you have your own support team assisting?" Something was off, but he wouldn't give me a straight answer with Martin still in the room.

"We'll talk in the morning. Good night." Ryan waved and let himself out of my apartment.

Going to the window, I watched him exit the building, tap on the patrol car's window, and get in the back seat. At least he was taking advantage of his armed escort.

"Alexis," Martin said my name, and I spun around to face him, "you can't do this." It sounded like an ultimatum.

"Despite your little act tonight, you're not my protector. I can do whatever I damn well please. You weren't in Paris. You don't know what really happened. Ryan saved me, and he's in a bind. Maybe I can help. Maybe I can't. But you don't get to tell me what I can and can't do." I didn't know where the ire came from, but he didn't deserve it. Unfortunately, the words already left my mouth, and I didn't feel like taking them back.

He glared at me, shooting daggers from his eyes. He looked away, fighting back whatever he wanted to say. Arguing wasn't advisable at this particular moment, and he knew it. We didn't have a submissive and dominant relationship. We were equal partners; even when one of us made an asinine decision, the other had to let it go. Instead, he swallowed another shot of scotch. "Fine, but I'm not leaving you alone tonight."

My resolve shattered, and my harsh exterior cracked a dumb smile. "Thanks. I could use the company."

He snorted, as if to say 'then why are you doing this' but simply shook his head and poured another finger of scotch.

EIGHT

Martin hadn't spoken a word since our brief exchange after Ryan's departure. He was sitting on my couch, doing something with his phone. I suspected he was going over information for work, but maybe he was playing a game or searching for porn.

I stayed at my computer desk, reviewing the names and information Ryan found earlier in the evening. There was more to the story. The ICC was a major entity. They had countless resources and pull with other law enforcement agencies. The fact that Ryan was out in the cold didn't bode well. Something was off, and I had no idea what it was.

Frustrated and angry, I clicked shut down and swiveled in the chair. "I don't like fighting with you."

Martin looked up, acknowledging me for the first time in hours. "But you're still going to do what you want, regardless of what I think." He put his phone on the coffee table. "You bust my balls about making unilateral decisions, but you do the exact same thing. Face it, sweetheart, the things that you don't like about me are the qualities you see in yourself."

Apparently, telling him I didn't want to fight meant he should start a fight. "Although, I'm sure you see this as none of my business. But, need I remind you, I'm the one who holds you in the middle of the night when you wake up screaming and can't catch your breath because you're so panicked you're hyperventilating?" His voice cracked, and he looked away.

"Martin." I hated how much this affected him.

"You're just like a junkie." He turned back to me. "You can't stop. The more dangerous it is, the faster you run toward it. This isn't saving a friend's kid or protecting someone you love. This is a freaking serial killer, but you'll find some way to involve yourself, more so than you already have. One of these days, it's going to kill you, and Ryan's failed to protect you before. He didn't have your back then, so what happens if he doesn't have it now?"

"I'll take precautions. It'll be okay."

"What if it's not?" he asked, but I didn't have an answer. He got off the couch and washed his glass, leaving it in the drain. "I have an early morning. I'm going to sleep."

"Go ahead. I'll be in soon."

I listened as he got ready for bed. We would be okay. I was determined to make that true. He knew what he was getting himself into, and for a little over a year, we managed to make it work. The problem was Ryan clued him in, hoping it would mitigate my involvement. Telling Martin the details of my job was something I tried not to do. There had been a couple exceptions, but that wasn't the norm. Maybe Ryan acted prematurely, assuming I would instigate myself into his case. It's not like I had any reason or resources that made me a useful candidate, but Martin was right. I was an addict. It was twisted and dangerous, and I couldn't stop.

Eventually, I crawled into bed. He was facing the wall, and I worried how much more we could endure. He hadn't been this close to a breaking point since my Paris case. Maybe Ryan's presence opened old wounds for both of us. Or maybe it was my undercover make-out sessions with Tommy that were threatening to be the straw that broke the camel's back. My internal voice snorted at the pathetic play on words.

Regardless of what it was, I couldn't sleep. If I woke up because of a night terror, it would only reinforce Martin's point. Instead, I stared at the ceiling, attempting to talk myself out of being so stubborn. It wasn't working. Sometime during the course of the night, he rolled over and wrapped an arm around my waist, snuggling against me. I couldn't lose him, and I couldn't lose me. When did I become this pathetic?

The next morning, Martin's alarm chimed, and he opened his eyes. He kissed my temple before climbing out of bed. I pretended to be asleep, not wanting to risk continuing the fight.

He spent a half hour running on my treadmill, followed by a shower, and then sifting through the single drawer and small portion of my closet that I gave him as a one year anniversary present. Opening my eyes, I watched as he stood in front of my mirror to knot his tie.

He caught my eye. "Maybe Ryan and I aren't quite so different after all," he said softly. I looked at him, confused and surprised, wondering if I was dreaming. "He was right yesterday. I'm just as guilty of putting you in harm's way. When you worked for me, you were almost killed." I opened my mouth to protest, but he shook his head. "Do what you have to. I'll be here to pick up the pieces if that's what you need," he sounded defeated, resigned to accepting what was beyond his control. "As always, just be careful. I love you, and the thought of something happening to you is unfathomable."

"Me too."

He came back to the bed and kissed me goodbye before leaving my apartment, assuming we wouldn't see each other until the situation was resolved. My fear for his safety was one point I would never yield.

* * *

I slept for a little over four hours. It wasn't ideal, but it was better than nothing. Phoning ahead, I stopped to pick up Ryan, so I could personally escort him to the OIO. Mark Jablonsky, my friend and former boss, was waiting for us. Interpol's liaison, Patrick Farrell, was in his office, and Ryan gave them the same information he had given me the previous night. Once everyone was up to speed, Farrell escorted Ryan away so they could make some calls to Paris and the ICC.

"Marty called this morning," Mark said once we were alone. "He's a mess. Whatever Donough said to him last night, it didn't need to be said." Of course, Martin called Mark. They were friends. Morbidly, I wondered who would get to keep Mark in the event of our break-up.

"Agreed."

"That being said," he continued, "what I'm about to say has nothing to do with Marty." He blew out a breath. "You've made it clear you have issues working out of this office. Every time you do, you lose a piece of yourself, or so you've said. I've asked a dozen times if you'll come back, but you always insist you don't want to be a federal agent anymore. You've left me no choice but to accept this fact. Therefore, this situation has nothing to do with you. You can't help Inspector Donough, Interpol, or the ICC."

"But–"

Mark cut me off. "No. You wanted a life in the private sector, and you have one. There's no overlap here. Director Kendall isn't asking you to consult for us, so go home. Maybe you can photograph some cheating husbands or something." His words stung. He was onc of the only people who could hurt me by showing disappointment or disapproval. This felt like both.

"Make sure Donough gets a ride back to his hotel." I headed out of the room.

"Parker, it's for your own good."

I didn't acknowledge him. Too many things were wrong with this situation. I just needed some time to myself to sort it all out. Everyone was pulling me in a different direction. The only consensus among my friends and colleagues was that I shouldn't be involved. That was easier said than done.

Heading to my office, I flipped the sign on the front door saying we were open and took a seat at my desk. There were no messages on the machine or mail in the box requesting my investigative skills, but I found a flyer for a new Mongolian restaurant with a coupon in the bottom corner. At least my day was improving.

"All right," I said to the empty room, "find a place to begin." The only thing I had extensive knowledge on was the GTA ring. Rooting through the drawer for pen and paper, I listed everyone involved, created a timeline for the local thefts, and diagrammed what I knew to be true. Flipping to the next sheet of paper, I made copious notations in shorthand on each of the players, not bothering to add Ryan to the list. This brought me to Reginald Barlow and his questionable travel plans.

On the next sheet of paper, I listed the locations he visited. I stared at the list, wondering what to do. This was the proverbial crossroads. If I went down this path, there was no telling where it would lead. Was I committed to helping someone who didn't ask for my help? How much was I willing to sacrifice for no damn good reason? Screw it.

I dropped my pen on top of the paper and picked up my keys. Maybe there was a Betty Ford clinic for former federal agents or something. Fuck if I know. The only thing I planned to investigate was the auto ring. Nothing else. Yes, the case was closed, but only the local thieves were apprehended. This was much bigger than Tommy Claxton and Robert Gregson, and there was no reason why I couldn't do some casual checking.

Arriving at the precinct, I bumped into O'Connell, who was on his way out. He had just come off shift and was ready to go home. "Parker," he blocked my entrance to the stairway, "what are you doing here?"

"Just wanted to get an update on the GTAs."

"Come on," he put his arm around my shoulders and forced me out the door I just entered, "I think you ought to buy me lunch instead. I'll drive." Nick wasn't taking no for an answer, so I grudgingly got into his car. He rambled nonstop about his wife, Jen, and the latest happenings at the hospital where she worked. It was distraction 101, and it wasn't working.

After getting our fatty burgers and greasy fries, he was forced to stop talking as he chewed. The filibuster was broken. Thank god. Not willing to waste the opportunity, I blurted out the first thing that came to mind.

"What's going on with the car thieves you have in custody?"

"Ongoing police investigation," he said, swallowing. "You know I can't talk about it."

"Dammit," I swore, "I can't catch a break." He

stared as if I were coming unhinged, which maybe I was. "You told me to stay away from Ryan. Martin told me to stay away from Ryan. Mark told me to stay away from Ryan. This is as far as I'm willing to compromise. It's not directly related to what he's doing, but it's on the outskirts. Please, Nick, I need something."

His eyes held the comprehension that no one else exhibited. Somehow, he understood. I felt there was a debt owed, and since I couldn't repay it, I had to do the next best thing.

"Tommy's the errand boy. There's so much evidence against him, but it's apparent he's not in charge. Right now, the DA's hoping to get him to flip on Gregson in exchange for dropping some of the more serious charges. It'd be nice if Gregson turned on Barlow since it seems he's the puppeteer in all of this, but the man is scared. We've tried threats, promises, and even offered protection, but he's stonewalling us. I don't think there's any chance of turning him."

"What about Barlow?"

He picked up a fry and chewed thoughtfully to buy time before answering. "We're being cautious around him. By the book. No offers. Basic questions with his attorney present." He picked up another fry. "Did you know he's not a citizen? We're holding him for now, but there are obvious complications. ICE is chomping at the bit, hoping to deport him to Canada. Aren't Canadians characterized by their lack of criminal behavior?"

"They're still human, aren't they?" I searched my mind for a better question to ask, but none surfaced. "Why are you being so careful around Reggie Barlow?"

"Alex," he shook his head and played with the straw

in his cup, "this isn't the time or place for that conversation. My guess is the car thefts will be handled properly. Tommy will turn on Gregson, and he'll go down for it. We'll press charges against Barlow, and depending on what else happens, either he'll be held responsible, or he'll be sent home. That's all you need to know."

He was right. It was all I needed to know. Nothing else was my problem or my responsibility. Overstepping my boundaries always led to trouble. Cars. I needed to focus on the cars.

"Any idea why they were stealing cars?" I asked.

"Because they're car thieves. Do you not see the correlation?"

"Any idea how many were stolen?" With the exception of the two I grabbed and the three from the dealership's delivery, all I had record of were the stolen APS clients' vehicles.

"Eleven that we know about. You brought us the data on the eleven, remember? It should have been twelve based on your statement, but Donough didn't deliver."

"How many vehicles were reported stolen from the time Barlow arrived in town until the raid Friday night?" Either I was on to something, or I was fabricating a plausible story to stave off my involvement with chasing the Camel, unless all roads led to the same place.

"You're neurotic." He leaned against the booth and stretched. "I've just come off a double thanks to the shit storm raining down on the precinct. The last thing I want to do right now is go back to work and read through burglary's files, but since I have to take you back to your car anyway, I'm not completely opposed to stepping inside and telling someone to have copies forwarded to my desk concerning all vehicular thefts for the last month."

"See, this is why you're my favorite, but don't tell Heathcliff."

"No, this is a quid pro quo." He pointed for emphasis. "You're not doing a damn thing until then." He snickered. "Why do I even bother saying such stupid things? I know you're incapable of listening." He reached into his pocket and pulled out his cell phone, typed something in, and put the phone down. "They should have it on my desk by the time we get back. Just promise you won't do anything other than investigate the car thefts."

"Not a problem. That's all I was asking."

He gave me a 'yeah, right' look and finished his lunch.

On the ride back to the police station, my mind turned over some facts that I should not have been considering. There was no reason to think the targeted vehicles had anything to do with the contract killer or leading us to a contract killer. The two were completely unrelated events. The only obvious flaw in my logic was the common denominator, Reginald Barlow, but Ryan said he didn't believe Barlow was the Camel. Stop it, Parker.

"Jen was wondering when you and Martin were free," O'Connell said, attempting to draw me away from spinning my wheels. Sometimes, I suspected he might be clairvoyant, or he was particularly apt at reading my body language and guessing my thoughts.

"When he's working, I'm free. And when I'm working, he's free. Why?"

"Because I promised Jen I'd ask you about our monthly double date night." He made an ugh noise which perfectly matched my sentiments. It was nice once we were out, but the planning and prep were the pits. Having couple friends and doing couple things was what the normal world did. Unfortunately, O'Connell and I didn't exist in a normal world.

"Maybe you should tell her to ask Martin. Although, I doubt we'll be going on double dates too much longer."

"How come?"

"Were you aware I had to lock lips with Tommy for a span of two weeks?" The burger I ate threatened to make a reappearance. "Plus, there's a lot of turmoil surrounding things I'm not supposed to be thinking about."

"You'll be fine." He dismissed my worry. "James Martin isn't an idiot, and he's probably the most secure person I've ever met. Frankly, it's downright annoying how cocky and arrogant he is. Hell, I've seen him flirt with my wife right in front of my face."

"That wasn't flirting. That's just him."

"Exactly. Goddamn arrogant." He shot me a smile. "If anyone's putting an end to our double date nights, my money's on you."

"Hey," I exclaimed, narrowing my eyes.

"You overthink, overanalyze, and make some dumbass moves. It's also why you solve as many cases as you do and stumble into these complicated situations." He pulled to a stop and got out of the car. "Wait here. I'll bring the information to you. There's no reason you need to poke around inside and stumble into an even bigger mess."

NINE

Every surface in my office was covered in paperwork. I dissected the police files and turned each incident into its own separate case, and then I worked each one separately. There were over fifty reported car thefts since Reginald Barlow arrived in town. Obviously, most of them had nothing to do with him. Unfortunately, the only way to determine this was to analyze each case.

"What are you doing?" I asked myself. I knocked out fifteen solved cases that had no connection to APS or Barlow's team. Sometimes, a stolen car was just a stolen car. There was no reason for me to do any of this, but my gut instinct insisted there was more to the story. Perhaps I hoped to find some kind of solid proof of the Camel's presence within Barlow's team, the connection that no one else had seen, or maybe this was just the best way of keeping busy in order to ensure I didn't instill myself into Ryan's case. Frankly, even I didn't know the reason for my current behavior.

After knocking out another dozen thefts as unrelated, I called it a night. It was after midnight, and there were half as many cases left to analyze in the morning. On the bright side, I knew what I'd be doing tomorrow. Briefly, I considered calling Ryan or showing up at Martin's, but both seemed like equally bad ideas. Arriving home, I tried to wind down for the night, but a thought lurked in the corners of my mind.

I woke in the middle of the night to the sound of my own screams. Having nothing better to do and hoping Ryan might still be on Paris time, I found my phone and dialed his hotel, requesting his room.

"Hello?" he asked, sounding awake but confused.

"Sorry I left you at the OIO. Obviously, you found your way back to the hotel."

"Alex," there was a brief pause, "I'm still in the U.S. Why are you calling at four in the morning?"

"Because you show up out of the blue, flip my world upside down, and I have no idea what's going on or what to do about it. When I shut my eyes, I'm back in Paris, and when I'm awake, I'm trying so hard to avoid what you're doing that I'm refusing to believe the investigation I've opened is connected to yours. But it probably is. I don't know. Maybe. And I don't know why I'm doing it. The point was to keep busy so as not to wonder what else might be happening."

"Breathe," he instructed, and I took a breath and shut my eyes. "Shall I come to you, or would you rather come here? I don't want to further aggravate your boyfriend."

"He's not here, but neither. I just had to vent to someone."

"This is my fault. What are you investigating?" He sounded interested, and with no reason not to share, I told him how I spent my day. "I haven't found a connection between the Camel and Barlow. We thought there was one, but like I told you, Barlow isn't our contract killer. The work you've done will help your police department's investigation in locating any remaining stragglers in the auto ring, but it should be safe to assume our paths won't collide."

"So I'm in the clear?"

"Seems like it. I didn't realize you'd have to work so hard to make sure you didn't involve yourself in my investigation," he quipped.

"See, I told you I wouldn't do more than advise." I thought about the few names we searched and how none of them led to anything solid. "How'd everything go with Interpol? Are you back on track?"

"Yes. As soon as things are cleared up, I will return home. Just another two or three days and you won't have any of this to worry about any longer. I'll be home, and you can investigate whatever you want."

"Did they recall you from the undercover assignment?"

"We shall see. After all, it's hard to maintain a cover identity when the group you've infiltrated is under arrest for thievery. At least I get to go home and retire Hoyt."

"I'm sorry."

"No reason to be. Maybe our intel was bad. Barlow wasn't the guy, and the last six months have been a complete waste of my time and the ICC's resources." His words sounded pained, and instinctively, I knew there was more to the story.

"I meant to ask," the voice in my head warned that I didn't want to know the answer, "where's your support team?"

"The Interpol agent I was partnered with was killed two months ago. Supposedly, it was unrelated to our assignment. Interpol thinks it was a mugging that went wrong."

"My god."

"This stuff happens. There wasn't even a blip on Barlow's radar afterward. Maybe that should have tipped me off that we were looking in the wrong place."

"I'm sorry, Ryan."

"Don't be. I barely knew the man." It was a coping mechanism to distance himself. I used similar techniques in the past, but it explained why he was so hesitant to tell me anything. He already lost one person and had no intention of losing more, and working with me was clearly taboo. "Agent Jablonsky is picking me up in a couple of hours, so I can continue my work with Interpol now that they've completely taken over the investigation from the ICC. He was your direct supervisor, wasn't he?"

"Yes."

Ryan chuckled. "That explains a lot. The way he was acting, you would think I wanted to marry his daughter."

"That's Mark for you. Fair warning, he's also Martin's best friend, so that's two strikes against you. I suggest you avoid a third."

"Baseball?" He seemed confused by the reference.

"Yes."

"See, I'm catching on." He paused again. "I have some work to do before he arrives. Don't you need to work or sleep?"

"A bit of both," I admitted. "Let me know if there's anything I can do."

"There isn't, but thanks."

Hanging up, I felt better about things. It was stupid, but hearing his voice and an explanation assured me he hadn't gone off the rails. He was searching for pieces to the puzzle, and it turned out he had the wrong picture the entire time.

After spending an entire day working on the car thefts, I decided to finish analyzing the information tomorrow as planned, turn over my findings to the cops, and mend some fences. Shutting my eyes, I slept soundly for the next eight hours, convinced everything was right in the world.

When I awoke, it was mid-afternoon. I spent a couple of hours working out and finding my center. I wasn't dedicated to yoga or meditation, but coffee and donuts were a decent substitute, especially after the five miles worth of cardio. Settling in at my office, I continued scanning through the cases. After another ten were knocked out of the running, I separated out the eleven I knew to be involved and began on the last few.

No matter how I looked at them, I couldn't get them to move. There was no way to dismiss any of them as unrelated. Not enough information was available to make that assessment. This wasn't supposed to be this daunting. When I looked up from the papers, the sun had set. I considered throwing in the towel. However, that would have made all the work I did up until this point meaningless.

Determined not to leave the office until I completed my task, I began conducting searches on the vehicles and contacting the insurance companies for further information. Regardless of the fact that I had no real authority in the matter, most of them were extremely helpful, probably because of their misguided belief that I was somehow involved in law enforcement. Who knows where they would have gotten such a crazy idea? I knocked out several other vehicles, narrowing my list down to four.

Checking the dates they were reported stolen, the estimated worth, and the similarities to the other heists Gregson orchestrated, I suspected they were related. While I would have enjoyed doing nothing more than proving it, I had restricted access since I wasn't working for the police department. Calling O'Connell's work number, I left a message and the case numbers, suggesting he pass the information along to the relevant investigator for further evaluation.

Disconnecting, I drummed my fingers on the desk. That was fun. Now what? Giving my computer a final furtive glance, I turned it off, locked the office, picked up a pizza, and went to Martin's.

After entering his security code, I parked in his expansive garage and went upstairs. The polite thing to do would have been to call ahead, grovel and apologize, and then show up. But as I expected, he wasn't home yet. I didn't have any desire to ask for forgiveness, but the longer we harbored a grudge, the worse it would be in the end.

Two slices and a lemon drop martini later, Martin came up the steps. "How'd you finish your investigation so soon?" He didn't bother to conceal his contemptuous tone.

"There's no case, but there is pizza." I pointed to the box on his kitchen table. "I wasn't sure if the offer to stay the week was rescinded. I can go if you don't want me here."

He let out a sigh, took off his jacket and tie, and unbuttoned his shirt.

"Are you planning to physically throw me out of your house?" I joked, tossing him a bittersweet smile.

"You know you are always welcome here. I just don't know what you expect from me."

"I don't expect anything."

"Dammit, why do you always have to be this difficult? For once in your life, just tell me what you're thinking."

"You're right. I can't stop. I don't know how, and I don't want to. You knew this when we met. Hell, that's exactly the reason we ever met, so you shouldn't expect me to change." My voice softened. "But don't think for a single moment that I didn't know what the dangers were when I worked as your bodyguard. You saved my life. It was stupid, unreasonable, and completely ass-backward, but that's what you did. So don't start rethinking everything. I'm the paranoid, neurotic, lunatic in this relationship, not you." He snorted, the relief was obvious on his face. "And I'm done arguing. We've had this fight before. This isn't about that. It's about what happened to me in Paris."

His jaw muscles clenched, and he pressed his lips together. It was his tell, indicating I was right.

"See, that's why I keep my work separate, besides needing to know you're safe. It's a lot to process, and a lot to handle. But I know the risks, and there is no reason in this world why you should worry more than you already do," I said.

"So you showed up to bring me dinner?"

"Yes," I looked away, "and because we had plans for this week, and even though there's a good chance that if I stay, I'll end up waking you up every night I'm here and not for any reason you'd enjoy, I can't sleep. When I try, I feel the electric current going through me and the rope cutting into my wrists, and I don't want to be alone."

"Sweetheart," whatever anger or argument he might have prepared dissipated as he enveloped me in an embrace, "it's okay."

"It's not Ryan's fault," I continued, my voice muffled against his shoulder. "Shit happens. Just like what happened when I worked for you." I pulled away from him. "That wasn't your fault. When I mentioned it to Ryan a year ago, it got blown out of proportion.

Okay?"

"Okay."

This conversation was beating a dead horse. We had some amalgamation of it over and over again. Besides the obvious issues, Martin believed he should protect me. Oddly enough, I had the same personality type, and it didn't mesh well when things became life or death.

"Sometimes, it's nice for a guy to know he's needed, even if it is just to scare away the demons. But, Alex, I can't bear the thought of the past repeating itself."

"You're such a sap." I nudged his ribs. "Fair warning, Ryan's case and the auto thefts have both grown cold, but if I'm invited to work on either, I'm not walking away. And you have to accept it."

"It's what you do. I couldn't reasonably expect any less." He turned his head to look into the kitchen. "By the way, how's the pizza?"

"It's not bad, but I think dessert will be better."

* * *

For once in my life, I was determined to stay out of trouble. I said my piece, but if there were any developments that I became privy to, I would blindly chase after them. But without further prodding, I was attempting to keep my nose out of everyone's business. APS paid for my services, and no one else was seeking to hire me. I earned some time off and was determined to enjoy the hiatus.

Ryan Donough hadn't made contact since my four a.m. phone call. Perhaps he was home by now, piecing together his real life away from the extended undercover assignments. No one from the police department, OIO, or Interpol called my cell phone which further illustrated how unnecessary my involvement in law enforcement matters had become. Alexis Parker, P.I., that's who I was now. Strangely, it was equal parts liberating and disappointing. Now that Mark had given up the struggle to have my federal agent status reinstated, I wanted nothing more than to return to my previous life. If this was his attempt to use reverse psychology, it was working incredibly well.

My self created vacation was beginning to fail horribly as the days passed. With nothing else to focus on or keep my mind busy, the nightmares were getting worse. They weren't just forcing me to relive ghastly memories, but now I was creating new demons in addition to the old ones.

Twice, I woke up hyperventilating, and once, I dreamt in vivid detail my final assignment at the OIO. It was heart-wrenching, experiencing the deaths of my partner, Agent Michael Carver, and Agent Sam Boyle all over again. This was the reason I resigned, and this was the nightmarish memory I relived over and over for the first few months after leaving. I wondered if the dream had more to do with the two year anniversary of their deaths, or if it was because a part of me was entertaining thoughts of wanting to return to the OIO. Or maybe it was because Ryan's Interpol partner had been killed when they were working undercover. Who knows?

By the fourth morning, I couldn't take it anymore. My subconscious wouldn't let me hide from a case. Instead, it was torturing me to get off my ass and do something about it. Martin didn't ask what my dreams were about, but the dark circles under his eyes spoke volumes. It was time I stopped hiding.

Returning home, I found three messages on my answering machine, all of which were cryptic. Mark called to check on me, which seemed strange because he could have phoned my cell if he was that concerned. The second message was O'Connell verifying he received the information and hoped to get together concerning a couple of points. The third was O'Connell again. All he said was *call me*.

"Idiots." I glanced at my cell phone which hadn't received a single call in the last four days. It wasn't like they didn't know the number. Dialing O'Connell, I waited for the annoying hold music to stop. When he answered, I didn't bother with the pleasantries. "It's the twenty-first century, and sadly enough, we're all tethered to the outside world via mobile devices. I hate it, but that's just how it is."

"Where've you been?" he asked, ignoring my diatribe.

"Hiding from the real world. What's with all the vague messages on my machine?"

"Parker," he stopped for far too long before continuing, "do you think you can get some information out of Tommy Claxton or Robert Gregson?"

"I can try."

"Come to the precinct and bring whatever getup you wore when you infiltrated their ring. The detectives in burglary want to have a word. Once you're up to speed, you might need to pull some presto-chango, turn-into-a-crook, magic act, and we'll put you downstairs with the two uncooperative offenders."

"Nick, what's going on?" He was still being vague. Something was brewing.

"Just get down here. We'll talk about it when you arrive."

I hated surprises, but O'Connell hung up without giving me the opportunity to wheedle any answers out of him. After tossing some dark eye makeup into my purse, I put on my leather jacket and my knee-high leather boots, decided that was badass enough for the return of Alexandra Riley, and left my apartment.

Going from zero to sixty would eventually result in a severe case of whiplash. Although, having something to occupy my mind might just be enough to stave off the nightmares. This was just a rough patch, and once I moved past it, everything would be back to normal. Whatever that is.

TEN

O'Connell looked up, attempting an unsuccessful smile. "I'm glad you prefer working with people who do actual police work, instead of those jerks in their fancy buildings with their fancy suits and fancy credentials."

"Y'know, I stopped working for Martin Technologies a few months ago." My brow furrowed as I tried to figure out where the animosity was coming from.

"Not them," he said as if I were supposed to know what he was talking about. "The idiots with their badges and sunglasses and three letter acronyms. I have some three letter acronyms for them." Thompson, O'Connell's partner, chuckled from the next desk. "Anyway," he still looked aggravated, "I'm glad you decided to grace us with your presence. We need someone to act as a go-between," he dropped whatever he was doing and gave me his full attention, "but off the books. The lieutenant doesn't have the budget to hire you to consult, but since you're already working this, you might not mind."

"APS and I split paths the day you arrested the car thieves." For some reason, I was ten steps behind. Maybe I wasn't even on the same planet. "Boredom was what made me dig through the other car thefts. But you know this. We had lunch. I ranted and raved. You got me the case files."

His face contorted in sudden comprehension. He didn't like the conclusion he reached. "What have you been doing for the last four days?"

"Camping out at Martin's, enjoying some time off, and driving myself absolutely crazy. Why? Where did you think I was?"

"Shit." He pinched the bridge of his nose. "Fuck. Fuck. Fuck." I raised my eyebrows and waited for something a little more telling than a string of expletives. "The four other car thefts you believed were related to Barlow were dead on. So dead on in fact that they traced back to two different homicides. You remember the morning you came here and asked for some information on identifying Barlow? The double homicide I was called away on was in direct relation to one of those four vehicles. Parts of one of the other vehicles you had a hunch about were recovered from the scene of a second homicide."

"The Camel?" Ryan's insistence that there was no connection was no longer true. Was he still here or did he get sent home? Who was investigating? What was being done?

"Camel, Jackal, I'm sick of fucking animal names. Let's call it what it is. We have a serial killer on the loose. Everyone's claiming jurisdiction. The European authorities want this guy. The FBI, OIO, and Interpol are throwing their hats in the ring. I swear I thought you were working on this with Agent Jablonsky and Frenchie."

"Is Donough still here? The last I heard, he was

ready to return to Paris."

He shrugged. "It's not like anyone thinks some lowly police detective should know a damn thing. Meanwhile, it's my job to protect this city. The lousy," he mumbled the rest too low for anyone to hear.

"Why didn't you call sooner?" But the question was already answered. He thought I was consulting for the OIO or Interpol. "Never mind. Point me in the right direction, and I'll get you whatever you need."

"Parker, this isn't your problem. Like you said, you've finished working this case."

I cocked a challenging eyebrow in his direction. I had to help. Lives were at stake. "Are Gregson, Barlow, and Tommy still in custody?"

"Yes."

"How much do they know?"

"I can't tell you." Nick slammed his palm on the desk. "You're a civilian, and it's an ongoing investigation." He turned and stared at Lieutenant Moretti's office door. "Give me two minutes." He stormed to the door and banged against it before going inside.

"Y'know, before you got here, O'Connell was bitching about how you couldn't be bothered to share any relevant information with us," Thompson said. "Bet he feels like a real jackass right about now."

"Don't say that too loudly. He has major issues with animal names."

While muffled words wafted from Moretti's office, I hopped into O'Connell's chair and opened a few of the files concerning the cars and the killer. Thompson didn't stop me, and no one thought my presence was strange. Despite my private investigator status, I worked so many consulting gigs for the PD they probably thought I was a cop. Unfortunately, the relevant information was safeguarded by individual password protection. I searched the various sticky notes and opened O'Connell's top drawer, but he wasn't inexperienced enough to leave information like that out in the open. Before I could ask Thompson for the login info, O'Connell returned.

"Get away from my computer," he ordered. "We're taking a walk."

As soon as we were out of the squad room, I turned to him. "What's the verdict?"

"You're a material witness and informant in an ongoing investigation, so the things you want to be privy to are considered need to know. Fortunately for you, I get to decide what you need to know." As he led me to burglary division, he detailed the two crime scenes. "I'll get the photos and evidence list to you soon, but it was gruesome." Considering he worked in major crimes and had seen a lot of nasty things, his assessment didn't bode well. "The way this guy does it is sick. I've read some of Interpol's reports. Contract killers normally favor execution style or even long-distance rifles. They like to remain detached. It's easier to get away. But this sick fuck gets up close and personal. He drugs them, dehydrates them, and floods their systems so badly the cells in their body literally explode. They turn into human soup."

"Have you ruled out Barlow and the others as being the Camel?" Maybe Ryan got it wrong. He didn't think they were connected, but coincidences never happened this frequently.

"The second victim, well third, since the first two were part of a double homicide, was discovered after Barlow's crew was in custody, but given the way the murders occurred, the medical examiner can't determine the time of death." He met my eyes. "This is a bad one. The only consolation is he only kills when he's hired, or at least that's what the reports indicate."

"Do we know how his clients get in contact with him? Are you sure he's in the city? What about working up a profile, physical and psychological? Do we know his country of origin?" My mind raced in a dozen directions.

He grabbed my shoulders to steady my thoughts. "Parker, look at me." I stopped and focused on his eyes. "The only thing you're going to do is have a chat with the car thieves. You can't let on about any of this. We don't know enough to risk tipping our hand or spooking him. Can you do that?"

"Yes."

"Okay. First, burglary wants to talk to you about the cars. Then I'll take you downstairs to holding and see if you can get anything helpful on the car thefts. We need to identify other players. Buyers would be great. If you can get any of the offenders to elaborate on their whereabouts over the last few weeks, that might be helpful whenever we get TODs. We're taking this one step at a time."

"Afterward, I'll make a few calls. Since you're the only one bothering to clue me in on the actual situation, I'll share my information with you."

He opened the door to burglary division and held it. "I was out of line, telling you to avoid Donough. It's not my place, especially now that we might need his assistance."

"The only thing I've learned from the last four days is avoidance is never the answer, and too much free time leads to utter misery. Idle hands, O'Connell. Idle hands."

After I explained to the lead detective in charge of the car thefts how I had drawn my conclusions, he attempted to bore me with unimportant details on security tracking systems, chop shop activity in the region, and the utter disregard manufacturers have for the ease of hacking into a car's computer system and stealing it without any muss or fuss. Having extensively done my homework on all of these points and a good portion of his job for him, I didn't care. I answered the few remaining questions, passed along the contact information for APS, Islind, and the legal counsel who negotiated with the DA's office. From this point on, the stolen vehicles were secondary to locating and identifying the contract killer.

"What's the difference between a serial killer and a contract killer?" I asked.

O'Connell lingered just outside the restroom while I applied dark eye makeup. "You're seriously busting my balls because I referred to the Camel as a serial killer?"

I shrugged, even though he couldn't see from the hallway. "Fine, the Camel's a ritualistic contract killer or a comfort serial killer, if you prefer. He likes to stick to a similar M.O. when he performs his hits. Honestly, he fits the bill. More than two murders have occurred as separate events and were committed for a reason, albeit financial gain. That doesn't mean I have a problem with the state bringing him up on serial murder charges in addition to contract killing, conspiracy, and murder for hire."

"You left out assault, assault with a deadly weapon, attempted murder, conspiracy to commit, some type of drug charges since he drugs his victims, kidnapping, and screwing with the wrong people."

I checked my reflection in the mirror, ensuring I looked like Alexandra Riley and spun on my heel. "Are you doing the honors?"

He nodded, considering his handcuffs. "How are you these days when it comes to restraints?"

"Wait until we're downstairs and closer to holding

before you slap on the cuffs, and maybe don't tighten them too much either." Absently, I rubbed the barely visible scars. "The more work there is, the better off I am. It sucks though. I've been nightmare-free for quite some time. Then I see Ryan, and it's like Paris happened two weeks ago. Do the skeletons ever stay buried?"

"No. They don't. We all have our triggers, but we find ways to avoid them or at least deal with them faster. Donough's one of your triggers, just like any type of restraint." He cracked a smile. "Be thankful Martin's not into bondage."

"Really? That's where you want to take this conversation?"

"No. I'd like to take it downstairs and let you chat with a few incarcerated gentlemen." Leaving the restroom, we went down the stairs to holding. O'Connell made quick work with the cuffs and took them off almost immediately, throwing me into an empty cell adjacent to Tommy. "Now, behave yourself while we get this sorted out."

"Screw you, pig."

"Alex?" Tommy brightened almost immediately, scurrying across the cell and standing a foot away from our shared bars. "I thought you got away."

"Shut up." I glanced at the officer who pretended to pay no attention. I moved through the empty cell in order to be closer to Tommy. "Why am I here?" I whispered angrily. "Did you squeal on me?"

"No, babe. I didn't say nothing."

"What about Robert? Did he say something?"

"I don't think so." He tossed a glance behind his shoulder. Gregson was as far from Tommy as humanly possible, and I didn't spot Barlow. Maybe he was being interrogated. "We aren't narcs."

"Damn you." I sighed loudly and sat sideways on

the bench, wrapping a hand around the metal bar. "I wanted a life, Tommy. This shit isn't supposed to come back and bite me in the ass." I looked away, staring at the light until my eyes watered. I turned back to him. The tears ran down my cheeks, and I wiped them away. "What are we involved in?"

"Babe," he knelt on his side of the bars and brushed his fingers gently across my knuckles, "I didn't say nothing about you. What'd the cops say when they busted you?"

"Not much." I shrugged and let him pry my hand from the bar and interlock his fingers with mine. "They said I was under arrest in connection with a car theft ring. Big surprise." My lip quivered slightly, selling the tears. "The police know too much, Tommy. How could they know about the garage and which vehicles we stole unless someone told on us? Are you sure Robert's not a cop?"

"No way." He frowned and edged closer. Reaching through the bars, he brushed my hair out of my face. "It wasn't either of us." The wheels started turning in his skull. With any luck, he'd reach the conclusion on his own, without my prodding. Scratching his neck, he looked to the side, remembering something.

"What is it?"

"Nothing. It's nothing."

"Tell me. Please."

"Robert always has buyers lined up. Normally, more than one, but all these jobs we've been pulling were for one guy." He turned to make sure the cops weren't eavesdropping.

"Reggie?"

He nodded. "I barely know the guy, but he's some international car broker or some shit like that. Everything we've been taking was either because one of his clients was looking for a specific replacement part or because he can't locate a car for sale that fits the bill. Y'know, like that Mustang you boosted. Reggie had it on his master list."

"Shh," I hissed. He immediately shut his mouth and looked at the cop. After making sure the coast was clear, I continued, "Where did Reggie get his list? Do you think one of the buyers is a rat or a cop?"

"I got no idea. I've never seen the list. Reggie guarded it, but he'd pull it out from time to time to mark stuff off. When he first approached Robert, he already had the list of cars lined up that he was going to need. We grabbed some of them before you and I hooked up, well, almost hooked up. Do you think they allow conjugals between prisoners?"

"This isn't funny. What about the rest of the cars? The 911s didn't seem planned."

"They weren't. Before we completed his wish fulfillment, he added another six cars to the list." Something dawned on him, and he dropped my hand, considering the ramifications of his thought. "I bet he found another buyer."

"How? Didn't you say he was a European broker?"

"I don't fucking know." His helpfulness was coming to an end. "All I know is I didn't implicate you in nothing. Nothing. And I don't think Robert did either. I don't even know why I didn't. You broke my heart, Alex. You said we were done, and my last chance to change your mind ends with me behind these bars."

"Maybe when we get out of here, we'll see what happens." That wasn't a possibility, but I didn't know how else to get more information out of him.

"Yeah, right. I got pinched with a hot car. How come they didn't grab you the same night?"

"When I heard the sirens, I bolted. The cops busted Robert's garage two minutes later. I hid in an alleyway. After the coast was clear, I took a cab home and went to work the next day like nothing happened." I trembled, reliving the horribleness of this fictitious event. "They always say you have to act natural, so I did. That's why I was surprised when they dragged me from work in cuffs. Are you sure you didn't give me up?"

"I'd never give you up."

The only helpful tidbit Tommy gave me was Barlow found another buyer, and for all any of us knew, that might not be true.

Twenty minutes later, O'Connell pulled Alexandra Riley out of holding for a follow-up. The police planned to apply more pressure to Gregson. Maybe he knew more than Tommy, but I wasn't holding my breath.

ELEVEN

I was sitting at O'Connell's desk, listening to Mark Jablonsky list all the reasons why the questions I asked were none of my business. When he stopped for air, I considered hanging up the phone. Unfortunately, there was the old adage about honey and flies, and hanging up was grounded in the vinegar symbolism.

"Mark, this isn't about me. This has nothing to do with your misguided attempt to protect me from the cold, cruel world. In case you've forgotten, there was a time you valued my input on these types of matters."

"There was also a time when you held federal agent credentials and reported to me."

"So let's play pretend. What have you gotten from Barlow? Have you ruled him out as the contract killer known by the affectionate dromedary euphemism?" While I was talking to Tommy, the OIO requested a prisoner transfer and interrogated Barlow.

"Parker, back off."

"I can't." Emotion eked from my words. "I just

can't. The last time I left an investigation involving an international criminal, things didn't turn out so well." I lowered my voice to something barely above a whisper. "The fact is, right now, the only way I'm keeping it together is by working. So unless you have a friend who needs someone to tail his cheating wife, I need access to this case."

"Alexis," his tone softened because when I quit my job at the OIO, he had seen firsthand how quickly I could spiral to rock bottom if I didn't have a focus, "you don't play fair."

"Funny. You taught me that trick."

"First of all, I don't like it. Second, I know I can't stop you. Meet me at my office in an hour. We'll talk then."

* * *

Riding in the elevator to the OIO floor, my mind immediately ran through the pros and cons of leaving this job behind. There was a time when my entire life was nothing but the job. Maybe if things hadn't turned out the way they did, it still would be. No matter how much I insisted I was doing what I wanted, I missed it. Ached for it. And fought back the desire to concede this was where I belonged. Shaking off the melancholia that wormed its way into my soul, I exited when the doors opened and strode to Mark's office. I knocked and opened the door without waiting for permission.

"What do you have for me?" I asked.

He slid a folder across the desk but didn't say a word. As I read, he left the office, shutting me inside. Maybe unfriendly was catching. The preliminary report didn't provide any new information. I flipped through the pages, looking for something new, interesting, or damning. A moment later, Mark returned with Patrick Farrell and Ryan Donough.

"Ms. Parker," Farrell greeted, "it's nice to see you again. You look well."

"Thanks, you too." I glanced at Ryan before settling my gaze on Mark.

"Inspector Donough believes he made an incorrect assessment," Mark said. "Our evidence against Barlow is circumstantial at best." He reclaimed his chair. "Gregson and Tommy confessed to the car thefts. But the two subsequent murders have no direct connection to either of our thieves. At least none that we've found."

"Interpol would like to investigate further," Farrell said. "After discussing the matter at length with the ICC, they've turned the case over to us, and since Donough was originally assigned to an Interpol joint task force, he will remain here."

"Donough's brought it to our attention that a Ms. Riley," Mark glowered at me for using a cover identity I had been assigned half a decade ago while working for the OIO, "might be instrumental in assisting him." Ryan touched my shoulder, and Mark's eyes diverted to the physical connection. "Gentlemen, give us a minute." Just as quickly, Ryan's hand disappeared, and he and Farrell left the room.

"Have you changed your mind about letting me consult?"

"I haven't changed my mind, Parker." His eyes smoldered. "This is coming from above my pay grade because if I had my way, you wouldn't even be in the same time zone right now."

"What is your problem, Jablonsky?" This was far beyond the scope of overprotective. "You trained me. You know I have what it takes to get things done."

"This is a dangerous assignment." He fought to

keep his anger in check. "This isn't some insignificant local crime. We're talking international contract killer with a penchant for inflicting pain and unnecessarily torturing his victims, and your head isn't in the game. You're emotional and raw. Every second you spend in Donough's presence makes it worse. I see it. The way your posture shifts. The way you react to his touch. The person who thinks it's a good idea to send you back to the car thieves is a fucking imbecile. Your shit's all over the place. When's the last time you slept through the night?"

"Don't you dare," I hissed. "What do you want me to do?"

"I want you to walk away. Say 'screw this, it's not my problem' and walk away."

"I can't do that."

"Please, Alex." He leaned forward, defeated. "I've lost a number of good people in the past. I have no desire to add any more names to that list, especially yours." He chewed on his thumbnail. "This requires a hundred and ten percent, and you're not there. Not even close. You're not bulletproof."

"Clearly, since I have scars to prove it." I tried to lighten the morbidity, but he wouldn't budge. "Thankfully, my eighty percent is equivalent to everyone else's hundred and ten percent. I'll be fine. Promise." I stared until he willingly met my eyes. "The first time I sat in this chair, you offered to be my emergency contact and made me swear I would never need an emergency contact." I smiled at the recollection. "Don't worry, sir. I won't need an emergency contact."

"How about a psychological evaluation?"

"I'm batshit crazy. No reason to waste an expert's time on reaching the same conclusion." I winked. "Now, would you like to tell me who gets the thank you note for letting me on this case?"

"Director Kendall approved you as a valuable asset after some insistence from some of the higher-ups in Interpol who seem to hold the misguided belief you're a capable investigator." He rolled his eyes, grumbled to himself, and went into the hallway to drag Farrell and Donough back inside for a proper briefing. One way or another, I never strayed too far from my roots.

"Parker, are you ready to get to work?" Farrell asked from the doorway. "You have a lot to catch up on before we throw you to the wolves."

"Let's get started."

I followed Farrell and Donough down the hall. In Farrell's office were dozens of printouts, international reports, and a world map with various marks and notations. Farrell rolled a chair from an adjacent office into the room and indicated that I should take a seat. Once the three of us were situated, he passed a thick dossier across the desk.

Before I could pick it up, Ryan put his hand on top of the folder. "Alex, are you sure this is what you want? I'm not dragging you into another one of my investigations if you don't want to be here."

"Too late." I scooted the folder out from under his grasp and looked expectantly at Farrell.

"Welcome to the team, Ms. Parker," Farrell said. "As you can see, we have extensive amounts of research, photos, and evidence pointing to an individual dubbed the Camel, but we're still narrowing our leads." I quickly flipped through the photos, witnessing the graphic nature of the murdered victims. Human soup, just like O'Connell described it. How anyone could be this sick and twisted was revolting. It was pure evil and completely sadistic. "Originally, we thought Reginald Barlow was our contract killer, but as I'm sure you're aware, there is no proof of this."

"Hang on." I held up a hand before he could get any further in his explanation. "What was the original impetus that led to Barlow?"

"We tracked passport stamps and travel itineraries throughout the EU in regions where bodies had turned up."

"How were TODs established? The medical examiner is having difficulty pinpointing time of death since the remains are so badly," I struggled to come up with an appropriate term, "damaged."

"They used rough estimates," Ryan replied. "Death was narrowed to within a week based upon when the bodies were discovered and when they were reported missing."

"How do we know this is murder for hire and not some indiscriminate psychopath?" I asked.

"I was getting to that," Farrell said. "Maybe it would be best if I start at the beginning." He shifted into a more comfortable position in his chair. "Victim one was found a year ago inside a storage unit in Frankfurt, Germany. It took investigators almost two months to identify the remains. After running extensive searches, by some strange happenstance, they discovered an online message board containing a conversation between two individuals. The majority of the conversation was deleted, but they recovered most of the correspondence and discovered the victim's spouse was searching for a hitman."

My eyes brightened. "Then we must have an actual lead, right?"

"You would think." Ryan snorted, disgusted. "The spouse was brought in and questioned extensively. That led to unearthing a wire transfer. No matter how many experts examined the account, they all reached the same conclusion. It's untraceable. The money went in and out so quickly it turned out to be another dead end. We don't even know how long the account was established prior to payment, but it was closed for almost three months by the time we found it."

"The remains of a second victim were found before the first victim's spouse was even in custody. Who knows how many hits the Camel's performed that we don't even know about yet?" Farrell continued. "Every time a law enforcement agency gets close, or thinks they're close, it turns out the Camel's already four steps ahead."

"It took five months before the ICC became involved. By then, there were seven victims," Ryan said. "Victims eight and nine were Parisians, and that's when I became involved."

"The ICC and Interpol searched for matching travel itineraries, and the list was narrowed to a few dozen individuals. After closely monitoring their financial records, establishing surveillance, and installing listening devices, the list dwindled," Farrell said. "When Inspector Donough was sent to infiltrate and monitor Reginald Barlow's car business, we were almost certain he was the Camel or in direct contact with the Camel."

Ryan cursed and rubbed his face. "It was a bloody miracle we even made it to that point, but we were wrong."

"But guys," they were forgetting the most important piece of information, "we've identified two local victims. You're here because Barlow's here, but so is the Camel. Clearly, he's operating in this city, so you can't be wrong."

"It's not Barlow," Ryan argued. "I've been with him constantly. He didn't have time to abduct his mark and do this." He pointed to the photos in the folder.

"What about the rest of Barlow's team? Did he

bring anyone else along for the ride?"

"He goes through people so quickly," Ryan shook his head, "it isn't likely. There've only been a couple of constants, and even they haven't been that constant. None of this makes a damn bit of sense. We've run everything, looked into every one of them, and nothing. It's a coincidence because it bloody well can't be anything other than that." He stood, shoving the chair out of the way, and stomped out of the office.

"Donough blames himself for the Interpol agent who was killed," Farrell said. "For him, this has become personal. I understand the point you're making, Ms. Parker, but we've gone over it a hundred times and none of it pans out. It doesn't make sense these solid leads aren't solid, but I don't know how else to explain it other than coincidence."

"You're missing something. You have to be missing something. Give me the file, and I'll talk to Ryan. He can help me play catch-up. I know this is Interpol's case, international murder for hire shit, but I need to run some things by the local cops. Right now, two men are in custody on a dozen counts of GTA, and they might be the only two people who can provide insight into whatever piece of information we're overlooking. If you want to end this, you'll need local help in addition to your foreign surveillance."

"Parker," Farrell exhaled, "the only reason you're assisting is because Donough wants to go back undercover with whatever's left of Barlow's gang. Since you have a pre-existing cover established as a car thief, he thought you might be able to excise some additional information due to your dealings with Robert Gregson. This doesn't mean you're investigating or that we expect you to go above and beyond to solve this case. You're simply assisting Donough. Jablonsky has given me constant reminders that you are not an agent, and no one expects you to act like one."

"I won't walk into a situation blind. I've done it before, and I almost didn't walk away. So either you give me everything so I can make informed decisions before risking my neck, or I walk out that door and you risk letting this sick piece of shit continue to kill indiscriminately."

He nudged the folder forward, providing the only answer I would accept. "Watch your back."

"I always do." I turned, finding Donough standing behind me. I didn't know how long he'd been there or how much he heard, but from his pallor, I suspected he heard every word I said. "Ryan, we have work to do." I jerked my chin toward the door. "It's your turn to buy dinner, but it better not be soup."

TWELVE

Since Ryan's hotel room was the size of Martin's closet and I had no desire to become a sardine, we picked up dinner and went to my apartment. My burger remained untouched in its wrapper, seeing as how my appetite vanished after examining the graphic crime scene photos. All avenues led to Reginald Barlow, but Ryan insisted he was with Barlow nonstop. It wasn't physically possible for Barlow to be in two places at once.

"But we don't have a TOD." Frustrated, I slammed my desk drawer. "How can you tell me you were with him when this happened when we don't even know when it happened?"

"Because I've been with him the entire bloody time. He's only been out of my sight when he was with Gregson in the garage."

"What about when he met with clients, when the two of you parted ways for the night, when you were in the shower or whatever?" Ryan had to be overestimating his own skills.

"We have audio and video surveillance on him. Interpol and the ICC have agents monitoring the feeds and keeping tabs on his movements. I planted the bugs myself, and we've done countless checks. They're all working. His only opportunity was when he was with Gregson, and he was with Gregson." He ground his teeth in frustration.

"Maybe Gregson's assisting."

"Bollocks." He slammed the file down on my coffee table. "You would have noticed. Even that twat, Tommy, would have noticed." He turned his back to me and stared out the window. "I don't know what we're missing."

"Neither do I." I reconsidered my conversations with Tommy, my brief encounters with Robert, and tried to think if there was something I missed. "Gregson's afraid to roll on Barlow."

"So?"

"Why not snitch on Barlow? First of all, ICE wants to deport him. Second, if he's the middleman, why not turn over the broker in hopes of a reduced sentence? It's not like they know each other. This is a business transaction that failed. Wouldn't it make more sense to cut your losses and move on?" I gnawed on my pen cap, trying to think of other reasonable explanations. "How did Barlow get in contact with Gregson anyway?"

Ryan folded his arms across his chest, considering the question. "I have no idea. He said he had a number of buyers lined up and needed a guy who could locate the items. The next thing I know, we show up at Gregson's garage, and it's like they're old friends. Are you sure they didn't know each other before?"

"I have no idea." I picked up my phone and dialed O'Connell. When he answered, I asked, "Want to come over and join my super secret crime fighting club?"

"Parker?" O'Connell sounded perplexed. "Are you on the sauce?"

"No, but Inspector Donough and I have questions concerning the two gentlemen you have in holding and what the precise connection is between Robert Gregson and Reginald Barlow, and since you're great at detecting things, you won't mind pitching in on this determination."

"I'll see what I can dig up, and I'll drop by after shift," Nick promised.

"Thanks." I hung up and met Ryan's eyes. "He'll get back to us, but in the meantime, you can read me in on your investigation and Barlow's backup players."

"Frankly, there's not much to tell. In the last six months, I've encountered over a dozen individuals. They come and go. Each location has a different team, like Gregson, Tommy, and you. I've been around for the last six months and so have three other people. Two, really. The third is Barlow's concubine, who's been in and out of the picture. Wendi Hu. She's in Amsterdam, I believe." He rolled his eyes. "Other than that, there are two men who transport the vehicles and parts over borders and across seas, Chase Devereaux and Virgil Mallick."

"You just listed three new possible identities for our deranged hitman. Most people would consider this progress."

"It's not them." He was back to being a defeatist. Maybe he needed a prescription for an antidepressant. "Virgil was serving the last few months of a five year sentence in Denmark during the first two contract killings, and according to Chase's passport records, he was in Canada until Barlow hit Paris."

"What about Hu?"

"Do you honestly believe a woman is responsible for this?" He pointed to the photos, agitated.

"Since when did you become a sexist? Are you saying I couldn't be a contract killer if I wanted to?" Where that comment came from, I wasn't entirely sure, and I rubbed my eyes. Maybe I was losing it. Exasperated, he mumbled some long rant in French. "English, s'il te plait."

"Stop being so bleeding ridiculous. Look at the statistics. The majority of serial killers are men."

"Maybe it's not probable, but it is possible. What do you know about her?" Something flashed across his face, and I wished I hadn't seen it. My gut said he liked her. Maybe he wanted to save her, or maybe he was screwing her on the side. Regardless, it was making clear, level-headed judgment unlikely.

"It's not her," he insisted.

"Then tell me what you know so I can reach that conclusion on my own, and we can get back to business."

"Fantastic." He shuffled through the files and handed one to me. As I read, he stared out the window. From the photographs, she was a slight woman. Given that the Camel drugged his victims, tortured them, and dumped what was left of their remains, she wouldn't have the physical capabilities herself. When I flipped to a few close-up surveillance photos, I also saw the extensive scarring on her shoulder blade. She probably didn't have much use of her right arm. "See," he didn't sound smug; he sounded protective, "it can't be her."

"Why is she with Barlow?"

"He made some kind of deal to get her out of her home country. They were torturing her, using her for all kinds of unsavory things. He promised to keep her safe. She loves him because she believes he saved her."

"Maybe he did." Was Barlow a contract killer with a heart of gold? Stranger things had happened, but human soup and rescuing women didn't coalesce.

Ryan let out a horrible sounding snort. "First, you insist Barlow's the Camel, and then you have the audacity to say he's a hero. Incroyable."

"How long has she been traveling with him?"

"Not long. They met in different hotels when we were in the EU, but she hasn't left Europe. She didn't make the trip with us. She doesn't have legal documentation, and any overseas travel would come under too much scrutiny. Instead, he established an apartment and a couple of bank accounts for her to use while he's away. He keeps her comfortable. But don't be fooled. She's his prisoner."

"Calm down." The warning bells blared in my brain. "You just hit on something." I studied him. "How emotionally compromised are you when it comes to her?"

"I'm not."

"Yes, you are." If anyone knew what emotionally compromised looked like, it'd be me. "Don't deny it, but can you work past it?" He nodded. "All right, let's get a full workup on Wendi Hu. Every alias she's ever used, and everything Barlow's set up for her. We need access to every account, property, travel arrangements, everything she has. I don't believe she's the killer, but maybe the Camel is filtering his funding through her. She might not even know it."

"Interpol's already checked her out. They didn't find anything."

"We can check again. It doesn't hurt to be thorough. It's not like we have anything better to do."

I typed in her name and conducted a search. Ryan

remained motionless in front of my fire escape window. Without looking up, I grabbed the pad of paper and pen off the corner of my desk and flung them in his direction.

He knelt down and picked up the thrown items. “She’s not involved. If we dig too deep, it might raise red flags and result in her deportation. Or it could tip off Barlow to a rat on his crew.”

“Newsflash,” I stopped typing, “Barlow’s not in charge anymore, and if what you said about her history is true, I’m sure some nation will grant her asylum. You’re working with the ICC. Pull some strings.” I went back to focusing on the computer, asking offhandedly, “Are you sleeping with her?”

“How can you ask that?” He sounded betrayed, so I dropped the topic. At least he was scribbling information on the notepad. We remained working in the hostile, tense atmosphere of my apartment as I hit dead end after dead end. Every name, alias, and address he provided led nowhere. “It’s not me. I was always suspicious of every person Barlow interacted with,” he swallowed, “but Grenauldo fell for her.” My head shot up, and I stared at him. “My partner, Interpol Agent Josef Grenauldo, fell in love with her. The night before he died, he made me promise to keep her safe. Safe from Barlow, the authorities, all of it.”

“Ryan,” my mouth was dry from the implications his words held, “did Grenauldo break cover? He told her who he was, didn’t he?”

“He wanted to get her away from Barlow. Josef had a plan to take her somewhere safe, so she could be free, not caged in some paid for apartment with monetary shackles.” He rubbed his eyes. “The day after he tells her his true identity, he was gunned down in the street like a dog. I should have been there. I should have stopped it.”

"He broke cover." I tried to reinforce the obvious, but Ryan shook my comment away.

"The investigation into his death ruled it a coincidence. His murder was unrelated. They didn't want to admit he botched the operation. Maybe it was just a mugging. We've been to some seedy hellholes."

"I don't understand why you're protecting a woman who might be to blame for an agent's death."

"Because he made me promise," Ryan spat. "She didn't kill him. There was no talk of such matters within Barlow's crew. No one ever mentioned a snitch or payback or making an example. She was surprised when she heard Josef was killed. She cried hysterically for days."

"Do you think Barlow killed him or had him killed because he was screwing his girlfriend?"

"I don't know." Ryan collapsed on my couch and buried his head in his hands, grasping for something tangible.

I sat down next to him, unsure of how to proceed. "You need to take a break before you have a breakdown."

Going into my bedroom, I pulled an extra set of sheets, pillows, and blankets out of my closet and brought them into the living room. I knew the toll losing your partner could take. When I lost Michael and Sam, I never recovered. Not really. And my recent nightmares proved that. I couldn't imagine what it must be like during an undercover assignment when the only people to lean on for support were those responsible for your partner's death. I collected our notes and files and put everything into my messenger bag.

"Where are you going?" he asked, observing me and the bedding.

"You need to decompress, and that shitty hotel isn't

the place to do it. There are clean towels under the cabinet in the bathroom and brand new travel-sized toiletries in the vanity in case you want to shower or get cleaned up. I'll meet O'Connell elsewhere, and we'll work on some leads. I'll be back sometime tonight but make yourself at home. Whatever's in the fridge or liquor cabinet is fair game." I put on my shoulder holster. "If you need anything, you have my cell number."

"Alex, I don't want to chase you out of your own apartment."

"You're not. But you haven't had a moment to breathe, let alone grieve, or remember that you're Ryan Donough, Police Nationale Inspector, not Hoyt, some lowlife car thief. Consider this your sanctuary. It's not much, but it makes a great hideaway from the rest of the world." I slung the bag across my chest and opened my front door. "You can stay as long as you like. If you go out for whatever reason, there's a set of keys in the drawer next to the kitchen sink."

"Thank you."

Ryan was on the verge of losing it, and people thought I couldn't handle the stress of this situation. Ha. As I descended the six flights of stairs, I called O'Connell. We'd meet at his place to go over the case. I just hoped the brief reprieve would be enough to steady Ryan.

* * *

Before coming off shift, O'Connell took another crack at Robert Gregson, even though Gregson refused to incriminate Barlow. It was apparent there was a long-standing relationship between the two men. Gregson owned a reputable garage, but on the side, he dealt extensively with car thieves. Over the years, his name had surfaced with every major auto theft ring, but until now, the police never had enough evidence to charge him.

My consulting work with APS and the sting operation I helped orchestrate provided enough evidence and corroboration to have the charges stick to Robert. It was about damn time. If only he would connect his operation to Barlow, then we'd be set.

"Since Gregson's been doing this for years," I glanced at his jacket and burglary's suspicions over the last five years, "he must have dealt with Barlow before."

"That'd be my guess," Nick said. "Since Barlow's an international traveler and broker, it'd be difficult for him to make the proper connections to acquire such a long laundry list of vehicles. He's not asking for run-of-the-mill cars that can quickly be scrapped or resold. He only deals in rare finds and insanely expensive new vehicles. I'd say they've known each other a while."

"Do you think Gregson knows about the contract killings? Could he be funneling money or passing messages to the Camel?"

"Search warrants have been issued for his property, and Moretti's sent Gregson's financials and phone logs to be analyzed by IT. We're even scanning his internet usage and checking his browser history." The first known hit was arranged via a message board. Browser history might shed some light on the situation. "So far, we've found a lot of car sites and your basic porn addiction. Nothing that screams out hitman for hire."

"Any information on the overseas accounts Barlow was supposed to establish as payment for Gregson, Tommy, and me?"

"Nothing, but we're hoping Interpol will pass along

that information as soon as they convince Barlow to turn it over." Before I could ask my next question, he read my mind. "The same is true of the client list or buyer list. Frankly, without Barlow, we're missing vast amounts of information. All we have is the garage owner and some knucklehead."

"Can you lean harder on Gregson? Maybe I can take a crack at him."

"You or Riley?" he asked.

"Whichever gets the job done. At this point, probably Riley since I have to keep my cover intact for Donough's operation." Then I filled him in on everything Ryan and I discussed concerning Wendi Hu, Virgil Mallick, and Chase Devereaux.

"I'll dig up what I can on Wendi Hu." Nick made a note for himself. "But our best bet is getting something conclusive out of Gregson. Moretti already handed Barlow over to Interpol, but they aren't releasing him to ICE until we have a handle on the murders. Just because Barlow wasn't there doesn't mean he can't tell us who was, especially if he's working for a serial contract killer."

"I'd love to take a run at him. Maybe Tommy too."

"Parker, you're assisting Interpol. You have no jurisdiction."

"Actually, I'm mostly assisting Donough." I pressed my lips together and glanced at my phone in case I missed a call. "He's in bad shape. He wants to fulfill his dead partner's wishes, but the reason his partner is dead might be because of the woman he broke cover for." I let out an exhale. "And I'm not completely convinced Ryan doesn't have a thing for her. Maybe not a romantic thing, but she has one hell of a sob story, and all you men are alike."

"Amen to that," Jen said from the front door. She had just come home from work and found us at the kitchen table with a pile of paperwork between us. She kissed her husband and smiled at me. "Are you staying for dinner, Alex?"

"No, I should give the two of you some privacy." I closed the folders.

"Don't leave on my account. I'm going to take a shower anyway." She cringed and looked down at her nurse's scrubs. "You wouldn't believe how many times I've been puked on today. I've changed three times." She left the room, adding, "I hate flu season. Plus, it's Nick's turn to cook."

"I make a mean steak," he offered.

"Well, in that case." Once the water turned on, we got back to the topic at hand. "Donough believes it's his responsibility to save Wendi from Barlow, the authorities, and the freaking boogeyman since Grenauldo can't do it. Meanwhile, it comes down to basic math. Her relationship with Grenauldo most likely resulted in his death. It might have blown Ryan's cover out of the water and done irreparable damage to determining the Camel's identity and next target."

"Where's the inspector now?" O'Connell opened the fridge and took out the marinated steaks.

"Just call me Victor Hugo."

"Huh?" He tossed a puzzled glance over the fridge door.

"*The Hunchback of Notre Dame*. Sanctuary. Sanctuary," I elaborated, and he let out a slight snort at my theatrics and found a broiler pan. "I told him to stay holed up at my place while he gets his head on straight."

"Speaking of which, you actually seem good. On top of things. Dare I say it? Calm, even."

"Strangely enough, I am. Maybe after spending so much time with Ryan, I've been desensitized to my triggers. Or there are more important matters to deal with."

"I'll pass everything along to the guys at the precinct, and I'll dig into the names and connections you've given me." He stopped the food prep and found Ryan's scribbles on the table. "Are all of these aliases and connections for Hu, or is he holding back in some misguided attempt to protect this woman?"

Pondering the question, I hated to think Ryan wasn't being truthful. He was one of the good guys. "I'll let you know when I find out."

I cleared the table while Nick made dinner. It didn't matter that it was almost eleven when the three of us sat down to eat. He was a cop. Jen was a nurse. And I was glad to have an excuse to stay out of my apartment. After dinner, I washed and dried the dishes. It was the least I could do.

Jen took the final stack of plates and put them in the cupboard. "How's James? It's been a while since the four of us have gotten together for a date night," she wheedled. Maybe O'Connell picked up some pointers on interrogation techniques from his wife.

"He's okay. Busy with work. Y'know, the usual." I shrugged. "We haven't been talking much lately, so I'm not certain what his schedule looks like. Although, I don't know what my schedule looks like either."

"Oh, please," she rolled her eyes, "the two of you are a broken record. You work and avoid him, and he gets annoyed. What do you think is going to happen?" I opened my mouth to respond, but she shushed me. "Remember, I'm married to a cop, and I work at a hospital. Anything you come up with, I've seen or heard before." She sighed dramatically. "He loves you. You love him. Stop making everything life or death. Give him a call, and let's get something arranged for this coming weekend."

"But..." I looked to O'Connell for help, but he ducked out of the room.

"If you don't, James and I will come up with extensive plans for Saturday. Maybe we'll start with a matinee, a stroll in the park, an early dinner, then on to dancing, and finish up with a nightcap at one of those swanky hotspots that will only let us in because he has a black card in his wallet," she threatened.

"If the two of you go out, does that mean Nick and I are off the hook?" I joked.

"Call him, Parker," Nick yelled from the other room. "I'm not leaving my wife alone with your boyfriend."

THIRTEEN

I stopped at a twenty-four hour supermarket on the way home and picked up basic supplies. Since I had company, I needed to act like a decent host and provide more than an old jar of mustard and a few bottles of beer as nourishment. When I arrived home, Ryan was asleep on the couch. His posture was rigid, and his body was pressed firmly against the backrest.

Silently, I put the groceries away and went into my bedroom. After spending the next few hours performing my due diligence, I mapped out Barlow's movements for the past year, his encounters with Wendi Hu, and the reported auto thefts and murders that took place in each location. It wasn't much, but it was the building blocks for the entire investigation. Sure, Interpol and the ICC were already aware of these facts, but it helped to build my own theory from the ground up. Glancing at the clock, it was nearing five a.m. Ryan was snoring and letting out random whines, so I left him to battle his demons as I drifted off to sleep.

I woke suddenly to a loud clang. Instinctively reaching for my nine millimeter, I saw my bedroom door was closed and remembered I had a houseguest. Ryan was in the kitchen, arguing with the frying pan. He smiled, looking slightly better than yesterday.

"Crepe?" He attempted to hold up the pan as the thin pancake slid across the Teflon.

Confused and bleary-eyed, I shook my head. "Did you need the bathroom?" I jerked my thumb at the room, and he shook his head. "I'm going to take a shower." It was too early in the morning to be awake or cooking.

Collecting some clean clothes, I shut the bathroom door. When I came out, it was a little after nine. No wonder I was barely functioning. I set the coffeemaker to brew and retrieved the work I did the night before. Ryan was at my kitchen table with a plate full of crepes and some type of fruit and cream cheese filling. When did I buy cream cheese?

"I didn't hear you come home last night." He took a bite and nudged an empty plate toward me. "Did," he searched his mind, "Detective O'Connell have anything insightful to add to my investigation?"

"He's looking into a couple of things. I'm sure by tonight he'll have something to add." I poured two cups of coffee and brought them over to the table. "How'd you sleep?" Rumpled bedding covered my couch.

"It's the first night I can say I actually slept." He chewed thoughtfully. "I owe you an apology and a debt of gratitude."

"You don't owe me anything." I reached for the crepes, skewered one, and put it on my empty plate, taking a tentative bite. "There's no way I had ingredients for this in my kitchen."

"I found a can of fruit compote in the cupboard,

along with some flour. Eggs and butter were in the fridge, and—" He was going to continue, but I held up my fork to stop his rambling.

"I hope you checked the expiration dates on everything."

He smiled at my joke, even if it wasn't a joke. Hopefully, neither of us would die from botulism.

"Can we continue where we left off yesterday?" I asked. His posture shifted, and he sighed. "When is Barlow's crew expecting you to resurface? Have you been in contact with them since your arrest?"

"Yes. Tomorrow, I'm supposed to meet Virgil and Chase at a gentlemen's club. We have to decide what to do with the vehicles we've already acquired and what our next step will be."

"Has Barlow found a way to get word out to any of you?"

"Not to me, but I've been busy. Thankfully, Interpol leaked that I've been in custody for the last few days. Before you agreed to assist, I made contact with Virgil about setting up a meet."

"I'm going with you." I wasn't sure if I meant it as a question or a statement.

He sat back and assessed me for a long time. The scrutiny was uncomfortable, and I focused on my breakfast instead of his eyes. When there was nothing remaining on my plate, I had no choice but to look up.

"How do you want to do this?" he asked. "We need to be intimately aware of each other's cover story. Do you want to go first?"

"Sure." I cleared the table while he grabbed a pen and paper to take notes. "My name is Alexandra Riley, but you can call me Alex." I attempted to recall everything that I said to Tommy and Robert over the last few weeks. When I was finished, Ryan dropped the pen and reread his notes. "Any questions?"

"Your cover has no priors, correct?" He was considering some kind of snag.

"No priors. No history of any kind. Riley's a clean slate."

"Why would two known car thieves, both with significant past offenses, trust you?"

"Because I make leather and eyeliner look good, and I didn't approach Tommy with the intention of getting on the crew. I was looking for some action. Unfortunately for him, that turned out to be boosting cars instead of doing the horizontal mambo." I considered my first two meetings with Barlow. "Did Barlow buy it?"

"I'm not sure, but the blue sports car sold you as a thief. Most people don't have access to two hundred thousand dollar cars, and when Tommy held the gun to the back of your head and no one came to the rescue, it was rather convincing that you weren't a cop."

"I'm not a cop."

"Semantics." Something dark passed behind his eyes. "As far as I know, Barlow never doubted your false identity. Therefore, Virgil and Chase shouldn't have any reason to doubt whatever it is I tell them."

"What are you planning to tell them, Mr. Hoyt?" I took the pad of paper, ripped off the top two sheets he used, and grabbed the pen from his hand. "It'd be nice to start with a first name."

"Ryan." He winked. "It's so much easier when our fake identities have the same first name. Wouldn't you agree?"

"Ryan Hoyt," I tested the name on my lips, "car thief extraordinaire."

"Nothing that sexy. Hoyt's a wheelman. If you steal it, I can drive it." He rested his elbows on the table and rubbed his forehead. "There's a long history of misdemeanors and felonies in my past. Everything from joyriding to GTA, and if I'm not mistaken, three assault charges, one weapons charge, and one count of vehicular manslaughter." He stopped rubbing his face and rested his head in his hands. Ryan was a pro. There was no mistaking the crimes his cover persona committed.

"All around badass."

"Makes it easier to establish a background when you aren't sure what the boss wants you to do or what skills you may need to possess."

"What did you do for Barlow?"

"Whatever needed to be done." This was never the easy part. "In Paris, he needed a couple of guys roughed up. It was his way of vetting me."

"Congratulations, you passed." There was no mirth or teasing to my words. It was hard maintaining the line, especially when you had to do physical harm or break the law.

"Lucky me. Aside from that, I've been his delivery driver."

"How have you stayed in contact with Interpol and the ICC?" I wondered aloud, even though it wasn't part of his cover. After all, Capt. Reneaux had lost contact with his star inspector.

"Dead drops, burner phones, the usual methods. It's unlikely Barlow has any idea who I am. Even though Grenauldo broke cover, he didn't break mine."

"How can you be certain?"

"Because I'm not dead."

"Dammit, Ryan, yesterday, you preached your partner's death was a coincidence, and Hu wasn't behind it. Here we are twelve hours later, and you're changing your story. I need the truth."

"I don't know." He winced at my increased volume. "Alex, I don't know what's true anymore. Grenauldo's dead. That's true." He blinked and looked away. "My superiors said it wasn't related. Barlow didn't let on that he knew or had anything to do with it, but," he focused on my eyes and didn't look away, "how likely is it?"

"Fine, how long has it been since his death?" I read the file earlier this morning, but he was pissing me off. So double-checking his story wouldn't hurt.

"Seven weeks. Barlow never replaced him on the crew, but like I said, there's not much stability with his team."

"Has he changed his attitude toward you?"

"No. Everything's the same."

He had to be right. If Grenauldo blew both their covers, Ryan would no longer be breathing. Needing space and something to do, I cleared the dishes and scrubbed the cookware. When I turned around, he was in the shower. I wanted to scream, cry, and throw glass objects into brick walls. Instead, I dialed Mark.

"Parker, what is it now?"

"Something's off when it comes to the dead Interpol agent Donough was partnered with. Can you get a hold of his personnel file, the police report, and the autopsy records? Interpol said it was coincidental, but you've always told me coincidences don't happen."

"Fine." The drawer in his desk slammed shut. "What have they talked you into doing?"

"I'm only playing a minor supporting role in the film adaptation."

"Too bad you think you're a leading lady. Look, just be careful. I'll pull those records and see what I can find. In the meantime, watch your back."

"Thanks. I will." Hanging up, I noticed Ryan standing in the bathroom doorway, dressed in his clothes from yesterday with his hair dripping. "What?"

"I just thought of something." Whatever realization he reached wasn't pleasant. His expression was grim. "There wasn't any surveillance in the bathroom, and often Barlow and Hu would lock themselves in there for hours. I assumed it was a romantic interlude."

"But it might have been when they were discussing other matters, such as contract killings."

"Bloody-fucking-hell." He slammed his fist into my bathroom door with a resounding thud and an awful crunch. Just what I needed, a partner with a broken hand. The impact didn't have any effect as he continued his string of expletives. "Grenauldo falls for her bullshit story and convinces me it's legitimate, and then she makes arrangements to have the lovesick moron killed. Either that bitch or Barlow is the contract killer, or they know exactly who is."

"Slow down." I approached him, fearing his anger would lash out at a moving target. "Grenauldo wasn't killed by the Camel."

"How the hell do you know that?" It was a fair question. "Because he wasn't left as a poor imitation of blood pudding?"

"Did he tell Hu he was pursuing a killer?" This detail was very important, and Ryan nodded. "Oh god." If Hu knew, Barlow did too, and if he was in communication with the killer or if he was the killer, the entire situation just became insanely more complex.

"I'm such a blind, imbecilic," he was starting to unravel, so I hugged him and refused to let go, "useless, washed-up, piece of shit." His breath came in heaving gasps, and I held him tightly until he pulled himself together. "Alex," he whispered as the self-loathing and anger ebbed, "how could I be so stupid? Why? Why didn't I make the connection before?"

"Shhh," I soothed. "You were too close. Your

partner made a mistake, and you didn't want to believe he was wrong. It's hard to think ill of the dead." I released him from my grasp. "Not to be morbid, but this might lead to an actual break in the case." Lifting his already swollen hand, I added, "And perhaps a few broken bones."

"It's nothing." He pulled his hand free. "I need to talk to Farrell. Interpol needs to be aware of my mistake. Maybe they can find something damning from the scene."

"Finish cleaning up," I insisted. "I called Mark He's looking into the matter for us. He'll talk to Farrell. They both have level heads. Neither of them is compromised. Let them figure it out. He'll get back to me. Besides, O'Connell is collecting information on Hu. This is about utilizing resources and outsourcing the investigating. You're an undercover operative," I tried to give him a playful smile, not quite succeeding, "start acting like one."

He went back into the bathroom and took advantage of the brand new, travel-sized toiletries Martin filled my drawer with in the event he ever forgot to bring something with him for one of our sleepovers while I paced my apartment, annoyed by Ryan's earlier deception and his insistence I was wrong about Hu. He had been wrong but too blind to see it. He saw it now. One night in a safe environment probably made him realize more than just that.

When he came out, I plopped a bag of frozen peas on top of his hand while he went over the other details about the crew, the jobs they'd pulled, and every tidbit of information surrounding his deceased partner. None of it was useful to the investigation, but at least we trusted one another again. By late that afternoon, we were making progress. At least Ryan was. The more we discussed things, the clearer the picture became. Maybe the only thing he needed was to bounce ideas off someone.

"I'm sorry," he concluded, ashamed. "I lashed out because of the accurate assessments you made. I've barely been keeping it together, and I'm sure that detective noticed. Stable people don't remain silent in custody, and they don't suddenly decide to call in favors from people they're already indebted to."

"Apology accepted." No wonder everyone warned me to avoid Ryan. Clearly, I was just as blind when it came to distancing myself from those I've worked with. "Funny story," I passed along Mark, Nick, and even Martin's assessment. We were rebuilding trust, and sharing something far less morbid might put us on a more even keel.

"Then why are you assisting?"

"Because you're a friend in trouble. Face it, we're both soft-hearted saps. One of these days, it will kill us. Let's just make sure that day isn't today or tomorrow."

"That's it? Your high hopes are for the next forty-eight hours?"

"I'm a realist. Let's take things one day at a time and see how it goes. Frankly, two is kind of pushing it."

Having recovered enough to work amicably, we began laying the groundwork for our meeting with Virgil Mallick and Chase Devereaux which was scheduled for tomorrow. The men didn't know I was in the picture or tagging along, which meant we had to make Alexandra Riley an incredibly useful asset. Hu was our best bet for finding the connection between Barlow and the Camel, but first, Ryan had to get back in the team's good graces.

There had to be a way to get some uncompromised backup to assist from the inside, and with any luck, that's where I'd fit in. Since Jablonsky, Farrell, and O'Connell were capable of working the investigation and tracking leads, they'd need new information, additional proof, and irrefutable evidence, and the best place to get that was from the inside.

"Parker, open up," Jablonsky called from my front door. I didn't hear a knock, and judging by Ryan's expression, neither did he. "C'mon, this thing is heavy." Dashing to thc door, I opened it to find Mark holding three file boxes. He brushed past me and into my apartment. "Nothing can ever be simple with you, can it?"

FOURTEEN

"I thought you were going to read the reports, not raid Interpol's files," I said as Mark pulled file upon file from the boxes.

"Shut up and give me a hand."

I opened a second box and removed the contents, skimming the tabs as I placed the files on my coffee table. Ryan remained in the kitchen with his hand under the bag of peas. In the battle of the bathroom door versus Ryan's fist, the bathroom door was victorious. When all three boxes were empty and my coffee table was no longer visible, Mark slumped on the couch and took a deep breath.

"You got any coffee?" He was being short with me, probably still miffed about the current circumstances.

"Do we need oxygen to breathe?" I asked, dutifully pouring him a cup.

After handing him the mug, he looked at the rumpled sheet and blanket on my sofa. "Are you sleeping on the couch again?"

"No, that was me," Ryan replied. Mark attempted

to hide his shock by keeping the glare firmly in place. "Sorry, I didn't get a chance to straighten up the mess I made."

"It's fine." I took a seat on the floor next to the stacks of files. "Now can you tell me what this is?" I asked Mark.

He scooped a thin file off the top of one of the piles. "This is the official report concerning the investigation into the death of Interpol Agent Josef Grenauldo."

"What's the rest?" Ryan asked.

Mark met my eyes, communicating silently what I already suspected. "It's the unofficial report," I supplied, and Ryan threw a confused glance my way.

"Not unofficial so much as everything Interpol has on Grenauldo and you. Your movements, everything on the current investigation, surveillance, suspicions, bank records, camera footage, profiles, possible suspects in Grenauldo's homicide, and the actual cause of death. Everything," Mark corrected.

"What?" Ryan's brow furrowed. He didn't understand how there could be so much information on his investigation that he didn't know about. "That can't be. They told me what happened. It was ruled an unrelated event. What do you mean bank records and suspicions? If they had information, they would have," he shook his head, standing up from the table and coming toward us, "told me."

"It looks like you don't need that blanket anymore," I deadpanned. "Jablonsky's bringing you in from the cold."

Hours later, there wasn't a single file that wasn't dissected. Ryan was up to speed. I was up to speed, and Mark was hoping he didn't make a horrible mistake by giving me access to this information. Silently, I replaced the folders inside the boxes so I could eavesdrop as Mark and Ryan discussed in graphic detail every aspect of his assignment. The version Ryan recollected earlier was the censored, tamer account. The grittier truth involved violence, drugs, and women traipsing in and out of the picture.

Reginald Barlow was a pig. He was smooth and calculating, a real businessman at heart. He wouldn't risk his capital gains on something stupid, but after receiving a payoff for delivering a vehicle, he partied hard. Recreational drugs, prostitutes, whatever struck his fancy. And the next day, it was back to business as usual. I shut the lid on the third box and listened as Donough laid it all out.

"Everyone or just Barlow?" Mark asked.

"Just Barlow. Sometimes, Wendi would show up, and the rest of us would be excused for the evening. I'd return to my room and monitor the surveillance." He looked at me. "The other guys probably went to the bars to find someone to celebrate with. I don't really know."

"Why wasn't surveillance on them?" Mark asked.

We went through all the folders. Interpol was aware of the likelihood that Wendi's accounts were transfer lines for the Camel. They also knew someone on the crew was the Camel or in direct contact with him. There was far too much circumstantial evidence for it to be anything else, and it infuriated me to think they didn't share this information with Ryan. What infuriated Mark was the lack of information they shared with Farrell, after the case was dumped in his lap. If I didn't ask them to investigate matters in such detail, we'd still be acting on the so-called official version that said Ryan's investigation was a complete waste of time and resources.

"They came and went too quickly," Ryan said. "I was told not to waste my time and effort and to focus strictly on Barlow." He slammed his palm down, wincing at the forgotten injury. "How the bloody hell could they neglect to tell me they thought my partner was dirty?"

"Easy, kid," Mark insisted, flicking his gaze briefly to me, "they thought you were dirty too."

"Bloody-fucking-hell. Until they brought me in to assist on the investigation, they didn't have any idea who I even was. They asked me to investigate, and then they turned into paranoid lunatics who don't even trust their own asset."

"Ryan, you can't take it personally." I reasoned with him. "They didn't know, and from the autopsy, you could have popped Grenauldo yourself. Barlow's business is insanely lucrative. Money's a great incentive to turn otherwise good men bad. That's why they left you out in the cold, to monitor you and make sure you were free from suspicion."

He was rightfully angry, and he fumed. I knew that feeling all too well. Hopefully, he wouldn't take his rage out on my bathroom door again. His ego couldn't handle another defeat.

"And what? Now they decide I'm not in the Camel's pocket anymore?" he asked.

"They thought you might be working for Barlow, not the Camel, unless the two prove to be one and the same." Mark sighed. "You've been cleared. After the debriefs, working with Agent Farrell," he jerked his chin at me, "and this one's insistence that you're one of the good guys, the asinine powers that be decided you were just doing your job to the best of your ability."

"Fantastic," Ryan retorted.

"Actually," I took a seat next to Mark, "it's a good thing you were so insistent that you possessed accurate information. If you realized it was bullshit or tried to buck the system, they might have painted you as a turncoat. At least until everything was sorted out."

"They've been watching you," Mark added. "You've seen the photographs. While you've been keeping your eyes peeled for any sign of the Camel, they've been monitoring your movements. Obviously, you're clean. Let it go. You still have a job to do."

"Some job." Ryan didn't like getting jerked around, and ever since he arrived, I'd been getting the same treatment.

"Suck it up, Donough. You're pissed. They screwed you. It happens. But right now, that doesn't matter. In less than twenty-four hours, we have to be prepared for the arranged meet. What you need to focus on is what we're going to do."

Obediently, he sat still, having been chastised like a wayward child.

"Parker," Mark cautioned, "maybe it's time to throw in the towel. If Donough wants to step away from the assholes who screwed him, he can do that. I've talked to Captain Reneaux. He had no idea what the situation was, but now that he does, he wants his best inspector back in Paris ASAP."

Ryan shifted his gaze from Mark to me and back again. "No, I agreed to stop an international hitman, and I intend to."

Mark stood. "Devise your play, and if you need additional support, the OIO is prepared to back you. Understood?" Ryan nodded. "Parker, walk me out. I could use a hand with these boxes."

Grabbing one, I followed Mark to his car. After he shut the lid of his trunk, he hugged me. "It looks like we still have the good cop, bad cop routine down pat."

"I was always better at playing bad cop."

"Yeah. I'm just relieved your old pal, Ryan, is not." He pressed his lips together, searching my face for something. "You're no longer frantic. Should I assume you've found something else to focus on besides Paris?"

"You knew I would."

He nodded and opened his car door.

"Hey, Mark, I've been thinking about how much I miss the OIO, but all this crap with Josef Grenauldo reminded me of my last official case before I resigned as an agent. It always comes back to how we lost Michael and Sam. How *I* lost Michael and Sam." My chin quivered slightly, and I looked away. "It's easier to get over what happened in Paris than it is to get past what happened to them."

He pressed his lips together. "How many times do I have to tell you that wasn't your fault before you accept it as true? If you want to blame someone, blame me. I left you in charge. I forced you to make the call."

"You didn't do it."

"Neither did you." He blinked and looked away. This was a difficult topic for both of us. "Shit, Michael even said it wasn't your fault before he died." Those words made the tears sting my eyes. "Is this because I said I accepted that you were never coming back to the OIO, and that none of this shit," he gestured obliquely in the direction of my apartment, "has anything to do with you? What does your last case have to do with your French boyfriend?"

"He lost his partner. He's losing himself. And it's scary how easily I can relate." I took an unsteady breath and stared at a pebble on the sidewalk. "Every time I've come back to the OIO to assist on something, regardless of how brief, the bodies pile up. I can't deal with any more loss."

His voice was soft when he asked, "Why did you fight so hard to help?" I let out a snort, and the bittersweet smile erupted on his face. "No matter how far or fast you run, you've never left the job. You can't leave the job. You don't know how. You don't know anything else. But every time I ask you to come back, you refuse. When the dust clears, you and I are having a chat. Maybe it's a couple of years too late, but..."

"Okay." It was the first time I agreed to listen or talk, and it caught him by surprise. He nodded and shut the door. As he drove away, I sat on the sidewalk, reminding myself to be strong for Donough. The only people I could help were the living.

"Alex?" Ryan came outside to see what was taking so long. "Is everything all right?"

"I just need a minute."

He sat down on the cold concrete, waiting patiently for me to say something else.

After a time, I let out a sigh. "You have to promise me something."

"Anything," he responded, leery of what I was about to ask.

"Don't die. Not on this case. Not for Grenauldo or the Camel or Barlow or even me. No matter what, you cover your own ass and keep breathing."

"D'accord, but you have to play by the same rules. You came a little too close last time."

"Eh," I shrugged, standing, "what are a few jolts every now and again?" He stood and studied me until I finally responded, "Fine, I won't die either. Now let's go back inside before we catch our death of cold."

* * *

We'd been going round in circles over the same few points for the last hour. "Look," Ryan said, "the only reason you are coming with me is because I need to ensure Hoyt's cover is intact."

"Right," I nodded, "you might need backup."

"No," he gestured emphatically and massaged his temples, "Riley adds legitimacy to my cover."

"But if your cover is blown, you'll need backup," I insisted.

He muttered to himself and skulked around the living room.

"Y'know, the two of you make a great comedy duo," O'Connell said. He arrived twenty minutes ago and had done nothing but watch us argue.

"Since you want to be helpful, Nick, why don't you translate for us? Obviously, we can't get over the apparent language barrier," I said.

"I have to do everything, don't I?" O'Connell asked, looking smug. "Alexis, Donough wants you to approach Barlow's gang as Alexandra Riley in order to remove any hint of suspicion they might have that he is an undercover agent." He said each of these words in a slow, sing-song voice.

"Exactly," Ryan exclaimed, relieved someone understood.

"But they don't know me from a hole in the wall. How am I making your cover look more legit? For all they know, I'm your handler."

"You're American," Ryan responded as if I were incompetent.

"And?"

He looked to O'Connell for assistance, but he lost Nick with that last comment too. "Fine, let's not worry why you're tagging along. Let's just get our story straight," Ryan said. He knew Riley's background history, semi-romantic relationship with Tommy, and ability to steal cars. "We were pinched during the heist. The cops didn't have enough evidence, so we were released. You have a hot car stashed somewhere and hoped to find a buyer. Since I was Barlow's right-hand man, you propositioned me."

"And since your assets are currently frozen, thanks to the authorities, you need the money to pack up and go home. Fake documents can be pricey," I added.

"As soon as I have their trust back, you're out of the picture," Ryan warned.

"See, that's where you keep hitting the snag," O'Connell piped up. "That's a foreign concept for her."

"That's all, Alex," Ryan said, "and if you can't agree, I'll do this on my own."

"If you could do this on your own, you never would have asked for my help."

Ryan looked like he wanted to hit something again, probably me. "You volunteered. You practically begged."

"And you needed it."

Nick snickered. "Damn, this is gold. Do either of you care if I record this?"

"Fine," I said to Ryan. He was right. I begged, but he needed help. "This is your operation, Inspector, so I'll follow your lead." O'Connell dropped his jaw in mock amazement, and I shot him a dirty look. "Now, Detective, enlighten us with your genius or get the hell out of my house."

"Jablonsky and I have been sharing intel, probably because we both hold your well-being in such high regard. Go figure. Anyway, not to bore you, but Hu's financials are a mess. Whoever set them up was brilliant. Of course, it doesn't make life easier when they're under bogus accounts with transfers in and out at every turn. It'll take forever to get them sorted, so in the meantime, I've run backgrounds on Chase and Virgil. They aren't the kind of guys you want to meet in a dark alley. Assault, suspected murder, armed robbery, possession with the intent to distribute. Need I continue?"

"Well-rounded crooks," I surmised. "Any idea if either of them could be the Camel or in cahoots with the Camel?"

"Cahoots, probably. My gut says our hitman is smart enough not to get pinched for doing stupid shit. These guys aren't that smart," Nick said.

"They're henchmen," Ryan added. "Barlow likes people willing to do whatever dirty work he has. Virgil has no problem getting his hands dirty and working the physical angles, and from what I know, Chase works the other angles, ensuring transport, payment, and making sure we always have adequate documentation for the stolen vehicles." Ryan squinted, considering some things. "Given their previous offenses and Chase's alleged connections, were either of them enforcers for any crime syndicates?"

"Virgil used to work for some loan sharks," O'Connell replied. "His file implies that was the motivation for his unlawful infringements. It's also what led to his five year stretch in Denmark. Chase has stayed off the radar the last few years. Not much to go on from his records. He became a ghost. So maybe he got a little smarter, but not by much, since he's cavorting with car thieves and contract killers." I took an uneasy breath, and Nick assessed me. "Parker, they don't have organized crime ties, so it should be okay." I nodded, relieved to have one less thing to worry about. "Unfortunately, that doesn't mean they won't put two in the back of your heads come tomorrow night."

"Then we'll have to be convincing," I surmised.

"Where are you meeting?" O'Connell asked.

As Ryan gave him the location and time for the meet, the wheels began turning in Nick's head. He would swing something to make sure we were covered, even if he wasn't telling Ryan that. Donough was skittish. His partner died, and Interpol had suspected he turned. His current trust issues were understandable, but we didn't need to add stupid to the mix. By the time I went to bed that night, we had a plan A and a plan B. With any luck, we wouldn't need to have a plan C.

FIFTEEN

"How do I look?" I emerged from my bedroom in full Alexandra Riley garb. Ryan's brow furrowed, and he shook his head. "Not enough eyeliner?"

"If you're wearing pasties and a G-string underneath your clothing, they're going to confuse you with a stripper."

"Don't you say the sweetest things?" I checked my gun, wondering if there were metal detectors at the strip joint. It was a risk I had no problem taking. I slid the weapon into my shoulder holster and covered it with my leather jacket. "Shall we?"

He gave a curt nod, and I led him out of my apartment. Hailing a cab, we gave the address to the driver and sat quietly, running through our internal pre-op rituals. When the cab came to a stop outside the bright neon pink sign, I took a deep breath. This wasn't my show. It was Ryan's. I would follow his lead.

"Allons-y," he said. Stress probably made him revert to French, or perhaps it was something Hoyt did. Stop it, Parker, my internal voice warned. Ryan is Hoyt. There is no differentiation. I repeated this a few times as we went inside and found the two men sitting in a private room.

"Ryan Hoyt," Virgil eyed me, "good to see you're a free man, and obviously, you haven't been wasting any time."

"Are you planning to take your clothes off and give us a dance?" Chase asked.

"Easy," Ryan growled, "she works for Gregson. Alex Riley, my associates, Chase and Virgil." I gave them each a nod but remained silent at Ryan's side. "Take a seat," he instructed, but before I moved an inch, Chase intervened.

"Why doesn't she grab us a few drinks instead?" It wasn't a question.

Ryan jerked his head toward the bar, and I walked away. He was in charge, so I was appearing to be subservient. But it didn't mesh with my natural inclinations.

Things were not going well. Leaning against the counter, I studied the two men. Virgil Mallick was built like a bull, large and intimidating, with a shaved head, some ink creeping over the neck of his t-shirt to camouflage a nasty scar across his throat, and clearly packing on his right hip. Chase Devereaux reminded me of a lawyer. He was slim, coifed, and exhibited an air of superiority. He believed he could have whatever he wanted through any means necessary, and I wasn't sure anyone ever disproved his theory. It seemed obvious who the muscle and the brains were in this operation, but since they both worked for Barlow, neither was meant to be the brains. They could probably both be muscle or at least shooters. Guns and weapons tended to be great equalizers. Wordlessly, the bartender dropped four long necks on top of the bar and scooped up the cash I left.

"Want a dance?" one of the strippers asked, strutting close by.

"No, thanks," I responded absently, uncertain if I should wait any longer before making a reappearance. "Hey, how long have those guys been here?" I jerked my chin toward the table. "The ugly one is my sister's ex."

"They got here about thirty minutes ago. Paid for the room, but they haven't taken advantage of the privacy."

"Thanks."

She continued past, looking for a more generous patron, as I scooped up the bottles and went back to the VIP area.

"Sit," Ryan commanded as I put the beers on the table. I sat on the edge of the semicircular booth next to him. "I've talked it over with my associates, and we believe we can move the merchandise for you."

"How soon?" I asked, my eyes shifting from Virgil to Chase before settling on Ryan.

"First," Chase interjected, "we need to renegotiate percentages. It sounds like you're in a bind, Alexandra Riley." I didn't like the way he said my cover name. "The police are looking for evidence against you, and you want to unload a sizzler. We're prepared to move it, but it'll be an eighty-twenty split."

"Twenty? Is that a fucking joke?"

"We're assuming the risk," he said.

"Sixty-forty and you can have until next week to take delivery," I bartered. Ryan and I went over tactics last night since it was important I didn't look overly eager.

"No." His smile looked like a licentious sneer. "Seventy-thirty and you blow me."

"Blow yourself. Or better yet, get your friend to

blow you. He looks the type." I watched Virgil, but he didn't say a word. Ryan let out an amused snort. "What? You wanna blow him instead? Be my guest."

Ryan smirked. "Twenty-five and not a percent more." I looked torn. Chase looked smug, believing I might agree to prostitute myself to him for a better deal. "If you don't like the offer, get the hell out of here."

"Deal," I reluctantly agreed.

"Ryan, Ryan, Ryan," Virgil shook his head, "you know we don't like surprises." He shifted his gaze to me. "But this one's been a load of fun." He turned and stared at the naked woman spinning on the pole. "Now, I think it's time we have some fun before we work out any more details." He caught the attention of one of the waitresses walking by and whispered something to her, slipping her three hundred dollars. A moment later, four women in nothing but thongs and pasties appeared at the entrance to the roped off area we were occupying. "Two for me, and two for you," he said to Ryan as the girls grabbed their hands and dragged them away. Ryan didn't make eye contact as he left, leaving me alone with Chase Devereaux.

"Funny how things work out." Chase picked up one of the beers from the table and took a sip. "I'm confused. What kind of girl doesn't want to make a few thousand dollars just by giving head?"

"I'm a thief, not a tramp. Even I have standards."

"Everyone has a price." He was cold. His rationality was so calculating he could find justification for anything. Sociopath, my mind filled in the blank. I reached across the table and picked up one of the beers, feeling the reassuring shift of the gun against my side.

"I'm sure one of these lovely ladies would be accommodating."

"Are you gay?" he asked, still trying to comprehend the rejection.

"No." We analyzed one another in silence. Talking too much would lead to trouble, so I kept my mouth shut, hoping Ryan would come back soon and not wanting to think what could be bought for three hundred dollars.

"How long did you work for Robert Gregson?"

"A few weeks." My heart skipped a beat. It wasn't a long time, and after the raid, it'd be easy to assume the newest member of the team squealed to the authorities, but I couldn't risk lying either. Reginald Barlow had plenty of time to update his team about me before his incarceration. "How long have you worked for Barlow?"

Something sinister passed behind his eyes. "Not long. Every now and again." He shifted his focus to the newest main attraction taking the stage. "Barlow's in a bind this time." His cold eyes met mine. "Any idea how that happened?"

"Not in the least," I responded with just enough annoyance and ire below the surface to mask my involvement. "And now I'm forced to deal with assholes like you and yours to unload this smoking gun."

He snorted as if it were a joke. "It could be worse."

"How? Your two guys are upstairs getting laid, and I'm sitting here getting interrogated by you. How is that fair?"

"Strippers have standards," he threw my own words back at me. "They're getting lap dances while we have a conversation. I don't deal with strangers. It's an unsavory business to work with someone you can't trust."

"I agree."

"So how come you approached Hoyt?"

Hesitating, I took a slow breath and repeated the story Ryan and I worked out. When I was finished, I caught the look on Chase's face. He fell for it. Ryan was back in their good graces, and my part in this was almost over. We watched the girls spin and gyrate while we waited for Hoyt and Virgil to return.

"Everything okay?" Ryan asked, following Virgil through the detached velvet rope barrier.

"Lovely," Chase replied, and I gave a barely perceptible nod. "Let's take this conversation someplace private to work out the logistics."

Ryan picked up one of the untouched beers and took a swig. "Are you ready to get out of here?" he whispered in my ear. It was part of the code we devised in case things went sideways.

"Whenever you're ready," I said. Chase bought the story. All systems were go.

* * *

"Is Barlow picking up the tab?" I asked as Virgil ushered me into the suite at one of the five-star hotels. No one said a word, so I entered and strolled through the room as if I'd never seen anything quite so magnificent before. "I guess I was working for the wrong guy."

"Quiet." Chase went to the window and looked outside, opened both bedroom doors, and scanned the room for signs of tampering before taking a seat on the couch. He was cautious, maybe slightly paranoid. Was that his nature, or did something spook him? Ryan took a seat on the opposite couch, and I sat next to him. "Okay," Chase said, "it will take a couple of days to locate a buyer. Make delivery on Wednesday, and you'll get your cut then."

"That's thirty grand," I leaned forward, "wire

transferred to an offshore account." He nodded. "Don't screw with me."

"Thirty grand," he repeated. "What's your account number?"

"You'll get it Wednesday, and once the money is verified, you'll get the car. I don't know you, and I don't trust you. I'm not giving you the opportunity to sell me out."

He cast his gaze at Hoyt. "You've seen the merchandise?"

"It's clean. The VIN's been removed. No trackers or identifiers. It's ready to move." He briefly turned and appraised me. "She's a thing of beauty." It was part of the cover, and I had to hand it to Ryan, he was excellent at the slight nuance.

Chase's unyielding stare was harsh. "It better be exactly as you say." I sensed the power play. Chase was trying to assert his dominance over Ryan too. But from what I knew of Hoyt, he was Barlow's right-hand man for the better part of six months and would make a stand to knock Chase down a few rungs.

Ryan leaned back, his posture open and his lips curled back in a silent laugh. He shook his head slightly. "Chase," his voice was rich with malice, "who the bloody hell left you to run things?" Without warning, he kicked the coffee table across the expanse into the couch Chase was occupying. "Barlow left me in charge, and I've let you get away with a lot since I was delayed. But don't you think for a bleeding moment that's the new status quo. You work the business angles and make the connections, but this is my show now." Ryan barely moved, but Chase cowered slightly. I spotted Virgil, hand resting closer to his hip, but he decided not to intervene. If a fight were to break out, I wasn't certain if it'd be every man for himself or if Virgil was Chase's bitch. "Right now, we're regrouping and licking our wounds." He tossed a glance at me. "But our priority is Barlow's release. These damn yanks are planning to deport him, so we'll get him freed on our end. In the meantime, behave in front of our guest."

"Yes, sir." Chase's words held loathing and hate. There was no doubt in my mind he wouldn't cut Ryan's throat in his sleep if he thought it would eliminate the competition. Ruthless, that's what he was.

"Brilliant." Ryan stood, offering me his hand. "I'll let the two of you keep this suite. I have someplace much more welcoming to stay and a side deal that needs closing." I took his hand, and he escorted me to the door. Tommy would be so infuriated to know that Hoyt was getting into Riley's panties tonight. "Wait in the lobby, Alex."

I didn't like leaving him alone with two potential killers, but it was his operation. I went to the elevator and pressed the button, listening for sounds of a struggle or weapons discharge. There were some raised voices, but it sounded business related. By the time the elevator car reached our level, Ryan exited the hotel suite. The door remained ajar, and he was very much in character.

"I told you to wait downstairs," he snapped.

"I'm waiting for the elevator. Do you want me to take the stairs?"

"No." His voice was low and angry, and I signaled with my eyes that Virgil was watching us from the doorway. "I'm sorry about my partners." He grabbed my wrist and spun me into the elevator, pressing me against the wall, and covering my mouth with his as the doors closed. Once the elevator started to descend, he released me. "Sorry," he apologized, back to Donough.

"It's all right. They'll probably be monitoring us as we leave the hotel."

He nodded, drained from acting as Hoyt. "We'll take a cab back to my hotel, and you can grab a ride home from there. That'll make it harder for them to track you, just in case."

"Ryan," I began, but he shook his head.

"Not now." As the doors opened and we left the hotel, he shifted back into Hoyt. He didn't relax again until he let himself into his hotel room.

"If you need a place to crash—"

"Not tonight. In case Chase tries something, you don't need to be caught in the crossfire."

"What if you need support?"

"Farrell has agents positioned throughout the hotel. It's secure."

"Okay."

He took a seat at the table, his back to me as if he were isolating himself from everything and everyone. Maybe it was how he coped. I didn't know everything that happened tonight, and now wasn't the time to ask.

"I'll see you tomorrow."

He nodded but didn't turn around.

I let myself out of his room. Leaning against the wall to collect my thoughts before heading home, I heard the chair squeak against the floor and the lock slide into place. Being Hoyt was destroying whatever was left of Donough. This needed to end soon while there was still something to salvage.

SIXTEEN

"You don't need to be present for the wire transfer," Ryan said. We were in Farrell's office, being debriefed about yesterday's meet. "Since Hoyt's screwing Riley, I can easily instill upon Chase and Virgil that you trust me enough to make the transfer."

"Do you honestly believe Chase wouldn't put a bullet in the back of your skull and keep the car and cash for himself?"

"It's better than having him put a bullet in both of us." Ryan's eyes were puffy and dark. I didn't think he slept last night. I know I didn't, and the lack of sleep made both of us edgy.

"Parker," Mark said from behind, and I swiveled to see him standing in the doorway, "do I have to separate the two of you?" I glared at the insult. "I'm going to take that as a yes. Now walk with me." Farrell jerked his chin at the door, and I went with Mark.

"What?" I asked as he closed his office door.

"Give me the unofficial version of things. How stable is Donough?"

"He hasn't flipped. How many times do I have to say it?"

"That's not what I meant. I've been listening to the two of you argue for the last forty-five minutes." He looked like he wanted to say something but thought better of it. "The man looks like he went through hell, and frankly, you don't look much better. I need to know if this operation should be scrapped."

"There's a contract killer on the loose."

"That detail is not what I asked."

"Ryan can hold it together for now, but the other two men Barlow employed," I pressed my lips together and took a deep breath, "they're sharks that smell blood in the water. He needs support. Tactical support."

"You're not it, but we'll figure something out." He assessed my expression for a moment. "What aren't you saying?"

"He's pushing the envelope. He's fighting so hard to be Hoyt and to separate out his own humanity. I don't think he can keep it up much longer. It's killing him. On the inside, it's killing him."

Mark swallowed and shifted his gaze to the door. "Only you would recognize the signs in others." The implication of his words resonated in my gut, but I brushed it away. "Finish up with Farrell and go home. This building doesn't agree with you."

"Well, I'm not overly fond of it, either."

* * *

"I'm sorry for yelling at you earlier," Ryan said. After he finished the debrief and strategizing with Interpol, he detoured to my apartment. "God," he put his head in his hands, "I don't know what's wrong with me." He let out a harsh breath. "Virgil called this afternoon.

We're supposed to figure a way out of this predicament. He said Chase has some connections. He's lining up papers and IDs as we speak."

"When are you supposed to see them again?"

"Tomorrow morning. Don't worry, Farrell and Jablonsky are keeping eyes and ears on me. Agents are stationed throughout my hotel."

"Where do they think you are now?" I was asking about Barlow's goons, but it took Ryan a moment to realize that.

"With you. Well, Riley. You expertly sold that line of bullshit to Chase."

"I do remember a couple of tricks. And you're one to talk. Hoyt is one scary son of a bitch."

"But is he scary enough to make a power play?"

I sat on the coffee table directly in front of Ryan. "What are you doing? How is pushing Chase's buttons going to force the Camel's hand? Have you lost sight of the reason we're doing this?"

"Either I force Chase to give up his connections and one of them will lead to the Camel, or he'll do something to remove the obstacle."

"Dammit." I got up to pace. I knew last night that was what he was thinking, and I was in no position to stop it. "Why would he waste the time and resources? Why wouldn't they just end you the same way they ended Grenauldo?" I didn't mean to say it, but the words tumbled out before I could stop them. The pain those words caused ripped through him, but he hid his flinch masterfully.

"Regardless," he sounded cold, Hoyt-like, "it will lead somewhere." I stopped mid-stride to determine what to say or do. "Alexis, I don't want you anywhere near this. You gave me the perfect cover story and reason to be distant, but Interpol and I will finish this."

"Understood." I offered a wry smile. "I didn't sleep last night, so I'm going to try to get in a catnap. Afterward, I'm meeting with O'Connell to discuss the current findings on the two bodies that were discovered. If you want to crash here, I'll give you an update later tonight before you meet with Chase and Virgil tomorrow. More information couldn't hurt, right?"

He smiled, one of the brief glimpses into the Donough I knew. "You just want to make sure I keep your couch cushions warm."

"Absolutely." I smiled. "Get some rest, Ryan. You need to keep it together," I turned in the doorway of my bedroom and added, "and you need to stop yelling at your only friend in North America. Mark was afraid we might come to blows."

"Well, it wouldn't be the first time you've knocked me around."

"And it probably won't be the last if you keep being so boorish and surly. But let's make sure it's the last time you hold me at gunpoint and handcuff me to a table." I winked and shut my bedroom door.

Since I exiled myself to the bedroom for Ryan's benefit, I reread my notes and the limited information I was given on the two bodies from the double homicide. The Camel's bank account must be traceable. We just needed to figure out where to look or how he passed along the accounting information. Right now, I didn't know much about the crimes, other than the victims were turned into blood soup, and O'Connell still hadn't given me copies of the report. Hopefully, he'd remember to bring them tonight.

As usual, the men in my life had the misguided notion of wanting to protect me, and I was bumbling around in the dark. It felt like the only thing I'd done since Ryan arrived was argue, and I argued with everyone. Sighing, I put my notes away and flattened out on the mattress, staring up at the ceiling. No matter how I tried to spin it, I knew the problem wasn't anyone else. The problem was me.

For the last two years, I swore off the OIO and insisted on being rooted in the private sector, but I had nothing to show for my efforts. I quit my only stable civilian job at Martin Technologies, and I consulted for the PD and OIO enough to know my heart was still in law enforcement. I was doomed.

Closing my eyes, I curled up on my side and dreamt about my final assignment at the OIO. I saw the explosion and felt the fear and dread grip my insides as I raced to the warehouse. Not Michael, please, not again. Agent Sam Boyle was already dead, bloodied and burned under a sheet, and Michael was in the ambulance dying.

"Alex, wake up." Ryan held me against the mattress as I thrashed and screamed. "Alexis," he repeated more forcefully.

I opened my eyes and stopped fighting. Inhaling swiftly as I fought to catch my breath, I brushed the tears from my eyes and tried to shake off the nightmare. "Sorry," I mumbled.

"Jesus Christ," he sat on the edge of the bed, "I thought someone was killing you."

"Not me." I shut my eyes, embarrassed. Only Martin knew how bad my nightmares were, and even he didn't know exactly what they were about. "Someone I lost when I was still on the job."

"I'm sorry about Michael," he whispered, and my eyes shot to him, confused how he knew. "You were screaming his name." He stood, comprehension dawning on him as everything gained perspective. "That's what this is about. Tu comprend."

"What did I tell you about keeping your comments in English?" I snapped to cover the frantic, debilitating upset that my dream caused. "Were you asleep?" I crinkled my nose. "This is why I don't normally have houseguests."

"How long have you had that nightmare?" Maybe he was asking out of morbid fascination or because he was suffering from the same infirmity.

I let out a nervous laugh. "They are so many. It's hard to keep track. This is the longest running at over two years. But my subconscious likes to mix it up every now and again. Some of my other greatest hits are fighting mercenaries, Martin almost bleeding to death," my chest constricted on that one, "and of course, let's not forget Paris and being tortured. I don't typically talk about this stuff, so if you don't mind." I shifted my gaze to the door, and he nodded.

Taking a few deep breaths, I looked down at my hands. The tremors were subsiding. Checking the time, I climbed out of bed and rummaged through my closet, pulling out a pair of dark jeans and a black sweater. Dressy enough for a Saturday night at the bar, but casual enough to be comfortable. O'Connell sent a message and asked if we could meet at six at the Irish pub. I didn't know why he didn't just come over or make plans to meet at our normal bar across from the precinct or the one near my place, but maybe he didn't want to talk about the case at one of our usual haunts.

When I exited my bedroom, Ryan was slumped against the couch cushion, aimlessly flipping through tv shows. Things were awkward after the scene in my bedroom. His best chance of relaxing would be when I wasn't around.

"You're more than welcome to join us," I offered, stowing my handgun in my purse. A shoulder holster seemed like overkill tonight. "Nick probably has something new since he's normally not so cryptic about our meetings."

"That's okay." He sat up and turned off the television. "I've invaded too much of your life."

"No, you haven't. Stay here. Watch tv. Sleep. Make dinner. Whatever. I'll read you in when I return," I said. He looked like he was about to protest. "You're not kidding anyone. I know you can't sleep in that hotel of yours, and since the banshee who owns this place is leaving for a few hours, take advantage of the quiet. I insist."

"Merci," he grinned, "I appreciate everything you've done."

* * *

Getting out of the cab, I tipped the driver and entered the bar. It was early enough that there were still a few tables and booths open. I grabbed the one in the back corner. As I waited for O'Connell to arrive, I analyzed Ryan's plan for exposing the Camel and realized I would do the same thing. The two of us were eerily similar in our undercover work. It was scary.

I checked my watch and took a sip of my drink. O'Connell was already twenty minutes late. He probably got bogged down at work. My eyes roamed through the patrons, making sure we weren't just missing one another. My gaze stopped on a man with perfectly styled dark brown hair, amazing green eyes, a strong, toned build, and wearing nothing but black. Black dress shirt, unbuttoned at the collar, black suit pants, and shiny black Italian shoes and belt.

"What are you doing here?" I asked.

His eyes studied me, trying to determine if it was a joke. "Do you want me to leave?" Martin asked, sounding hurt. My face drew into an 'oh, shit' expression because he added, "If you'd rather spend date night alone with Nick and Jenny, I'll go."

"I forgot. When Nick left a message to meet, I thought he had something new on the case." I scooted to the inside of the booth, making room for him to sit down. "I didn't think about it."

"It's fine." From his tone, it wasn't. He ordered a scotch from a passing waitress and angled in the seat to face me. "How have you been? You weren't doing so well at my place, and I haven't heard from you in a couple of days."

"Don't do that," I said. He was being too polite, like he wanted to fight but not in public.

"I'm not doing anything." Anger flashed in his eyes. "I thought you didn't want to be alone, but you took off. I told you I'm here to pick up the pieces. Thankfully, I don't need my super glue." He cocked his head to the side, seeing something unsettling reflected on my face. "Unless I'm wrong about that."

"Nightmares." I took another sip. "Before I left my apartment, I was taking a nap. I think everything with Ryan and being back inside the OIO building is screwing with my subconscious." I wasn't ready to verbalize my desire to go back to work, especially since I wasn't even sure if that was what I wanted.

"What's going on?" he asked. I looked away not wanting to give him any other reasons to worry. "Talk to me." I wasn't sure if it was being trapped in the booth, the remnants of my earlier nightmare, or everything else, but all of a sudden, I couldn't breathe. I gasped for air, and he pulled me against his chest. "Breathe," he whispered. "Slow and easy. It's okay. I'm right here. You're okay."

I couldn't imagine what we must look like to the rest of the crowd at the bar, but it didn't matter. My mini panic attack vanished almost as quickly as it appeared. "I'm sorry," I whispered against his neck.

Before I could say anything else, Nick cleared his throat. "Are we interrupting something?"

Jen slapped his arm, and the two of them sat down across from us. I scooted away from Martin and stared at the table, hoping the embarrassment would fade quickly from my face. Martin shook hands with Nick and gave Jen an awkward one-armed hug from across the table.

"You okay?" Nick asked me.

"Yeah, fine." I felt Martin's hand on my thigh, and I grasped it tightly. "Any progress?"

"No," Jen interrupted sharply, "the two of you are not talking about work all night. We are here to have fun." She stared at Martin, hoping for moral support from another civilian. "So no shoptalk."

"Yes, dear." Nick gave her a peck and got up to grab the two of them some drinks.

Martin was his usual outgoing and pleasant self and made sure the conversation was light. As the evening progressed, some force of nature drew us closer together, and I didn't notice how or when I ended up curled against him as he continued to find Jen's recent hospital stories fascinating.

The story ended, and silence temporarily filled the void. O'Connell snickered. He and I hadn't said much all evening. Being barred from the only topic we wanted to discuss, we provided the bare minimum of conversation, but at least we were smart enough to laugh at the right places. But since we were the only ones who made a sizable dent in the appetizer platter, it was obvious we used eating as another excuse not to talk.

"How'd the two of you meet?" Jen asked, pointing her fork at Martin and me.

"Honey, you've heard the story." Nick knew it wasn't something any of us liked to talk about.

"Right, I mean I know how you met, but," she looked mischievous, "when did you realize you were interested in him?" Apparently, telling Jen that Martin and I weren't communicating made her believe her R.N. credentials translated into a licensed couples' therapist.

Martin shifted to the side, so he could see my face. "I'd love to hear this one."

"Jerks," I teased but found his eyes. It couldn't hurt. Maybe it would help smooth the waters after all the turmoil I'd put him through with Tommy and my nightmares. "The first time he kissed me."

"In the car?" he asked, surprised.

"That wasn't the first time you kissed me," I corrected. O'Connell emitted an odd sound, and Jen kicked him under the table. "You might have been too drunk to remember. It was the night after we had that horrible fight in your office and you took a leave of absence from work." The vaguest recollection crossed his features. "You told me how you knew Mark."

"If that's when you decided you were interested, why'd it take a year for us to start dating?" Martin asked, but it was playful.

"I didn't want you to think I was easy."

O'Connell and Martin both let out a snort at that one, and I wasn't sure who to glare at first.

"Well, Ms. Parker, I knew the first night we met that you were exceptional." Martin ran his hand along my arm. "You were stunning in that lavender blouse and black skirt." That had been at my dinner interview to become his security consultant.

"How do you even remember that?" I barely remembered what I had for breakfast or if I had breakfast.

He smirked and tapped his temple knowingly. "Steel trap."

Jen looked sappy, like one of those women who swoons at romantic films. Normally, I tended to fall asleep within the first five minutes. But it was date night, so I played along. She turned to O'Connell with a challenging look.

"C'mon, babe, I remember precisely when we met and what you were wearing. Light blue scrubs." Nick shot a glance across the table and rolled his eyes. "Now, can we please talk about something far less nauseating because I think I'm going to be ill?"

Having appeased Jen with enough romantic mumbo-jumbo, Nick and I began discussing the case while Martin distracted her with less morbid tales from the civilized world. The coroner conducted a chemical breakdown of the drugs used in the murders and dismantling of the remains. Only a handful of chemical and pharmaceutical companies produced the materials, and the purchases were being traced. With any luck, they'd have a list of potential suppliers and buyers soon. It could only help.

"Narcotics is asking around. If we can locate some street-level dealers who might have heard something, it will be faster than going through the more official channels," Nick concluded.

"Why would local drug dealers know anything about this?"

"They're cooking all kinds of crap nowadays. Or they buy from these New Age chemists who watched one too many television shows and think they should manufacture their own meth, bath salts, and god knows what else."

"Do we have any idea what we're dealing with or the quantities needed?"

"It's some kind of benzodiazepine derivative mixed

with a few other things. The ME's not sure, but our killer either injects his victims with the drug or has them ingest it. We're assuming the combination must knock the vics on their asses. Then he abducts them, holds them in some undisclosed location for a few days, long enough to cause severe dehydration, and before death occurs, he somehow floods their bodies. Maybe intravenously or in some perverted waterboarding torture method. It's sick. The whole thing is fucking sick."

"What about cross-referencing the chemicals, drugs, whatever, with the vehicles or vehicle thefts. There's bound to be an overlap." I blew out a breath, and Martin gently rubbed my back. Apparently, their conversation concluded, which meant ours should too. "Sorry, I can be somewhat obsessive," I apologized to Jen.

"I'm used to it when he and Thompson get together." She rolled her eyes. "I guess I'm guilty of gender bias. You're one of my gal pals, so I forget this aspect of your life takes priority."

"It has to," Martin said, surprising me. "Nick and Alex deal with more than either of us can imagine, and quite frankly, we probably don't want to know about all of it."

The conversation halted, and Nick looked at his watch. "It's getting late. How about we call it a night?" He looked at his wife. "The next time we do this, I promise we'll schedule it when we're not in the midst of something huge, okay?"

"Fine," she agreed.

Martin picked up the tab, and the four of us went outside.

After bidding the O'Connells good night, Martin turned to me. "Do you want a ride home?" I nodded, glad for a few minutes of quiet with him. He signaled to Marcal, and the car came around. He opened the door, and I climbed in the back. He put up the privacy screen. "You don't have to talk to me about any of this. All I know is you're struggling with something, and I can't do anything to fix it." He looked away. "It's frustrating as hell. So I push, and you pull away. But, sweetheart, I just want to do something to make everything more bearable for you."

"I know, but most of the time, I don't even know what I'm doing. What do you want from me?"

"Nothing. I just want you. Because sometimes it feels like I've never had you in the first place."

"You're the only one who's glimpsed behind the curtain, but there are so many things I can't talk about, that I don't want to talk about, but knowing you're there is enough."

He smiled and ran his thumb across my cheek, and in the privacy afforded by the tinted windows and the screen separating us from the driver, we enjoyed date night in the back of his car. "Should I stay at your place?" he asked.

"Ryan's upstairs. He's been so worked up that I offered him a safe place to get his head on straight."

"Well, if you need a safe place to stay, you're welcome at my house anytime."

We kissed goodbye, and I grabbed my purse off the floor, where it had fallen, and went inside.

"Ryan," I called. I shut the door and flipped the lock. "Ryan?" The bathroom and bedroom doors were open, but there was no sign of him.

Confused, I went to the kitchen counter and searched through the drawers for my extra set of keys to see if he had gone out for a while. The keys were at the back of the drawer under layers of junk. I scanned the counter and notepad on my fridge for a message or some clue where he went, but still, I came up blank.

Thirsty, I took a sip from the water bottle on the counter and glanced at the fire escape. Even though it was closed, maybe he stepped out for some fresh air, and the window got stuck. So I went to check.

Jeez, it's like an oven in here, I thought as I tried to slide the window open. No wonder he probably stepped outside. The exertion from trying to open the window made me a little dizzy. I stood up straight to steady myself. The room spun, and suddenly, I felt sick. Supporting myself against the furniture, I made my way to the bathroom and knelt in front of the toilet just in time. If I had food poisoning, I was going to be so annoyed. As I tried to recall how much I drank at the pub, I used the vanity to pull myself off the floor and rinse my mouth in the sink.

As soon as I straightened up, the floor pitched forward. Finding comfort in the cold tile, I shut my eyes against the harsh glare of the lights and hoped the room would stop spinning. Soon, I was too exhausted to move.

SEVENTEEN

"Alex, please," Martin begged, "open your eyes. Please, sweetheart." He sounded panicked. "Alexis. Alexis. C'mon, look at me." My head throbbed. "Dammit, open your eyes." I forced my eyes open, fighting against my heavy lids, but I immediately shut them tight against the harsh, nauseating light. "Alex?" Something cold and damp touched my forehead. "Open your eyes."

My eyes opened again, and he looked relieved. "Why'd you let me drink so much?" I croaked.

He frowned and ran his hands along my body, from my neck to my hips, pressing gently and watching my reaction. "Stay with me. Focus." He lifted me into a seated position and held me in his arms. "God, I thought I lost you." His words made no sense. I closed my eyes, wanting to shut out the light and go back to sleep. "No, don't do that." He shook me slightly. "You have to stay awake."

"So tired," I whispered. Since when was sleeping considered a high crime?

"James? Alex?" There was another voice in the distance. It might have been Nick, but I wasn't sure, nor did I care.

"In here," Martin called. I slumped against his shoulder, glad for the reprieve from his nagging. Maybe now I could go back to sleep.

"Parker," O'Connell was more annoying than Martin, lifting my eyelids until I kept them open on my own, "stay with us." He stepped back, and Martin hauled me to my feet, supporting almost all of my weight. "Her pupils look like saucers. What happened after I left?"

"I don't know." Martin dragged me into the living room. "When you called her cell, I found it in my car. When I showed up to return it, she didn't answer. I found her unconscious on the bathroom floor."

"How long ago?"

"Twenty minutes. I dropped her off maybe an hour ago." He shook me again. "Alex, c'mon, why do you always have to be so difficult? Eyes open, sweetheart."

"This is a losing battle. Maybe sit her up on the couch." O'Connell pressed his fingers against my neck. "Her pulse is slow but steady. Her breathing seems fine. She's definitely drugged, but I don't think we need to worry about an overdose. How far out did dispatch say the EMTs were?"

"Thirty to forty-five minutes. They're backed up due to a multi-car pileup," Martin said.

When I opened my eyes again, I was sitting sideways on Martin's lap, and there was a sharp pain in my arm. I tried to move it, but he held my elbow firmly. I focused on the person standing next to me, holding the needle as the clear tube rapidly filled with a dark reddish substance. Glancing around the room, I watched colorful swirls float endlessly through the air. Why did everything have an odd glowing haze around it?

"I need to know exactly what's in her system," O'Connell said. "Take two complete panels. I'll personally bring one to the crime lab for a rush."

I resisted the urge to close my eyes because every time I did, I lost minutes or hours. I couldn't be sure which was more accurate.

"Welcome back." Nick crouched down to my level. "I need you to focus for a second. What's the last thing you remember?"

"The bathroom floor," I managed.

"What about before that?"

"Getting out of the car."

My head ached, but the rest of my body felt numb. A gloved hand poked at my temple with a long cotton swab. I wanted to jerk away, but in Martin's arms, there wasn't any place to go. Everything seemed fuzzy, in a swirly mist that I never remembered noticing before, but I didn't have the energy to decipher the cause. There was something important I was missing, but I couldn't figure out what it was.

"I'm calling Jablonsky. We'll tear this place apart to figure out what happened," O'Connell said. "I don't know what's going on, but maybe it'd be safer if you take her to your place instead of the hospital. She doesn't have a concussion or signs of an overdose, so she just needs to sleep this off."

"Sleep." I smiled and nestled against Martin.

* * *

My head throbbed, my body ached, and I was nauseous beyond belief. I took a deep breath and shifted my gaze from the ceiling, deciphering my surroundings. How did I end up in Martin's bedroom? His hand rested against my ribcage, and his upper body was wrapped around the top of my pillow as he pressed a cool rag against my forehead. Looking at him from this angle made his face appear almost upside down, and I thought I might be sick.

"Drink this." He leaned across to the nightstand and produced a cup with a straw in it. "You have to balance out your electrolytes. It's important you stay hydrated."

"How'd we end up here? Why'd you let me get this drunk?" I forced a sip of the too sweet liquid down my throat and hoped it wouldn't make a reappearance.

"You're not drunk," He shifted downward so I could look at him without getting dizzy. His eyes were haunted, plagued by something unimaginable. "You really don't remember what happened?" I shut my eyes, trying to recall, but everything was jumbled. "Go back to sleep. It'll be okay."

When I opened my eyes again, it was still dark, but my nausea wasn't as prevalent. Martin's hand was still pressed firmly against my ribs, and as my breathing shifted, he brushed my hair out of the way. His eyes were clouded in pain, and I was certain something horrible happened.

"What's wrong?" I asked, struggling through the confusion.

He swallowed. "Nothing," he smiled, but it wasn't convincing. "What do you remember?"

"The car, but how did I end up here? Didn't you drop me off at home?" He didn't say anything as I searched the recesses of my mind for a solution. "Wait, you were at my place, and Nick was there." I squinted, and my head throbbed. I rubbed my forehead and felt a bandage at my temple, noticing a piece of gauze rolled up and taped to the crook of my arm. "What the hell happened?" My breathing suddenly felt labored, and the room was bathed in an eerie, unnatural glow. Gasping, I fought against the panic.

"Shh. Easy." He reached over to the nightstand and placed the cool compress against my pounding skull, and I calmed slightly. "You must have dropped your cell phone in my car. I was on my way home when Nick called to say he was dropping off some information on the case. So I figured I'd bring your phone back and save you a trip." He still looked tortured. "You didn't answer the door."

"When?" I was having issues following along.

"Tonight." He inhaled and exhaled slowly. "Thank goodness I have a spare key. When I entered your apartment," his jaw clenched, "you were on the bathroom floor, bleeding. You must have hit your head, but for a moment, I thought someone attacked you. And then," he looked away, "I spent twenty minutes trying to get you to wake up. Those were the worst twenty minutes of my entire life."

I clutched his hand over my ribs, realizing he never moved it because he needed to make sure I was breathing. "Well, I'm awake now." I gave him an encouraging smile. "But what happened?"

"I don't know. You were dosed with something. Right now, Nick and Mark are tearing your place apart to determine what happened. They'll be here in a few hours to ask you some questions." He reached across for the glass, and I drank, familiar with the annoying routine. "How are you feeling?"

"Not great, but better than before. If this is what a residual low feels like, I have no idea why anyone uses drugs. The supposed high was equally terrible. Dizzy, vomiting, and everything was hazy. Hell, everything still is."

"You should get some sleep," he insisted. "It'll help." I shut my eyes, and his grip tightened.

For the next several hours, I would wake sporadically, and he'd force me to drink. Then I'd shut my eyes and lose unknown amounts of time. In between conscious and unconscious, I knew there was something important I was missing. Unfortunately, I couldn't hold onto the thought long enough to force it to the surface.

When I finally came out of the fog, it was mid-afternoon. Martin hadn't slept, and he looked distraught. "Sweetheart, are you okay?" he asked, getting out of bed and opening his closet. I nodded as he found a clean shirt. "I'm going downstairs to talk to the guys. They just got here." He changed his shirt and ran a hand through his hair. "Can I get you anything?"

"I'm all right." My head felt like it was used in a ping pong tournament, but that was to be expected.

He nodded and left the room.

Taking a deep breath, I slowly got out of bed. At least the room wasn't spinning, but a few colorful blobs floated through my vision. Martin left my overnight bag next to his dresser. I managed to get cleaned up and changed without too much hassle. I peeled the tape and gauze off my arm and checked the scrape at my temple. It wasn't a big deal. I just wished I could remember if I hit the vanity or the floor with my head. What was I even doing before that?

Suddenly, the thought that I had been chasing all night surfaced. Ryan.

EIGHTEEN

"Mark," my voice sounded frantic, even to my own ears, "where's Ryan?"

I bounded down the stairs in such haste that my head pounded in time with my heartbeat. Martin, Nick, and Mark were seated at the kitchen table, and from the looks of things, Martin was giving his statement. They exchanged a look, and my stomach flipped.

"Come on, Alex," Mark guided me into the living room, "you need to take it easy." He stared into my eyes. "God, you're still higher than a fucking kite."

"Where is he?" I asked more fervently. I crumpled onto the couch, fearing the world would pitch again if I remained upright for too long. Mark sat next to me, studying my features. I squinted, willing my mind to process rational thought.

"He was supposed to meet with Virgil and Chase this morning."

"Did he? Have you talked to Farrell? Interpol was supposed to be watching his back. You said you would watch his back." I sounded crazed. Everything was garbled in my head, and I struggled to filter through the static. "Ryan was at my place yesterday, and when I got back," I squeezed my eyes shut and shook my head, "I think he was gone."

"Alexis, start at the beginning. Tell me everything you remember from yesterday," Mark said. I didn't like being questioned when I just wanted reassurance that Ryan was okay, but whatever happened was part of an official investigation. He wasn't safe. I shuddered and relayed everything I knew and the bits and pieces I remembered. Mark waited until I finished before he spoke. "Last night, you were drugged. The water bottle on your kitchen counter was laced with the same benzo derivative found in the two homicides O'Connell is investigating."

"Oh god."

"Are you sure Ryan wasn't there when you got home?" he asked, drawing me from the horrible thoughts I couldn't shake.

"No. I don't think so." I pressed my lips together.

"Are you sure he didn't do this to you?"

"He wouldn't." Hot tears stung my eyes, and in my impaired state, I couldn't control them. The last clear memory I had of Ryan was when he woke me from that nightmare. "They're going to kill him. We have to find him. We have to."

My chin quivered, and I moved to stand up. There was too much to do. I couldn't hang around here. I needed to be out there, searching for him. How long was he gone? Who took him? Was he still alive?

Mark grabbed my arm and pulled me back to the couch, holding me still. "We will find him, but right now, you're not in any shape to do anything. From the toxicology report, this particular cocktail lingers for forty-eight to seventy-two hours. You have to sit this one out because you're a liability."

"I can't lose someone else."

"You won't." He released me and stood up. "I'll get a team together. We'll scrub the footage from your building and the surrounding areas. We'll check his hotel and do the same. We even have the surveillance feed from Barlow's hotel room. We'll find him."

I nodded, holding my head in my hands and forcing my brain to retain this information. I was barely aware of Mark's departure. O'Connell and Martin were still discussing last night in the kitchen, but I couldn't hear them or focus on their words. I couldn't even stay focused on developing solid leads to locate Ryan. I needed to pull it together. This wasn't the time for fogginess.

"Parker?" Nick said, and I lifted my head out of my hands and looked at him. "Can I ask you some questions?"

"Yes." Obediently, I followed him into the kitchen.

"You need to eat something," Martin insisted. "Maybe it'll help soak up whatever's floating around in your system."

"Sure," I could be agreeable since the only thing I needed was a clear head, "and some coffee."

Martin puttered around the kitchen while I answered the same questions Mark already asked. By the end, I had a basic foundation of what transpired after Martin dropped me off at my place.

Apparently, the water bottle had been dosed. It was run for prints, but the only sets on it were Ryan's and mine. I couldn't remember if Ryan brought it with him or if I'd taken it out of my fridge, and we had no way of knowing how the drugs got inside it. More importantly, someone else must have been in my apartment. But who? And when?

"Alexis," Nick sighed, "just take a minute and think

this through. Are you absolutely certain Donough didn't drug you? His prints were on the bottle. He had access to your apartment. And now we don't know where he is."

"He wouldn't do this, Nick." I bit my lip to fight back the tears. I was a mess. "Barlow's guys must have him. Chase wants him dead. I know it."

"I'll do my best to make sure that doesn't happen." He squeezed my shoulder before heading for the door. "Get some rest. Once you're functioning, we could use your help."

Martin put a plate in front of me, and I forced down a few bites. But I was too queasy and upset to eat, even though I'd try anything to feel normal. Unfortunately, breakfast had little effect on my woozy state. My head ached, and I didn't want to take anything for it. Who knew what kind of interaction that would cause? Martin was stingy with the coffee, believing a stimulant mixed with the depressant mixture wasn't smart, so I drank two glasses of juice, ate a banana, and drank some water. The only thing I could do was rest and give it time. Too bad that was something I couldn't spare at the moment.

* * *

After spending all day and night practically incoherent, I was ready to pound the pavement. Hopefully, it wasn't too late. Martin refused to leave my side, but he still looked plagued. The constant throbbing in my skull hadn't stopped, but my ability to focus and process thoughts was back, and the world was no longer turning itself into a swirling, glowing haze. Checking my pupils in the mirror, I saw they were reactive to the light, signifying my drug-induced hiatus was over.

Reaching for the phone, I dialed Mark. When he didn't answer, I tried Nick. "Come on," I begged, hoping the ringing would be answered. I hit end call and gritted my teeth.

"Give them a minute," Martin insisted, "I'm sure someone will call you back."

"We don't have time for this. We have to find him." I inhaled an unsteady breath. "This can't be happening. Maybe I should go to Virgil and Chase's hotel suite as Alexandra Riley. I bet they know where Ryan is. Chase probably ordered the hit himself." I considered going to the precinct and questioning Tommy and Gregson about the possibility of Barlow being able to identify the Camel or pinpointing some of his buyers. Someone had to know something that would lead to Ryan. Suddenly, images of the two victims popped into my mind, and I shuddered, swallowing the bile that tried to escape my body. That could be Ryan. "Oh god."

"Alex," Martin cautiously touched me, "they'll find him."

"Before or after?" I couldn't finish my statement.

Angrily pacing the room, I stared at my phone. Someone needed to provide a solution. I didn't have time to wait around. At this moment, Ryan could be turning into human soup. Rubbing my face, I fought back the tears. The drugs left me raw, emotional, and weak. Whoever did this would pay, especially since I didn't like being out of control.

"Sweetheart," Martin embraced me, "stop." I tried to push him away, but he held on tighter. I fought against him, but he wouldn't let go. Soon, I was sobbing uncontrollably, and we sunk to the floor. "Let it out." I clung to his shirt front. This wasn't helping, and it wasn't bringing us any closer to locating Ryan, but I couldn't stop. "It'll be okay." His voice sounded so convincing that I chose to believe it. Those words had to be true. They just did.

After crying myself out, I was sedate. No longer frantic and much more capable of dealing with the crisis. Yes, there was a ticking clock, but missing something would be just as detrimental as running through all leads half-cocked. The first thing I needed to do was get back to my apartment, read through the investigation Mark and Nick conducted, check the surveillance feed to see if I could figure out who drugged the water, where it came from, and where Ryan went. Did someone drug and abduct him from my apartment? Or did he accidentally drug himself with the contaminated water and blackout on his way out of my apartment?

My gut said this was Chase Devereaux's doing, but going straight at him wouldn't save Ryan. It might kill him faster. I recalled the few facts about the Camel's M.O. His victims were kept for a few days in order to become that dehydrated before he reversed his process and drowned their cells. We had a small window to find him. There was no other option. That twisted piece of shit screwed with the wrong person this time.

"I'm sorry." I pulled away from Martin's drenched shirt. "I know I scared you the other night, and the last thing you want is for me to chase after the asshole responsible. But he has Ryan." I bit my lip. "Every time I step foot in the federal building, someone ends up dead. I promised myself after Michael and Sam that this would stop. I quit my job because they were never coming back, and I wasn't going to either. But this is happening all over again."

He nodded, his green eyes understanding. "Fine. Where do you want to start? I'm coming with you."

"No." My jaw clenched, and I shook my head

vehemently. “I can’t risk losing you.”

“So you’d prefer to put me through more torment? I thought our history of traumatic, near-death experiences was over, but it sure as hell didn’t feel like that two days ago.”

“That’s different. You’re a businessman. This isn’t the life you signed on to. I’m a...” I wanted to say federal agent. More than anything else, at this moment, I wanted that to be true because I needed the resources, the badge, the gun, and the power to change things. “I’m...nothing.”

“Jesus Christ,” he swore, “no wonder you’ve always been so adamantly opposed to drug use. You’ve gone off the deep end.” He was attempting to lighten the morbidity, but it wasn’t working. “You’re not nothing. I know you’ll do whatever it takes to bring him home alive, but don’t forget for a single moment that he isn’t the only one depending on you. You saved my life once, and you make it worth living.”

“Martin,” I took his face in my hands and kissed him, “I could use a ride.”

* * *

“What’ve you got?” I asked, sitting in Det. Thompson’s chair and swiveling to face O’Connell. Martin lingered unobtrusively nearby.

Nick glanced up, first at me and then at my escort. “Do you realize you have a shadow?”

“Hazard of passing out on the bathroom floor and not being able to operate heavy machinery. Are you going to read me in, or do I have to go downstairs and request a copy of the report you filed? By the way, I’m missing a couple of nine millimeters, and I need them back, preferably now.”

“How are you feeling?” He softened, digging out a

folder with the full report concerning my dosing and sliding it across the desk.

"Long division's no longer kicking my ass."

"All right. Read this while I get the paperwork on your private property." He disappeared down the corridor, and Martin sat in his empty chair as I skimmed the report.

The water bottle contained a cocktail of heavy sedatives, hallucinogens, and paralytics. Thankfully, my immediate reaction was to purge as much of it from my system as possible. Perusing my toxicology screening, I noted the small quantities of each in my blood system, along with alcohol from dinner. It was estimated that less than two hundred milliliters were missing from the bottle, so Ryan couldn't have consumed much. Unfortunately, even a small amount knocked me on my ass, so it probably did the same to him.

"Sign this," Nick said, and I dropped the folder and filled out the release form. When it was complete, he disappeared again, and I resumed reading.

There were no prints in my apartment besides Martin's, O'Connell's, and mine. The only sign of Ryan ever being in my place was on the water bottle. Did they dust everywhere for prints or just the bottle? Putting the folder down, I rested my chin in my hand.

"What is it?" Martin asked.

"Ryan's prints weren't in my apartment." Squinting, I flipped through the pages, searching for photographs. "Do you remember seeing a blanket? Since he was staying with me, I pulled some sheets and blankets out for him, so he could sleep on my couch. But," I shook my head to shake away the cobwebs, "they're gone."

"I don't remember seeing them, but I was preoccupied with you."

"Here." Nick produced a single evidence bag containing my two handguns, unloaded, with the bullets removed from the magazines. "Ballistics checked to see if they had been fired or if any prints were on the casings. Nothing."

"Did you dust my entire apartment?"

"Top to bottom. Your prints were on the doorknobs, all over the kitchen, the tables, the window to your fire escape, and the bathroom. Martin and I left our prints on your front door, bathroom, and living room. But no unfriendlies or unknowns."

"And no sign of Donough except for the bottle." I rubbed my forehead. "Ryan's been all over my place. The bathroom, my bedroom, the kitchen, living room. Whoever took him must have spent some time cleaning up after themselves. What about the trashcans? Maybe they left something behind."

"We checked everything, Parker. Whoever's responsible is a professional. They didn't make any stupid mistakes. Jablonsky's working on security cam footage from your building and nearby locations. They can analyze the data faster than we can."

"Have you heard anything from Mark?"

"Not a word."

"Okay," the precinct was useless, "any leads on identifying the Camel? Have you gotten anything out of Tommy or Gregson?"

O'Connell tossed a look at Martin. He wasn't supposed to be discussing ongoing investigations in front of civilians, even if they were friends. He wasn't supposed to be discussing them with me either, but that ship set sail a long time ago. "Not really."

"Take another run at them. If Riley needs to make a reappearance, I'm game, but in the meantime, I'll check out my old stomping grounds and see where we are on finding the inspector."

“Be careful, and don’t forget your bodyguard.” Nick chuckled. “Didn’t this start out in reverse?”

I wasn’t in a playful mood, but Martin let out an amused snort. When Ryan was safe, then I’d laugh.

NINETEEN

"What the hell is this?" Mark asked. "And you," he frowned at Martin, "if anyone could talk some sense into her, I thought it'd be you."

"Sorry," Martin replied, "she has a gun." He pressed his hand against the small of my back and leaned in, whispering that he was going to get some coffee and wait in the car. "I'll see ya around, Jabber."

We waited for the office door to close before speaking. "Any leads?" I asked.

"Alex," he slumped against the back of his chair, "this isn't helping. You're not even forty-eight hours sober yet, and you're sticking your nose where it doesn't belong. You've even dragged Marty into it. Who are you and what have you done with the paranoid, overprotective, former federal agent I know?"

I wasn't in the mood for his rhetoric. "I haven't dragged him into anything. And this is my business. Interpol asked for assistance on Donough's case. I was supposed to have his back, and I didn't." I sighed, feeling the pain of failure and fearing the outcome. "Not to mention, you didn't wake up on the floor with no recollection of how you got there and no idea who's responsible. So don't tell me this doesn't concern me. Everything about this situation concerns me."

"They weren't looking for you. They just wanted Donough. We've scrubbed the feeds from the time he left the OIO building. Apparently, he picked up a tail a few blocks from here. A dark-colored Jeep with unmatched stolen plates. Two guys were following him, but we never get a clear shot of their faces. Luckily, they probably thought he was on his way to visit his girlfriend, Alexandra Riley, and not planning a way to take down their operation." He blew out a breath. "At least I did one thing right by sending you home early on Friday."

"Don't." From Mark's perspective, my well-being was more important than Ryan's, and I adamantly disagreed.

"DOT cams caught sight of two men exiting the Jeep and heading in the direction of your apartment a few minutes after you got into the cab. Twelve minutes later, the same men are carrying what appears to be a rolled-up carpet. They shoved it into the trunk. The footage is grainy and black and white, but it could have been Donough."

"Where'd they go?"

"I don't know. We lost them in traffic. We're checking for reflections and better angles, but it doesn't look promising." He folded his hands and studied me. "There were no signs of a break-in at your apartment, so Donough must have let them in." What if I left the door unlocked? Did I let them get the jump on him? "Parker," his voice dragged me from my reverie, "there were no signs of a struggle either. The place was wiped, but Donough's a decent-sized guy.

Nothing was broken or damaged. The only blood we found was on your bathroom floor." His eyes went to the butterfly bandages at my temple. "It wasn't much, and it was yours. He would have fought. Plus, from the looks of things, they were only after him. They waited to get him alone."

"Chase Devereaux and Virgil Mallick, Barlow's guys. When we met with them on Thursday, it was a power play. Chase wants to take over. He must have taken Ryan."

"The drugs in the bottle are the same cocktail we believe the Camel uses."

"So let's get complete profiles on these guys. We need a full workup. Are they being monitored now? If we have eyes on them, more than likely, they'll lead us to Ryan. You need to have another chat with Barlow. Hell, I need to chat with Barlow. I can make him talk."

Jablonsky exhaled uneasily, before firmly adding, "Farrell and Interpol are monitoring the situation."

"You promised we'd find him."

"No. I promised I would find him. Go home with Marty, and let me do my job. And stay the hell away from your apartment. Right now, you're not thinking clearly, and the last thing Donough needs is a liability."

"I'll be back tomorrow. Please," I pressed my lips together, trying to stabilize my breathing, "you taught me everything I know. If anyone can find him, Mark, it's you."

"I will." He ushered me to the door.

I took the elevator to the garage. My mind was already piecing things together. If Barlow's guys had Ryan, there must be a way to rescue him. I climbed into the back of the town car and rubbed my eyes. Robert Gregson seemed like our best bet to figuring out where Ryan could be stashed. If he knew Barlow personally, or even if it was solely a business relationship, he might know where the cars or car parts were kept prior to transport. Maybe Barlow had some safe houses no one discovered. Any one of them could be used to hold Ryan captive.

"How'd it go?" Martin handed me a cup of coffee, my first one in two days.

"Can you drop me off at the precinct? I'm sure one of the detectives will give me a ride." I took a sip and continued to process through my thoughts. "They took him from my apartment. They waited until I left, and then they came for him." I thought about the rolled-up carpet comment and my missing blanket. Poor Ryan.

"Sweetheart, you're not to blame for this."

"I know, but it doesn't make me feel any better." Why didn't Ryan fight back? Why would he drink anything they brought? No, the water bottle must have been from my fridge. It must have already been on the counter when they mickied him. Why did he let them inside? "Shit, his cover's been blown. Mark practically said as much upstairs, but I missed it."

This wasn't about taking over. This was about revenge. They tracked him out of the OIO building. They knew he was Interpol. How did they find out? Did Grenauldo say something before they killed him? Or did something recent tip them off?

I dialed Mark and waited for an answer. "What is it now?" he asked.

"They know he's Interpol. Do we have a leak? Or does this track to Grenauldo? How long have they known? Have you swept for bugs at his hotel?" A new thought formed in my mind. "What about tracing his phone? You could trace their phones."

"It's too soon to know anything, but I don't think it's a leak. Not from our end, anyway. His phone's been turned off, and we don't have enough information on Chase Devereaux or Virgil Mallick to positively identify their phone numbers or carriers. They probably picked up burners when they arrived. Maybe they've been tailing him all along. If they were, that'd explain how they determined he was working against them instead of with them. After the arrests, they probably got paranoid."

"Listen, you and I go in circles, but if there is something I can do, tell me."

"Frankly, I don't know yet. We're still gathering intel, so get your head on straight and get some rest. I'll pull you off the bench if I need you."

"Thanks." At least that conversation went better than the one in his office. Unfortunately, I wasn't planning to listen. There was no reason to sit out another inning when I had some cop friends who might let me play.

"What are you going to do?" Martin asked. He heard most of the conversation and knew I wouldn't sit around and wait. I was incapable of such action.

"I'll start at the beginning. This began with a couple of car thieves. With any luck, they'll lead to a couple of thugs, who will lead to Ryan."

* * *

"We've been over it and over it," O'Connell griped. After hours of research, he found me sitting in the corner of the evidence room reviewing everything APS provided the precinct, the interview transcripts with Barlow, Gregson, and Tommy, and the manifest of the items found during the raid at Robert's garage. "Do you even know what you're looking for?"

"I'm looking for leads. Gregson must know Barlow. It has to be more than just a business transaction. If not, he'd have flipped on him. What do you have on Gregson? I can't find his rap sheet, but the precinct's computer system doesn't acknowledge me as a valid user. Can you believe that?"

"Parker, the brass isn't happy you're camped out in evidence. You're not a consultant, and a week ago, you looked good for a few counts of GTA. You need to clear out of here. I'm off the clock, but most things are computerized nowadays. We can take this party elsewhere." He offered his hand and helped me off the floor.

After everything was replaced on the shelves, Nick drove to my office at the strip mall. I unlocked the door and turned on the computer. This wasn't the ideal place to work, but my apartment was out of the question.

"Did you ever identify the manufacturers and distributors of the drugs?" I asked, surrendering the chair, so he could log into the precinct database and open the relevant case files.

"It's a fairly complex compound. Narcotics is busy identifying street dealers who sell the stuff, and major crimes has been placing calls to dozens of companies who manufacture this shit. But as of yet, we can't trace it to one supplier. Honestly, it's probably not a single supplier since it's made from three different compounds." He opened the Gregson interview files and scooted away from the desk. "What are you thinking?"

"That this is the worst time for my brain to be fuzzy," I muttered. "Robert Gregson and Reginald Barlow have to be connected. Maybe Gregson can identify the Camel or lead us to Donough." I clicked through the various interview transcripts. "How many passes did you make at him?"

"Four. I think Thompson and Heathcliff might have

tried once or twice." He leaned over my shoulder. "They should be listed."

"They are." I skimmed but didn't see anything useful. "What were your impressions? You know there's so much more behind an interview than what gets recorded as verbal communication."

"He's hiding something. I don't know what, but with a killer for hire and Donough missing, it could be anything. Originally, I thought he had other garages or chop shops he was protecting, but clearly, the game has changed."

"Maybe not." I shut my eyes, recalling my encounters with Robert and Tommy. "Tommy always stayed in the neighborhood. He lived, worked, ate, chopped, all within a ten block radius. But maybe Robert has other garages elsewhere."

"Wouldn't that be very entrepreneurial of him?"

"Tommy said after Barlow gave Robert the initial shopping list, six more cars were added. We thought that was because he found an additional buyer." C'mon, think, I coaxed my brain to work. "What if one of Robert's other chop shops couldn't deliver, so he passed it along to me and Tommy since I'm apparently a kick-ass car thief?"

"I'm going to pretend you didn't just say that." O'Connell picked up his phone. "Let me call around to a few of the other precincts and see what kinds of busts they've made recently. Do you think one of Gregson's other locations is where they're keeping Donough?"

"I don't know. They need someplace secluded." Why didn't I ask Ryan about this before? Since he went everywhere with Barlow, he might have had valuable insight into the car theft ring, but I didn't care. My job with APS was over, and he was busy working on identifying an international hitman. "It doesn't make any sense, but I keep thinking Barlow's buyers or clients or whatever they are somehow link to the Camel. Like maybe that's how the money is transferred when a hit is ordered, or it's code for something. After all, two homicides with the same M.O. linked to stolen car parts." I paced my office. "We need to take another stab at Barlow."

"Why don't you ask Jablonsky for some assistance?" O'Connell waited for his call to be redirected to burglary. "They've taken custody of Barlow, or at least some federal agency has."

I let out a bitter laugh. "He said Interpol's handling it. Mark doesn't want to assist me or let me help. Do you know how many times I've walked out of that building, proclaiming to quit and refusing to come back? I've used up all of my influence by acting like a spoiled brat. After last time," I thought about yet another of my screwups, "it makes sense why Mark isn't helping."

He held up a finger, speaking into the receiver and asking for information on chop shops. After a time, he disconnected, having been given another precinct to check with. "Funny, he showed up to work your apartment before Martin even got you out the door, so I'd say he's helping." He dialed another number and opened a search box in the police department's database. "I've found Gregson's record. You said you wanted to take a look earlier."

I hated how I forgot this between the drive from the precinct to my office. At least O'Connell was doing a decent job acting as my sticky note reminder.

Sitting down in front of the desk, I began reading as he continued placing calls. Maybe it wouldn't lead anywhere, but it made me feel better to think I was doing something. Waiting around was much more painful than running through dead end leads. Plus, something substantial could be gained. There was no way to know for sure.

Robert Gregson had a record for assault and theft, but nothing serious and no auto-related crimes. It seemed strange, but maybe he was just that good. Drumming my fingers on the desk, I performed a search for his property records, hoping to come up with some additional locations he owned or operated, but it came up blank.

When the phone calls were concluded, O'Connell pulled up my client chair and sat down. "Now what do you want to do?"

"I know you're in the middle of countless investigations. The cars, the drugs, the dromedary killer, but can you tell me what you know?"

"When I lose my badge because of this, I'm hoping Martin will pitch in to support me and Jen when I'm unemployed or in jail."

"Bonus, I'll make sure he tosses in legal fees for some high-powered defense attorneys," I added, grinning.

"That really doesn't help." He studied me for a moment. "All right, make a pot of coffee. We're going to be here awhile."

The two bodies that were discovered with the stolen vehicles suffered from extreme dehydration followed by a sudden excess of fluids which caused the cells to burst. It was painful, slow, and a horrible way to die. It was also the method used by the Camel. Based upon missing person's reports, the double homicide victims were identified as frat boys who disappeared during a weekend getaway almost a month ago. TOD occurred somewhere within a two week time span.

"Any idea why someone would want to put a hit on two college kids?" I wondered.

"Well, it turns out they were Ivy Leaguers. Their

parents have tons of money, power, and could buy their sons out of trouble, which they did. A year ago, they were accused of aggravated sexual assault. It looked like the local police had a decent case." His cheek twitched with disdain. "They had a rape kit, DNA, and photographs, but the charges were dismissed. The case was dropped."

"Small town?"

"Close-knit community. Things were handled out of court."

"What about the girl's family? If it was my kid, I'd hire a hitman too."

"We're checking, but they're just as affluent. Without solid evidence and zero proof they hired someone to do the job, we can't get a warrant or subpoena."

"That's why you need to see their financials." That was the trick. The evidence needed to obtain the warrant could only be obtained with a warrant. "What about tracking their internet history and seeing what turns up?"

"Same problem." He looked away. "We need to stop this killer, and we need to get your friend back. But under the circumstances, I can understand seeking a third option."

"I'll pretend you didn't say that." I understood too. There was a psycho on the loose, and he might have Ryan. "Okay, so we'll assume the two frat boys are the most recent kills on the Camel's list." I stopped, a thought suddenly flashing brightly in my brain. "What kinds of auto parts were found with the bodies? You said they were rich."

"Audi parts, I think."

"What did they drive?"

"The parts weren't from their cars. The parents said all their vehicles were accounted for."

"But what did they drive?"

"I don't know." The light bulb clicked on, and he opened the DOT database. "Let's find out."

TWENTY

The two homicide victims also drove Audis. They were frat brothers that owned the same model vehicle. It was also the same model of parts that were found with the remains. It couldn't be a coincidence. Maybe it was the Camel's calling card or verification that the job was completed.

"What about the other murders? Do we know if the victims were left with random cars or automotive parts nearby?" I asked.

"I don't know." O'Connell picked up his phone. "I'll pass it along to Heathcliff and see what he can run down. They aren't our files, and whatever copies we've been granted access to are at the precinct. He can check when he has some downtime. With any luck, it'll be a quiet night."

I wanted to look myself, but it was after midnight. I had already been thrown out of the police station once, and repeating the process wouldn't help matters. I pulled my legs up on my rolling office chair and sat sideways, leaning my cheek against the backrest. After O'Connell hung up, I let out a yawn. "What else can you tell me?"

"Gregson and Tommy barely said anything helpful. Barlow kept his mouth shut too. We're working on the double homicide and the stolen vehicles and trying to find the drugs, but there's not much to go on."

"What about my place?"

"We swept it. Minimal prints, no bugs, no blood, no signs of a struggle. With the exception of the water bottle, there was no evidence Ryan Donough was ever in your apartment, and there's no indication anyone else was either, well besides the two of us and Martin.

"Jablonsky said there's surveillance footage indicating two men waited until I left before going inside my building. They tracked Ryan from the OIO all the way to my place. I'd say they dosed Ryan's water when he wasn't paying attention, waited for him to drink, and carried him out, wrapped inside the blanket that was on my couch. So he must have known who they were." I knew who they were too. "Virgil Mallick and Chase Devereaux."

"The two men you met on Thursday?"

"Yep." I shut my eyes and slumped further in the chair. "We need to put eyes on them, monitor their movements, and hope they lead us to Ryan. Jablonsky insists Interpol has it under control. But Ryan's cover is blown. They followed him out of the federal building. They must know he's Interpol, and the only reason I'm not knocking down their door is the fear they'll kill him faster. Farrell, the Interpol liaison, is supposed to be tracking them and searching for Ryan, but who knows what's really going on. Interpol already screwed Ryan once when his partner was murdered. They're probably doing it again."

"We protect our own. I can almost guarantee their doing what they say, but I'll make a couple of calls to see what I can dig up. Then maybe we should call it a night."

"We're running out of time, and I'm useless."

"You're not useless, not completely. Face it, the best investigators you know are working this. We'll get to the bottom of it." O'Connell began making calls, and I let the white noise shut out my fear and dread.

The phone rang, and I jumped. O'Connell was sitting behind my desk, running information on the computer and answering calls. I looked around the room, trying to figure out exactly when the sun came up and how I missed it.

"Morning," he said. "Obviously, you're still not at a hundred percent because the Alex Parker I know doesn't fall asleep in the middle of an investigation." He appeared to be in a much cheerier mood than normal. "I phoned Martin so he wouldn't flip out. You're welcome."

"Thanks."

"You're lucky I have today off, and Heathcliff and Thompson have made some major progress in the last six hours. If not, I'd be pissed for working through the night while you caught up on your beauty sleep. We've gone through the ICC's and Interpol's files. Each of the Camel's victims was discovered in a stolen vehicle or with some kind of car part in the vicinity. It's the connection to Barlow they've been missing all along. Frankly, I don't know how they missed it."

I sat up, and my back popped painfully. "They weren't worried about auto thefts."

"Still, don't they train these Europeans better?" He went to my coffeepot and poured a cup of cold coffee. "I'll admit it's not much, but it's more than what we had last night."

"The six additions to Barlow's wish list mean six more hits," I said as he put the coffee on the desk in front of me. "Wait," my brain pinged on something, "the American muscle car I stole, those are hard to find. If we can identify owners with similar vehicles, we might be able to identify the next victim. We might be able to stop the Camel before he kills again."

"Precisely." Smiling, O'Connell clicked a few keys. "I'm running vehicle registrations. Can you get a list of any recent thefts from Auto Protection Services and pass it along, just in case?"

"I'll try." Just as I reached for my desk phone, my cell rang from inside my purse. Getting stiffly out of the chair, I noticed the blocked name on the caller ID. "Hello?"

"Alexandra," the familiar Irish brogue sounded hoarse and weak, "I'm sorry I left without a goodbye."

"Ryan," I exclaimed, grabbing a pen and scribbling 'trace' on the sheet of paper before shoving it at O'Connell, "where'd you go, babe? I've been looking all over for you. How are you?"

"I had some things to take care of. I'm gonna be busy, so you probably won't see me before the exchange." From his tone, they were forcing him to make the call. Nick stepped to the back of my office, giving his badge number and requesting an immediate trace. "Remember, we're doing it Wednesday morning. If I'm otherwise detained, Chase will finalize the deal. Just make sure you deliver."

"Are you okay? You sound strange." They were listening, so I had to remain in character. But I needed to keep the conversation going as long as possible.

"When did you become such a bloody hen? Everything's fine. It's early, and I'm busy."

"Yeah, well, so am I. I have a day job, and searching through patient files can be tedious. I don't have time for some asshole to disappear from my apartment out of the blue. Did you meet some other bird? Maybe one of those skanks from the strip club?" I tried to sound angry, like I had no idea what was going on, but the tormented sound of his voice was breaking me. Hopefully, he'd understand we were searching for him and give us some clues where to look.

"No strippers. Just business with the guys." Okay, so Chase and Virgil took him. That was progress. "Alex, you and I both know this was just a way to kill time. We were having a fling until the deal was finalized. It's not every day I find a talented car thief as sexy as you. And my god, you were good in the sack." My cover was intact, and he was making sure it stayed that way. "You bloody delivered on that one. Now don't forget to deliver on the car or my partners will be very disappointed."

"Ryan," I said, knowing they were seconds away from disconnecting us, "you made me a promise. I'm holding you to it. Do you understand me?" I swallowed, forcing the tremor out of my voice. He promised he wouldn't die, and I needed him to assure me we had more time to find him.

"I'll do my best, but I don't know if Chase will go for another three percent." The call ended before he could say another word.

"Chase Devereaux has him. That son of a bitch has Ryan. Tell me we have a location."

"I don't know," O'Connell was still on the phone, awaiting verification, "but at least he's alive."

Rubbing my face, I paced the room. Three percent. Did that mean something, or did Ryan just come up with something feasible to use as a cover story? He had been gone since Friday night. It was Monday. Maybe he just regained consciousness. I knew I was sensitive to drugs and medications, and thankfully, I vomited up most of what I ingested, but it had been a rough two days. Maybe they kept him doped up until they could figure out what to do with him.

Temporarily veering off course, I thought about Martin's blue sports car and the alleged vehicle I was supposed to be delivering on Wednesday. They must be using the car thefts to finance their operation in between supplying a hitman with his calling card.

"The Camel must be one of their buyers."

"Seriously?" O'Connell asked, tapping his pen impatiently.

"He's probably not on their crew, but he's been using them to get whatever he needs to verify his kills. It would explain why they traveled to the same countries around the same time bodies surfaced. Like Ryan said, they never found anything solid linking Barlow to the Camel."

"Call Jablonsky, tell him everything you know and everything that just happened. We'll take another run at Barlow, and we won't stop until he gives us an identity." O'Connell offered me a reassuring look. "Hey, this is good. It means the Camel doesn't have Donough."

"No, but two other sickos do." As I filled in Mark on everything that just transpired, Nick shook his head and fought the urge to throw his phone across the room, instead crushing the rectangular object in the palm of his hand. We didn't get a location. "We don't know where they've taken him," I said over the phone, and O'Connell verified with a nod. "But Riley's still in play. Ryan kept my cover intact, either to protect me or to give us a method of getting him out."

"Looks like you're back again," Mark said, less than pleased. "Why don't you and O'Connell head to the precinct and update the brass. They established a task force for tracking the Camel. I'll grab a hold of Farrell, and we'll meet you there. With any luck, we'll figure out a way to break Reginald Barlow."

"Oh, I'm sure I can come up with some creative ideas. Make sure you get the locations on Chase Devereaux and Virgil Mallick. They have Ryan, and we need to figure out where they are holding him." I disconnected, feeling like I was splintering in a million directions.

"C'mon," O'Connell insisted, "you can call APS from the road." I locked my office and followed him to the car. "How are you holding up?" He watched as I fidgeted with the seatbelt, my phone, and everything else.

"I'm fine." After phoning Islind, I was told the records were being sent to the precinct for further analysis. "I just wish we had more time." The adrenaline kickstarted my morning more than any cup of coffee ever could. "Ryan said three percent. I can't figure out if it was just something to say or if it means something."

"Three percent?" O'Connell zoomed through traffic, hitting the siren periodically in order to avoid stopping for red lights. I gave him the context from the Thursday night meeting with Chase to compare to what Ryan said on the phone today. "Could there be three guys? Or maybe he meant three days. He's been missing for three days. Or maybe he was just saying something to make sure you didn't blow your cover. Since they know he's Interpol and you were talking about promises, maybe they thought he was pulling a Grenauldo and promised to take you away from the life. It might have been nothing, but I don't know."

"We should have devised some kind of codeword." I thought back to our Thursday encounter. We devised signals for that night in case things went south but nothing in regards to three percent. "If it didn't mean anything, why did they disconnect so quickly?"

"You're overanalyzing."

"Fine." A plan was formulating in my mind. There was a decent chance it would be dismissed as too risky, but it might just work. "Nick, before this becomes super official, I want to run a theory by you, but let's just keep this between the two of us."

"I already don't like it." He glanced at me, waiting for whatever stupid thing I was about to say.

"If my cover is solid, I could show up at their hotel suite. Maybe I want to renegotiate the deal. After all, Ryan promised me another three percent."

"And for your trouble, you could end up joining him."

"But we might get eyes on the situation. They could have records linking to the Camel, and more importantly, they could lead us to Ryan. Who knows? Virgil or Chase could have a key to a storage unit or a receipt from a parking garage, something that will tell us where Ryan's being held. But the only way we'll find out is if I go in."

"You're insane." Which was probably true, but O'Connell didn't say I shouldn't do it. He probably didn't have a better suggestion. The only problem was there would be no support or backup. He pulled into his normal parking space and shut the engine. "For once in your life, let's do this by the book. We go inside, and you act like a cooperating asset. You divulge everything you know to anyone who asks, and you let those of us with badges make some judgment calls."

"I thought Moretti didn't want me lurking around his house."

"That was an exaggeration. He can't afford you."

"Well, it's about time I did some charity work, don't you think?"

He grasped my forearm and stared into my eyes.

"Are you up for this? I want the truth."

"I'm good to go. Are you ready for this?"

He nodded, aware that I spent the night asleep in my office chair while he worked. "Who needs a day off anyway?" He released my arm and opened the door. "But Heathcliff and Thompson will be pissed they have to pull doubles."

"Well then, we better make sure it's not in vain."

TWENTY-ONE

"They haven't taken him back to the hotel," Farrell said after we finished going over all the recent developments. "The surveillance hasn't picked up anything of interest either, but if Donough's been exposed, they're probably too cautious to speak openly."

"At least we have solid leads on the Camel. I don't know how you people could have missed this for the past year." Moretti sounded exasperated, but none of us knew exactly how gruesome the European crime scenes were or how obvious the evidence was. "You kept my guys in the dark, yet we're the ones solving this case for you."

"Parker helped," I chimed in. Jablonsky sighed, and O'Connell rolled his eyes. "Look, I know everyone's opposed to my assistance, but Ryan's still out there. Your focus has to be on getting a contract killer off the streets. Mine's on bringing Donough back alive. Face it," I looked at Moretti, "you could use an extra set of eyes on this."

"You're right."

"Except Friday night you accidentally dosed yourself," Mark said. "You're being reckless."

"I am not. It was a water bottle in my empty apartment. It could have happened to anyone. I'm fine now." I turned to Farrell. "You cleared me to assist Donough with the meet on Thursday. My cover's intact. There's a good chance I'm the only one who can get inside without raising suspicion."

"When are you scheduled to meet?" Moretti asked.

"Wednesday morning, I'm supposed to deliver a stolen car." I shook my head. "Wednesday's too late. Does anyone have any idea how long the Camel keeps his victims before they die?"

"The Camel doesn't have Donough," O'Connell pointed out. "You said so yourself. Chase Devereaux has him."

"And they aren't one and the same," Farrell said.

"But the cocktail I drank and Donough probably drank is the same one the Camel uses, isn't it? That means two things. First, Chase's in contact with our serial killer, and second, he must be taking pointers from a professional."

"All right," Mark took control like he usually did, "Interpol's main focus is on identifying and apprehending the Camel. The FBI and OIO are supporting them. An international hitman is federal jurisdiction. When we nail this son of a bitch, there will be issues of extradition, international laws, et cetera, et cetera. So," he turned to Moretti, "Dominic, your guys are free to work on the car thefts, finding Donough, and if it comes down to it, apprehending Mallick and Devereaux. If they lead to our killer, it's your collar but know that you'll lose jurisdiction after processing."

"Like I give a shit," Moretti said.

"Parker's yours for now," Mark added. "Good luck." Farrell and Mark collected the pertinent files and headed for the exit. "We'll work Barlow over for answers. We need locations and buyers. With any luck, it'll lead to the Camel and Donough. Alex, you'll find him, and if not, we will." He tossed me a reassuring nod over his shoulder.

"Lieutenant, am I allowed to consult?" I asked. "This is personal."

"Guess we could use the help." He looked around the room at the small group of detectives gathered in his office. "O'Connell, Heathcliff, and Thompson are okay working with you. But after you were instrumental in cleaning house a few months back, some of the other guys aren't happy to see you skulking around. Watch yourself and try not to make any more enemies."

"I'll do my best," I shut my eyes briefly, "since my friends might be dwindling."

* * *

I slipped my nine millimeter into my shoulder holster and tucked my backup in the bottom drawer of Nick's desk. We went over the facts again and again. It was the same information Nick and I already discussed this morning. In addition, APS sent over files on two more recent thefts which Thompson was in the process of tracking. Frankly, I had no place in this investigation, and I never did.

"Hey," Heathcliff came up behind me, "I heard about Friday night. Is everything okay? I wanted to check on you, but things have been hectic."

"I'm okay." My eyes darted around the room as I tried to come up with something relevant to say. "This was supposed to be a private sector job for a car security company."

"I know." He sunk into O'Connell's empty chair. "Can I ask why you aren't getting temporarily reinstated at the OIO for this? Does it have anything to do with the mob boss you pissed off the last time you held federal agent credentials?"

"Maybe that's partially why Mark's been so adamant that I stay away." I blew out a breath and made sure we were alone. "Honestly, Derek, it's because Ryan's partner broke cover and got killed a couple months back. Ryan feels somehow guilty or responsible, and I can relate. When I was still on the job, I gave the order that killed my partner and another agent." I pressed my lips together and felt my jaw clench. Since Heathcliff lost his partner to suicide, he could also relate. Frankly, it was scary how similar we all were. "Jablonsky was my supervisor at the time, and he's afraid, given my questionable past with Donough and my ability to sympathize, that I'm too emotionally compromised. Just don't spread it around."

"I've seen you emotionally compromised." He stood, rubbing my shoulders. "You're not. Now get the hell out of here and do what it is that you do. You have my number. Moretti's keeping a rapid response team on standby. Just make sure I don't have any other funerals to attend."

Nodding, I collected my belongings and asked for a ride to my apartment. My car was still at my place, and I needed transportation. On the way, I ran through every tidbit of Alexandra Riley's cover that she fed to Tommy and Gregson, and then I made sure it coincided perfectly with what Barlow knew and what Ryan and I told Chase and Virgil. Sometimes, it was difficult to keep the facts straight, but this wasn't. Maybe it was because of the importance it held or the number of times I ran through it by myself and again with Ryan and Interpol. Regardless, by the time I stepped out of the cruiser, I was Alexandra Riley.

I went into my apartment and swept the area for anything amiss. Everything had been torn apart by an investigative team comprised of the few people I trusted, but nothing else was off. Donough's abduction was a snatch and grab, and here I thought kidnappings were meant to be more difficult. Refusing to eat or drink anything in my fridge or pantry, even though almost everything had been confiscated and tested, I went to my closet, donned some leather, put on heavy eye makeup, and found an arsenal of weapons to conceal on my person.

I stuck my nine millimeter in my shoulder holster, a blade at my ankle, and pepper spray in my purse. I stared at the taser, wondering if shoving it into my jacket pocket would be overkill. Instead, I stowed my lock picks in my purse, along with a few more tricks of the car thievery trade to help sell my cover when I was searched, and studied my reflection in the mirror. The butterfly bandages at my temple could help sell some kind of bar fight or brawl, even though it was only a small scrape.

After giving my place a final once-over and making sure I had all the essentials, I went to the hotel where Ryan and I spoke to Chase and Virgil. The elevator ride to their floor lasted an eternity. My thoughts wandered to Ryan doing all he could to sell himself as Hoyt. What did he say to them after I was dismissed? Did Chase threaten him then, or did Ryan throw down the gauntlet?

I rapped against the door. "Chase, open up. It's Riley." I stared at the floor, watching for the light patterns to change, but nothing happened. "Open the damn door. Hoyt's avoiding me like the plague, and we have business matters to discuss. I don't have all freaking day." I heard movement inside, and I did my best to look annoyed in case they checked the peephole.

"Alexandra Riley," Virgil Mallick answered, looking like a snake, "why don't you come in before you tip off the entire hotel to your presence?"

"Whatever." I sauntered past and went to stare out the large windows. "Where's Hoyt? That piece of shit had the audacity to call this morning to tell me he was busy after he stepped out Friday night. The damn coward." I spun on my heel and glared at Virgil. "Let me guess, he asked you to cover for him."

"Hoyt's not here. Neither is Devereaux." A wicked smile slowly crept onto his face. "And I don't cover for anyone."

"No, you're just the son of a bitch who bought him god knows what from some skank stripper the other night." I let out an exasperated growl. "For three hundred dollars, I hope it was a good lay." My maliciousness was concealed in my faked jealousy. "But it doesn't matter. This is about business. I'd like to renegotiate the price. Ryan promised another three percent." Still, the three percent irked me.

"We settled on twenty-five." Virgil sat on the couch, studying me. His eyes were cruel. I could only imagine what he was thinking.

"Can I ask you a question?"

He nodded, cocking his head to the side like a cobra preparing to strike.

"Barlow was running the show, but he got pinched. It seemed like Hoyt was his right-hand man, but Chase's pretty sure of himself. I'd go so far as to call it cocky. Shit, he offered five percent more if I blew him. So who's in charge?"

"It's not that simple."

"Make it that simple." I took a seat on the other end of the couch. "Hoyt or Chase?" I returned the vicious smile. "Or maybe I should ask if you're calling the shots now, Virgil."

Something sparked in his eyes, and in one swift move, he leapt the distance between us and bent me backward over the arm of the couch, opening my jacket and removing my nine millimeter. I didn't flinch, waiting to see what he would do. "Why the heavy artillery?" he asked, his arm pressed along my clavicle to hold me in place.

"Girl in my line of work needs some protection. Why?" I crinkled my nose playfully. "Were you afraid I was going to shoot you?" I laughed. "If I planned to shoot anyone, it'd be the asshole who screwed me over on Friday."

"In that case," he released his grip, "you'll be happy to know Hoyt is no longer in a position to make any decisions."

"Great." I watched Virgil manipulate my gun in his hands. The way he stared was as if the metal were something tantalizing and sexual. There was no doubt in my mind he liked power, and he liked to kill. "So who do I have to sleep with to get a better deal? You or Chase?" My words caught him off guard, and his eyes shot up. "Glad I got your attention." I stood and held out my hand. "Tell your boss I'd like another meeting. How about tonight at the same strip club? Maybe he'll get what he wants, after all."

Virgil gripped the barrel and reluctantly handed back my gun. "Expect a call in a few hours but don't expect to get a better deal."

"We'll see. Maybe I've found something else to offer."

His eyes lit up, and I wondered what he was expecting, more cars, sexual favors, or perhaps a trunk full of artillery.

"I'd suggest the two of you figure out who's in charge between now and then. I don't like renegotiating." I went to the door. "When should I expect to see Ryan again?" My stomach clenched tightly, but I kept the cool façade in place. "I still owe him a little something."

"He's busy, but since he's not calling the shots anymore, I'd say you don't owe him anything."

"Oh, I owe him something all right." I let my hatred drip from every word.

The best conmen and grifters always said you couldn't hide raw emotion, so use it. And that was precisely what I was doing. It was a misdirect, but it came across clearly. And the venomous monster inside of Virgil brightened.

TWENTY-TWO

I didn't know where to go or what to do. There was a good chance Virgil Mallick was monitoring my movements as I left the hotel, so I couldn't risk letting him track me to the precinct. Plus, I wanted to keep a lookout for Chase. The greatest chance of locating Ryan would be to follow Barlow's minions back to him, but if I was being watched, that would be even more difficult. As it was, Farrell's team was already keeping tabs on the hotel suite, so they knew I stopped by. Thankfully, no one called to bitch me out.

Every muscle in my body was tensed, ready for a fight. That look of absolute bliss on Virgil's face when he caught sight of my rage scared the shit out of me. I doubted there was anything he wouldn't take pleasure in doing. He was a cold-blooded killer. As if we didn't have enough of those on the loose.

I got in my car and drove to the nearest diner. There was zero chance I would be able to stomach anything at this point, but I needed a reason to stay in the vicinity. Getting out, I zipped my jacket to conceal my holstered gun and went inside. After finding an empty table near the window, I phoned Heathcliff.

"Hey, I need you to meet me. Can you bring my backup handgun that I locked in O'Connell's bottom drawer? Also, bring an evidence bag and gloves, and whatever you do, make sure you don't look like a cop when you get here."

"Okay." He hesitated before asking, "Did you shoot someone?"

"No, but he put his fingerprints all over my weapon. Maybe something will ping in IAFIS. There could be other crimes or aliases we don't know about." I tried to recall if Virgil had an alibi for the time of Grenauldo's murder. More than likely, no one bothered to consider him since they were so focused on the Camel. "My guess is Barlow has his own protection plan. Maybe he's afraid of the people he does business with."

"I'll be there soon. I have to change first."

"I'm wearing leather and chains. Coordinate appropriately." We disconnected, and I exhaled the breath I'd been holding since the elevator.

Ordering a soda, I took a few tentative sips while I wrapped my mind around everything. The phone call this morning changed everything. Ryan was alive, or at least he was at eight a.m. From what we gathered, the Camel wasn't one of Barlow's teammates. Ryan would have figured it out, but the contract killer could be a buyer or client. If we could get our hands on his list, we'd be able to identify the contract killer and maybe even a few of his targets.

Tommy Claxton didn't know much. He was an idiot lackey who stole cars and pointed guns at people. If I had been smarter, I would have made Robert Gregson my mark, but I didn't realize what I was getting myself into at the time. Frankly, I still didn't know what I was involved in.

My only objective was to retrieve Donough by any means necessary. The PD could track the targets, find wonderful excuses to arrest Chase and Virgil, and otherwise assist Interpol while Mark and several federal agencies identified and apprehended the Camel. The only downfall was too many cooks in the kitchen. Any interference on any of these fronts could sabotage the other operations in play.

"Hey," Heathcliff slid into the booth across from me, "I changed, but unfortunately, I couldn't grow a five o'clock shadow between the precinct and here."

"It's okay. At least you tried." I laughed because if I didn't, I might cry. "We'll make the trade in the car."

"How'd it go?"

"It was fine. I'm hoping to arrange a meet this evening." I put a few dollars on the table and stood. "Let's go someplace quieter."

We sat in Heathcliff's car, and I exchanged my nine millimeter for the backup and explained what happened with Virgil. Unlike the others, Heathcliff respected my abilities and didn't argue that I shouldn't go alone to meet Chase. More important things were at stake, and my safety wasn't a concern as long as my cover remained intact. However, he started the engine and parked across from the hotel, so we'd have a better view in case Chase reappeared.

"We're running all the stolen vehicles and matching the more unique cars to other owners. Then we're checking the databases for anyone reported missing. It's a long shot, but even if we find just one, it'll make a ton of difference."

"You should have another go at Gregson. Tommy's useless. But Gregson knows more than he's letting on. He has a relationship with Barlow, even though the logistics are foggy." I turned around in the seat and watched a dark-colored sedan pull up. An elderly couple exited. "Any word if you'll get another shot at Barlow?"

"Jablonsky's all over his ass. He promised to send transcripts over ASAP."

"Good." I shut my eyes and tried to come up with a reason to keep Heathcliff close by. It was stupid, but I didn't want to face Virgil alone. He was physically intimidating, well over six feet and a good hundred pounds more than me.

"Do you need your entourage to kick someone's ass?" Heathcliff teased.

"No. I'd like to do the ass-kicking myself, but someone should be there to hold my purse while I do it. Never mind. I'd feel better if I had some idea where Ryan is and how he is. For all I know, they could have killed him right after the phone call. Virgil said Hoyt wasn't in any position to call the shots."

"That doesn't mean anything. Look, if his cover's blown, they'll want answers," Heathcliff said while I flashed back to Paris when my position and Ryan's were reversed. "We have time. We'll find him."

"Do you have any idea," I shook my head, "no. I'm not going there. This isn't Paris. Ryan isn't me. This is completely different." Even though it didn't feel different. "If I get Chase's number, can you put a trace on it and get a location?"

"Yeah. We should have enough, given this entire shit storm."

"All right. Get back to work. I'll call you as soon as I have something concrete, and don't forget to run those prints. If you can bring that rat bastard, Virgil, in, it'll be one less to deal with."

"Sure," he drove back to my car and double-parked, "but do me a favor. Check in every two hours so I know you're okay."

"Okay, but you can never tell Martin I agreed to those terms."

* * *

A few hours later, Chase appeared in a dark-colored Jeep. He tossed the keys to the valet and continued inside. As the valet pulled the car into the hotel's garage, I scribbled down the plate number. Maybe it was the same Jeep that was spotted outside my apartment around the time Ryan was abducted. After a few minutes and no sign of movement from Virgil or Chase, I phoned Heathcliff with the updated information.

"The Jeep is a rental." He gave me the rental agency's information. "The plates don't match the Jeep that was outside your apartment at the time of Donough's abduction, but it doesn't mean Chase or Virgil didn't switch them. I'll see what I can dig up on the rental. Maybe it'll lead somewhere."

"Thanks, let me know what you find." After we disconnected, I debated whether I should call the rental company directly or if I should call APS and see if they could pull some strings. "What the hell." I dialed information, got the phone number, and called the car rental agency.

"How may I help you?" a man asked.

I turned on the charm and lied through my teeth, claiming to be an airheaded bimbo who locked her boyfriend's keys in the car. While I continued with my spiel, I drove into the parking garage and found the Jeep. Parking beside it, I waited for the man to come back on the line.

"You're in luck, Miss. It's equipped with an onboard computer. I can unlock the door remotely from here. Can you provide the name on the account?"

"Well, his name is Chase Devereaux, but he rented the vehicle for work, so I'm not sure who's actually on file. Oh man, he's going to kill me for being so stupid." I tried to sound panicked and on the verge of hysterical tears.

"That's okay. We'll just keep this our little secret."

"Aww, thank you so much. You're a total doll." The doors unlocked, and I put on my gloves and climbed into the passenger's side. "I'll make sure I come to you the next time I need a rental."

I hung up and accessed the built-in GPS, but Chase was smart enough to disengage it. However, he wasn't smart enough to disable the vehicle anti-theft tracking system. Finding the hood release and locating the device, I recorded the serial number and other relevant information before getting back inside my car and phoning Islind at APS.

"This is Alexis Parker. The police department greatly appreciates the assistance you've provided in apprehending the car thieves, but I have a small favor to ask." I gave him the relevant information and asked if he could pull up the tracking information on the current vehicle. Who would have thought my consulting gig would be beneficial?

"Do you have a pen?" Islind asked.

"Yeah," I dug one out of my purse and recorded the coordinates for the last ten locations, "thanks."

"Oh, Ms. Parker, we've issued the reimbursement check for Mr. Martin's vehicle. He should be receiving it by the end of the week."

"Thanks again."

Starting my car, I gave one last look to the hotel's top floor window where Virgil and Chase were staying before exiting the garage. I'd run the coordinates and determine locations, check to see if any of them might be where they were holding Ryan, and turn over whatever was left to the police department. They shouldn't have a problem receiving information, illegal or otherwise, since I wasn't technically an employee and it was willingly divulged.

I went to my office, ran the list of coordinates, checked the computer for aerial views of the locations, and numbered them based on their likelihood to conceal a hostage. Just as I locked my door, my phone rang.

"I thought you weren't a whore," Chase sounded smug, "but now you want to renegotiate terms."

"That doesn't make me a slut. It makes me smart. Was there a coup? Because according to Virgil, Hoyt's no longer in charge."

"No, he's not."

"In that case, the deal's off until whoever's in charge makes a new offer. Twenty-five percent is a joke. And obviously, you're having issues in your house. Wouldn't it be in everyone's best interest to do this quickly and quietly?"

"I prefer loud and messy, and I want you on your knees." His voice dropped an octave. "And that's nonnegotiable."

"Fuck you."

He snickered. "No, that's what Hoyt did to you. Now it's my turn, Riley. Thirty-five percent. It's the best deal you'll get, but I get what I want."

"When?"

"Aren't you impatient? Tomorrow night, my suite at the hotel. I'll even let you stay the night, and we'll make the trade in the morning as planned." He really thought he was holding all the cards. "Or you can walk away. The clock's ticking. Yes or no? You have ten seconds to decide."

"Yes." And I hung up.

Immediately dialing Heathcliff, I passed along the phone number and gave the briefest update on the situation. He said they just got a judge to sign for the rental car agency's records, and a few uniforms went to collect the information. I didn't bother to mention I already had what we needed since I wanted to see where it would lead before turning it over. The PD had enough to do without botching their investigation with a rescuc attempt.

TWENTY-THREE

I had driven to three of the ten locations. One was a small business which produced fake passports and other forms of identification in the back room. The next was a pawn shop, and the third was an abandoned garage.

After thoroughly snooping around the garage, I didn't find any signs of Ryan or a place to stow hostages. This was one of the other chop shops Barlow did business with. Maybe Chase was collecting funds or paying for additional products. There was no way to know what state Barlow's former business was in with him behind bars and his team turning on themselves.

Reordering the next few locations on my list, I set out for the most secluded destination. If they were smart, they wouldn't keep Ryan chained up in a back room or inside a garage where any random passerby could hear him calling for help. Entering the coordinates into my GPS, I set out for the fourth location.

When I arrived outside a house in a tiny neighborhood, I double-checked the information APS provided with the corresponding numbers I entered. This didn't look right. There was no cover outside the house, and no cars in sight. Considering my options, I approached the front door, feeling the reassuring weight of my nine millimeter at my side. I rang the doorbell and strained to hear, but no sounds came from within.

I rang the bell again, but there was nothing but eerie stillness and silence. I rang the bell incessantly, knowing if someone was inside they'd do something to stop the raucous, but no one came to the door. Maybe no one was home.

This location was pretty far down the list. Maybe it was from the last person who rented the car and not from Chase. Still, something didn't feel right. The area was full of dilapidated and condemned houses. There were no signs of life on the street. The neighborhood was downright creepy.

I tried to twist the doorknob, but it was locked. Cautiously, I stepped away from the front door, studying the house. It was a small ranch style dwelling. I went around the side in search of other entrances. Since I made such a wonderful car thief, there was no reason why I shouldn't add B&E to my pending rap sheet.

The rear of the house took me by surprise. A greenhouse addition was attached directly to the back porch. The makeshift metal door remained closed by a single latch that broke easily when I threw my shoulder against it. The door swung open, and I managed to regain my footing before tumbling forward. No one was around.

I scanned the contents of the potted plants as I made my way to the back door. There were a few flowers and some herbs, but nothing I recognized as illegal. Frankly, the greenhouse was a joke. It was ten feet by twelve with very few plants.

I didn't spot any surveillance or alarms, but that didn't mean they weren't there. *Parker, what are you doing?* I was about to break into someone's home because the coordinates were on the anti-theft system of a car Chase Devereaux rented. I had no solid proof Chase visited this location, but an undeniable force urged me on. Either I was insane, or something about this house screamed psychopath.

Glancing down at my gloved hands, I knew I wouldn't contaminate any evidence or leave proof of my illegal activities. Upon twisting the doorknob, I was surprised when the door miraculously opened a few inches before the security chain stopped it. Carefully reaching inside, I pushed the door closed against my hand, thankful for slender wrists and fingers as I slid the chain out of the lock and reopened the door.

The door opened into what must have been a breakfast nook at one point. Now it was practically gutted, except for the counter. A thick layer of dust and drywall littered the floors from here to the front door. There was minimal furniture. A few large ceramic flowerpots stood in the center of what must have been the kitchen, and numerous glass instruments and vials were spread across the counter. The entire area from the front door to the back was empty and gutted. Even the walls were torn down, leaving nothing but a wide open space. What was this place?

My mouth went dry, and my heart raced. This wasn't right. None of this was right. Logically, I should have gone outside and phoned Heathcliff, but curiosity got the best of me. I unholstered my weapon and edged toward the non-demolished portion of the house.

The only standing walls opened into a narrow hallway. Two doors were on the left side of the hall, and three were on the right. I crept to the end, turned around so my back was against the wall, and tried to turn the first doorknob I found. It was a bedroom, small and empty, just another abandoned area. Closing the door as silently as possible, I continued to the next doorknob, but it didn't open. Not wanting to waste too much time, I tried the next knob to discover a bathroom. Sink, tub, toilet, and glass instruments and a few syringes on the counter. Carefully, I picked up the plastic wrapper containing a syringe and checked for a hospital code or purchase information, but it was blank. My mind ran to dark places, and I shuddered, imagining a few of the more gruesome scenes from horror films.

Maybe I was insane and the owners were remodeling the house before putting it up for sale, but my stomach twisted into even tighter knots. I fought to keep the tremor out of my hands. Opening the next door, I found a single straight back chair in the center of the room next to an I.V. pole with bags and tubing hanging. Was this the Camel's den? And if it was, where was Ryan? Was Chase the Camel? We had gone through this before, but my thinking was mangled by this unsettling discovery. The reason we ruled him out eluded me at the present.

Shutting the door, I feared what else my search would turn up. I opened the next door to find a staircase. What was down there? What was in the locked room? *Make a decision, Parker.*

Carefully, I went down the steps. The second one creaked loudly, and I halted my procession, afraid some unforeseen entity had heard me. When I heard no other sounds, I continued downward. The basement was dark. The only light came from a few tiny, barred windows at ground level.

As my eyes adjusted, I spotted various car parts, a few car magazines, and a metal table and bench. Large barrels, the size of oil drums, lined the back wall. Nothing on this earth could bring me to look inside them. With any luck, they were empty, but if they weren't...I shivered and refused to consider the thought that formulated in my mind. If Ryan was in there, I didn't want my last memory of him to be like that. Frantically dialing Heathcliff, I held the phone to my ear, waiting for ringing, but heard nothing. I had no bars and no reception in this hellhole of a basement.

After one last look, I went upstairs as quickly as I could, avoiding the creaking second step. There was only one place left to check, and that was behind the locked door.

I tried the knob again, but it still wouldn't budge. I didn't want to waste time picking the lock, but shooting it was too loud and damaging. I had no other choice. Shoving the metal pins into the lock, I barely managed to pop it open with my shaking hands.

"Ryan," I exclaimed. He was unconscious, duct taped to a chair. The room was small, and there was nothing inside except the chair in the center. "C'mon, Ryan, wake up." I knelt in front of him, checking his pulse. It was slow but steady. He had a few bruises that looked like they were in various stages of healing and no other signs of injury. But he wouldn't open his eyes. "Dammit, Donough." I shook him. We didn't have time for this.

Using my knife to cut through the tape and free his hands and legs, I noticed injection marks on his arm. They must have hooked him to whatever shit was hanging in the other room. I had to get him out of here before whoever was keeping him came back, but he was too heavy for me to carry. Maybe I could drag him out of the house.

"Ryan." I shook him again, but he remained unresponsive, sliding down in the chair now that he wasn't being held by the tape.

Unsure how to proceed, I slapped him. He jerked his chin up, but his eyelids remained too heavy to open. He didn't even make a sound.

Grabbing my phone, I saw two bars and dialed Heathcliff. I needed help. But before the call connected, the front door opened.

"Shit," I cursed, knowing there was no place to hide. Whoever was here must have seen my car out front. It was already too late. They knew they had company. Slipping my cell into Ryan's shirt pocket, I knew that no matter what happened they'd at least be able to track it and find him. He would be okay. It was the only comforting thought I could muster as I hid behind the door. Pressing my back against the wall, I waited for his abductor to find us.

Footsteps moved through the house. I heard them in the hallway, opening doors and checking each room. Straining to listen, I wanted to determine if it was one person or a group of people. It sounded like one. One made decent odds, depending on how well armed he was. The doorknob turned, and I braced myself. *Wait a second, Parker. Just half a second longer.* The intruder took a step forward, and I slammed into the door with all the force I possessed, knocking him back and hearing something tink against the floor.

Throwing the door open, I was poised to fire, but the bastard rammed his shoulder into my chest, knocking me backward into the room. Heavy footsteps ran down the hallway. Emerging more cautiously, I didn't see him. Where did he go? There weren't many places to disappear inside the gutted house. Keeping my back against the wall, I crept forward toward the open kitchen and living room. Something sounded close by, and I lunged to the other side of the hallway, afraid he was inside one of the rooms and about to reappear.

We were playing a deadly game of cat and mouse. It was a screwed up form of hide and seek. When I found him, one of us would be fighting to survive. I made it to the end of the hallway, still searching. Jumping out from his position against the side wall, he grabbed the barrel of my gun, pulled it down, and punched me in the face.

The suddenness and force of his actions caused my eyes to tear, and I fought my natural reaction to panic and flail. He grabbed the collar of my jacket and spun me, shoving me face first into the wall. He yanked my arms behind my back.

My grip slipped, and my gun clattered to the floor. I kicked off the wall, propelling myself backward and sending the two of us careening across the open expanse. His balance was off, and I landed on top of him, my back to his chest. Bucking hard, I got free from his hold and lunged for the gun. He grabbed my forearm and used my own momentum to throw me into the edge of one of the ceramic flowerpots.

My back made contact, and something crunched and broke. The cracked ceramic hit the floor. Hopefully, my spine was in one piece. The impact knocked the wind out of my lungs and left me dazed. Gasping, I didn't have time to react before he was on top of me. He pushed me harder against the pot, bending me backward over it.

"Mallick," I hissed. Until now, I didn't get a good

look at him.

An evil grin erupted on his face, and he laughed, pushing me further into an inverted U over the top of the flowerpot. He was determined to snap me in half, and I didn't doubt he'd succeed. Instinctively, I tried to push him off of me, but he was too strong and too heavy. Fighting that inclination, I brought my hands to the ground behind my head. Using it as leverage, I pulled my legs up and kicked him in the stomach, sending him sprawling across the room and flipping myself backward over the ceramic planter.

"Riley," he snarled, getting off the ground, "what do you think you're doing here?"

"I was looking for Ryan." Standing up, I winced. "What did you do to him, you sick son of a bitch?"

He smiled, circling closer. I teetered slightly, moving backward, hoping to grab one of the glass implements from the counter to use as a weapon. He lunged, and I barely got out of the way in time.

He skidded to a stop near the wall. Letting out a chortle, he picked up my gun, moving like a cobra, slinking back and forth, forcing me further backward into the far corner of the room. He fired, and I dove out of the way. The large room was devoid of furniture, and he fired again. I rolled, barely avoiding the gunfire. He fired again and again. Each time getting closer to hitting me.

The only cover position was behind the row of flowerpots. I slid behind one as a bullet ripped past. That was too close. He fired four shots into my ceramic cover, each time breaking chunks away.

I tried to keep count of the bullets, knowing how many were in my magazine and how many should be left, but when he hit particularly close, I jerked as a large portion of the pot turned to rubble, showering me from behind. I wasn't going out cowering in fear.

He fired again, and I leapt from my spot and dove for him. My unexpected move caused him to react defensively. He batted me away before I made contact. I was nothing more than a ragdoll to him. Even that slight shove sent me across the room.

I landed against the counter and grabbed a large glass thermometer. I launched myself at him, intent on stabbing him in the chest. He deflected, breaking the end and leaving me with a smaller, jagged piece of glass. I kneed him, and when he doubled over, I hit him with an uppercut to the jaw, knocking him backward a few feet. The force should have put him out cold, but it didn't.

He didn't react to pain the way normal people did, and despite the hits, he recovered quickly and kept coming. He grabbed my shoulders, and I stabbed him in the thigh with the glass, hoping to hit an artery. Unaffected, he slammed into me with such force that I was momentarily airborne before crashing into the wall. My vision blurred, and I struggled to fight through the pain and dizziness. I clawed for purchase against the tile floor. As I overcame the jarring pain in my back and got to my knees, Virgil hit the ground.

"It's about bloody time," Ryan whispered, sinking to the floor.

I grabbed my gun and pointed it at Virgil, noticing the hypodermic needle shoved in his neck. "Don't you dare go back to sleep, Donough," I ordered, struggling to stand and grabbing Ryan's arm and trying to drag him to his feet. "I can't carry you, and we need to get out of here." Virgil was out cold, but I didn't know for how long. If my moral compass became any more skewed, I might put two in the back of his head just on principle, but instead, I focused on Ryan. "What'd you give him?"

"Hell if I know. I just found it." He was barely

coherent, fighting to remain conscious.

I knew how hard it was to resist the drug-induced haze. As he collapsed on the floor, I tried to brace him, but it was no use.

TWENTY-FOUR

My eyes never left Virgil's unconscious form, even as I tried to drag Ryan across the room to the front door. Grabbing his wrists, I tugged, but I only pulled him a few centimeters before crippling pain shot through my back, forcing me to stop. "Okay, this isn't going to work." The only thing I could do was call for help. I went to Ryan's pocket and retrieved my cell phone. It showed it was connected, and I pressed it to my ear. What would I do if Chase showed up before I freed Ryan?

"Heathcliff?" I asked uncertainly.

"Shit," he cursed, "it's her." He spoke to someone in the background. "Are you okay, Parker? We're on our way. I scrambled a unit after you placed the call. Thank god, your phone has GPS."

"I found Ryan. He's okay, I think. I don't know. He's unconscious again. He's been drugged. I can't carry him."

"Okay, we'll get him out of there, but I heard gunfire on the open line. Are you okay?"

"Yeah, I guess. I need to get Donough out of here before anyone else shows up. It was Virgil. Virgil Mallick. He's here. He came to the house. This fucking creepy house. It's like something out of a horror film. It would be perfect for disposal. Maybe it's the Camel's. I'm not sure. There are syringes and drugs, oil drums downstairs for who knows what purpose. I couldn't look," I rambled.

"Alexis, take a breath." Never before had I heard such a calm, authoritarian tone from Heathcliff. "Are you okay? What's the situation?"

My breathing was labored, and I realized I was panting. No wonder he was freaking out. "Yeah, I'm okay. Virgil showed up while I was freeing Ryan, and we scuffled. But Ryan intervened. I'm not even sure how that happened. He's so far gone."

"Hang on, Parker. We're two minutes out."

While I waited for the cavalry to save the day, or at least carry Ryan out of the house, I checked his vitals. He was barely coherent, but with enough shaking and coaxing, I could convince him to momentarily open his eyes. Virgil was face-down on the floor. I was too afraid to go near him. Not much scared me in terms of physical threats, but the way he threw me around the room encouraged me to keep my distance. Unconscious or not, he was dangerous.

When the rapid response unit burst through the front door, I jumped, automatically aiming my weapon. "Stand down," O'Connell ordered, stepping between the tactical assault guys and me. Heathcliff maneuvered around them and took the gun from my shaking hand. O'Connell went to Ryan, and the tactical unit surrounded the unconscious Virgil, evaluating his injuries and slapping on the cuffs.

"I thought you said you were okay." Heathcliff examined my swollen and bruised visage.

"Comparatively speaking. After all, I'm the only one wide awake." I turned to see O'Connell crouched next to Donough. "Can we move this shindig somewhere else before any more killers show up?"

O'Connell caught my eye and checked Donough for injuries. Heathcliff didn't move an inch, uncertain how fine I really was.

"I'm okay. My nerves are shot to hell, but at least I'm not. Why don't you help Nick get Ryan out of here?" I threw a final cursory glance at Virgil. "If he moves, I vote someone shoots him."

One of the tactical guys snorted and tossed a smirk my way.

"Okay, let's get you out of here too, Annie Oakley," Nick said as he and Heathcliff draped Ryan between the two of them and dragged him to the front door. "Give your keys to one of the officers outside. You're riding with us."

"Sure." I did as I was told and slid into the back seat of the cruiser next to Ryan. Sometimes, it was nice to have someone else save the day.

"Alex?" Ryan squinted against the bright sunlight. "There was gunfire, right?" All those rounds must have been enough to rouse him and force his adrenaline to kick in. That gave him the energy and strength to walk out of the room, down the hallway, and stab Virgil with the needle.

"Yeah, there was gunfire. Eleven shots, I think."

He nodded, closing his eyes and drifting into the abyss.

When we were a decent distance from that horrible house, O'Connell hit the siren and flew through traffic. Heathcliff was on the phone and radio, simultaneously relaying orders and news. The rapid response team had already taken Virgil into custody and cleared out. A surveillance unit was positioned to keep eyes on the house, but with any luck, my rescue wouldn't be enough to scare away anyone else who might be using the house, like the Camel or Chase. The police wanted to grab whoever showed up, so hopefully, Virgil didn't call to report the news and the police didn't spook them.

"This morning, you got a call from Donough, and by dinnertime, you've single-handedly located and rescued him." O'Connell glanced at me through the rearview mirror. "I've complimented your skills in the past, but this is insane. How did you pull it off?"

Maybe it was the fact that my body was still in shock from the fight and near-misses, but everything from confronting Virgil at the hotel to illegally obtaining the Jeep's GPS coordinates and checking the locations spilled out of my mouth. When my story was over, I took a ragged breath, exhausted from the retelling.

O'Connell stopped the car in front of the emergency room, and since Heathcliff called ahead, a stretcher and doctors were waiting for Donough. A second cruiser parked nearby, along with a government-issued SUV. "Moretti's assigned Donough a security detail. Jablonsky's done the same. Do you want to stay here with him or come back with us?"

Spotting Agent Farrell hovering outside the door, I knew Ryan would be safe. "I'll stick with you guys. Chase is expecting Riley to show up tomorrow night." Normally, I wouldn't want to leave Ryan's side, but I'd been through too much in the last hour to wait inside a hospital with a dozen armed LEOs.

After Ryan was carried in, I stretched out on my side. My back was sore, and I was suddenly too exhausted to remain upright. It was just the adrenaline crash, but there was no reason not to take advantage of the entire back seat.

Heathcliff turned and studied me. "There is no way you're confronting that son of a bitch by yourself. Why didn't you give us the information from his rental if you already had it? Aren't we on the same team? Don't you trust me? Shit, Parker, you called me to run prints on your gun and deliver your backup. You should have realized I had your back on this." Apparently, since I was safe, he decided it was okay to yell at me.

"*We*'d have your back," O'Connell corrected. "Sure, we have some legal guidelines to follow, but eleven shots." Even though he was facing forward, I could see his head shaking.

Heathcliff ejected the magazine from my commandeered weapon. "All eleven came from your nine millimeter." He raised a wary eyebrow. "Since when do you miss eleven times?"

"Since I wasn't the one firing," I said.

Heathcliff rubbed his face, and O'Connell let out an exasperated grunt.

"What? You gave Donough your gun, and he's an awful shot?" Heathcliff asked, certain this wasn't the case.

"Oh, come on. Did you see Virgil? The guy must be 6'4 and two hundred and twenty pounds of muscle. He's twice my size, and yet, I kept him at bay, even after he wrestled my gun away from me." I shuddered, recalling the desperation.

"You needed backup," O'Connell said.

"When I got there, the place was abandoned. How did I know he was going to appear? I sure as hell didn't invite him."

"Yeah, but you couldn't carry Donough out of there either. He's probably got eighty pounds and six inches on you, Parker. You needed help," Heathcliff argued.

"You're right, but I wasn't about to ask for it if it meant blowing your chances of apprehending the

Camel. So how much progress have you made since this morning?" I asked, changing the subject.

"Not much," O'Connell began, and as the conversation shifted, my eyes closed. The car came to a sudden stop, and I rolled off the seat and onto the floor. Damn, that hurt. "It's state law to wear a seatbelt inside a moving vehicle. Maybe we should ticket you for the violation," O'Connell suggested.

"Bite me." I winced as I climbed back onto the seat and waited for one of the detectives to open the back door.

"Y'know, if we leave her in the car, at least we'll know where she is at all times and be able to keep tabs on her," Heathcliff suggested. "Plus, she can use the time to nap."

"Guys, let me out. Ryan's been recovered. I have no reason to do anything alone from here on out. If you want me off the case, I'll walk away."

"Yeah, right, you'll walk away," O'Connell muttered, opening the door. "That's total bull, and you know it." I dragged myself out of the car, achy and limping. "However, you might actually be invaluable since you already have a meet set with Chase Devereaux. It just depends on what Moretti wants to do. Until then, you're not allowed out of our sight."

Heathcliff nodded in agreement, and the detectives escorted me to major crimes.

* * *

Hours later, I was debriefed by Moretti, the detectives assigned the Camel case, and by Mark Jablonsky and a team from his joint task force. Luckily, no one arrested me for my questionable investigative tactics. Sometimes, the ends justified the means. Farrell phoned with Donough's condition. He been drugged with the same benzo derivative and suffering from dehydration, but he'd be right as rain in a couple of days. Until then, he had a platoon of federal agents and uniformed police personnel stationed in his room, the hallway, and throughout the hospital.

"Are you sure Chase Devereaux is calling the shots?" Moretti asked.

"I guess. When I encountered Virgil at the hotel, he seemed more intrigued with the aspect of physical violence than he did with taking over Barlow's business. He must have relayed my desire to renegotiate to Chase because he called a few hours later." I chewed on my bottom lip, thinking. "That house, the I.V. bags, Donough being drugged, they have to be getting this from the Camel if neither of them is the Camel." Which I was having a hard time believing, but their alibis suggested otherwise.

"Virgil's in custody now," Mark said. "We've moved him to an undisclosed location. He's under armed guard. But from what the medical staff said, he'll be out for a couple of days. He's lucky he's a big guy, or the dosage would have killed him. We have to get a court order to supersede medical advice before we can question him."

"What?" I cocked my head, confused.

"We need permission to shoot the bastard up with something else to get him wide awake and talking. Given the circumstances, I'm sure we'll get the go-ahead, but we have to wait. Everything's gotta be on the up and up."

"Until we have something more substantial, I say we use what we have," one of the Interpol agents said. "Ms. Parker, you have a meeting scheduled with Chase, so we should plan to send you in tomorrow night."

I saw three sets of concerned looks. Mark, Nick,

and Derek needed to relax. Ryan was out of danger, and I had no desire to be reckless with another member of Barlow's team, particularly after all the sexual demands Chase had made since the first time we met.

"I'll do whatever you guys want. I'm here to follow orders."

"Great," the Interpol agent said, "but since it's almost midnight, and you've been through quite the ordeal today, let's reconvene in the morning."

"Sounds good," I replied as a few people stood up from the conference table.

"Just for the hell of it, I'm assigning a detail to you, Parker," Moretti announced. "Since your car's been brought to the station, why don't we give you a ride home and make sure you have a peaceful night."

"Sounds even better," I said, surprising Mark.

He narrowed his eyes but shook it off and excused himself since a team was sitting on that house, and Mark was set to meet with them. The warrant was signed, so it was just a matter of snooping without spooking.

Heathcliff offered to drive me home, and a patrol car followed us to Martin's. "I'm glad you found the inspector," he began, "but do you have any idea how frantic you made our department when that call connected this afternoon and you weren't on the other end?"

"Aww. You were worried."

"Damn straight. Constant gunfire, no response, and before you came on the line, sounds of a struggle. It's not what I want to hear when you call me. Do you understand that?"

"Absolutely." I peered out the window as he parked in front of Martin's house. "Why'd you bring me here instead of home?"

"Because after a day like today, you shouldn't be by yourself. It's okay to ask for help. Even when it might mean letting a killer go free. There are always other opportunities to catch him, but you may not always get another chance to remain breathing." He exhaled. "Finding Donough was your priority, but you should realize, we're a tight-knit group, just like when we banded together to rescue O'Connell's niece. We protect our own, and that includes you."

"Thanks," I opened the door and added as an afterthought, "you should keep eyes on my apartment. Maybe Chase will make a run at me since Virgil has disappeared. Apparently, Alexandra Riley is an awful influence on Barlow's team."

"Jablonsky's already assigned multiple units to do that. It turns out a few of the coordinates we pulled from the Jeep tracked to your neighborhood. It looks like Chase abducted Ryan from your apartment, after all." He glanced at Martin's house; the lights were on inside. "Both of your weapons are in evidence right now, but we'll put a rush to get them back to you by the morning. Until then, the unis will keep an eye out, but I don't imagine Chase knows enough about you to look here. It's just precautionary."

"I know."

"However," he turned serious once more, "if you hear so much as a peep, pick up the damn phone and call it in immediately."

"Yes, sir." I saluted and stepped out of the car.

TWENTY-FIVE

The next morning, I woke up, draped across Martin's chest. One of his hands was on my neck, and the other was on my thigh. He took extra care to avoid touching my back. Yesterday played through my mind, and I felt at peace for the first time in weeks. His alarm clock chimed, and he reached over and turned it off.

"Can you skip the workout this morning?" I murmured, tracing the ridges on his chest and abdomen. "You're already ripped. You can afford to miss one day." He brushed my hair back carefully. "Plus, I'd like to stay just like this a little longer. For once, everything is perfect."

He kissed my forehead. "That's the first time you've ever said that."

I shut my eyes and remained in the peaceful bliss. It was an over-embellishment, but I didn't care. Donough was safe. I was alive and breathing and so was the guy playing with my hair.

"I'm sorry we didn't get a chance to talk last night." Martin traced circles on my leg. "I didn't expect you to be here. You went up the stairs so quickly. By the time I realized what was going on, you were in the shower, and then when my conference call concluded, you were practically asleep. You just mumbled some random things and rolled over."

"We found Ryan. He's okay."

"Thank god." He shifted beneath me. "But why is there a patrol car out front?"

"They're patrolling," I deadpanned. His torso jumped as he chuckled, and something in my back pinched painfully. "I don't remember talking to you last night. I barely remember the shower. That's where the hot water comes from, right?"

"Is that why you came here? For the hot water?"

"Heathcliff thought it'd be best to drop me off. The next thing I know, I'm using you as a body pillow." I searched my memory, but I didn't remember Martin coming to bed or saying a single word to him.

"Well, it was the only position you found comfortable." His voice took on a slight edge. "You were twisting and turning, letting out these pitiful whimpers. When I touched your back, you practically screamed. I thought holding you would help. Honestly, I was surprised you didn't wake up. What happened?"

"I must have been tired." I shrugged, still not moving from my spot against him. "Just so you know, none of this fits with my previous statement that things are perfect."

"Sorry, I had no intention of destroying your fictitious utopia."

"Y'know, I found Donough in a similar condition to the way you must have found me on the bathroom floor. I realize how disconcerting that must have been, and," I looked up at him, "I also came to the realization that things need to change between us.

We've known each other for over two years, and we've been dating for half of that." He tensed beneath me, fearing what I had to say. "You've spent far too many nights contending with my nightmares and various injuries. Clearly, my plan to shield you from all of this has never worked."

"Alex?"

"Donough told you how crazy this case was, and it upset you. I thought it was because you didn't understand this is what I typically do. But that wasn't it, was it?"

"I told you we're not fighting anymore." He brushed his lips against my hair. "You do what you think is best."

"I'm guessing by keeping you in the dark, you assume the worst all the time. So I'm going to tell you what happened yesterday because you asked, and when I'm done, you will search every cabinet in this house until you find some extra strength muscle rub and ibuprofen because my back hurts like a son of a bitch."

When I was finished, he eased himself free, set me gently on my stomach, and lifted my shirt. "Are you sure you want me to touch you?" he asked.

"Why? How bad is it?"

"You're swollen and bruised." He gently ran his finger along my side, and I jerked and gritted my teeth. "Maybe you should get a few x-rays."

"No. Just slather on the analgesic ointment or whatever. I'll be fine."

He disappeared and returned with the gel. As carefully as possible, he coated my back and pulled my shirt down. The cotton immediately stuck to the cooling cream, and I sighed. Before I could turn to face him, he disappeared into the bathroom. While the burning coldness numbed my aching muscles, I contemplated the rest of my day. After a few minutes, I got changed and phoned for a ride to the precinct.

* * *

"Were you walking like that yesterday?" O'Connell asked as I made my way across the bullpen. "Why didn't you say something? I would have taken you to get checked out."

"That's why I didn't say anything." I sat in Thompson's empty chair and leaned forward against the desk. "I'm fine. Just sore." He didn't look convinced, but I soldiered on. "Has anyone devised a plan for tonight?"

"It seems you're Interpol's bitch. They're going to do whatever they want with you, and they've taken over on this front now that you rescued their guy. Moretti's pissed. Our role gets smaller and smaller every time he turns around," Thompson replied, annoyed that I stole his chair.

"Better them than Chase. Any word on Ryan's condition?" I asked.

"Stable. They have him on fluids. He'll be discharged tomorrow. From what Jablonsky said, Donough's still pretty wonky, but that's to be expected," O'Connell said.

"Parker," Moretti bellowed from his office, "I need a minute." Carefully standing, I went inside and shut the door. My nine millimeters were on top of his desk. "We matched the ballistics to one of the slugs the OIO pulled from the wall in that house. The prints on both weapons match Virgil Mallick."

"I wasn't making that up. He took my gun and shot at me."

"No, I guess you weren't." The corners of his eyes crinkled. "I interviewed Mr. Gregson and Mr. Claxton this morning. Interpol is trying to pull the rug out from under my feet, so I thought they might have something more substantial." He flipped open the interview notes and pushed them across the desk. "Claxton's ready to get out of here. He might be willing to turn, but I don't think he has what we need."

"Tommy was the idiot of the group." I flipped through the pages, not seeing anything damning. "What about Robert?"

"Can I persuade you to have a chat with him?" He slid a pile of paperwork across the desk with a pen. "Standard consulting contract. You know the drill. Sign the bottom, and we'll get to work."

I signed, breathing deep and enjoying my now official role in the investigation. "Quick question, how does this impact my ability to aid Interpol?"

"How should I know? There's nothing in this about exclusivity. With any luck, whatever paperwork you sign with them will have the same easygoing feel and you can share information across the board." His eyes held a knowing look, and I was again thrust into the role of go-between. Why couldn't federal agencies and local precincts get along? "Do you want company for the interview?"

"No, just make sure he's secured to the table. Is anything off limits?"

"Use whatever leverage you have but don't rough him up. He might be the only collar we get on this crime ring."

"You got it, boss."

* * *

"Good afternoon, Robert." I sauntered into the room as if this was my domain. "How has your stay in lockup been? I see they've been running you back and forth from central booking. That must be tedious."

He glared. "I told Tommy you couldn't be trusted."

"Well, Tommy's an idiot, but I'm sure you already knew that." I pulled out the chair across from him, flipping it around and sitting backward. Smiling like a Cheshire cat, I stared at him.

"What do you want, Riley?"

"Wow, Tommy's not the only idiot." But I didn't bother to make a real introduction, just in case. "This is going one of two ways. Either you go down on a dozen counts of GTA and a double homicide, or you tell me who's pulling the strings."

"I never killed anyone. You can't make that stick to me."

"Wanna bet?" I gave him the smile again, leaning forward against the backrest. He inhaled slowly, meeting my eyes and shaking his head. "Barlow's scared you shitless, hasn't he?" I waited a beat. "He's in custody, and if he gets released, it won't be within the continental U.S." Still, Gregson didn't speak, but something flickered behind his eyes. Hope. "His lackeys are dwindling. Hoyt and Virgil are in custody." Since Ryan kept my cover intact, there was no reason to divulge the truth unless it would prove useful.

"Virgil?" He feigned confusion, but relief read in bold letters across his face.

"You know exactly who I'm talking about. I'd go so far as to say you also know a whole hell of a lot more about Barlow's business than you've let on. How long have the two of you been working together?" I raised an eyebrow. "A couple of years at least, I'd say."

"I don't know anything about Barlow. He was looking for some cars and found me based on reputation."

"I hate to burst your bubble, but if he found you

because of your reputation, the police would have busted your pathetic excuse of a chop shop a long time ago." My friendly tone went hard as nails. "Don't bullshit me." He leaned as far back in his seat as he could, given that he was chained to the bar in the middle of the table. "Let me ask you something." I tilted my neck from side to side, stretching, taking all the time I wanted. "Why do you think I was sent to infiltratc your team?"

"How should I know?"

"Take a wild guess."

He shrugged. "We got sloppy and took too many cars too rapidly."

"Hmm. Until this moment, I didn't peg you for a narcissist." His face showed confusion, so I continued. "We have bigger fish to fry. This isn't about a few cars getting chopped. If it was, do you think I would have been granted clearance to steal that classic Mustang? Or do you think the state would waste two hundred thousand on a brand new Ferrari just so you could chop it if we wanted to put an end to a dozen GTAs?" He swallowed. "That's right. They wouldn't. Give me something, and your problems will go away. Shit, if you give me something, your problems won't be able to get to you."

"Reginald Barlow selected the vehicles to be stolen. He paid cash up front. The overseas accounts he promised to establish for you and Tommy are out of a Swiss bank. The actual account information is inside a briefcase in a locker at the bus depot."

"I need an address and locker number."

He rambled it off. "There. That's everything."

I heard a faint acknowledging tap from whoever was monitoring the interview from the observation room. Turning back to face Gregson, I watched him fidget. "You know what else I want, Robert."

"What?"

"Don't play dumb. I want to know who dropped those two bodies. I want to know everything you do about the killer." It occurred to me he didn't request an attorney, and I briefly considered the possible reasons why. "We can protect you if you cooperate."

"Bullshit. Have you seen what this guy can do?" He shut his mouth so fast his teeth clacked together.

"Who?" I asked.

"You have the account numbers. Make me a fucking deal."

"It's not enough. I need more. Something concrete that absolutely guarantees you aren't a killer and you didn't coordinate the thefts for him."

"I want assurances and my phone call."

"You better not be wasting my time." I went to the door. "We'll get you that phone call, and the next detective who comes in here will continue where I left off. Don't screw with them, or I'll personally make sure your deal is off the table."

I shut the door and let out a breath. How much did Gregson know? Maybe it wasn't what I hoped it'd be, or it could be everything. At least we had the account numbers. That might lead to something.

TWENTY-SIX

I rode the elevator to the top floor to meet Chase Devereaux. Mark Jablonsky stood beside me, leaning against the wall next to the buttons and out of sight for when the doors opened. The police were sorting through the information I obtained from Robert Gregson. But before anything solid surfaced, Farrell showed up to brief me. He gave me a tiny earpiece and radio in order to stay in constant communication with the team outside.

"Are you sure you want to do this?" Mark asked. He wore a vest under his suit jacket and had his holster unclipped.

"Sure. No problem."

He didn't look convinced. "You remember the codeword. If there is even the slightest bit of trouble, say it. I'll break the door down if I have to."

"If things go south that quickly, we won't need a codeword, I'll just tell you to bust in. But it's one guy. I'll be fine."

The elevator doors opened. I strode toward Chase's

suite and knocked loudly. After a few moments, the light pattern under the door darkened, and Chase cautiously opened the door. I almost forgot how paranoid he was.

"Are you alone?" He glanced at the open elevator doors.

"Are you?" I brushed past him and into the suite. "Where's Virgil?" I spun on my heel. "And what the hell happened to Hoyt?" I made my way through the suite, glancing into the two bedrooms and bathroom. "This negotiation started out with Barlow, but he got pinched and took down my entire team. Then I renegotiate with Ryan because he's supposedly in charge, except he up and leaves, and now you've lost another one. Is there something I should know?"

"Alexandra." His eyes narrowed. "Alex, the reason no one is here is because I thought we could use some privacy." He poured a drink, attempting to derail my inquisition. "I'm not a monster. I'd hate to make you kiss and tell." He was amused by some sick thought. "Can I get you something hard?"

"The only reason I showed up was to tell you this deal is off. Your house is burning down around you, and I've found a better offer from a more reputable broker." The plan was to get details on the meet, the location, anything substantial that would trace to a buyer list or the Camel. The only way to do that was to renegotiate because asking too many questions would only fuel his paranoia. I went to the door, planning to open it, but he placed a firm palm against it. "If we do this, I want fifty and precise details, so I know this isn't some scam. Prove you aren't a cop, or I'm walking."

He snaked an arm around my waist, and I bit back my wince as he made contact with my back. He guided me to the couch and practically forced me to sit. "Take a seat. This meeting concludes when I say it does."

He believed he was in charge, and with no one around to disprove it, I guess he was. Briefly, I wondered if he knew what happened two nights ago with Virgil in that horrible house. Maybe he knew I was working with Ryan, but it was too soon to tell. Although, if he knew the truth, he was an excellent actor.

I slid forward, away from his grip, and sat on the edge of the couch. "Fine, but if you touch me again, I'll break your fucking hand. And that aspect is nonnegotiable."

"So you aren't a whore, after all." His voice lowered. "At least one that gets paid." He sat across from me. "What did you see in Hoyt?" He scrutinized my reaction, watching for any hint that I knew Ryan was a cop.

"He was charming and hung like a horse." It wasn't an answer, but there was no right answer to this question. "Obviously, he turned into an asshole." I returned the paranoid look. "Why would he let you take over for Barlow? You look like an accountant. Even that steroid freak, Virgil, would be a more likely choice."

Chase's eyes turned into slits, and he fumed over my insolence, the muscles in his jaw jumping due to the anger. Silently, I reminded myself of the codeword. And my hand moved to the armrest, so it'd be closer to my concealed handgun which was nestled in my shoulder holster. The stare off continued.

"Parker, you have incoming," Farrell said in my ear. "It's the concierge with a delivery."

I blinked, having forgotten how irksome it was to have an extra voice in my head besides my own.

"Why should I trust you?" Chase scanned the space immediately surrounding me as if he were assessing possible threats. "This was supposed to be a civilized meeting, yet you're packing."

"Civilized? After your demands, you have the audacity to call this civilized?" I opened my jacket, revealing my nine millimeter. "Do guns make you squeamish?"

"Not at all." He shifted, and the .32 on his hip became visible. "Are you sure there's nothing else you'd like to show me," his eyes flickered, "or anything else you'd like to see?"

"I'd love to know more about you, the money transfer, and exactly how I can trust you when the rest of your team has proven unreliable." Before he could respond, the concierge knocked. I threw a confused, nervous glance at the door. "I thought we were alone. Surprises are not acceptable."

"I'm not expecting company." He moved with caution from the sofa to the door, avoiding standing directly in front of it as he opened it, his hand near his weapon.

"Well, who is it?" I asked.

Chase accepted the small mug-sized box and shut the door, frowning. Ignoring me, he dropped the item into the melted ice bucket before opening it. Wow, even I wasn't that paranoid. Although, that might be a handy trick to keep in mind. His upper lip developed a slight sheen of sweat, and as I continued watching, a red laser sight bounced off the liquor bottles and glasses.

Reacting without thinking, I called out, "Chase, get down." I leapt from the couch and knocked him to the floor mere seconds before the window blew. Immediately, he rolled me off of him. We both aimed, prepared to return fire. Sliding to a cover position against the bedroom door, I noticed him taking up a similar position near the bathroom. "Who is shooting at you from across the street?" I asked, mostly for Farrell and Mark's benefit.

"We're en route to intercept. Stay down. Signal if you need support," Farrell said in my ear.

Chase shot daggers in my direction and crawled across the floor to get a better glimpse, stopping at another cover position against the sofa. Following suit, I edged along the ground to a place just below the window.

"Toss me a pillow," I said.

Chase was visibly shaken, not characteristic for a hired gun, but he complied. I held the pillow up, but no shots were fired. So I cautioned a glance out the window, but I didn't see anything.

"The shooter must have been on the opposite roof. It's the only vantage point, but he's gone now." I didn't know if I was speaking to the team of agents or Chase, but neither responded. Edging back to the mini bar, I quickly stood, cautioning a peek at what appeared to be an engine piston inside the box that Chase dunked in the ice water before ducking below the wooden stand.

Using the wet bar as cover, I turned to face him. His breathing was rapid and labored. He leaned against the side of the sofa, unwilling to break from his cover position.

"Shit." He rubbed his face.

"Who's shooting at us? It's one thing to steal cars and worry about being arrested, but it's a whole other story when someone's firing at me."

"I have to get out of here." His survival instincts kicked in. He crawled into the bedroom and grabbed his already packed bag.

"Oh no, you don't. Not until I know this psychopath isn't gunning for me too." He raised his gun, and I aimed at him. "I just saved your life, Chase. Normally,

I think that calls for a thank you." He didn't move, and neither did I. "Furthermore, that doesn't mean I won't hesitate to pull the trigger. Obviously, you have enemies. Are you sure you can afford to make another one?"

"I don't have time for this nonsense," he said. "I have to get out of here." Still, I didn't waver. "Fine, come with me. Let's just go." Nodding, I lowered my weapon, and he put his back in its holster. "Move."

"Where are we going?" I asked as he pushed the elevator call button, glancing nervously down the hallway. "Shouldn't we take the stairs?" If Mark was still inside the elevator, things would go south quickly.

"Shut up." The doors opened on an empty elevator car, and he shoved me inside. An involuntary whimper escaped my lips, and after pressing the button for the garage, he turned. "Who are you?"

"What?"

"No car thief reacts that calmly to a shooting." He pushed me backward into the handrail. The contact brought me to my knees as white-hot pain surged through my body. A brief look of amusement came over him. He believed he found my weakness and had the upper hand. "I'll ask again. Who are you?"

"It doesn't matter. The only question you need to ask is who was shooting at you, and how badly do you need my product to get you out of this city."

He looked torn, realizing I now held all the cards.

"I'm thinking a sixty-forty split sounds about right." I waited, seeing the desperation on his face.

"Where's the car?"

"How stupid do I look? If you knew where to get it, what would stop you from putting a bullet in my back?" I shook my head. "No. If you want to make this deal, I want details and information, particularly about that shooter. The only thing I'm concerned with is protecting my own ass. Deal's off the table once these doors open. Tick tock."

"Fifty-fifty and you take me to the car now."

"Fifty-fifty but you tell me everything I want to know before you see the merchandise." The elevator halted, and I pulled myself unsteadily to my feet. The garage was empty, except for a man searching in his trunk for something. Spotting Mark was a relief, and it made me even more brazen. "Fine, have a good life or whatever's left of it." I stepped forward, and he grabbed my arm.

"Deal."

"Great." I looked at his hand, considering the previous threat I made. There was a decent chance I'd follow through before the night was over. He released my arm and gestured that I go ahead. "Planning to use me as a human shield?"

"I'd be lying if I said the thought didn't cross my mind."

Stepping out of the elevator, I glanced around. Mark shut the trunk on the SUV, having buttoned an overcoat over his Kevlar, and went past us to the elevator. Just another hotel guest enjoying his stay.

"We'll take my car. It's the Jeep over there." Chase jerked his chin toward it, and we walked side by side to the vehicle, unwilling to let the other gain any type of advantage.

"Parker, voice your destination ASAP. We'll keep eyes on you as best we can," Farrell said through the garage static. In the last twenty minutes, things had become a lot more complicated.

TWENTY-SEVEN

Chase stopped at a bar across town. It was a small, seedy hole in the wall. I read the name aloud as soon as he parked. Since there was no way of knowing how many guys might be working for him or the Camel, I didn't need to take any additional risks.

He took a seat in the back corner, strategically located near an emergency exit, and kept his back to the wall. I sat across from him, not liking it, but hoping federal agents were keeping an eye out for me. We ordered drinks as soon as the waitress appeared. Neither of us looked at her. Chase focused on his surroundings, and I focused on him.

"Where's the car?" he asked.

"Close enough. What happened to your team? Are they gunning for you?"

"Listen to me. Your boyfriend was a rat. A snitch. A mole. Whatever term you prefer, and my associate is handling that situation."

I swallowed, pretending to be surprised by the news. "No way."

"Believe what you want, Riley, but think about it."

I gulped and looked around the room. Make it believable, Parker. "Jesus." I forced him to meet my eyes. "But I saw him in lockup."

"The authorities are tricky like that. Rest assured, I've handled the situation."

"But he called." I shook my head, still in disbelief. "He said he would get me a better deal."

Chase waved away my protest and clammed up on the other details. It didn't matter. Ryan was safe, and Chase wasn't the wiser.

"What about Virgil? Is he another cop?" I asked.

"No. He's cleaning up the mess Hoyt left behind." So maybe he didn't know Virgil was arrested and in custody, thanks in part to yours truly. "Are you satisfied? Can we get back to business?"

"Almost. Tell me about the buyer."

"It's a name on a list. Barlow's been in this business a long time. I've reached out to most of our clients since my boss is detained. We need to cut our losses and move on until we can regroup." He looked suspicious again, and his eyes settled on me. "I want to see the merchandise before we discuss this any further."

"Are you seriously that paranoid? An hour ago, someone was shooting at us."

His eyes narrowed further, back to tiny slits. "How do I know they aren't working for you? Who reacts that quickly?" A bitter sneer appeared. "Why would you risk your neck to save me? As far as I can tell, you can't stand me." Then he smiled. "You don't have another buyer. You need me just as much as I need you."

"What was delivered before they started firing?" I shot back, not liking the way his wheels were spinning.

He paled, and I contemplated the possibility the Camel was behind the shooting. But it went against his M.O. What was going on here?

"Take me to the car, I'll check it myself, and afterward, we'll meet with my buyer. You'll get your cut. I'll get mine, and this will all be over." Chase moved to stand.

"Not so fast."

"I've had enough of you. If I don't see the merchandise in the next hour, all your concerns will be pointless because I'll kill you myself. Let's go." He grabbed my arm and dragged me to my feet, pushing me in front of him and poking the muzzle of his gun into my back just to prove what an asshole he was. As if I hadn't read and reread that memo countless times by now.

"Fine, I'll take you to see the car. It's in an abandoned garage near the wharf." Hopefully, the OIO still used the same property to conduct sting operations because I didn't have a car stashed anywhere. "The place is hard to find, so I'll have to give you directions. It's like meandering through a fruit salad, trying to find a grape." That was the codeword. With any luck, the troops would rally at the proper location.

"Intercept?" Farrell asked in my ear.

"It better be there." Chase unlocked the doors and made sure I got inside.

"No, it'll be waiting for us. I'm sure of it," I said. Farrell had his response, and Chase wasn't the wiser.

"We'll set up. Delay as long as you can. We're pulling eyes off of you to reroute," Farrell replied before I heard another burst of static.

I gave Chase directions that took us in a large loop through the city. Thirty minutes later, Chase pulled up to an abandoned warehouse. It was pitch-black outside, almost midnight, and with the limited visibility from lack of lights, I didn't know if agents were on site yet.

"Where is it?" he asked.

"It should be over there." I indicated one of the locked doors.

"Open it."

"Hate to break it to you, Chase, but I left the keys in my car at your hotel." Stalling wasn't my strong suit, but I would find a way to make do.

He unholstered the .32 and pointed it at me. "I said open it."

"Abra-fucking-cadabra." I glared at him. "What do you know, it didn't open. If you give me a minute, I'll pick it." He gave a sideways nod at the door, and I pulled a set of lock picks out of my purse. "Are you in position?" I whispered, hoping he didn't hear me since I was turned away from him.

"Parker, I'm five minutes out. Interpol hit a snafu. My team was scattered on the house and our newest crime scene. I'll be there in five," Mark replied.

"Great." I spun to face Chase. "Y'know, this would go a whole lot faster if I had some light." His eyes darted to my back, assuming he could subdue me easily enough without a loaded weapon, and produced a cell phone he used to illuminate the otherwise darkened lock. "Thanks." Taking my time, I popped the lock two minutes later, blaming the dark for the delay.

"After you."

Before he could touch me again, I faced him. "Don't even think about it."

"How'd that happen?" he asked.

"Hoyt likes it rough," I said, my tone scathing, "which makes your bullshit story about him being a cop seem even less likely." I was trying to sow the seeds of distrust within his paranoid psyche, but there was no way of knowing how much he believed. "I hope you made that pig suffer." The rage bubbled to the surface. I wanted nothing more than to make Chase pay for the hell he put Ryan through.

"Absolutely." He said it with such certainty, I thought my teeth would break because my jaw clenched so tightly.

"Good," I put on a fake smile, "in that case, step inside and check out the merchandise."

He gestured me forward, and I walked into the dark garage. I didn't hit the light switch, needing as much time as possible. He followed, feeling along the walls. When the light clicked on, there was no car. The single hanging bulb did little to illuminate the garage, but the area was empty.

"Where is it?" he asked, gun out and poised. I aimed mine at his chest. "Is this a double cross?"

"You tell me. It was here the last time I checked." I paused dramatically as if a thought just hit me. "Hoyt came here. He must have taken it, moved it, or whatever it is cops do." Narrowing my eyes, I used the only play in the book. "You're one of them, aren't you? The next thing I know, this place will be swarming with police, complete with sirens and flashing lights." On cue, Mark hit the siren and lights on his SUV. At least backup arrived.

Chase panicked, stepping backward toward a secondary door. "What is this, Riley?"

"You tell me." My eyes remained focused on him. "Are you setting me up?"

"No," he shook his head, frantic, "this is because of you. The shooter at the hotel, insisting I come to some remote location, forcing yourself on me. No." He kept shaking his head, obviously rattled.

"I didn't force myself on you. You expected a

freaking blowjob when I knocked on your door earlier." My eyes narrowed further. He had to trust me and open up or else we'd have to do things the hard way. "This isn't me. This is one of those cops you were working with."

"I wasn't working with the cops."

"Hoyt," I screamed at him. "You said he was a cop." He stepped closer to the back door, and I took a tentative step forward. Our guns remained pointed at each other. "We have to get out of here."

"Parker," Mark said in my ear, "do I breach?"

"We need a moment to devise a game plan. An escape route. Running out the back door won't solve anything," I said.

"Affirmative, I'll cover the rear," Jablonsky said.

"Stay away from me, bitch. Everything was manageable until you showed up." Chase's gun didn't waver, and neither did his grip. But with his free hand, he reached into his pocket and dialed a number. Holding the cell to his ear, he waited, but whoever he was calling wasn't answering. I took another step forward, and he dropped the phone into his pocket. "Something's not right."

"The cops are outside. That might be part of the problem. We need to get out of here. Now."

He smirked, reversing his retreat. "Actually, the odds are better if I'm alone." He made it to the wall and flipped off the lights, plunging us into darkness.

"Don't do this." I blinked, attempting to force my eyes to adjust to the lack of light.

Somehow, I caught the slightest movement as he steadied the gun with both hands. His shot ripped into the cinderblock immediately to my right. I returned fire. My bullet made contact with some part of his upper torso, but it didn't slow him down. Instead, he ran for the front door.

"Mark, he's going out the front," I yelled.

Racing to the door, I fired again, but it hit the doorjamb, narrowly missing my target. I heard two more shots, wondering who was firing. Chase's door slammed shut. By the time I made it outside, the vehicle was already in motion.

Jablonsky came up from the side, and we both fired at the Jeep as the tires spun, shooting gravel into the air before launching itself forward onto the main road. Jablonsky got on the radio, calling in a description and location while we hauled ass to his SUV to pursue.

"Forget it," I stopped before climbing inside the vehicle. "He took out your back tires. Farrell, he's all yours." Then I yanked the earpiece and microphone free. I was tired of having voices in my head.

Mark let out a string of expletives, collected himself, called in a BOLO on the vehicle and Chase, alerted the teams sitting on the house, the hotel, and my apartment, and came around to the passenger's side. "Are you okay?" he asked.

"Yeah." I squeezed the bridge of my nose. "I winged him. We should alert hospitals, clinics, and the like to be on the lookout for a GSW to the upper torso."

"Okay." He passed along the new information and leaned against the rear door. "You used to be better at this." He bumped my shoulder and offered a teasing smile.

"Excuse me for being rusty. I wasn't expecting our op to get derailed by the Camel attempting to execute our only lead."

"What?" He met my eyes, looking bewildered.

"The concierge delivered a car part. A piston maybe. And then the bastard opened fire from the neighboring rooftop. I've been making it up ever since." I kicked my heel into the side bumper. "Dammit. Our best bet of finding the killer just got away."

"We have a team on the hotel, another one working the adjacent roof, and tactical is set up on the house where you found Ryan. We'll locate our asset. That's not even an issue."

"Good."

"Alex," this was the first time we had a moment of privacy since Friday afternoon before the shit hit the fan, "Donough's alive because of you. What are you still doing on this case?"

"Trying to make sure rescuing him doesn't result in a contract killer escaping."

He snorted.

"It's not funny, Mark. It's the truth. Maybe pulling Donough out and having such a close call with Virgil wasn't the best way to ensure Interpol's goal was achieved, but I won't apologize for rescuing Ryan. Still, I'll help end this any way I can."

"I know you will." He gave me a genuine smile. "C'mon, we might as well sit in the car while we wait for someone to pick us up." He held the door for me. "Plus, it'll give us a chance to have a proper debrief away from the prying ears of Interpol and the local PD."

TWENTY-EIGHT

"Five fractured ribs and a bruised spine," Mark read my medical report as we waited outside for the doctors to discharge Ryan Donough. After explaining everything that happened two days ago and the way Chase inadvertently brought me to my knees in the elevator, it seemed a checkup was in order. Plus, federal agent credentials tended to shorten the wait times for ER visits. "How does this translate into volunteering to go undercover for Interpol?" He gave me that bothersome, disappointed look again. "How are you even standing, much less chasing after a suspect and dodging bullets?"

"I feel fine."

"You'll have to spell out what that word means one of these days. Although, by now, I should realize when you say you're fine, you're anything but fine."

Rolling my eyes, I sat sideways in the SUV, glad to be out of the hospital and away from the x-ray techs. If they'd taken any more pictures, I'd glow in the dark. A group of federal agents escorted Ryan to the front of the building. They glanced at us, and Jablonsky flashed his credentials and handed one of them the official paperwork. Then Ryan clambered into the back seat.

"Alex," he smiled, the relief evident on his face, "merci." I snorted, and he corrected himself, remembering my insistence to speak English. "Thanks. By the end of this, I'll have no idea how to pay back all the things you've done for me."

"No need." I shifted my focus to Mark. "Where to, boss?"

"Funny." He rolled his eyes. "How are you feeling, Inspector?" Ryan didn't say a word, and I turned to assess him. "All right, boys and girls, we'll camp out at the OIO building, get an update on everything still in the works, and then we'll figure out where you're staying for the time being," he said to Ryan. "You," he shot a look in my direction before pulling into traffic, "need to be officially debriefed. Then I'll find someone to give you a ride to Marty's and keep a detail on you, just in case Chase feels particularly ambitious about tracking you." Before I could protest, he added. "You've been up for twenty-four hours. When we're done, you can recharge and then get back to work."

* * *

Jablonsky's brilliant plan didn't go exactly the way he intended. By early evening, he returned to his office and coughed loudly. I lifted my head off the rolled-up jacket I was using as a pillow and looked at him expectantly.

"Didn't I order someone to give you a ride home?" he asked.

"They were busy." I dropped my head back to the desk and inhaled carefully. "Truth?"

"That would be a nice change of pace."

"This is probably the most comfortable position I've found in days." Giving up on the possibility of napping any longer, I sat upright and met his eyes.

"Being back inside this building with countless federal agents for protection or sleeping at my desk?" He sat across from me and spun the computer monitor and keyboard around.

"Honestly, both." I moved to stand, but he held his hand up to stop me. "Where's Donough?"

"Farrell put him in a different hotel and assigned a team to keep him company." He stopped typing. "He's safe. No one can get near him. Tomorrow morning, he's back on the job. We got the go-ahead to override medical advice, and we plan to interrogate Virgil first thing in the morning. Assuming nothing shakes loose, I'd be willing to let Donough take a crack at him." He met my eyes, seeing the fury there. "If you behave, I'll let you take a crack at him too, figuratively speaking."

"You're no fun. It's not like I'm on the job. Assaulting a prisoner doesn't violate any statutes or laws, at least not if I do it."

"Regardless, that's not you."

"I've done it before."

"And you hated yourself for it." He glanced out the window into the main room where a few agents were still hard at work. I followed his gaze to my old desk, then to Michael Carver's old desk, and lastly to Sam Boyle's office. "Alexis," he hesitated, "a lot's changed around here in the last two years."

"So have I."

"C'mon, neither of us is any good here. Let's get a drink, and I'll take you home."

"You mean I actually get to go home?"

"No." He chuckled and shrugged into his jacket. "Marty called earlier. He's expecting you. At least you have somewhere else to stay, besides on my couch."

I waited for him to log off his computer and finish filing today's paperwork. Then we went downstairs. The federal building always made me uneasy, but I knew what Mark wanted to talk about tonight. Even though the case wasn't over yet, it was time we had this discussion. I avoided it for two years, but there was no hiding anymore.

He parked at the bar, the same bar we always went to after work. We sat in a booth in the back corner and ordered bourbon and stared uneasily at each other. I spun the glass on the tabletop. Bourbon wasn't my preference. It had been Michael's. I didn't know what Sam drank and suspected it depended on his mood.

"Two things happen every time I step foot in the OIO offices," I began. "I get hit by this crushing, debilitating wave of pain, guilt, and loss." I gulped down a mouthful of the burning liquor. "That's followed by an undeniable yearning to stay. To work. It feels like it's where I belong, but being there is torture." I stared at the table. "I want to come back, but I think it'll kill me."

"Alex," he sighed heavily, "you have to accept they're gone, and it wasn't your fault." I didn't say anything. I couldn't. So he continued. "Quite frankly, I think part of the problem is you need to blame someone because that's the only thing that makes any of what you do seem rational." I glanced up, thinking Jablonsky was just as crazy as me. "Nothing we do is sane. Normal people don't chase after contract killers, bombers, or arms dealers. This is the only thing you've ever done, so it seems normal to you." He shook his head. "But it's not. To make the risks seem negligible, you have to believe you're in control. That's how the instructors at Quantico and every debrief you've ever sat through has made it seem. That's why they always ask the same questions."

"What did you do? What could you have done differently?" I mimicked. "But," I began to protest, but Mark grasped my hand, shushing me.

"What happened to Carver and Boyle was out of your control. There was nothing any of us could have done. I was on-site when it happened, and I still couldn't do anything to change things." He blinked. "Boyle saw such promise in you, Alex. He was backing your promotion." He took another sip. "And Carver never blamed you. The kid had horrible luck. You saved him more times than not."

"And he saved me." I fought against the emotional response talking about this always led to. "But we found his letter of resignation afterward. He planned to leave. He never did because he didn't get the chance."

"That didn't mean you had to go because he wanted to."

"No, but you're one of the only people who saw firsthand what that explosion did to me." I leaned back, forgetting my current injuries. Oddly, I found the physical pain a relief to the emotional turmoil. "I couldn't stay." I pressed a little harder against the backrest, forcing everything into perspective. "Each time I've come back to consult, I can barely make it inside the building. So what do I do? I'm a basket case not being able to work and help on things like the Camel, but being in the building is unbearable. Even today, I had to hide in your office."

"Yeah, I noticed."

"Honestly, Mark, I don't think my soul can handle losing anyone else, especially if my order led to it."

"You have to find your peace with this. When you took the job with Marty, I thought it would give you your confidence back. You'd help out my friend, remember why you do what you do, and come back to work. I never imagined you'd face a hit squad and almost lose him in the process." I looked away, not liking thinking of that event either. Seriously, I wondered if I was jinxed. "Instead, everything had the complete opposite effect, and you ran even farther from your old life." He snorted. "Well, your old job."

"I can't seem to stray too far from my roots." I gave up on the bourbon and leaned forward, giving my sore back a reprieve. "I'm just stuck in purgatory."

"How long will it take before you realize you do more good than harm? Shit happens. That's not on you." He finished his glass and shook his head. "Let's be honest, if you weren't insane and completely insistent on finding Donough, he'd be dead right now. Interpol has their priorities skewed. Even now, they're more concerned with finding a killer than watching out for their own guy."

"Maybe."

"Shit, Alex, I wouldn't say this unless I wanted to hit my point home, but the only reason in this world James Martin is alive and breathing is because you saved his life."

"No. That isn't something you get to say. Not now. And not ever. The reason he almost didn't survive is because of me. This does not go the other way."

"He'd argue with you."

"Yes, and he'd also be wrong." I stood up. "Drop it. I agreed to talk about work, not about him. He and I made our peace with that a year ago. That's all that matters."

"So then, it's time you make your peace with the OIO. We need you back. Someone has to keep these Interpol assholes in line."

TWENTY-NINE

Chase was hiding. I didn't know if he was hiding from law enforcement or the contract killer he pissed off. It was hard to say for certain, and it didn't matter either way to me. Chase Devereaux would get caught or killed. He wasn't capable of going to ground and staying gone. It wasn't in his nature. He was too arrogant, believing he was the smartest man in the room, which he wasn't.

"Did you get anything out of Virgil?" I asked when Mark returned. I was in the OIO's conference room, skimming through the photos of Chase's hotel room and the roof where the sniper shot at us.

"Not yet. Farrell and Donough are working him over now." Mark sat heavily in the chair and flipped open one of the folders. "How are you feeling today?"

"Fine. Have you heard anything from Moretti on what the PD is doing to find Chase?"

"They have an all points on him, and since they've offered to help, we have them keeping tabs on your apartment and the hotel. Unmarked cruisers are positioned in key choke points near the house where you found Donough."

"Has anyone been inside yet? There's tons of evidence just ripe for cataloging. It might lead to Chase or the Camel."

He drummed his fingers on the edge of the table. "The only problem with going inside is spooking them."

"Chase must know we have Virgil by now, which means the only person we could spook is the Camel. I don't think he was behind the abduction. What did Ryan say? I wasn't allowed to sit in on his debrief, so give me the lowdown."

"Virgil and Chase showed up at your apartment unannounced. The next thing he remembers is waking up in the room where you found him. He only saw Virgil and Chase inside the house."

"What about the phone call he made to me?"

"I guess they woke him up for his phone-a-friend, but he doesn't remember it."

I considered our options. The shooter didn't leave any evidence on the roof, and Chase and Virgil's hotel room was clean. Spotless. Whatever incriminating evidence they had against the Camel was off-site or with them.

"I want to take a stab at Barlow. He's in charge. This is his crime ring, and these are his people. That son of a bitch shouldn't get off the hook that easily."

"I'll make it happen." Mark left the conference room, and I phoned the major crimes unit to give the boys an update on everything that happened yesterday. I doubted anyone else bothered to take the time to do it.

After my interview with Robert Gregson, the police searched the locker at the bus depot and found a briefcase containing numerous documents which led to the overseas accounts Barlow planned to use to pay us. Two separate accounts had been established, one for Tommy Claxton and one for me. Too bad the police department wouldn't let me keep the cash.

"We're still determining how Gregson got paid since he's not being forthcoming," Heathcliff said. "The accountants are looking things over, but it doesn't look like we can connect Barlow or Gregson to the accounts. Whoever set them up used fake IDs. Since it was done over the phone, it looks like Alexandra Riley and Tommy Claxton established the accounts themselves."

"That's funny. I don't remember setting up an account. Maybe some woman named Alexandra Riley is masterminding all of this."

"Ha. Ha."

"Keep digging. I'm about to speak to Barlow. I'll let you know what he says."

By the time I hung up, Mark had returned. "Shall we?" he asked.

"Sure." I followed him down the hallway.

"Just remember, we need info concerning the Camel's whereabouts, the identities of his victims, and any possible safe houses he uses. You know the drill."

"Is anything off limits?" I asked, wondering if we had to keep a lid on Ryan's identity or who we had in custody.

"I don't care what you tell him. Tell him we arrested his grandmother, if you think that'll get results." Mark opened the door, ushering me inside.

Reginald Barlow attempted to mask the surprise on his face. His attorney gave a curt nod to Mark, and after the briefest of introductions, I took a seat in front of Barlow, smiling brightly.

"Hey, Reggie," I looked around the room, "the two of us keep running into each other in the most unlikely of places. A parking garage, a repair shop, and now an interrogation room. My guess is the next time we meet, you'll be in a prison cell."

"Gregson thought you were a cop," Barlow said.

"Unfortunately, it didn't keep him out of lockup." I winked, getting up to pace the room. Mark held the attorney at bay with a stern look, so I was allowed to play. "Do you want to hear a secret? Gregson wasn't the only one who had a cop on the payroll." I waited for Barlow to meet my gaze. "You need to pick better associates. You should also select your clients more carefully." I let the threat linger in the air. "Maybe if you did, your team wouldn't be under arrest or running for their lives."

His lawyer shot a look in my direction. "Are you planning to ask a question, or do you want to waste time, spouting off narratives and conjecture?"

"You get paid by the hour, right?" I asked.

The lawyer shrugged. "Your point?"

"In that case, you shouldn't complain." I turned my focus back to Barlow. "Do you remember the first night we met? You were convinced I wasn't a cop because the authorities don't have the budget to let me steal a classic American muscle car. Realistically, that's true. The problem with your reasoning is you assumed we were only after shutting down an auto theft ring. None of this has anything to do with the cars you boosted." His attorney opened his mouth to protest. "Correction, the cars you hired Gregson to boost."

"We want names, locations, and means of contacting your clients," Mark said. "There's an AUSA on standby to cut you a deal."

Barlow shook his head. "No way."

"That's fine. It's just a matter of time." I slid the chair out and sat on the edge. "Y'see, not only do we have Gregson, Virgil, and Tommy in custody, but Chase's been incredibly helpful too. And let's not forget Wendi. Dear, sweet Wendi Hu. It's only a matter of time before the Camel eliminates everyone who connects the two of you. So the longer you refuse to cooperate, the fewer loose ends we'll have to deal with when this is over with." I stood. "Who knows, maybe we'll lose some evidence and cut you loose. It'd save us plenty of time and paperwork, but I doubt you'd survive more than seventy-two hours outside of custody."

Mark pushed his chair in and followed me to the door. "Fifty says Chase doesn't make it another twelve hours."

"You're on." I winked at Barlow. "Good luck, Reggie."

We left the interrogation room, but before the door closed, Barlow and his attorney exchanged frantic whispers. Hopefully, the Camel was a scary enough threat to warrant some cooperation, or they were devising legal strategy for after his extradition.

"That's it?" Mark asked. "I thought you were going to knock the guy's skull in or make him weep like a little girl."

"I don't know enough about Barlow to do that. Heathcliff offered to let me take another crack at Gregson now that additional evidence has come to light, but I'd much rather check out the crime scenes first. Interpol considers me a valuable asset, so I'd like to get to work."

"Stay here. I'll have a chat with Farrell and Director Kendall about putting a team together to go to the house. If we get approval, you're coming with us." He left me in the conference room and started down the hallway.

A few minutes later, Ryan surfaced. He opened the

door and took a seat at the table, giving me an odd look. "Why are you standing there?"

"I'm tired of sitting." I assessed the dark rings under his eyes and the paleness to his skin. "How'd it go with Virgil?"

He spat out a few French curse words. "On the plus side, he feels a hell of a lot worse than I do. They shot him up with a stimulant, and apparently, the drug interaction is incredibly painful. It wreaks havoc on the bloody nervous system."

"Great." I sat on the edge of the table, next to Ryan. "I take it you feel about as good as you look."

"Worse."

"I know that feeling. Friday night, when I went home, I didn't realize you were missing, and stupidly, I took a sip from the bottle on the counter. Next thing I know, Martin finds me unconscious on the floor. After that, it was two days of utter misery, and that was only because of a single sip." I patted his shoulder. "I finally pulled it together and found you inside that horror fest of a house. I can't imagine how you managed to shake off the drugs long enough to intervene, but you saved my life."

He tried to process what I said, but he didn't remember much of Monday evening. "All I know is I stabbed Virgil in the back with something. I'm glad I got there in time, but I wouldn't be here now if it wasn't for you."

"How 'bout we call it even then?"

"Do we know what the plan is now?"

"It seems the Camel is attempting to eliminate anyone who can identify him. The car parts are the Camel's confirmation of his kills. He leaves a part from the same make and model vehicle his victim drives with the remains. It's how he's connected to Barlow. We're pretty sure one of Barlow's clients is the contract killer, but he won't talk."

"I never saw the client list, and neither did Virgil. It's possible Chase knows who the killer is since he coordinated the business angles, but I can't be sure. When Barlow met with Gregson the second time, I think he brought the client list with him. Gregson might have a name."

As soon as the words left Ryan's mouth, I dialed the precinct and gave the newly acquired information to Lt. Moretti. Heathcliff and Thompson were at the hotel doing another sweep of Chase's suite and the neighboring rooftop. O'Connell was working the drug connection. It was about time we made progress and wrapped this up.

While I was on the phone, Mark returned with the okay to go to the house, so I promised to stop by the precinct after we finished analyzing the evidence inside the house. We would find our contract killer, maybe even before Chase became a corpse.

After the three of us, a tactical unit, and the forensic team arrived on the premises, I gulped down some air and worked the kink out of my neck. Scanning the neighboring area for any signs of activity and spotting no snipers or killers hiding amongst the trees, I entered the house, went to the back door, and explained in vivid detail my actions from Monday.

The large ceramic flowerpots, which were now decimated heaps, were the only real signs a struggle took place, aside from the numerous bullet holes and casings that covered the walls and floor. With a gloved hand, I opened the basement door. Just after I cleared the squeaky second step, my phone rang.

"It's Chase," I said, surprised. Mark immediately ordered a trace on the incoming call to my number. After getting the go-ahead, I answered. "Well, well, well, I didn't expect to hear from you again."

"Riley," Chase hissed, "I know you're a cop."

"If you're so sure, why are you calling me?" I let out a laugh. "Oh, you're afraid your contract killer pal is going to kill you. That's right. You pissed off the wrong person this time, Chase. So, what can I do for you?"

"Let's meet. Alone. Can I trust you to do that?"

"Why should I take the risk? The last time we met, you pulled a gun on me."

"I have something you want."

"Newsflash, Virgil's been eliminated, and Hoyt's safe. There's nothing you have that I want."

"What about information on the Camel? That's what you're after, isn't it?"

"Tell me who he is."

"Not until you provide me with protection. I want a deal. Full immunity. And protection from the killer."

"After what you've done, tell me why I shouldn't let your buddy turn you into blood soup. You nearly killed a friend of mine. If the Camel kills you, that's just karma."

"You're a cop. You protect people. I need protecting. And you need to stop a contract killer. If you don't, more bodies will drop. It's up to you, Riley. I'll find another way. This is just easier for me. A convenience."

I glanced at Mark, who'd been urging me to keep the conversation going while the trace ran. He gave me a thumbs up that they had a location, and I let out an audible sigh of relief. "Fine. If this is the cost of playing by the rules, then so be it. When and where?"

"The same bar we went to the other night. Nine p.m. If I see anyone suspicious, I'm out of there. And you'll never catch the killer." He hung up.

"Units are on the way to his location. With any luck, they'll arrive before Chase leaves," Mark said.

THIRTY

Instead of following the team to Chase's location, we continued with our plan to analyze the evidence inside the safe house. Property records had been pulled, but no one owned it. The house had been condemned, pending another inspection before the bank sold it or the city tore it down.

"Ryan," I examined the glass instruments and medical equipment littering the kitchen counter, "if you were Barlow's right-hand man, why did he give Chase access to the client list?"

"Chase was in charge of the finances. He set up the accounts and transferred the funds." Ryan rubbed his five o'clock shadow. "Before Chase hooked up with Barlow, he was an accountant or something, making him an expert at hiding money and concealing transfers."

"And Virgil was the muscle?" I asked.

"Not just Virgil."

"Okay, so you were both the muscle."

"Parker," Mark called from downstairs, "take a look

at this."

I went down the steps, finding him standing beside an open oil drum. "I'm sorry, but whatever is inside that container, I don't want to know about. I have enough nightmares as it is."

"Just take a look," he insisted.

I stepped forward with Ryan at my heels. Inside were dozens of photos, papers, and information. It wasn't at all what I expected to find in what I thought was the Camel's stewpot. Bending over, I snagged one of the papers. It was a photo of a woman I didn't recognize.

"Friend of yours?" I handed the picture to Ryan.

He shook his head. "I've never seen her."

While Mark continued to search the barrel, Ryan and I examined the worktable, various car parts, and the magazines that blanketed the rest of the basement.

"What is this place?" one of the techs asked, coming down the stairs to begin cataloging the evidence.

"One of the levels of hell, but I haven't read Dante in a while, so I'm not sure which one. Can you check the table for blood?" I licked my lips which were suddenly dry. "I'm hoping I'm wrong as to what the table and power tools were used for."

Not waiting for the results, I went upstairs. If I was right and the equipment in the basement was used to disembody the diseased before tossing them into the oil drums, I didn't want to hear about it. My psyche was already convinced that was the case since it made the most sense, but it was too horror film for any sane person to contemplate. Not that I was necessarily sane, but I didn't need anything else to fuel my frightening thoughts. My imagination worked far too well without outside stimulus.

Instead, I checked to see what the other team had found in the bathroom and bedrooms. The hanging I.V. bags contained saline, fluids, and potassium. The normal mix you'd find in any banana bag in an ER. The point was to rehydrate.

"They probably pumped the fluids into you to make you lucid," the tech said to Ryan, who appeared behind me.

"That's probably how you were awake enough to make the call." I considered the syringes and vials. "Afterward, they probably gave you another dose of that horrible concoction."

Ryan let out a long string of expletives. "Those bastards."

"Are you okay being here?" I shook my head. No one considered the impact this trip would have on his mental health. "We can go. You don't have to torture yourself further."

"How is it torture when I can't remember a bloody thing about being here?"

"Agent Parker," a voice called from the living room.

"Alex, not agent," I corrected, following the sound. "What can I do for you?"

The tech pointed a laser at the bullet holes in the wall, confused by their locations. I did my best to recall where we were when the shooting started and where we ended up. During my rendition, Mark returned from downstairs. More techs arrived to help bag and tag the evidence. Our trip didn't lead to a smoking gun, but maybe it was somewhere in the details. We just had to find it.

"Are you finished playing *CSI*?" Mark asked.

"CSU," I corrected, heading toward the door.

"No, *CSI*, like the tv show. They like to pretend to be cops too."

* * *

After our adventure inside the house, Ryan and I settled into an empty corner office. I studied the collected information and phoned Heathcliff to beg for something more exciting to do. Unfortunately, he told me to be patient.

"Why haven't they brought Chase here yet?" Ryan leaned back in the chair while he read the report from the hotel shooting.

"They missed him or killed him." Those were the only explanations I could think of. "How did your interrogation go this morning?"

"It went." He rocked slightly. "The only thing worse than being abducted by the targets is realizing how bloody incompetent I've been for the last six months." He smiled, but it was ugly and full of self-loathing. "Regardless of what happens, it's painfully obvious I need to go home. I lost sight of things. I need to get my head straight."

"There's no shame in stepping away."

"Then why are you still here?" He narrowed his eyes. "Oh, you thought you owed me." He slammed his palm down unexpectedly. "If anyone has a debt to repay, it runs the other way, Parker."

"I don't owe you, Donough. We're even. I'm here because I'm trying to prove something to Mark or myself. Or I'm a million times more screwed up than you can imagine. It doesn't matter. Right now, we're close. The group I infiltrated is in custody, and so is two-thirds of your team. We grab Chase, and the only one left is the Camel."

"You still don't get it. He's the only target I've ever been focused on, and I have no idea where he is or who he is."

"Hell, O'Connell made the car connection. After the

shooting at the hotel, we know the Camel is gunning for Chase. I'm hoping once Chase talks, we'll be able to freeze the Camel's assets. Without funding, he'll surface, and someone will locate him. We'll get him. Have faith."

"Yeah, sure." Ryan sighed. "Farrell's limiting my access, but since you have a reputation for failing to play by the rules, shall we partner up until the end?"

"Absolutely."

After we spent another few hours reviewing the new information the forensic teams brought us, a lot of things became apparent. When Heathcliff showed up to brief us on his latest interview with Robert Gregson, the pieces came together. First and foremost, Barlow might be the international connection to the Camel, but Gregson had his fingers in the cookie jar from the time the plane set down in the U.S. Barlow had been in the business for years and used Gregson numerous times before. The two men had an understanding, and any cars that Barlow couldn't find within the EU, Gregson found here. Barlow always took care of transport and shipping, but the two had a long-standing partnership.

"Gregson always received payment from Barlow in overseas accounts, the types with closed banking policies," Heathcliff said. "We don't have the current information because Barlow never gave it to Gregson. We must have intervened too quickly, but get this, the last payment was in German bearer bonds."

"What is this, a World War II movie?" I retorted.

"Like you've been saying since the beginning, Tommy's an idiot. Even Gregson finally admitted Tommy doesn't know anything. So he's offered to turn on his longtime friend for a deal," Heathcliff said.

"What does he want?" Ryan asked.

"Full immunity."

"No." I shook my head for added emphasis. "Robert Gregson might only be responsible for the car thefts and chopping the stolen vehicles, but if he thought I was a cop, he would have told Tommy to put a bullet in the back of my head. Nonviolent criminals don't order their lackeys to kill people."

"You know it's up to the DA." Heathcliff pulled up a chair and took a seat. "If Gregson gives us Barlow, there won't be any extradition, we can keep him here and prosecute him to the fullest extent. Right now, he's our best bet for locating the hitman."

"What did Jablonsky say?" Ryan asked.

"He told us to do what we have to." Heathcliff watched me carefully. "What are you thinking? I know that look, and typically, I don't like what follows."

"Chase Devereaux. Did you apprehend him?"

"No, he's in the wind," Heathcliff said.

"He wants to meet with me. Well, Riley, but same difference. We can leverage him to lure out the Camel. Our killer has already taken a run at Chase once and missed. I don't think he considers failure an option."

"Parker, you already got banged-up tangoing with the other creep. Are you sure this is a good idea?" Heathcliff asked.

"It's a wonderful idea. But I could use an entourage and a translator."

"You need approval," Heathcliff insisted. "I'm not losing my badge over this. Someone has to stick around to keep you," he tossed a glance at Ryan, "and your friends out of trouble."

"I'm in," Ryan said, breaking the silence.

"I'll talk to Interpol and Director Kendall and work it through the official channels," I said.

"Fine, I'll talk to Moretti." Heathcliff headed for the door. "How come you didn't ask O'Connell to help?"

"Because you do undercover better."

THIRTY-ONE

Once again, I developed an ingenious plan that no one liked. Oh, well. It happens. Heathcliff was inside the bar. He'd gotten there two hours earlier and was hiding in the corner, ordering drink after drink. Where he was actually putting those drinks, I didn't know. Jablonsky made certain I was wired, which fit nicely underneath the elastic bandage wrapped around my torso. In the event things soured and turned physical, I didn't want Chase to be able to use my current weakness for his own gains.

Ryan was equally outfitted with a GPS tracker and a radio, but since he didn't plan to leave my side, it seemed ridiculous that we were both equipped for some black ops gig. The surveillance team and a rapid response unit were close. Standing outside the bar, I peered inside to see if I could spot Chase. As predicted, he was sitting in the back booth near the emergency exit.

"Maybe you should stay out here," I suggested. "He said just me."

"Too bad. I have a score to settle." Ryan opened the door, leading the way inside.

Chase spotted us immediately, but he didn't run like I thought. Instead, he smiled. "Looks like you're still alive and breathing," he said to Ryan, gesturing to the empty booth. "Pity."

I bristled, but Ryan didn't react. He wordlessly took a seat and relaxed. No wonder I wasn't cut out for undercover work. Apparently, I had a temper. "I'd suggest you play nice since you're the one looking for an out." I noticed the faint blood stain on Chase's shirt near his shoulder. Guess I didn't miss, after all.

"This is what you think coming alone means?" Chase quipped. "Don't think I'm stupid enough to believe you don't have cops crawling all over this place." He swept the interior with his eyes. "We'll reconvene in ten minutes where you first met Reggie. I'll even let you bring Hoyt." Without another word, he disappeared through the emergency exit.

As soon as the door shut, Heathcliff and I radioed for someone to grab Chase, but somehow, he eluded us. "He had a car parked in the back alley. We missed it," Heathcliff said. "Where is he going?"

"I have the address, but it's a stretch to get there in ten. And he knows it. Tell our tactical team to get there as soon as they can, but go quietly." I turned to Ryan. "Ready?"

"Allons-y."

Tearing through the streets was more taxing this time than it had been at four a.m. People were still out and about, and they kept getting in my way. I didn't like Chase calling the shots, and meeting him on top of a garage wasn't the safest plan either. Things could go south quickly.

"In the glove box," I jerked my chin at it, "is a spare nine millimeter with a full magazine. I assume you know how to shoot."

He snorted. "Is this your way of adding insult to injury?"

I graced him with a smile before careening onto the sidewalk, knocking off a side mirror from a parked car, and launching back onto the main street before cutting through two lanes of traffic and pulling into the garage.

"We need him alive." I crept up the ramp, watching for signs of activity.

"Well, let's hope I'm not a very good shot then."

Parking diagonally to provide the most cover protection, I scoped out the roof of the garage. Chase was waiting inside his car. I stepped slowly out of my vehicle. Chase opened his car door and stood, sweeping the expanse.

"Isn't it much nicer to talk without company?" He glared at Ryan. "Fucking bastard. I told Barlow to end you when we took care of that other rat, but he wouldn't listen."

"What do you want, Chase?" Ryan asked. "You called Alex because you wanted protection, so I'd suggest you shut up." The two rattled arguments and insults back and forth in French while I stood there, hoping the delay would give our teams time to catch up.

As the two exchanged barbed words, I wondered why someone intent on turning himself in would go to such extremes to avoid the authorities. Frankly, Chase couldn't even be a hundred percent sure I was the authorities. Sure, it seemed obvious with Mark and me chasing after him the other night, but I never announced myself or showed him any credentials. Granted, I didn't have any, but he didn't know that. Something was starting to stink. I took a step backward, closer to the car.

A shot rang out, and I hit the ground, hoping Ryan had done the same. Another three bullets were fired in rapid succession. Based on sound alone, I knew they were from a long-range rifle. Chase grinned and ducked back into his vehicle.

"Shit, our sniper's back. North side of the garage," I relayed over the radio, watching helplessly as Chase started the engine. "Ryan?"

He edged around my car and fired, blowing the back window and the driver's side mirror off but not making enough of an impact to stop Chase. I saw the laser sight on him, and dove, knocking him to the ground.

More shots rang out. By the time I rolled off Ryan, the Jeep had crashed into one of the support pillars. Blood dripped down the window. Before I could ponder if Chase was dead, he crawled out of the car.

"Are you okay?" I asked Ryan. He nodded. "You have two options. The shooter or Chase?"

"The shooter." He crouched, taking cover behind my car.

"Fine. I'll get Chase." I lifted myself off the ground. This was not the best time for broken ribs. "I need cover fire. On the count of three."

On three, he fired in the direction of our shooter, knowing the handgun rounds wouldn't do anything to someone hundreds of feet away, but it was more about distraction than anything else.

Scurrying across the expanse, I ducked under the barriers and continued after Chase. Thankfully, he was leaving a decent blood trail to follow. He must have been hit by one of our shooter's bullets. At least I was in the closed portion of the garage, no longer susceptible to sniper fire, but Ryan was alone on the roof.

"Really?" I bellowed. "You made a deal with our

killer in order to save your own skin. How stupid are you?"

"Riley," I heard the evil laugh in his voice, even though I couldn't locate him among the cars and various obstacles, "you've made my life so much easier. You eliminated the competition. Now I'm in charge."

"There's nothing left of your auto theft ring."

"Who said anything about stealing cars? Brokering hits is a much more lucrative prospect."

"I doubt you have the cojones for it." I took a breath, noticing a blood droplet land on the ground beside a parked car. "Newsflash, your partner just shot you. Obviously, you're the victim of yet another coup. You really need to find a more stable career."

"Don't play mind games with me," he spat. "Hoyt shot me, no one else. But I'll promise you one thing. When this is all over, he'll be in a box."

Pissing me off was the worst idea Chase ever had. He probably hoped it would make me stupid, but it just eliminated my hesitation to make sure he stayed breathing. The longer we stayed here talking, the less chance he had of walking away.

"Believe what you want." I edged around the barrier, wondering if he was armed. There was one way to find out. "The truth of the matter is your friend, the Camel, is going to get sick and tired of your sniveling, pain in the ass, arrogant, self-aggrandizing ways. Hell, I barely know you, and I'm already sick of them." I stood cautiously, maintaining cover behind the support pillar.

"You have a smart mouth, Riley. It's a shame you never put it to good use."

A shot rang out in my direction, but because of the echo, I didn't know where it came from. As I ducked, the stairwell door swung open. I couldn't let him escape, so I broke from cover and ran after him. No wonder they called him Chase.

Two flights down, he teetered. The blood loss was finally getting to him. I took the opportunity to close the gap between us. He swung his gun toward me, and I grabbed his forearm and pointed it up. The bullet fired harmlessly into the ceiling above us. The wound he sustained was to the side of his upper torso, below the GSW I inflicted during our last meeting. I hit him hard in the bloodied spot, and he grunted, losing hold of the gun, which fell over the edge of the stairs and to the ground below. Unfortunately, he didn't go down.

Instead, he kneed me in the stomach. I lost my grip and doubled over. He charged forward, knocking me back against the railing. It hurt, but not as much as it would have if I hadn't been prepared. Using this to my advantage, I sunk to the ground, grabbed my gun, and shot him in the knee. He went down, howling.

"Do you want any more holes in your body? Or are you ready to give up?" I pulled myself to my feet. He didn't respond, and I retrieved the cuffs from my belt and chained him to the railing. Radioing in his location, I wondered if he'd bleed out before anyone freed him. Frankly, I wasn't too concerned. My only worry at the moment was Ryan.

Racing back up the stairs and to the roof, I didn't see him pinned behind my car. Listening to the radio chatter, I knew the rapid response team was storming the adjacent roof. With any luck, our shooter wouldn't escape again.

I edged toward my car, staying low. By the time I made it to the only cover position on the open-air roof, Ryan was gone. Requesting information, I waited, but no response came. As I considered my options, surveying as much of the area as possible, the radio chirped to life. Ryan had gone down the ramps and came up the other side, encountering our shooter just as he was driving away from the adjacent building.

The chorus of clears rang my earpiece, and I heard verification that Heathcliff had taken Chase into custody. An ambulance was on the way.

I climbed into my car, noticing the new scratches and dents, and drove to the bottom. Dozens of vehicles, lights, and tactical team members made the garage look like a carnival. Turning off the engine, I stepped out of my car.

"You shot a suspect in the leg," Mark berated, having heard Heathcliff's call. "Are you out of your mind? Either you shoot to kill or you don't shoot at all."

"Sorry, I missed," I brushed past him, finding Ryan. "Where the hell'd you go?"

"After the Camel." He held my gun out, but before I could take it, Mark intervened, confiscating that one and the one tucked in my shoulder holster. "I think I clipped him, but I'm not sure."

"We'll check the roof and surrounding area for evidence," one of the cops said.

"Where'd he go?" Mark asked.

"Dark sedan, license plate number two, seven, five, r—" Ryan stopped, "I didn't see the rest."

"Better than nothing," Mark spun in a circle, surveying the area. "We've got them all. The only one left is our contract killer."

"Yep." I rested my hips against the hood of my car. "Chase said he wanted to take over the hit brokering business. His words. I'm guessing that means Barlow was putting the Camel in contact with his clients. Maybe it was his idea to add the car parts as part of the signature."

"Are you good to drive back to the OIO?" Mark

asked, and I nodded. "Okay, the two of you get cleaned up, answer whatever questions we have, and we'll end this."

"It's about bloody time," Ryan said.

* * *

After the debriefs, Ryan and I split up. The federal agencies didn't need my assistance anymore. All our suspects were in custody, and it wasn't like Alexandra Riley had any reason to make a reappearance. Ryan was working with Interpol and the OIO on the details, questioning Barlow and Virgil while waiting for Chase to come out of surgery. So I went back to the precinct. Since Moretti gave me permission to consult for them, it was time they got some bang for their buck.

Heathcliff was slipping on his jacket when I walked into the bullpen. He looked up and tried to hide his smile. "We don't shoot suspects for the hell of it."

"I didn't shoot him for the hell of it. I shot him because he threw me against the railing. Since he was determined to put me down, I thought I'd return the favor."

He stepped closer so no one else would hear. "Next time, shoot him somewhere a little farther north."

"I almost did," I whispered. "Remember, he put me through hell, but we need him."

"I'm not fooled. You're one of the good ones, Parker." He continued out of the precinct.

It was late, and graveyard was just beginning their shift. I sat at Heathcliff's desk, hoping Thompson or O'Connell might be unlucky enough to be coming to work, but unfortunately, I didn't spot any familiar faces. After scanning the stack of files Heathcliff left for me, I was relieved to discover the police department found the drug connection.

It wasn't glamorous, but a few dealers who moonlighted as CIs remembered a guy asking about the ingredients used in the Camel's cocktail. It wasn't much to go on, but they'd given a basic description of the man. Very basic. He was white, over six feet tall, might have been a bodybuilder, and had a scar across his neck. From the notes, it sounded like someone failed to cut his throat.

A few units and some of the narcotics guys were keeping their eyes peeled for anyone matching that description, but it wasn't much to go on. With any luck, Chase Devereaux would talk. Maybe Ryan's license plate number and the description would lead to something, but I had my doubts. The car was probably stolen, or the plates were switched, like on the vehicle Chase drove. These guys were careful, meticulous, and a little scary.

When I ran out of reading material, I called it a night and went home. It was the first time I'd been back to my apartment for any length of time, and I was glad to be home. The ice packs were in the freezer where I kept them. The extra plush blankets were in the linen closet, and my bed turned into a blissful safe haven. The only things missing were my handguns, so I left the taser on my nightstand, popped some ibuprofen, and slept soundly.

THIRTY-TWO

Only when the knocking became unbearable did I clamber out of bed and limp to my front door. There was nothing wrong with my leg, but something in my back wasn't lining up properly. I stretched and shifted, listening to things pop and creak that should never pop or creak. Barely over thirty and I was already falling apart. Damn, I really needed a better job with medical and dental.

"Entrez-vous." I stepped away from the door.

Ryan squinted, confused by my sudden good mood, and Mark rolled his eyes and came in, dropping the heavy artillery on my counter.

"Did we wake you?" Mark asked, not at all surprised to find me in a t-shirt and pajama shorts.

"Maybe." I checked the magazines and slid them back inside their respective guns. "I didn't realize we had breakfast plans. Since you came empty-handed, someone should probably order out."

"Get dressed. We have work to do," Mark said.

"I'm pretty sure I'm off the case. Plus, the PD's

expecting me. They think I'm useful and brilliant."

"No, they think you're a pain in the ass, but they haven't figured out how to ignore your insane demands yet." Making himself useful, Mark measured out the coffee and added water to the pot. "C'mon, Parker, you know you want to."

I turned to Ryan who looked uneasy being in my place. It made sense, but feeling my eyes on him, he offered an encouraging nod. "Sorry to wake you. We have some solid leads on the financials, the current overseas account information, and Farrell's working to convince Chase to explain how he got in contact with the Camel. It's a lot to process. Our joint task force joined with the local police department, so you're back on board. Detective O'Connell requested your assistance."

"Then why didn't Nick make the trip himself? He would have brought breakfast in a brown paper bag." After giving up and returning to my bedroom to find the ice packs that needed to be refrozen and searching through my closet for something professional to wear, I reemerged to find the two men sitting at my kitchen counter, exhausted. "Did either of you even go home last night?" I stuffed the packs in the freezer.

"No, but it's fine. We stopped for espresso," Ryan said.

"I'm dropping him off at his hotel on the way back to the OIO," Mark declared as I made my way to the bathroom to shower. There wasn't time for long and leisurely. "I got a few hours on the couch since they finally moved it back into my office."

"Thank god," I called, not sure if he heard me through the door and over the running water. "I wondered what happened to that couch. It's a great couch. I'm calling dibs if today's indentured servitude turns into more than an eight hour workday."

*   *   *

"We've flagged Hu's assets, so if there's any account activity, our agents will be all over it," Farrell assured. "Also, during our raid of the locker Barlow and his team were using, some additional overseas accounts were uncovered. Right now, our forensic accountants are monitoring that situation and checking to see what other accounts might have been opened around the same time. More than likely, at least one of them will trace back to our contract killer." This was old news, but apparently, it seemed new to Interpol.

"As far as the drugs are concerned," O'Connell said, no longer blending into the background of cheap suits and sunglasses, "narcotics has eyes on possible dealers and suppliers. We didn't find any sales through official sources, so the Camel's cocktail must have been purchased off the street. One of our CIs provided a description. Even though it leaves a lot to be desired, it gives us a basis for identifying our guy if he shows up again."

"Facial recognition hasn't gotten a hit on the woman in the photos we uncovered from the house," Jablonsky added, "but based on the information we currently possess, we're assuming she's our hitman's next target."

"We're comparing her ID to the list of rare car owners that match the stolen vehicles, but it's a long list," Nick said.

"Did you ask Chase?" I chimed in. "Did we get anything out of him? Tuesday night, our killer shot at him, but last night, he told me they were working together, although the bullet in his body says differently."

"He's not talking. We're working him night and

day, but as of yet, he hasn't cracked," Mark said. "We're alternating guys and tactics and hitting up all of our presently incarcerated, but no dice."

"Funny, Barlow has a nice pair inked on his wrist."

"Any idea why our killer went from drug and drown to sniper rifle?" O'Connell asked. It was the question I'd been wondering since Tuesday, but no one had any ideas.

"We're assuming Chase Devereaux isn't a contracted hit. It's probably personal. A business deal gone bad or cutting ties with anyone who can identify him, so sniper rifle will get the job done quickly and efficiently," Mark theorized.

"Except it hasn't," I retorted. We were missing something. I felt it.

"We're running ballistics now," Mark said. "We have the slug we pulled out of Chase and a few stray shots that were left in his hotel and on the garage roof. With any luck, they'll lead us to a specific gun."

"All right," Farrell stood up from the conference table, signifying our tete-a-tete was coming to an end, "Interpol's working the money angle, the OIO's tracking the latest target and analyzing the evidence, and the police department is working on the drug connection. All our bases are covered." He left the room, phone already to his ear.

"Back to the grind." Mark gave me a furtive glance. "Are you sure you're fine?"

"Absolutely," I replied, and he nodded to Nick and left the room. "So, Detective, you requested my assistance?"

"Yeah," he squinted, "remind me to schedule a head CT."

"Ha, ha." I sat sideways and rested my shoulder against the backrest of the chair. "Are you thinking what I'm thinking?"

"That the shooter isn't the Camel?" He knew it just as well as I did.

"Actually, I was thinking we should get the hell away from this building, stop for breakfast, and talk to some of those dealers you have eyes on, but yeah, I don't think a killer would change his M.O. that drastically."

"All right, looks like the investigation is once again in the hands of the lowly police department." He snorted, demonstrating his disdain. "Not that we have any earthly idea what we're doing or how to do it."

"At least you're not at the bottom of the totem pole. That spot is reserved specifically for incompetent consultants."

Wordlessly, we left the OIO, got into O'Connell's car, and ended up in one of the shadier neighborhoods in the city. It was within the ten block radius of Tommy Claxton's place, and suddenly, I was ready to believe we were actually on to something.

"How are you holding up?" Nick asked as we sat in the cruiser, watching a dealer in the midst of a handoff. "Jablonsky asked how you were, and Martin's called a couple of times to see if you were at work."

"Seriously?"

"It's not a big deal, but something's going on with you. What is it?"

"A few cracked ribs and a bruised back. Y'know, the norm."

"Sure." He glanced at me before returning his gaze to the pusher.

"Next time Martin calls, feel free to remind him you aren't an answering service."

"Give the man a break. If I found Jen the way he found you, I'd have assigned a couple of unis to follow her everywhere. It's a guy thing. We like to protect our womenfolk."

"Egotistical maniacs are what you are." Unfortunately, he had a point. And as if being drugged wasn't bad enough, the next time he saw me, I wasn't exactly in one piece. Overprotective was one of the weapons I wielded very well, sometimes too well, so I couldn't fault Martin for having the same quality. "Do you have a composite on the buyer?"

"Yeah, hang on." He shuffled through the files. "Here." Before he even held up the picture, I knew who it would resemble. "Anyone you know?"

"The same guy I said you ought to shoot if he moved."

"I thought it looked like Virgil, but when I passed it along to the guys in the suits and sunglasses, they thought I was raving mad." O'Connell found another file which contained a photograph of Virgil Mallick. "Shall we see who the lunatic is?"

"Absolutely."

We got out of the car and approached the dealer. He grunted and glowered, not bothering to mask the disdain he had for the two of us. Nick asked the questions and paid for the information while I scoped out the area. This was a tight-knit community. The crews that ran this area knew one another and avoided rivals and other gangs.

"Obviously, I'm not the insane one," O'Connell muttered as we went back to the car. "The only problem is Virgil probably bought the drugs to use on Ryan which doesn't bring us any closer to identifying the Camel."

"Allegedly, when did the deal go down?"

"Two, maybe three weeks. These upstanding citizens don't concern themselves with dates and times since it's not like they are reporting their revenue to the IRS." He put the car in gear and drove a block away before parking. We wanted to stay in the vicinity since this was still our best lead. "You have a theory, don't you?"

"The cars started going missing around the same time, but it doesn't make any sense why Virgil would have bought the drugs to dose Ryan at that point. His cover was supposed to be intact, unless they made him." I shook the cobwebs free. "Shit. Chase said he told Barlow to end Hoyt when they took care of Agent Grenauldo."

"But by now, that's ancient history. Every bit of intel Donough gathered from the surveillance feeds after Grenauldo's death is probably bogus anyway."

"They've been leading Interpol in circles intentionally. That's why they let Ryan live. It's why they were skeptical of me when I entered into the picture and Ryan made the introductions. They knew he'd bring in backup support. It's why Chase was so emphatic about oral sex and why Virgil pushed the envelope to get a reaction."

The situation in Chase's hotel room before and after the shots were fired was designed to force me to show my hand. Even when he brought me to my knees in the elevator, he must have assumed backup would appear, but they didn't. Unless he made Mark, and that didn't seem likely. Although, when I failed to produce a vehicle, he had his proof that I wasn't a car thief. I doubted there was ever a buyer. It was all a ploy to figure out who I was and how much information Interpol already had on him and the Camel. Clearly, it wasn't enough, and the sudden appearance of the sniper worked perfectly to divert our efforts. After all, the Camel was a much more valuable target than Chase Devereaux.

"No wonder you shot the guy twice, but what does any of this have to do with locating our killer?"

O'Connell's words dropped off. "Jeez, it could be anyone if they've been jerking around the investigation."

Blowing out a breath, I wondered how to start at the beginning when everything we knew was tainted. As I stared out the window, I considered the original players I encountered.

"Can you get Tommy moved back to a holding cell in the precinct for additional questioning?"

"I can make a call. He's been sent through central booking, but the case is still open so probably." He started the engine. "What are you thinking?"

"Alexandra Riley's job isn't over yet. Phone in the request and then swing by my place. I need to change."

THIRTY-THREE

After applying enough makeup to look believable and finding a ratty shirt I didn't care to part ways with, we went to the precinct. O'Connell made sure our prisoner was on his way, and then they stuck me in a holding cell. My shirt was torn down the back, so the dark bruises and swollen places were clearly visible. Two things were true about Tommy. First, he was an idiot, and second, he was a softie. Even though things didn't work out between him and Riley, the thought of someone using her as a punching bag wouldn't sit well with him. The ploy was to ask enough questions to find out if he heard any rumors about the drug buyer or the contract killer after telling him about how one of Barlow's guys beat the shit out of me. At least some of it was true.

"Are you sure you can pull this off?" O'Connell asked, making sure the wire I was wearing was invisible and transmitting properly. "You've rejected this guy a dozen times. Don't you think he'll assume you got what you deserved?"

"I thought you men like to protect your womenfolk."

"True." He took a seat behind the counter, next to the sergeant on duty, and waited for the newest charge to be transferred.

I sat on the edge of the bunk, my back to the adjacent cell where they intended to place Tommy. Waiting was always difficult, especially when it was hard to stay in character when I could easily kill time by chatting with Nick and the other cops. Fifteen minutes later, a uniformed officer brought Tommy into lockup. He was cuffed. After uncuffing him and securing the cell door, the uniformed officer left.

I turned my head. "Tommy?"

"Alex," he rushed across the cell, "who did that to you?" His face contorted. "I swear to god, I'll smash his face in."

"It was one of Reggie Barlow's guys. The police released me because they didn't have enough evidence, and this guy just shows up." I looked away.

"Babe." He paced the small space in his cell, running his hands through his hair. He was more distraught by this news than I imagined. "I never should have brought you in on any of this. This is all my fault."

"Did you know Barlow was working with guys like that? Did you meet them?"

He checked to see if anyone was paying attention before sliding onto the bunk across the bars from mine. "I heard some stuff around the neighborhood about Barlow's guys looking for dealers. Crazy shit. Obviously, since they're psycho assholes. Was it the guy who helped us move the, uh, packages?"

"No, it was someone else. The cops say they have a description, but I don't know if they'll find him." I reached for his hand through the bars. "I'm scared what will happen when they let me out of here." I took an unsteady breath. "I think these guys might be killers." I exhaled rapidly, wincing and hoping the pain was selling the story. Who didn't like a good damsel in distress tale? "What do I do, Tommy?" I lowered my voice to barely a whisper. "Maybe I should confess just so Barlow's guys can't come back and kill me."

"It's gonna be okay, babe. I'll fix it. I got you into this. It's time I man up."

"Tommy?" I wanted information, and this sounded more like an eleventh hour scheme. "What are you going to do?"

"Officer," he announced loudly, stepping away from me and going to the front of the cell, "we need to talk. I got some things that have to be said."

O'Connell stood up, completely confused by this strange turn of events, took Tommy out of lockup, and headed for the interrogation room. Two minutes later, Thompson came down the stairs, opened my cell, and jerked his chin at the stairwell. "You're free to go."

"Hilarious." I stopped by the tech department to return the wire before going to the women's locker room to change into something decent.

By the time I made it to the observation room connected to the interrogation room, Thompson had joined O'Connell. This time, Tommy didn't ask for his lawyer. He wanted to confess. He said he'd tell them everything he knew. All he asked in return was that the asshats who beat up his girl were arrested. Like I thought, the guy was a sentimental idiot, but luckily, it paid off.

Tommy Claxton heard rumors about a few new guys in town looking to score. Their drug of choice wasn't the usual. It was a combination of psychotropic, paralytic, and prescription grade sedatives. No one in that neighborhood sold items of that nature. Typically, they dealt in the much more common crack, weed, and oxy. To top it off, Tommy positively identified the buyer as Virgil Mallick.

"It was just one guy?" O'Connell asked. Maybe Tommy had information to further inculcate Chase Devereaux.

"As far as I know. I'm not a dealer. I don't use, buy, or sell." He glared at the detectives. "I got better things to do with my time. I thought you were supposed to protect people. You bust a bunch of us on some car shit but can't protect a chick from some psychos." He poked at the tabletop with his pointer finger. "I want a guarantee you'll keep my girl safe."

"You're the only one who can protect her, man," Thompson said. "We need a name, description, and any other kind of information you can give us. The only way we can take people off the street is with evidence."

"Right, because the way her back looks doesn't count for shit." He glared.

"C'mon, get back on track," I hissed. Tommy knew something. He had to.

Sighing dramatically, he crossed his arms across his chest. They didn't think he posed a risk and didn't bother to cuff him for the trip upstairs. "Look, here's everything I know and everything I heard." He shook his head and shut his eyes, struggling with his decision. "Robert Gregson and I have a side business. We boost cars sometimes, and Rob chops them. It ain't much, but bills add up, y'know. Anyway, Reggie calls Rob one day and gives him a list. I've never seen it, but it had like a dozen or something cars on it. Whatever." He blew out a breath, annoyed with the police, himself, and the situation.

"Reggie?" Thompson asked.

"Barlow." Tommy scoffed. "Anyway, Reggie's got this other guy to help boost cars. Hoyt. I don't got a first name for him, but we called him Hoyt. Anyway, that's all we knew."

"We?" O'Connell asked.

"Me and Rob. So as I was saying, that's all we were told. The thing is I got family and friends in the neighborhood. Lived there all my life, and this is just how we are. Tight. So maybe I hear some stuff about that guy," he pointed to Virgil's picture, "asking for those drugs I told you about. People don't ask for drugs like that just out of the blue, y'know what I mean?"

"Not exactly," O'Connell said.

"I got to spell everything out, don't I? Some people start asking around, and there's some hushed words exchanged that this is some hardcore date rape shit. Like lose your memory, out for days, hallucinate pink elephants kind of shit. Then when the guy comes to pick it up, everyone's keeping an eye out. Maybe we're not the greatest spot in town, but we try to keep our kids safe. Anyway, this guy brings another guy with him. The other guy's driving Reggie's car."

"When did the pick-up happen?" Thompson asked, pen poised to record the information.

"I don't know." His eyes darted between the two detectives. "Seriously. I got no idea. But one of those two assholes came looking for revenge because their boss got pinched when we were stealing some cars for Reggie's pretty little wish list, and they came for my girlfriend, who had nothing to do with any of this. So get off your asses and do something about it."

"Only you could get a confession without even being in the room." Heathcliff startled me from the doorway, and I jumped at the sound of his voice. "Sorry. I thought you heard the door open. How'd you get him to confess to the cars and implicate everyone except you?"

"Riley made a recent reappearance in holding while wearing a crop top." I snorted. "O'Connell gave me the idea."

"So you seduced Tommy?"

"No, but I make a damn good damsel in distress, which frankly, scares the shit out of me."

The interview was over. Tommy spouted out everything he knew, solidifying the GTA case against him, Gregson, and Barlow. He even implicated Virgil as an accessory, and tossed a few accusations at Chase.

"Ryan should be in on this. He might have additional information to add or some questions no one has thought to pose. Can we get clearance to pick him up?" I asked.

"Later, you can make the call, and I'll give you a ride. It looks like O'Connell and Thompson have some paperwork to file. In the meantime, Moretti has a few questions to ask concerning the shootings at the hotel and the parking garage. It seems your federal agency doesn't believe in sharing intel."

"It's not my fault. The rivalry was going on long before I ever signed up. Plus, I'm very progressive in my thinking. Sharing information can only help an investigation, not hinder it."

He gave me a 'yeah, right' look but didn't comment as he ushered me out of the room and to Moretti's office. The lieutenant gestured to the seat in front of his desk, dismissing Heathcliff with a wave of his hand.

"What are we gonna do with you, Parker?" Moretti asked.

"Sir?"

"You bring down an auto theft ring that no one was

investigating, then you turn my city into the playground for an international hitman, and if all that wasn't bad enough, you throw in a sniper for good measure." Before I could voice a protest, he shook his head and rubbed his eyes. It was apparent no one was getting much sleep with the current situation. "My department's been granted limited access. The suits don't want us mucking about in their territory, but you're my consultant."

"I'm starting to feel like a whore. What do you need?"

"Answers. Has the shooter been identified?"

"No. They're working under the assumption it's the Camel seeking a personal vendetta against Chase Devereaux, one of Barlow's guys." I didn't believe it, and neither did Moretti. "Tommy Claxton just admitted he heard some of his friends spotted two guys buying the Camel's cocktail in his neighborhood a few weeks ago. The only two guys we know about are Virgil Mallick and Chase Devereaux."

"Let me guess, you think one of them is the Camel." He flipped through his notes. "Chase Devereaux, right?" I nodded, and he studied my expression. "Your pals don't agree?" he asked.

"Can I speak off the record? I don't want any of this repeated."

He leaned back. "Go ahead."

"Interpol's screwed up this investigation since the beginning. Once the ICC handed it over to them, they haven't had a clue what to do or how to do it. They missed major details at the crime scenes, like the car parts, and they should have pulled Donough out as soon as Grenauldo's body was discovered. But they left him in and tried to paint him as a turncoat. It's been one screwup after another, and instead of taking the blame, they're pointing fingers and spinning in circles. Most of the evidence they have is bogus. Chase practically admitted they knew Ryan was a mole ever since Grenauldo broke cover, so everything Interpol's collected or overheard was probably staged."

"Jesus."

"I'm not sure why a contract killer would be traveling with Barlow, but Virgil's out because he was incarcerated during a few of the murders. My gut says it's Chase. His passport says he was in Canada, but documents are easy to forge, particularly since one of the GPS locations I pulled from his rental led straight to a place that prints fake documents in a jiff. Maybe he was in Europe the entire time. I'm to the point where past crimes don't even matter. Truthfully, the GPS tracker in his car brought me to the house where they were keeping Donough. Virgil bought the drugs, but Chase has been calling the shots. We need Barlow to substantiate this, or we need to trace the funds paid to the Camel. Some bank accounts were recently uncovered. But I don't know if we got anything solid yet."

"Interesting, but what does this have to do with the sniper?"

"This might sound crazy, but I think Chase hired him to throw us off the scent." I knew how insane that was, but the angles were wrong for a professional sniper. "There was no clear shot into the hotel room from across the roof. And in the parking garage, Chase was at an angle. Sure, he was shot, but it seemed more accidental than intentional. Like the guy was trying to take out the back window and not shoot the driver."

"You don't have proof?"

"Not yet."

"All right," he didn't seem convinced, "we've pulled footage from a few cameras. With any luck, we'll identify the shooter and bring him in. Maybe he'll have something that corroborates that insanity you call a theory."

"Thank you, sir."

"What does Jablonsky think of this?"

"I haven't shared it with him yet. I've been afraid to say too much. With the way things are going, Interpol will get wind of it and claim I'm the Camel or someone's bound to order a mandatory psych hold since I've lost my damn mind."

He chuckled. "Get out of here. If anything new surfaces, bring it to me."

THIRTY-FOUR

As promised, Heathcliff picked up Donough. Ryan looked bored out of his mind, but that probably had more to do with his lack of sleep. He didn't want to be benched, and since Interpol was busy working its own leads, I thought he'd be more comfortable cooperating with fellow police officers, even if it meant watching hours of surveillance footage.

While I was explaining everything that happened in the hotel room, including my observations about Chase, I started reconsidering my earlier conviction. Inside the hotel room, Chase was scared. The layer of perspiration on his upper lip and the frantic need to escape were indicative that something spooked him.

"Maybe he thought he would get caught," Heathcliff suggested.

"Did anyone identify what automotive part was in the box?" Ryan asked.

"Hang on. I'll see if we have copies of those files. That is, if the other agencies bothered to share."

After Heathcliff left, I paused the monitors. "Fill me

in. What are you thinking?"

"I don't bloody know. Every step forward is six backward, mostly because Interpol is making me go in circles. When will this ride end?"

"Soon."

"Chase was afraid of what was inside the box before he even opened it. Either he's afraid someone's on to him, or he's been receiving threats. Virgil wasn't there, but Chase didn't know he was incarcerated."

"Isn't it strange they didn't have some kind of monitoring system set up at the safe house? How safe can it be if anyone can break in the back door?"

"Did anyone identify the woman in the photo from the steel drum?" Ryan asked.

"I don't know. I've been here."

Heathcliff returned, empty-handed. "We don't have those records. We're lucky to have copies of the surveillance." He slumped into the chair. "Look," he pointed to the frozen monitor, "that's when you left the parking garage."

"Yeah, so?" I asked, seeing Chase beside me made my blood boil.

"For someone who was just shot at, he doesn't look scared anymore. He looks smug," Heathcliff said.

"Maybe the reason he was nervous upstairs was because someone was about to take a couple of shots at him," Ryan suggested. "He probably feared he'd have to take a bullet."

I tapped my fingers against the arm of the chair. It seemed plausible. My memory of that evening was off because I was too busy reacting instead of monitoring. The hazards of taking fire and setting up a sting simultaneously. "So, he was scared but not because the Camel was going to kill him?"

"No, he doesn't strike me as suicidal," Ryan said, and I realized we both believed Chase was the contract killer. "Let's figure out a way to prove this. I'd like to go home."

"Well, I would offer the two of you a crack at Barlow's guys, except we don't have access to them," Heathcliff said. "But maybe if we ask nicely, we can get a manifest of what was discovered in the house."

Ryan looked torn. "It's gonna be bullshit. Assuming our assumptions are accurate, this is all part of the contingency plan. The only way we'll be able to nail Chase is with evidence we gather that he hasn't led us to."

"All right. We need to find the woman from the photo, look into the overseas accounts again, and talk to Virgil," I surmised. "We just can't do any of that from here."

"The guys and I will review Tommy's confession and talk to Gregson again. If we uncover anything, I'll give you a call. Once we get a positive ID on the woman, I'll pass along that information," Heathcliff said.

"Derek, I trust Mark and the guys here, but I don't trust Interpol. Last year when I was working in Paris, things weren't sitting well back then. Based on Donough's experiences, I'm guessing they've only gotten worse. Everything you guys read in those files, take with a grain of salt."

"Will do. Hey, Parker," he called before I made it to the stairwell, "if you need backup, give me a call."

"Absolutely."

* * *

Steeling my nerves, I followed Donough into the interrogation room. Virgil Mallick was chained to the chair. The federal agent monitoring him offered to shackle his ankles too, but I didn't want him to think I was scared. Maybe I was, but no one needed to know that. Something about this guy creeped me out, probably the fact that he had come close to literally snapping me in half.

"Virgil," Ryan said with such maliciousness, even I was surprised, "how are you feeling?"

Virgil shifted his gaze briefly away from me before settling on Ryan and smiling. "I liked you better unconscious."

"Personally, I can rest easy knowing you'll never see anything except the inside of a prison cell. Unfortunately, you're not the focus of this investigation." Ryan weighed each of his words carefully.

Virgil continued to scrutinize me, and no matter how hard I tried to ignore it, I couldn't. Yanking one of the chairs away from the table, I glowered at him.

"How many?" His eyelids lowered, and he stared through the narrow slits, relishing in some devious thought. "How many of your bones did I break?" He observed the way I held myself, enjoying every minute of it.

"I'm not breakable, but I'm positive by the end of the day, you'll be broken," I replied, low and calm. "Let's put it this way, right now, you're in a room in a federal building, but there aren't any agents inside. I'm not carrying a badge, and neither is Ryan. So we don't have any protocols to follow. Whether you make it out of this room alive or not is up to you."

He laughed, not believing my threats. "The only thing I understand is violence." His eyes focused on my holstered gun, smiling again like the snake I knew he was.

"Oh, you like shiny things, huh?" I went around the table and pressed my knee into the bandage on his thigh. He howled. "How'd you like the glass? Was that shiny enough for you?"

Ryan shifted behind me, and I stepped back. This was the first time Virgil displayed a normal response to pain. I wondered if that was a result of the mix of drugs they'd given him to get him conscious or if whatever methamphetamine he normally used was no longer prevalent in his system. I stepped away. My point was made, and I was done.

"Word of advice, I wouldn't piss her off. Then again," Ryan sat on the side of the table, leaning down to Virgil, "you shouldn't piss me off either."

Realization struck in Virgil's reptilian brain, and his eyes darted between the two of us. "We've known for quite some time you were an Interpol agent, but once we determined you weren't a threat, we decided you could be eliminated."

"Who's we?" I asked.

"Who do you think?" Virgil asked. Ryan shoved our prisoner's chair backward, stopping it with his foot before Virgil's skull cracked on the ground. Virgil laughed. "It sure as hell wasn't Barlow."

"Chase?" Ryan knocked the tilted chair forward to an upright position. It teetered due to Virgil's mass but stabilized. Physical danger and pain wouldn't tip the scales in our favor.

"You know, don't you?" Virgil met my eyes, impressed and satisfied. "I've been waiting for someone to make the connection. Barlow thought I'd be the protection, the enforcer, but instead, that twat had to prove what a badass he could be."

"We need details," Ryan ordered.

"What for?" Virgil asked. "You've been with us for months now. Don't you know everything there is to know about Barlow's car deals?"

"I don't give a bloody fuck about the cars," Ryan yelled.

I sat across from Virgil. "What do you want?" I asked. Trades were a far too common occurrence, and after everything Ryan had been through, he wouldn't offer or budge. I didn't blame him. Letting this snake get away wasn't something I wanted to do, but we had to find some kind of leverage if we wanted him to talk.

Ryan stepped back, fuming. He glared and slammed his palm into the wall.

"Oh," Virgil smiled, "you're in charge." He turned his head to face Ryan. "It sucks never calling the shots, doesn't it?"

"What.Do.You.Want?" I tried again.

Virgil leaned back. The power in the room shifted. "I don't know. I'll think about it." He grinned, and Ryan lost it.

Ryan shoved Virgil, still in the chair, across the room and against the wall. Jablonsky and two agents burst through the door. I should have attempted to intervene or pull Ryan away, but the way I figured it, even if I tried, I wouldn't have been able to. The two agents struggled to drag Ryan from interrogation. I averted my gaze. I'd been there before. I understood.

Mark raised an eyebrow, but I remained in the chair, waiting for answers. "I'd suggest you think faster," Mark urged. "The next agent you piss off won't be that easy to drag away."

Virgil's eyes never left mine. We stared at one another for what felt like a millennium. "How many?" he asked again.

Shoving a pen and paper in front of his handcuffed hands, I leaned over him. "Not until you tell us exactly who Chase Devereaux is."

He manipulated the pen in his bound hands, drawing an image on the paper. When he was done, he put the pen down. The vicious smile never left his face. Mark glanced down and spun the pad in my direction. On the paper was a rudimentary sketch of a one hump camel.

"Five," I responded.

He shut his eyes, inhaling a long, blissful breath. "Amazing."

I left the room, wondering how admissible any of that was. Then again, it wasn't like I had a badge. Maybe rules were important. They balanced the violence, the rage, the desire for revenge that didn't need to be explored. Those scales had been tipped one too many times in the last few months, and I feared how much worse it would get if I didn't find a balance. After glancing at Michael's old desk, I ducked inside Jablonsky's office and found Ryan.

"I'm sorry," he whispered, his face buried in his hands.

"I get it." I sat sideways in Mark's chair. "It scares me sometimes how much violence I'm capable of inflicting. Don't be that guy, Ryan. Someone has to wear the white hat and ride in on the horse to save the day. I'm only up for that about seventy percent of the time. The rules exist for a reason. Regardless of what I said to Virgil, we'll be lucky to make it out of here with our asses intact."

"It doesn't matter."

"It should. You've seen me close to rock bottom, and you kept a tight leash on me. Unfortunately, I didn't extend you the same courtesy. I'm sorry about that, but after you left, Virgil provided us with a nice doodle."

"Doodle?"

"Yeah, of a camel."

"Bloody hell. How'd you get him to say it?"

"Virgil Mallick isn't your typical criminal. I'm not even sure he's sadistic in a traditional sense. Honestly, I'd wager he has an inferiority complex. The only thing he seemed concerned with was proving he was the toughest, meanest, biggest badass in the room. The guy pumps iron. Shit, he probably eats it for breakfast, takes who knows what, and all of that is to walk around being some tough goon. He wanted to bitch and moan about Chase because, all of a sudden, he wasn't the biggest badass anymore. That's why the only thing he wanted was reassurance that he was still physically threatening. That's why he kept asking how many. He needed me to tell him that he snapped my ribs like they were twigs. His ego needed stroking."

"Be thankful that's all you had to stroke," Mark said from the doorway. He shook his head. "Kid," he turned to Ryan, "we don't assault handcuffed prisoners in interrogation rooms, particularly when the interview is being recorded."

"D'accord."

"Fine," Mark blew out a breath, "we'll chalk it up to something being lost in translation." He sighed loudly. "Parker, any reason you didn't move a single muscle to intervene?"

"My back hurts. Movement's not what it should be. I can't help it if I'm injured, especially when Virgil was directly responsible."

"Just FYI, if you ever decide to come back to the OIO, you can't assault suspects, detainees, or prisoners," Mark casually added.

"Duly noted, sir."

THIRTY-FIVE

After the way our interview with Virgil Mallick went, Ryan and I weren't permitted to go anywhere near Chase Devereaux. Despite Virgil's lovely little drawing, we still didn't have solid evidence or corroborating eyewitness accounts that Chase was the Camel. So while Farrell and Jablonsky went to work on Virgil and Chase, Ryan and I reviewed the recently acquired information and checked to see if the forensic lab had any idea who the woman in the photo was, where the bank accounts would lead, or if something obscure could give us a location to scout.

"Nancy Shepherd," the tech said, handing over the pertinent file. "We just started a full workup. It'll be a while before we have anything solid."

"Thanks." I took a quick snapshot of her driver's license and led the way out of the room, my phone to my ear. "Hey, we found a match to the woman in the photos. Nancy Shepherd. I just sent you a copy of her ID. The OIO's working on a profile but start checking into her close contacts, friends, family, ex-husbands, whatever, and see who has something to gain by ordering a hit. Ryan and I will be there in twenty." I disconnected from my brief call with Heathcliff and made sure Ryan was still with me.

"Back to the precinct?" he asked.

"Unless you'd rather stay here and keep Mark's couch warm."

"I'm a cop. The precinct is where I belong."

"Have I mentioned it's nice to have you back, Inspector?"

He smiled. "It's nice to be back."

When we arrived, Heathcliff and Thompson were knee deep in research materials. Not only were they compiling a list of known associates for Ms. Shepherd, but they were also reviewing the files Interpol sent over. As it turned out, Ms. Shepherd was the proud owner of a 1967 Mustang, the same model Robert Gregson made me steal as part of my initiation into his car boosting ring. At least we found a connection between Gregson, the Camel, and one of the Camel's intended victims.

"Where's Nick?" I asked.

"Unrelated case," Thompson said. "He caught a triple homicide at the scene of a burglary. I'm supposed to meet him there in a couple of minutes."

"Tell my pals in burglary I said hello," I deadpanned, and Heathcliff snorted. Most of burglary still blamed me for the dirty cop scandal that rocked the city not too long ago. "Is Moretti around?"

"Office." Heathcliff pointed.

I left the men with their research while I knocked on the door. "Lieutenant," I began once I was situated, "I thought you'd like an update." After telling him everything we gained from interrogating Virgil and the information on the woman, he gave us permission to track her down and investigate any pertinent leads, with two stipulations. First, Donough was my responsibility, and second, someone with a badge needed to accompany me at all times. It looked like I'd be involved in a threesome, after all.

By the time I returned to Heathcliff's desk, Thompson was gone and Ryan was getting reacquainted with his investigating chops. It had been months since he'd been behind a desk in a police station, and while this wasn't the Police Nationale, I could already see his years of experience and training taking over. Some things you never forget.

After careful study, a few things became painfully clear. First, the piston that arrived in Chase's hotel room was a match to the make and model of the vehicle registered to Nancy Shepherd. Also, the techs found a set of prints on the metal that matched Robert Gregson. Now we had our proof Gregson was supplying Barlow's team with cars and the Camel with his calling card. Second, based on the photographs, the oil drum, and all the other nasty equipment found in the house, we were working under the assumption Ms. Shepherd was the Camel's next target. Lastly, a court order was in the works for her financials. We were trying to determine who would have ordered the hit, but it was too soon to say.

"Shall we take a ride?" Heathcliff asked as soon as I stopped typing.

"Either that or send a couple of uniforms to bring her in," I suggested.

"No, we should go," Ryan insisted. "Chase is in custody, but on the off chance we're wrong or he hired someone to carry out the contract, we don't want to risk spooking and losing the hitman."

"Agreed," Heathcliff said. "I'll have an unmarked car follow us, and I'll notify ESU to be on alert. But first things first, we need to determine who wants her dead."

On the drive to Shepherd's apartment, we debated on possible suspects. She had an ex-husband who was paying a pretty penny in alimony. A twenty-year-old stepson who was suspended from college for drug abuse, and since she operated her own interior decorating business, it was possible a subordinate had an axe to grind.

"What about disgruntled customers?" Donough asked.

"Do you think someone would pay thousands to kill her because she didn't get the right carpet?" I asked.

"Probably not," he admitted.

"Don't forget, spurned ex-lovers and current flings," Heathcliff added.

I squinted into the distance. The Camel was expensive. His methodology was brutal. Whoever would go to such lengths wanted revenge and probably stood to gain quite a bit. If not, there were cheaper ways to have someone killed.

"How old is she?" I asked, not remembering her DOB.

"Thirty-five. Her ex-husband is in his fifties." Ryan chuckled. "She's young enough to be one of his children. I'd say he's our best bet."

"Let's talk to her first before we start theorizing," I suggested. Although, there were dozens of reasons I could think of as to why he might want to kill her.

Pulling up to her place of business, Heathcliff nodded briefly to the officers in the other vehicle and signaled that they remain on standby while the three of us went inside. The office was small, not much larger than my own, with samples and books filling half the space. Shepherd's assistant glanced up from the desk, smiling warmly at the three of us.

"How may I help you?" she asked.

"We need to speak to Ms. Shepherd." Heathcliff flashed his badge.

"She just stepped out for a minute, but she'll be back soon. What is this about? Is she in trouble?"

"Nothing like that," Ryan said, and the woman beamed at him. Obviously, she thought there was something sexy about him. My money was on the Irish brogue. "We just have a few routine questions that need answering." He lowered his voice and leaned in to the desk, turning on the charm. From the few words I heard in between her answers and giggles, I knew he was asking about the business, some of the clients, if Shepherd had a boyfriend, and if her assistant ever met the ex-husband.

Heathcliff rolled his eyes. "Is he going to ask her to drop her panties too?"

"Derek," I hissed, stifling my laugh, "he's working. Plus, it's an excellent distraction."

As Ryan continued his flirtatious questioning, we perused the items on her desk, flipped through her appointment calendar, and otherwise searched the entire office space without the assistant ever noticing. Heathcliff pointed to her appointment book, and we scanned the times and locations, looking for something that hinted Shepherd met with Chase. Just as our search concluded, the bell above the door chimed, and Shepherd entered the office. Her classic Mustang was parked out front.

"Can I help you?" she asked, putting her sketchbook on top of her desk.

"Ma'am, we were hoping to ask you a couple of questions." Heathcliff identified himself and introduced Ryan and me.

"Sure, no problem." She bit her lip, slightly nervous, and asked her assistant to pick up lunch.

Once the four of us were alone, she sat behind her

desk. Heathcliff asked some basic questions about her vehicle, how long she owned it, if she received any threats, and what her relationship with her ex-husband was like.

"Why are you asking me any of these things? Did something happen to Scott or Nathan?" Scott was her ex-husband, and Nathan was her stepson. Ex-stepson. The proper terminology was lost on me.

"Nothing like that," I said, knowing my male counterparts thought I'd be better at the coddling. "Have you ever encountered a man named Chase Devereaux?"

She frowned and shook her head.

Heathcliff tapped on his phone, bringing up a few photos. "Ma'am, do you recognize any of these men?" He showed her pictures of Barlow, Virgil, and Chase.

"I'm not sure."

"Ms. Shepherd," Ryan said, "are you scheduled to meet with any new clients this week?"

"Yes."

"Would you happen to have their contact information? It's vital to our investigation."

She flipped through a few pages on her calendar, wrote out a list of appointments, and opened the contacts tab on her computer. After scribbling a list of names and phone numbers, she handed it to him. "Is this what you wanted?" She swiveled, assessing the three of us. "I want to know what this is about."

"We have reason to believe someone conspired to have you murdered," Heathcliff said with a calm, authoritarian voice.

She gasped, horrified. Panic etched her otherwise flawless skin.

"Have you received any threats or believe anyone is holding a grudge against you?" Heathcliff asked.

She shook her head, flummoxed.

"Ma'am," I tried a different tactic, "if something were to happen to you, who stands to profit from your death? I'm sure this is a lucrative business."

"It pays the bills, but it's not worth much. I'm not worth much," she said as an afterthought. "I don't even have life insurance. There was never any need since I don't have children. Well, except for Nathan, but he's Scott's son. Scott always took care of him. Of us." She shook her head, shocked and in utter disbelief. "This can't be. You must have the wrong Nancy Shepherd."

"Always a possibility," I said, hoping to reassure her. Denial could be just as calming as hope. "We can take you in to protective custody or keep a unit on you to make sure you're safe."

We remained in her office while she changed her mind half a dozen times. Nancy was fairly sedate about the situation, not frantic or angry, but in utter disbelief this was happening to her. When her assistant, Emily, returned, Nancy sent her home for the day. Thankfully, she gave us permission to search her office, snoop through her financial records, and delve into her private life. There were no current boyfriends or any significant scorned lovers within the last year. Her divorce was still fresh, less than two years old, and she hadn't felt the need to start dating yet.

"Was it amicable?" Ryan asked. "Marriage is messy, and divorce can be a disaster."

"At the time, it was messy. Scott accused me of having an affair with one of Nathan's friends."

"Were you?" I asked.

She looked away, reddening. "Yes."

"Yeah, that counts as messy," Heathcliff said. "But you're still receiving alimony?"

"Scott never had solid proof." She wouldn't meet

our gaze. “He has family money, and I didn’t ask for half of it or anything like that. But there is a level of comfort I’ve grown accustomed to.” It sounded like her divorce attorney had programmed her with some key phrases. “He will continue to pay until I make more than he does, which will never happen, or I remarry.”

Ryan glanced smugly in my direction. Yeah, it was probably the ex-husband. “Did your husband collect cars?” Ryan asked.

She scrunched her brow together, shocked. “How did you know that?” She looked out the window at the classic muscle car. “Oh. That was part of the settlement.”

“We’re going to need his address and contact information,” Heathcliff said. “Also, we need to move on this, so what’s it going to be? Protective custody or a protection detail?”

She focused on me. “What would you do?”

“Your chances are better in custody.” Although, I wouldn’t willingly agree to either of those things. Unfortunately, decisions like that were never left up to me, probably for that exact reason.

“Custody it is then.” She nodded resolutely, and we let the unmarked car take her in.

“I’m calling to get the paperwork started on Mr. Shepherd’s phone and financial records,” Heathcliff said.

While he did that, I phoned the OIO and gave Jablonsky an update. Regardless of my thoughts concerning Interpol, this was still a federal matter.

THIRTY-SIX

"Have you been here all night?" O'Connell asked when he came in the next morning to find Ryan and me camped out at his desk.

"You mean to tell me it's morning?" I asked.

"That's what that bright yellow thing in the sky means," O'Connell said, amused. He turned to Ryan. "How do you take your coffee?"

"In a cup."

I burst into a hysterical fit of giggles. We'd been up all night, and the lack of sleep made me slightly insane. While I got myself under control, O'Connell filled a few mugs and brought them to us.

"Merci," Ryan replied, not bothering to look up from the report he was proofreading. He stuck the paper into a file and stretched in the chair. "I'll call Farrell with an update." He disappeared into the empty roll call room with his phone and mug.

"The Camel's newest contracted hit is a woman named Nancy Shepherd. After extensive questioning, we think her ex-husband hired the Camel to kill her.

Heathcliff brought him in yesterday afternoon. The guy's a day trader. His lawyer got him released late last night. I think they're filing a harassment suit against the department."

"That's nice," O'Connell muttered. "Do we have hard evidence yet?"

"Not yet. We subpoenaed his financial records and phone logs. After spending far too many hours reviewing every call this guy placed, nothing tracks to the Camel or any suspicious numbers. Heathcliff thinks he purchased a throwaway phone or used an online message board to hire the hitman. I don't know how much progress has been made on tracking his internet history." Taking a long sip, I rubbed my eyes.

"What about his financials?"

"Did I mention he's a day trader? Every forensic accountant on staff here, at the OIO, and the local Interpol office is hard at work, crunching the numbers in search of the account connection. With any luck, one of those overseas accounts Chase or Barlow established will link to a transfer Scott Shepherd made, but until then, Moretti ordered we back off him."

"Where's Heathcliff?" O'Connell asked.

"He went home around three. We were all supposed to go home, but Ryan and I got sidetracked. For the last four hours, we've been searching for a connection between Chase and Mr. Shepherd. Shepherd's a car aficionado. We're assuming he must have crossed paths with Reginald Barlow at some point. It's the only way we've come up with to determine how he got in touch with the Camel."

Nick sat at Thompson's desk since I was still in his chair and logged onto the computer. "If that's true, he might have used a third party to get in contact with Barlow or Chase or whoever."

"Maybe Robert Gregson?"

"Maybe. We have Gregson's phone records somewhere around here. I know there were a few different calls from burner phones. Maybe one of them will trace back to Shepherd. If we run the numbers, we can determine where the phones were purchased and pull security footage if it hasn't been that long."

"Sounds like a lot of work," Ryan said, returning from his call. "But that's what we do."

"Have Jablonsky and Farrell made any progress on finding the sniper?" I asked.

"Not yet."

"I can help on that," Nick said. "We've identified the type of weapon. We're tracking gun sales, but I doubt its registered. Instead, we're looking at ammunition sales. Bullets like this aren't too common. We might get lucky."

"Great." I stood up, gasping at a sudden sharp pain. Ryan hovered closer in case I collapsed. "I'm okay. The damn ibuprofen wore off a few hours ago."

"Why don't we take a break?" Ryan suggested. "I could use some sleep."

"What do you think, Nick? Can we take a break?" I asked.

Nick nodded toward the door. "Get some rest. I'll hold down the fort."

I patted his shoulder on my way out. "Call if something concrete surfaces."

"Absolutely."

I dropped Ryan off at his hotel. The threat of being followed or abducted a second time seemed particularly slim based on our assumption that the Camel was in custody, even though we didn't have enough proof to file charges. At least one psychopath was off the streets. All we needed was to prove it and find the sniper. I was certain Scott Shepherd screwed up. Once we found out where or when, we'd have the evidence we needed. As I considered my options, I dialed Martin.

"Do you mind if I crash at your place?" I asked. There was no reason why I couldn't go home, but Martin should be at work now. And since O'Connell said Martin had been worried and calling for updates, maybe I could alleviate some of his worry.

"Since when do you ask permission?"

"Okay, well, I'm taking a break and need to get some sleep, so I'll be there for a while. I'll probably be gone by the time you get home, but if I leave a mess, I promise to come back later and clean up."

"Are you okay? How are you feeling?"

"I'm fine, just sore from sitting behind a desk all night." I put on my signal light and turned, heading for his house. "Maybe you can point me in the right direction to find that muscle rub from the other morning."

"It's in the master bathroom next to the sink."

"Thanks. I'll see you sometime tonight, unless I stay at work all night again."

"I'll see you later."

* * *

"Alex?" I opened an eye at the sound of Martin's voice. He knelt next to the couch, attempting to determine where I began and the layers of ultra plush blankets that I was using as a cocoon ended. "I thought you'd be in bed."

"This is the first comfortable position I've found." Somewhere in this mess of blankets were a few ice packs which no longer felt cold. Stretching, I realized it was one o'clock. "You're home early."

"I came home for lunch." He sat on the edge of the couch. "Forgive me, but I wanted to make sure you were okay."

"Yeah, I heard. O'Connell said you've been asking for updates." I sat up, realizing I had to leave soon. "Martin, now's not the best time for this conversation, but I've been thinking about going back to work. For Mark. At the OIO. For good."

"What prompted this?" he asked, failing to keep the bitter tone out of his voice.

"My nightmares. Ryan. The fact that I'm tired of running away from the one thing I've always wanted. No matter how much I tell myself I don't want that life, a part of me still does. That job is the only one I know how to do. Even you pointed out that I can't stop myself from doing this."

"When?"

"I don't know. I don't even know if it'll happen, but I've been thinking about it a lot lately. I just thought I should share since you've been hounding me about what I've been thinking." I winked, trying to make it sound playful.

He ran his thumb across my cheek. "Do you want some breakfast?" He looked at his watch. "I'll make you pancakes before I go, okay?"

"Sure." Obviously, he wasn't ready to talk about this right now, but at least I put it out there. Whether or not it ever came to fruition was beside the point.

After breakfast, Martin covered my back and sides in muscle rub and left for the office. I changed clothes and picked up Ryan. On the way to the OIO building, Farrell called and informed us of a plan being set in motion. Detouring, we arrived in time for the briefing.

"All right, people," Jablonsky said, "as you know, we've discovered the apparent link between the Shepherds and our contract killer. The automotive part which was delivered to Chase Devereaux the night Parker went to his hotel suite matches the make and model of the vehicle Nancy Shepherd drives. Based upon her infidelity and the exorbitant alimony settlement she received, our prime suspect is her ex-husband, Scott Shepherd."

"Mr. Shepherd claims he has nothing to do with the crime, and since we don't have a body and slim evidence that a hit was ever ordered, it's been difficult to ascertain enough clear-cut evidence for an arrest warrant," Farrell added.

"Furthermore, we're assuming Chase Devereaux is our euphemistic dromedary killer, but he isn't talking. Reginald Barlow and Virgil Mallick, his two associates, have been pandering. Yesterday, Parker convinced Virgil to open up. He drew this." Mark held up a copy of Virgil's doodle. "But it will be difficult to convince a judge this is legitimate."

"That's probably why he did it," Ryan muttered.

"However, given the automotive parts and Barlow's business, we're threatening to pin the murders on him unless he gives us Chase," Farrell said. "An AUSA is on the way."

"In the meantime," Mark said, "our biggest problem is the appearance of a yet to be identified sniper. We have to assume it's someone Chase contracted. We're reviewing his financials, phone records, and checking into his contacts, but as of yet, we don't know who this guy could be. Ideally, we locate the sniper and bring him in."

"How do we do that?" someone asked from the back of the room.

"We send in a decoy. The real Nancy Shepherd is in protective custody, so we'll send an agent in to impersonate her. We'll keep tactical teams on standby and position agents near the possible vantage points.

Then we wait," Farrell said.

It didn't sound like a great plan, particularly since I thought the point of the sniper was to throw suspicion off Chase. As soon as the room cleared, I voiced this to Mark.

"It's all we can do," he said.

"Your time would be better spent surveilling the locations Chase used for his business. Maybe he made contact with someone about procuring drugs or finding a shooter to throw us off the scent."

"Then you and Donough go do that," Mark said before leaving the room.

"I say we go back to the precinct. The detectives have a better handle on this than anyone." Ryan tossed a contemptuous glance at the other agents, and I couldn't help but laugh. Sometimes, they really were a piece of work, and it seemed Ryan finally realized it.

THIRTY-SEVEN

"We've got the son of a bitch." Heathcliff darted out of his chair and into Moretti's office. A few minutes later, the lieutenant and Heathcliff emerged. "The sniper's been identified as one of Robert Gregson's associates."

"Big surprise," Thompson muttered from his desk.

"Do we have a name?" O'Connell asked, prepared to pull records.

"Elmer Neville," Moretti said. "He was identified buying the bullets used in the rifle. I'll send uniforms to question the store owner, and I've already requested a transfer of Mr. Gregson for another round of questioning. Do you think you can break him this time?"

"We'll do our best, sir," O'Connell said.

The LT disappeared into his office, and Ryan spun to face us. "I'd like to speak to Gregson."

"We can make that happen." O'Connell nodded, and we went back to work.

While we waited for Gregson, the OIO called with an update of their own. One of the calls Chase received from a burner phone traced back to a purchase made at a convenience store a couple of blocks from Scott Shepherd's office. Upon careful review of the footage, Shepherd was identified as purchasing the phone.

Farrell and Mark took another crack at Chase, but he wasn't talking. Instead, they presented this information to Shepherd and his attorney. In exchange for Shepherd's cooperation, they agreed to drop the conspiracy to commit and attempted murder charges.

"The police identified the sniper," I relayed to Mark. "Elmer Neville. They're bringing him in now. With any luck, we'll have everything wrapped up in a nice neat bow by dinnertime."

"Parker, it's been nice having you on board, despite what I may have said earlier," Mark admitted before disconnecting.

Carefully stretching, I stood up from the desk and went down the hallway to the observation room. While I was on the phone, O'Connell and Ryan left to chat with Gregson, and I didn't want to miss out on the fun. Just because I already questioned Robert Gregson once, that didn't mean I wouldn't enjoy watching actual cops do the job the proper way.

"Care to explain why you're the proud owner of German bearer bonds?" O'Connell took a seat and tossed a glance at Ryan. "It seems a strange way to get paid, especially when everyone else was handed overseas bank accounts."

"Does my deal still stand for full immunity?" Gregson asked.

"Yes, sir."

"Fine. Then I'll tell you." Gregson leaned back in the chair. "Reggie and I had an arrangement. We're comfortable with one another, but within the last two years, he's dealt with internal strife. He needed more products, locations that could provide safety away from prying eyes, establishments that could produce realistic documentation that wouldn't come under scrutiny by Customs, and another six vehicles delivered immediately. Some major changes were taking place within his business, and it didn't smell right to me."

"So you requested the bonds?" Ryan asked, understanding they couldn't be traced or questioned. It was a brilliant way to exchange money during illegal endeavors while remaining under the radar.

"Yep," Gregson said.

"Spell out every location, name, and item you gave to Barlow." O'Connell placed a pen on top of a blank notepad.

Gregson listed the safe house, the drug dealers, Elmer Neville, the name of the store that produced fake passports, and a few other relevant items. No wonder Barlow moved with such ease. Since Chase ran Barlow's business, he had access to everything he needed to carry out his hits: the drugs, the documents, and his signature calling card.

The only thing Gregson didn't give us was Barlow's client list. We still didn't know who else ordered a hit or planned to purchase a stolen car. So not everything was a slam dunk, but all the important things seemed to be, particularly after Gregson decided to cooperate.

By the end of the evening, everything was crashing down around Chase Devereaux. Although the man was supposed to be one of Reginald Barlow's lackeys, he was a hitman for hire. He and Barlow met years ago when Chase was still creating his killing persona. Wanting a unique angle, as if the method of murder and body disposal weren't unique enough, he began leaving automotive parts as calling cards. This led to an unsteady partnership of sorts forming between the two men.

Barlow was all about the cars. He was a dealer, sometimes legit and other times not so much. He didn't care what Chase was doing just as long as it never interfered with his business. Chase was in and out of the picture for the last year and a half, but when the investigation into the string of murders heated up, he stuck around for the protection Barlow offered. I wondered if that was because he feared Barlow would turn on him.

Agent Josef Grenauldo wasn't even close to determining any of this, but he discovered the Camel's calling card. However, he never had a chance to tell Ryan about it because he let his heart take the lead. He told Wendi his true identity, and after she told Barlow, Virgil killed him. This was the beginning of the internal power struggle. Chase was supposed to be the seasoned killer. He wanted the power, prestige, and to one day take over the car ring Barlow was building. But the flaws in his plan became apparent when Virgil took the lead, murdering an Interpol agent.

After that, Ryan 'Hoyt' Donough was kept out of the loop on all things. The internal feuding was kept under the radar. So when Barlow planned the trip to the U.S. and got pinched for the GTAs, Chase saw the perfect opportunity to take over, resume his role of killer, become an exotic car broker, and eliminate Hoyt, the other spy within their midst. Chase was willing to tolerate Virgil only as long as the muscle-headed snake was willing to follow orders.

Once we had enough solid evidence, Virgil took a deal and turned into our greatest asset. His voicemail contained damning evidence against Chase, asking if Hoyt had been eliminated and whether or not

Alexandra Riley proved to be connected to Interpol or the investigation into the Camel.

Someone should have taught Chase to keep his mouth shut if he didn't want to incriminate himself when his business burned to the ground. Virgil also provided bank accounts for Barlow and Chase. Like I suspected, the accounts Barlow established for Wendi Hu were initially used to filter the funds to Chase for the jobs he was hired to complete, but when he became paranoid that Interpol was closing in, he ceased that activity and set up his own accounting network through numerous international banks, completely separate from Barlow's business and associates. Part of the reason Chase allowed me to get so close was to determine how much Interpol knew.

Everything Chase did was to cast aspersions. Barlow or Virgil could have easily been blamed for being the Camel. Also, by hiring the sniper, Elmer Neville, Chase hoped to paint himself in the clear in case he was ever caught. The greatest flaw in his plan was kidnapping Ryan. His rented vehicle led to the house, and that led to a heaping pile of shit raining down on him.

After extensive questioning by the police, Neville said he was hired to show up, take a few shots, and disappear. He was in his early twenties, dishonorably discharged from the army, but still wanting to play soldier. Originally, Neville helped move merchandise for Gregson, and the same day Chase and Virgil bought the drug cocktail, they stopped by Gregson's and found the kid there. They struck a deal, and the next time Neville surfaced was to blow out the windows of the hotel suite.

Now that everyone was arrested, Gregson offered up whatever corroborating testimony he could, but there wasn't much to it aside from a few additional bank accounts to investigate. By the time O'Connell and Ryan finished their paperwork for the evening, the PD had basically closed the Camel and GTA cases.

"D'accord," Ryan replied and hung up the phone. "Interpol has closed their investigation. I'm escorting Chase back to the EU tomorrow."

"What?" That was fast. Too fast. "What about the double homicide he committed here?" I asked.

"I don't know, but I have my orders."

"Are you going alone?" I was glad it was over and Ryan could return home. But this felt so sudden, and truth be told, I would miss him.

"No. There will be many agents accompanying us." He took a deep breath, smiling. "It's over."

* * *

The next morning, I went down the stairs and found Martin and Ryan in the kitchen, prattling on in French. Completely confused as to how Ryan appeared at Martin's and even more confused why they weren't speaking English, I narrowed my eyes and concentrated on determining a few of the words. Quickly, I realized I was the topic of discussion. Pouring a cup of coffee, I sat at the table and waited for the conversation to die down.

"What did I tell you about speaking English?" I teased.

"Pardon," Ryan replied, grinning. "I wanted to say goodbye. Jablonsky dropped me off on his way to fill out the paperwork and finalize everything for Chase's transfer."

"I'm sure you're ready to get home."

"It's about bloody time." He exchanged a brief glance with Martin. "Thank you, Alex."

"Don't mention it. Let's just say it's a debt repaid."

The garage door opened, and Mark arrived to collect Ryan. "Promise me the next time you visit, it's just a visit and not another undercover assignment."

"Okay. Although, I think it's your turn to make the overseas trip." He stood, and I hugged him. He kept his hands on my shoulders so as not to hurt my back. "I think I'm getting too old for these undercover assignments. After spending the last few days at the precinct, I'm starting to remember why I wanted to be a cop in the first place."

"Good. I'm glad I could help." I spotted Mark lingering near the stairs. "Your ride is anxious to go."

"Donough," Martin extended his hand, and the two exchanged a few more words, not in English, before Ryan went to the stairs, "thanks for keeping her safe."

Ryan smiled, and he and Mark went down the steps.

"What were the two of you talking about?" I asked, turning to Martin. "And remember, even if I'm not fluent, I do speak some French."

"What do you think we were talking about?"

"Me."

He smirked. "Guilty as charged. We needed to clear the air and exchange some Alex is awesome stories. I'm glad Ryan's alive. You saved him. You do that a lot." He started clearing the breakfast dishes, and I realized Ryan must have been here for at least an hour. Someone should have woken me sooner. "Sweetheart, you've made a life for yourself by consulting. Are you sure you want to give it up to carry a badge and deal with agencies that are more concerned with covering their own asses than finding the truth?" Wow, Ryan must have said a lot more about the case than I imagined.

"I don't know yet." I absently spun the coffee mug in a circle. "There isn't a day that goes by that I don't miss Michael. He was my partner, my best friend, and a huge pain in the ass. It's time I come to grips with what happened."

"That doesn't mean you have to destroy the life you forged in the aftermath. If this is something you want to face, then I'm here for you." He scooted his chair closer, kissing my temple. "Why don't you tell me about him?"

After discussing things, I found myself parked at the cemetery. I never came here. The last time I was here was the funeral. Dropping off some flowers on Sam Boyle's grave, I swallowed and continued to the grey tombstone. *Michael Carver, beloved son, hero, he will be missed*. No shit.

"Hey, Michael," I said, feeling stupid for talking to a slab of granite over a decaying corpse. Why did people do this? It's not like their loved ones were still around. Then again, I spoke to inanimate objects frequently, so this shouldn't be that much different. "I miss you." Swallowing, I glanced around, but the place was pretty much dead. Snorting at the cheesy pun, I tried to figure out what I thought this would accomplish. "This is such a waste of time."

Turning to leave, I couldn't help but feel like this was another epic fail in the long list of failures and disappointment that had become my life. Spinning, I realized more than anything that I was angry. "This wasn't supposed to happen. You and I were the top of our class at Quantico. We should both be at work, driving each other crazy with your damn competitive, arrogant streak." I bit my lip, fighting back the tears. "How could you leave me? Why the hell did you say it was okay. Nothing has ever been okay since you flatlined in that ambulance two seconds later."

I kicked at a pebble on the ground. "This isn't supposed to be my life. You and I made fun of consultants and private eyes, and now look at me. I'm a consultant. Nothing has gone the way it was supposed to. Everything that's happened in the last couple of years never should have been."

Sudden realization hit me like a ton of bricks. Martin. I wasn't one to believe things happened for a reason, nor did I believe that somehow the world was better without Michael Carver because it wasn't, but there was no way of predicting how things would have turned out. Maybe Michael would have left the OIO. Maybe I'd be dead by now. Maybe Martin would have died if I wasn't his bodyguard. Then again, maybe he would have never been shot in the first place.

"How could you leave me?" I asked again. It was the one question that was never answered. I blamed myself, but he should have fought to make sure it was okay. "It's not fair." I shut my eyes and rested my hand on his headstone. "Wherever the hell you are, I hope it's peaceful because nothing here ever is."

* * *

When Martin came home from work that night, he found me sprawled on the sofa. Since he knew my plans, he would have checked on me if I returned to my apartment, so instead, I decided to share the misery with him. There were ice packs underneath my back and a glass of bourbon suspended from my fingertips. The bottle was on the ottoman. This was either my third or fourth. On the plus side, my broken ribs and bruised spine no longer hurt. At this point, pretty much nothing hurt anymore.

"I didn't think you liked bourbon." Martin scrutinized me with a level of concern.

"I don't." I set the glass on the floor before it could slide out of my grasp. "Michael did." I looked up at him. "I went to his grave like you suggested. That was a pretty dumb idea. Your lunatic girlfriend spent twenty minutes screaming at a gravestone."

"Did it yell back?"

"No. Instead, I realized there are so many things beyond my control. It's all just a roll of the dice, isn't it? No wonder Barlow has a tattoo of dice on his wrist. He probably has life figured out. You steal cars, hook up with some assassin for hire, and then it's just a tossup to see if you get killed, or arrested, or stabbed in the back, or whatever."

"Sweetheart," he sat on the edge of the couch, "what happened?"

"Nothing. What did you think was going to happen? He would pop out of the ground like a zombie in a horror film? He's dead, and I have no earthly idea what to do to fix it."

"You can't." He stroked my cheek. "I'm sorry."

The alcohol made my thoughts more haphazard than usual. "If Ryan had gotten killed, I don't know what I would have done. It seems that chances are better from the outside looking in that more shit like that will happen."

"What?" He raised an eyebrow, and I knew I wasn't making much sense.

"The reason I want to go back to the OIO is because that always seemed like the best way to make a difference, but it isn't. Not really. I don't need the badge to do what I do. In fact, it can be a hindrance, but it also comes with rules to keep me in line."

"Alexis, you don't have to make any decisions right now."

"Do you want to know what my scariest thought was?" I challenged. He gave a curt nod, waiting for the answer. "I don't know if you'd even be alive if Michael still was."

"Alex," he wrapped his arms around me, "don't think like that. This isn't a trade-off. I don't want you to resent me because of insanity like that. This is the bourbon talking. Not you."

"It's not the liquor, and I don't resent you. You're the best thing that's ever happened to me, minus the parts we'd both rather forget. I've never been able to find balance or stable ground. You pointed it out not that long ago. I believe you called me an addict." Resolve dawned on me, and I pulled away from him. "I know I tried returning to the OIO temporarily, just to see. And I've consulted a few times, but it's time I do this for real." The sadness in his eyes was hard to stomach, but I soldiered on. This wasn't about him. This was about me and maybe a little bit about Michael and Sam too. "I need closure. I don't know how else to get it."

"Where does that leave us?"

"It doesn't change us. I won't let it."

THIRTY-EIGHT

Over the course of the next two weeks, there were a few loose ends that Interpol and the PD needed tied up concerning the GTAs and the Camel. Donough phoned a few times since he was back at work. Except, for once, he seemed relieved to be behind a desk. Even though he mostly worked undercover, maybe he could change. Maybe so could I.

Ryan was instrumental in working to ensure Wendi Hu was granted temporary asylum until the authorities determined her exact level of involvement with Barlow and Chase. From the way it sounded, she would be allowed to remain as a refugee since she had been coerced, threatened, and beaten by the men who supposedly rescued her from the same type of torment elsewhere.

"It's what Josef would have wanted," Ryan said. "I can't deny his dying wish."

"How involved do you think Wendi really was?" I knew she was more than likely responsible for Josef's murder, even if it was unintentional.

There was a long silence before Ryan finally spoke. “Does it matter? He asked me to protect her. It’s the only way I can make peace with failing to protect him.”

“We aren’t supposed to live for the dead. We’re supposed to live for ourselves.”

“Let me know when you plan to follow that advice. Martin said you were reapplying to the OIO. That’s not about you, Alex. That’s about Michael.”

“Maybe it’s about me too. Maybe leaving was about him and returning is about me.”

“Do you really want to go back?”

“Honestly, I have no idea.”

* * *

When it was all said and done and the contract killer was behind us, I spoke with Director Kendall at the OIO. Since it had been two years since I quit my job and a year since my first consulting attempt, there were numerous hoops to jump through. There was no guarantee I would get my old job back, but Kendall was willing to go to the mat for me if I passed the physical and mental requirements. As usual, I worried about the mandatory psych evals more than the physical tests. This time, my concerns were inaccurate.

After wrapping my torso in an elastic bandage, I popped a few OTC pain relievers and sunk onto the couch. You can’t win for losing, Parker. After spending almost two hours struggling to get into a comfortable position, someone knocked on my front door. “Who is it?” I called, really not wanting to get up.

“It’s me,” Martin said. “Are you screening your guests in addition to your calls?”

“It’s locked, but if you can let yourself in, I won’t

stop you."

He opened the door and cocked his head to the side, confused by the position I was in. One leg was thrown over the back of the couch, the other was curled underneath me. I was tilted sideways, balancing my weight on a couple of pillows underneath my hips and shoulders.

"What?" I asked.

"Are you auditioning for Cirque du Soleil?"

"No, but for some reason, this is comfortable. Nothing else helped." I shut my eyes and shook my head, knowing why he was really here. "I failed my physical and my drug test. On the plus side, I didn't make it far enough to fail the psych eval too."

"What happened this afternoon?"

"The damn cocktail I drank that night apparently has properties that linger for at least thirty days. That was strike one, especially when the federal government frowns on any and all illegal drug use, regardless of if it's intentional. Then to make matters worse, after suffering through a mile and a half around the track, I collapsed on the first round of push-ups."

"You have five broken ribs and a bruised spine. What do these morons expect from you?"

"Perfection."

He muttered expletives under his breath. "What did Mark say?"

"I haven't talked to him yet. On the bright side, I'm still really great at shooting things." I met his eyes. "It's okay. Honestly, you would think I should know better. Drug use is law enforcement 101, and given my recent run-in with Virgil, I should have waited at least another two weeks before scheduling this. Maybe it was subconscious sabotage. I don't know."

"Or maybe you were in a rush to get back out

there."

"Since I'm an addict."

"I'm sorry I said that." He took a step back, but I grabbed his hand before he could walk away. "It wasn't a fair comment. How about I order dinner while you strategize on what your next move will be?"

"I'm not moving. Did I not mention this was the first comfortable position I found all day? But a girl's gotta eat, and I could kill for some spicy crab rolls."

"Well, since you're still an excellent marksman, I'll pick them up. The last time, they arrived warm. Anything else?"

"Hibachi shrimp and some miso soup. Plus, whatever you want, just grab the cash out of my wallet."

He tossed an offended glance my way and let himself out of my apartment.

When he returned, he had a large shopping bag from the drugstore and a smaller bag containing our takeout containers for dinner. Still not moving, I managed to eat without dropping or spilling most of my food. Martin watched, slightly awed by the contortionist act I was performing.

After we ate, he stood at my kitchen table, doing something. But since he was behind me, I couldn't figure out what it was. Finally, he stepped back into view with a large gift bag.

"What's this?" I sifted through the contents, finding ice packs, heating pads, bandages, scar repair cream, antiseptic, muscle rub, and dozens of other items. "Is there anything left on the drugstore shelves?"

He smiled. "Hey, this stuff might come in handy, especially when you go back to work. It'll happen if you want it. You do know that, right? Although," he knelt down on the floor next to me, "I much prefer when you stay in one piece, so hopefully, this is only preventative." He pulled out a tube of superglue. "Prepare for the worst and assume the best, but let's try not to need this stuff, okay?"

"Okay."

DON'T MISS THE NEXT NOVEL IN THE
ALEXIS PARKER
SERIES.

LACK OF JURISDICTION
IS NOW AVAILABLE IN PAPERBACK AND
AS AN E-BOOK

ABOUT THE AUTHOR

G.K. Parks is the author of the Alexis Parker series. The first novel, *Likely Suspects,* tells the story of Alexis' first foray into the private sector.

G.K. Parks received a Bachelor of Arts in Political Science and History. After spending some time in law school, G.K. changed paths and earned a Master of Arts in Criminology/Criminal Justice. Now all that education is being put to use creating a fictional world based upon years of study and research.

You can find additional information on G.K. Parks and the Alexis Parker series by visiting our website at
www.alexisparkerseries.com